D0388819

Q-SQUARED

STAR TREK
THE NEXT GENERATION®

Q-SQUARED

Peter David

POCKET BOOKS

New York   London   Toronto   Sydney   Tokyo   Singapore

POCKET BOOKS, a division of Simon & Schuster Inc.
1230 Avenue of the Americas, New York, NY 10020

 STAR TREK is a Registered Trademark of Paramount Pictures.

This book is published by Pocket Books, a division of Simon & Schuster Inc., under exclusive license from Paramount Pictures.

Library of Congress Catalog Card Number: 94-65679

ISBN: 0-671-89152-9

First Pocket Books hardcover printing July 1994

10 9 8 7 6 5 4 3 2 1

POCKET and colophon are registered trademarks of Simon & Schuster Inc.

Printed in the U.S.A.

TO GUNTER DAVID

Happy Birthday

INTRODUCTION

I generally write two different types of *Star Trek* stories.

The first type is your more standard adventure in which the characters (Original, Next Gen, whichever) get involved in some sort of series of events centered around a problem and have to resolve it. *Rock and a Hard Place* and *The Siege* are examples of those.

The second is the more ambitious novel, in which I endeavor to look at the long history of *Star Trek* and try to tell a story that weaves together various threads and adds to the concept of *Trek* as a vast and intricate tapestry. Some fans love this sort of story, while others declare it to be "fannish" . . . which is odd, since I write all my books for myself, and I *am* a fan. Examples of this latter type of book are *Vendetta* and the work you now hold in your hand.

In composing *Q-Squared,* I felt somewhat intimidated by the success of my previous hardcover, *Imzadi,* and my previous Q-related adventure, *Q-in-Law.* I wanted to avoid slavish imitation of either, but by the same token produce something that had enough of the familiar elements that made the previous two so popular. The result is the longest, and most complicated, novel of any genre that I have ever produced.

I also kept in mind that many readers tell me that they sit down and shoot through one of my books in several hours. I freely admit that I'm banking on that this time out, because—not to scare away anyone who is faint of heart—but there is a *lot* going on in this one. You may consider yourselves duly warned.

I thank the usual suspects for this one, including Kevin Ryan and the cooperative folks at Pocket Books (whom I could call up urgently and say, "Quick! I need a copy of the script for *Yesterday's Enterprise!*" and, lo and behold, I would have it the next morning); the incomparable reference volumes from Mike and Denise Okuda and Debbie Mirek; the many fans whose letters have been of tremendous support and encouragement; and, as always, the intrepid Myra (my wife) and the three kids, Shana, Guinevere, and Ariel, who know when to stay away during one of my intense writing binges.

And so: *Q-Squared*. A book I give you with an admonishment that's applicable to most aspects of life:

Assume nothing.

Q-SQUARED

The child looked up at the adult eagerly, wonderingly in that way that children had. That way which made you aware that you comprised the entirety of their universe.

"What are we going to do today?" asked the child.

The adult smiled down. He had known the child since his birth . . . since before his birth, in fact. This was a child of destiny, of that he was most certain. This was a special child, for whom many possibilities would be open. In a galaxy of infinite potentialities, he was certain that the child would choose that with the most potential. The child would explore it, and savor it, and make it his.

It would be glorious.

"What are we going to do today?" the adult echoed, seeing so much of himself in the smiling, mischievous face. "My boy . . . there is nothing that we are not going to do today."

The boy frowned. "Isn't that a double negative?"

"No, my boy," boomed the elder. "That . . . is emphasis!"

He paused a moment, and then added, "Tell you what,

1

boy . . . I leave it to you. What would you like to do this fine day? Create a star? Traverse a galaxy? Reshape a cosmos? What occupation shall consume this day's endeavors?"

The boy considered a moment under the adult's watchful eye. And then he said . . .

"I want to understand."

"Understand what?"

"Everything," said the boy.

"Everything?" The adult was momentarily taken aback. Perhaps the boy did not quite grasp the entirety, the breadth, of what he was saying. "Everything as in . . . ?"

"Everything as in everything," said the boy firmly. And there was something in his voice that the elder noticed for the first time. A hint of stubbornness, a taste of intransigence.

"Everything," echoed the adult once more, studying the child as he would a microbe. "Very well, then . . . everything it is."

"And what shall we do after we understand everything?"

The adult did not hesitate. "Die, most likely."

ALL ABOARD

TRACK A

1.

"Jean-Luc . . . there's something I've been wanting to tell you."

Picard put down the book of Shakespeare sonnets he'd been skimming and leaned back in his chair, eyebrow raised in curiosity. Crusher stood in the doorway, shifting uncomfortably from one foot to the other and looking more apprehensive than at any time Picard could recall.

"Problem?" asked Picard. He gestured to the chair opposite the desk. "If there's anything I can do to help, you know I will."

"Thank you, Jean-Luc. It's good to know that, in times of stress, there are friends I can count on." Crusher crossed quickly and sat down, ramrod straight . . . but, a moment later, was up and pacing. Picard sat patiently, not rushing his longtime friend and associate. Then Crusher stopped, faced Picard, and said, "A woman is coming aboard the *Enterprise* whose presence is going to make me extremely uncomfortable."

5

"Former lover?" asked Picard.

"Ohhh yes," said Crusher. "Yes, she certainly was that. And I hate to say it, but even now when I think about her, she makes me . . ."

Picard waited, but then prompted, "Nostalgic?"

"Itchy, actually," Crusher said sheepishly. "Silly, isn't it? After all this time?"

"So who is it?" asked Picard. "Natalie?"

"No, not Natalie."

"Amanda, then. Or Lucy perhaps? Don't tell me it's Lucy; she came after me, you know, after you two broke it off. The woman was . . . determined, shall we say."

"Actually, 'legendary' is probably the more accurate term," said Crusher.

" 'Legendary' is not too bad a term to ascribe to yourself, actually," Picard said, smiling. "You've had a formidable number of amorous encounters in the years since you broke up with . . ."

Then he understood, for Picard didn't even have to say the name. The merest oblique reference was enough to take Crusher's face and taint it with a layer of pain.

"Beverly," said Picard.

Crusher nodded.

Picard considered his next words carefully . . . not that he was one to toss off utterances rashly under any circumstance. One did not, after all, become the first officer on the Fleet's flagship without making a habit of proceeding with caution. Rather than addressing the obvious emotional pitfalls immediately, he opted to approach the matter slowly. He asked what was, really, the least important question he could come up with. "When did this happen?" he asked.

"The assignment came in late last night. I've been spending much of the night stewing over it. I'm going to be

6

a delight on the bridge this morning, I can promise you that."

Picard smiled sympathetically. "I have every confidence in you, Captain."

Crusher laughed softly. "I wish *I* did. You're not to quote me on that, of course. If anyone ever asks you, I am the apostle of aplomb."

"Those very words have been used to describe you on any number of occasions."

Picard felt a measure of relief. At least Crusher seemed to be regarding the situation with a degree of gallows humor . . . which was preferable, certainly, to deep depression. Now, though, was the time to move forward. To explore just how in the hell this situation had come about. "What position will Beverly . . . is it still 'Crusher' . . . ?"

The captain shook his head. "No. She went back to 'Howard' after we split up."

"All right. What position will Dr. Howard be assuming on our fair vessel?"

Crusher smiled thinly. "CMO, of course. Nothing but the best for my ex."

Picard was not successful in dissembling his lack of enthusiasm for that piece of news. "Jack . . . I don't know if that's such a good idea. The chief medical officer and a starship captain . . . they have a special relationship on a vessel. They have to work smoothly together. They have to be a team. When you and Beverly split, it was not on the happiest of terms. . . ."

"You're telling *me?*" Jack Crusher tried not to laugh. "I was *there,* Jean-Luc, remember?"

"We were both there, Jack."

"I know, I know." Crusher endeavored to sit, but the closest he came was leaning on the back of the chair.

"Does Beverly know you're in command of the *Enter-*

prise?" asked Picard. "We're newly commissioned, after all. Only been in space a few weeks. It's possible . . ."

"No, it's not possible," said Crusher, shaking his head. "You don't seriously believe that Beverly would take an assignment without knowing who her CO is going to be, do you?"

"Not the Beverly I remember, no," admitted Picard. "But why would she accept the assignment, then, knowing that you're here?"

"Are you kidding?" said Crusher. His face was round, the additional years having added a few pounds to his previously square-jawed face. His once-thick brown hair was seriously thinning on top and graying at the sides, a condition that elicited absolutely no sympathy from Picard. "This is the *Enterprise* . . . the prestige and the history that's attached to that name . . . what reasonable officer could pass that up?"

"I certainly could not have," agreed Picard. And then he added a bit ruefully, "Not that I had many options . . ."

Crusher sucked in air between his teeth, a long-standing habit when confronted with unpleasant truths. "Do we *really* want to go down that road again, Number One?"

"No, of course not," said Picard. "We were speaking of your problems, not mine." He tried to keep the bitterness out of his voice, and was only partly successful. Mentally he chided himself. With all the practice he'd had at trying to control his frustration over his career track, one would think that he'd be more accomplished at bottling his feelings by now.

If Crusher picked up on Picard's tone of voice, he did not let on. "My problems, Jean-Luc, are your problems," said Crusher. "I'm a big believer in the pass-along theory of aggravation." He let that sink in, and then continued, "Now, as we've already made painfully clear, Beverly would have to be crazy to turn down the position of chief medical officer on the *Enterprise*. My loving ex-wife may be many things, but crazy she most definitely is not. Another thing that she is 'not' is afraid of confrontations. And if the only impediment to her taking a position is that it might bring her friction from her superior officer, then I assure you, Picard, that's no impediment at all."

"She's not on the ship yet, however," Picard pointed out after a moment.

"You're right, Jean-Luc," said Crusher in wonderment, as if the thought had not occurred to him. He leaned forward and whispered conspiratorially, "We'll tell the whole crew to hide. When she comes aboard, she'll find no one here, and then maybe she'll leave."

Crusher maintained such a deadpan expression as he spoke that it was all Picard could do not to laugh. "You know what I mean."

"Yes, I know precisely what you mean," said Crusher. "You mean that, as captain of the *Enterprise,* I could block her appointment to this vessel. Raise a fuss, and there's no way that Starfleet will ram her down my throat."

"Correct."

"Yeah, well, there's two problems with that. First, I don't want to be that petty. And second, the simple fact is that Beverly Howard is the best person for the job. Period. Her record is outstanding and unblemished. This ship, this crew, deserves the best, and I'll be damned if I let my personal history stand in the way of this crew's best interests."

"That's very noble of you, Captain."

"Like hell. I just don't want to put myself in the position of taking on a CMO who's not the best. Because the very first time a crewman dies, I'll start second-guessing myself that maybe Beverly could have made a difference.

Wouldn't matter if God himself came down, looked at the dying crewman, and said, 'Sorry . . . nothing I can do to help, I'm afraid.' I'd still be thinking, 'Damn . . . should have had Beverly aboard.' "

"That's quite a lot of expectations to put on the woman's shoulders."

"She has broad enough shoulders. She can handle it."

"Yes, but can you?"

"Guess I'll have to."

Crusher rose from the chair and started for the door, when Picard said, "If I might make an offer, Captain . . . ?"

He turned. "Yes?"

"I would be perfectly happy to . . . run interference, for lack of a better way to put it. I'll handle most of the interfacing between commander and medical."

"Are you implying that I can't handle her, Picard?"

"Not at all. I am saying, however, that no captain can handle everything. And if you should choose to delegate this responsibility to me, I would be more than happy to assume it." When Crusher did not reply immediately, Picard noted, "Might I point out, Captain, that you were considerate enough to honor my request that I not deal directly with the children aboard the ship. I made my concerns plain to you. You said you understood, and were perfectly comfortable with assuming that responsibility yourself. I see this as simply returning the favor."

Crusher nodded slowly. "I suppose you've got a valid enough point there. All right, Number One. I don't want to be perceived as hiding in my ready room, of course. If our soon-to-be chief medical officer wishes to meet with me at any time, she is of course welcome to do so. You are not to interfere in that regard. But for simple day-to-day interaction"—he gestured expansively—"she's all yours."

"Whatever you say, sir."

Crusher gave it a moment's more thought and then said, "You know . . . actually, we're not completely even. After all, there's a bunch of kids. There's only one Beverly Howard."

"Quite true," agreed Picard readily. "There's only one Beverly."

TRACK A

2.

Selan looked up from the latest set of test results and rubbed the bridge of his nose with his thick fingers. He glanced out the narrow window that was the sole source of exterior light in his small, cramped office. The sun was starting to set, and it would be night within several hours. The angle of the light highlighted a thin haze of dust motes dancing in the glare. The walls of the office were a depressing shade of brown, and Selan made a mental note . . . once again . . . to repaint the place before it drove him into a fit of deep depression.

Then he stood and stretched, mildly annoyed that he was feeling creaks and aches in his muscles that he would not once have felt before. It was annoying to him. He kept himself in good shape, and took pride in himself. Nor was he all that old. Barely middle-aged, in fact, for a Romulan.

Perhaps it was the coolness. It was a brisk day on Rombus III, positively nippy at seventy-eight degrees Fahrenheit. Selan clapped his hands together, rubbed them smartly. Poor blood circulation. That was it. He felt only the faintest tingling in his fingers.

Maybe he was due for a checkup.

Rombus III certainly had the facilities for it. In terms of medical technology, there was no place better. Selan was very aware of that, considering that he had been the one who had set it up and managed it all these years.

One of his aides entered, a rod-thin Cardassian. Selan looked up and nodded his head in acknowledgment. "Good evening to you, Turo. It promises to be cool tonight."

"Good," said Turo. The weather was something of an ongoing debate between the two of them: Where the Romulan was at his most comfortable, Turo felt ill at ease, and vice versa. Poor luck on the part of Romulan and Cardassian metabolisms.

Divided as they were by such things as climate, however, they did at least share one thing:

A fascination with pain.

Not their own, of course. That would be sick. That would be inappropriate. No, what intrigued them was the pain of others.

Turo was carrying a computer padd, and he glanced at it for reference. "I understand that we lost Subject Twenty-two today."

"Yes," sighed Selan. "I'm afraid so. A pity, really. I feel that she was capable of enduring so much more, but she simply gave up." He rose from his chair and clapped a hand on Turo's shoulder. "That is what I find to be so intriguing about the many species we study here, my friend: the great variety in terms of personal determination."

Turo smiled thinly. "You misspeak, Selan. You make a

false assumption. Kindly do not address me as 'my friend.'
I am not your friend. Were we not thrust together through
the mutual bond of our governments, I doubt seriously
I would be speaking to you at all. At most, we share a mutual taste for the distasteful. Do not make more out of it
than it is."

"Forthright as always. You might want to consider, from
time to time, the notion of tact."

The Cardassian cocked his head. "Why?"

Selan laughed once, curtly, almost like a bark. Then he
looked back at his computer screen, and tapped it. "I
think," he said slowly, "it's time to turn our attention back
to good old Number Eight."

"You think so?"

"I believe he's healed enough from our last experiments," Selan said thoughtfully. "His endurance is remarkable, wouldn't you say?"

"For a human? Nothing short of amazing." He regarded
Selan with curiosity. "What is it about humans that you
find so fascinating, anyway?"

"I am a student of all biologies," said Selan almost
regally. Then he paused and nodded. "Still, I must admit,
Terrans do hold a certain allure for me. Did I ever tell you
about the first ones I encountered?"

"No," said Turo. "When was this?"

Selan leaned against the desk, crossing his legs at the
ankles. "You've heard of Narendra Three, I presume?"

Turo frowned for a moment, the name clearly familiar.
Then it clicked into place for him. "Of course. A Klingon
outpost, wasn't it?"

"That's right. Or at least, so the Klingons claimed when
they established it over twenty years ago." Selan made a
twisted face that showed very clear just how contemptu-
ously he held that claim, even after all the time that had

passed. "The fact was that it was established purely for the strategic purpose of being able to spy in through the Neutral Zone. Oh, the Klingons maintained their innocence in the matter, of course. Klingons excel at prevarication. But we knew what their intentions were. It was a slap in the face to the Romulan Empire. Well, naturally we had no choice but to retaliate."

"Naturally," said Turo, when Selan paused long enough to make clear that he expected some sort of affirmation. "Clearly they were testing you. Any other action would have been perceived as a sign of weakness."

"There, you see?" Selan slapped his thigh. "You understand! What a remarkable race you Cardassians are. So . . . we attacked them, as we clearly were justified to do. We did them quite a serious bit of damage, too . . . until we were interrupted by a Federation starship. *Ambassador* class, what was the name . . . ?" He searched his memory. "Oh yes. *Enterprise*. Our forces . . ."

"You were there, then?" asked Turo.

"Merely as an observer," said Selan. "I was part of the Emperor's personal staff, and was frequently present at such major maneuvers. As I was saying, our forces destroyed the ship rather handily, although the vessel put up a tremendous struggle. So much so, in fact, that its performance hastened the alliance between the Klingons and the damned Federation. That was the downside of the escapade. The upside was, as I said, we did considerable damage to the Klingons. And, furthermore, we did end up capturing a group of the Terrans who had been crew members aboard the *Enterprise*. There was a feisty group, let me tell you. I found them truly fascinating."

"In what respect?" asked Turo.

Selan leaned forward, stroking his lower lip thoughtfully. "In terms of sheer physical makeup, Terrans are a rather pathetic lot. Soft epidermis. Bones that break under minimal pressure. Rickety circulatory system with vastly insufficient built-in redundancies. Average physical strength substantially less than norm."

"I know." Turo was shaking his head. "All things considered, it is wondrous that they accomplished as much as they have."

"My thoughts precisely. I found them—at least, the first ones I was exposed to—to be driven by an almost indomitable will. A will that seems to transcend their many frailties. It might be a sort of evolutionary means of making up for everything they lack."

Selan then headed for the door, and Turo fell into step behind him. They exited the office and walked across the small compound. "The Emperor shared my interest, and was very supportive when I broached the idea of setting up this facility to study the physical and ethical limits of various species in general and humans in specific. The captives from the *Enterprise* are long gone, of course. But the Emperor has been most generous in keeping me supplied with a steady stream of subjects. Number Eight, though, has been absolutely exceptional."

"Exceptional?" Turo laughed derisively. "Phenomenal is more like it. I swear I don't know what keeps him going. He's been here, what, four years now?"

Selan shook his head. "Six, actually. Almost seven."

Turo whistled. "Is there anything *left* to him?"

"That's the amazing thing about this one," said Selan. As they walked, their booted feet sent up small clouds of dust. Selan nodded in acknowledgment to other scientists passing by him. "He has reserves of inner strength that are unmatched. I don't think he remembers who he is anymore, or what he was like before he came here. All of that has been stripped away from him, and instead he's focused on one thing and one thing only: survival. Focused on it, in fact, to the exclusion of all else. I doubt he recalls *why* he wants to live, but it's become such an imperative that it is all he dwells on. I look in his eyes and all I see burning in them is pure, naked determination."

Suddenly Turo placed a hand against Selan's chest, stopping him in his tracks. Clearly a thought had struck him, and Selan waited for it to work its way to the Cardassian's mouth. "How far would he go to survive?" asked Turo.

"Could you be a bit more specific?"

"Was he a man of high moral character when he came here?" asked Turo.

"Very much so, yes."

"Is he still?"

"I don't know," confessed Selan. "My specialty is survival instinct and the amount of endurance various life-forms have in regard to—"

"Yes, yes." Turo waved impatiently. "But what about the more subtle aspects of moral behavior?"

"I'm a scientist, not a philosopher."

"Well," said Turo with an air of mischief in his voice, "do you not think that expanding one's horizons is a laudable goal? Hmmm?"

Selan gave the matter some thought, and then said, "What precisely did you have in mind . . . ?"

Prisoner Number Eight dwelled in darkness. Darkness of the room, of the soul.

Once upon a time, a very long time ago, there had been light. He was sure of that. He could not recall the details of it so much as the sensation. Buried deep, deep within him was the knowledge that there had been a period where he was so much more than he was now.

Now there was no light, but only fire. Fire burning in the pit of his stomach, fire behind his eyes, fire in his mind. Fire that seared him and drove him forward even when every other instinct screamed for surcease.

He was covered in his own filth, for they had never provided him water with which to bathe. He stank. His hair and beard were long and matted, his fingernails ragged from his having bitten them off. He was clothed only in the tattered remains of a uniform that had once meant a great deal to him.

The wounds from the last beating had all but healed. Plus the pain from the previous week's electrodes had faded completely. They had clamped the leads all over him, to his fingers, to his chest, to his genitals, and then they had sent electricity ripping through him. His screams were so deafening that it seemed at the time as if they must have been coming from a source outside of himself. A place very far away, where some poor devil was suffering terribly, and wasn't it a pity that there was nothing, simply nothing, that he could do about it.

By the time he realized that the screams were issuing from his own mouth, they had already finished with him and tossed him back into his cell like a bag of garbage. And all the time, all the time, the gray-haired man with the pointed ears had been jotting down notes and nodding his head and saying, in his alien tongue, things like "Impressive" and "Very good" and "Yes." How odd. Here he was being complimented. Usually compliments were a positive thing that made one feel good about oneself. But the man in darkness didn't feel good. No, not good at all.

Then his nostrils twitched. Ferally, they scrutinized the air, for something had flickered past them ever so tantalizingly, and he . . .

Yes. Yes, there it was again, stronger this time. It was

approaching his cell, and it was an aroma that stirred primal memories.

The smell of cooked meat.

He was too far gone to recall the last time he'd sat down to a thick steak, the juice flowing out of it at the first pass of the knife. At best, the smell was harkening to something as basic as his prehistoric ancestors, grouped around a fire and cooking the meat (which was a novel idea as opposed to just eating it, raw and dripping, off the bones of the newly deceased animal carcass . . . and even that wouldn't have seemed too shabby a concept. Not in the dark man's current state of mind, if such a word as "mind" could be reasonably attributed to so pathetic a creature).

Cooked meat. He could not recall the last time he'd eaten anything other than simple, meager sustenance.

The door opened, and the smell that wafted through almost drove him mad.

And then something was shoved in.

It was a woman.

He was not appalled by her appearance. He was beyond caring about such things. She was skin and bones, a shredded green dress barely covering her nakedness.

She did not, however, have the look in her eyes that he carried in his. She gazed up at him, and his stare almost devoured her. All that her eyes said to him was *End it end it enditenditendit* . . .

From just beyond the doorway, the Romulan was staring in at him. The Cardassian was just behind him. In the Romulan's right hand, he was holding a force prod that could easily drive Number Eight back if he decided to try anything. In his left hand was a plate, and on the plate was the source of the aroma that was driving Number Eight even madder than he already was.

"I have a treat for you," said the Romulan. "It's out of

respect for you, Number Eight. Out of respect and consideration for your remarkable durability. This meat, cooked to your . . ." He wrinkled his nose slightly. ". . . taste. You merely have to do one thing in order to get it."

The dark man's eyes narrowed.

The Cardassian pulled a knife out of his belt and tossed it across the floor. It landed several feet away from the dark man and skidded, coming to rest right in front of him.

"Kill her," said the Romulan.

Number Eight's gaze flickered from the Romulan to the knife to the woman and back to the Romulan again.

The woman gave no reaction at all to the Romulan's request for her death. It didn't seem to matter to her particularly.

Still Number Eight didn't move.

"She won't give you any trouble, I assure you," said the Romulan softly. "She doesn't have the stamina or the interest. In fact, I daresay you'll be doing both of yourselves a favor."

Slowly the dark man picked up the knife. He was still in his crouch on the far side of the room. He held it up, staring at the blade. It was shining, glittering in the dimness of the chamber.

Outside, night was falling.

So were guards. Falling quietly, unobtrusively. Fingers coming from the darkness, swords flashing. Cries were cut off before they could develop into full-throated alarms.

Through the darkness moved deadly figures dressed in black.

Selan wanted to step back outside the door and reactivate the forcefield, just to play it safe. But Turo was blocking the way, craning his neck and trying to see clearly in the darkness. The stench in the room was oppressive, and Selan made a mental note to have it washed out.

Number Eight was hunched at the far end of the room, and he had just picked up the knife. He was staring at it thoughtfully. He regarded the woman. She was nothing to him. Hell, she wasn't even a Terran; she was a Bajoran, named Kara or something like that. There was no reason for any sort of loyalty on his part.

The only thing that might stop him was a sense of ethics. Of morals. Killing a woman, or anyone for that matter, just to get some food . . . once upon a time, it was nothing that the pathetic creature known as Number Eight would ever have thought himself capable of.

But that was a long time and many torturous sessions ago.

She wasn't moving.

Neither was he.

Damned if Turo hadn't been correct. It was stimulating to see whether or not Number Eight would throw off his ethical training. Selan found himself holding his breath, fascinated to see how the scenario would play out.

Number Eight moved.

Like a panther, he vaulted across the space between himself and the Bajoran woman. He knocked her back and she went down without the slightest noise. Her head thudded on the hard floor, her arms fell listlessly to her side. The dark man was over her, the knife poised to strike.

He brought the knife down across her throat and made a swift slicing gesture.

Turo leaned forward farther, anxious to see the first jet of Bajoran blood splatter on the floor.

This was a mistake . . . one of two that would be made within the next sixty seconds.

For the dark man had suddenly flipped the knife around,

and there was barely time for it to register on Turo that Subject Number Eight was holding the knife by the blade, which was a pretty inefficient way to cut someone's throat, and just where was the blood anyway?

And then the subject's arm was a blur, and Turo felt a sudden pressure against his head. That was when he thought, *Oh, I see the blood now,* except it wasn't coming from the Bajoran woman. In fact, she seemed in fairly good health, all things considered, and she was twisting her head to look around and clearly her throat had not, in fact, been cut.

But where's the blood coming from then? Turo was wondering, and then it dawned on him that it was, in fact, coming from higher up on his head. He turned to see a horrified—and yet fascinated—expression on Selan's face, and then Turo reached up and touched the still-quivering hilt of the blade which was now solidly embedded in his forehead.

He looked in wonderment at Number Eight—the starved, desperate, pathetic wretch—and to his surprise all he could think of to say was "Good throw!" At least that was what he tried to say, but it came out more as "Nychhhhhohhhh," and then Turo pitched forward, dead before he quite made it to the floor.

His face twisted in fury, Selan jacked up the power on his force prod and took a step forward, his every instinct being to punish Number Eight for this hideous transgression.

That was the other mistake.

Number Eight charged forward with an animal growl, and the only thing that stopped him from getting his hands around Selan's neck was that he tripped over the outstretched arm of the Bajoran woman. The stumble was a brief one, but it was enough for Selan to stab forward with the prod, filling the dark man with enough of a charge to, at the very least, dispatch him into unconsciousness. Indeed, depending on the subject's condition, it might even have stopped his heart.

It sent the dark man to one knee.

That was it.

That was all.

And then a deranged howl ripped from the throat of Number Eight, and Selan suddenly realized that after all this time, all these years, he had finally found a boundary that he should not have crossed. For waiting for him on the other side of that border was a creature that harkened more to the days when man was a brute of pure, unreasoning emotion and instinct. And every instinct, Selan immediately understood, was focused on getting hands or teeth or something around Selan's throat and pulling or ripping or squeezing or doing whatever it took to make sure that the Romulan was dead.

Selan backed up.

The dark man moved. He vaulted clear of the Bajoran woman and came in fast.

The Romulan was through the door and reached quickly to activate the forcefield. It flared to life just as Number Eight reached it, and he was caught in the arc. Energy from the forcefield pounded through him, trying to drive him back. But year upon year of torture had elevated the dark man's threshold of pain to levels he would never have dreamed possible.

Against all instinct, against all odds, he managed to drive a step forward even as he felt his brain starting to close down. But he overrode the urge to slip into unconsciousness, and then there was a second step, muscles refusing to yield, and then a third step, and this one was the hardest because it was dragging through the rest of his body.

Then he was past the forcefield door, his breath ragged and forced, his heart racing. But he was past.

He tried to get up.

He could not.

Nothing was working. His overtaxed nervous system had simply shut off. He ordered his arms to push him forward, his legs to bring him to standing. Neither occurred. Instead he fell forward, slamming his face into the floor. He didn't feel the pain. He didn't feel anything except a surge of fury at his helplessness.

Selan sagged against a wall, and shouted, "Guards! *Guards! In here, quickly!*" He waited for the pounding of feet, but there was nothing. Where the hell *was* everyone?

Devil take it. He'd do it himself.

"Number Eight," he said coldly to the spasmodically twitching body on the floor, "I am sad to say that you have proven yourself to be a hopeless subject. I am afraid I shall have to terminate you." He twisted the rod to its maximum power. Stop Number Eight? At this setting, it could likely have blown a hole through the wall. "It is nothing personal, you understand. Believe it or not, I will very much miss you. You were a magnificent subject."

He jabbed forward toward the helpless Terran, and the dark man did nothing to block it.

That did not stop it from being blocked.

A blade, long and lethal, had swooped in and deflected the blow. The prod sent a charge through the blade, but the handle was insulated and the wielder was unharmed.

Selan turned and faced the new opponent, and he felt the blood drain from his face.

It was a Klingon.

He was a young one, that Selan could tell immediately. He was dressed in black, and his hair was long and wild.

Both hands were holding the vicious curved blade defensively in front of him.

For a moment neither of them moved.

"You are Selan," he said after a moment. His voice was low and gravelly.

"And you are dead," Selan responded. "My guards will—"

"Your guards are in no condition to aid you," replied the Klingon evenly. His fighting stance was perfect; he balanced lightly on the balls of his feet. Alert and yet relaxed. "The rest of my group has disposed of them. You may die fighting, if you wish."

"You are too kind," said Selan. "How did you know my name?"

"I have spent my life memorizing your face," he said, sounding rather matter-of-fact. "I am Worf, son of Mogh. My parents died in the Romulan raid on Narendra Three, when I was only three years old. I understand that you ordered that raid."

"You are misinformed," said Selan.

Worf blinked in slight surprise at this. "You did not order it?"

"No." Selan shifted his grip slightly, not letting down his guard for a second. "I was merely an observer on behalf of the Emperor."

"So you were there."

"Yes, but—"

"That will suffice."

The blade flashed. Selan brought the prod up quickly to block it, but Worf drove the blade forward with such force that it sliced through the prod without slowing.

The prod clattered to the floor.

Selan's head joined it a moment later.

The rest of Selan's body followed shortly thereafter.

Worf stood there a moment, taking it in. From outside he heard the sounds of pounding feet. If the other Klingons in the raiding party were making that much noise, then the likelihood was that all of the Romulans and Cardassians were dying, or dead, or wishing they were dead.

He slung his weapon and turned to the slightly twitching person lying on the floor. He knelt down beside him and turned him over, looking into his eyes.

What he saw there frightened even him.

"Poor bastard," he murmured. "What did they do to you?"

His lips moved, and it seemed as if he were desperately trying to remember how to form words. And finally he managed to get out one word:

"Home."

"Yes," Worf said, nodding. "Do not worry. I shall get you home. What is your name?"

The dark man stared at him for a long while.

"Deanna."

Worf frowned. "I do not think so. I believe that is a woman's name."

"Deanna," said the dark man again. And it was not his name, of course. But it was the only one that meant anything to him.

Unfortunately, he could not recall why.

TRACK **A**

3.

"**T**erminus?" Picard blinked in surprise. "I thought we were to be en route to Farpoint Station."

In the captain's ready room, Jack Crusher came around from behind his desk. Picard had never seen Crusher stay behind the desk for more than a minute or so at a time. Jack liked to be in motion. Aware of that tendency, he had once joked to Picard that it made him a much more difficult target. Picard had wondered how much of that joke had a serious edge of truth to it.

"We have been rerouted, as Starfleet is wont to do," Crusher replied. "We are going to be taking on a most interesting passenger: one Lieutenant Commander William T. Riker."

Picard frowned. "Riker. I know that name." Then his face cleared. "My God. Missing in action, wasn't he?"

"Good memory, Jean-Luc. Six years ago. The *Hood* was on a routine exploratory mission, and had an away team down on the planet Falcor, when they ran into some serious trouble with unidentified attackers. Most of the away team was slaughtered. A handful was never found, and Riker was one of them."

"That's right. And there was a tremendous brouhaha at the time because the belief was that the Romulans were behind it. That's why I remember it in particular. There was all sorts of talk that it was a harbinger of a new Romulan incursion."

"Yes, well, they were partly correct." He rapped briskly on the desktop . . . a long-standing habit ever since he'd taken up the drums at an early age. "There was no Romulan incursion, but it was the work of Romulans, all right."

"They had him for six years and he's still in one piece? That's phenomenal."

"In a sick sort of way, he was lucky . . . although it's a pretty broad definition of luck, I suppose. I mean, if he were really lucky, the whole nightmare wouldn't have happened in the first place. The thing is, on the rare occasions when Romulans do take prisoners, they just torture them for information until they die. That's not what happened to Riker, though. Here, look for yourself." He turned the computer screen around so Picard could see for himself. "I shouldn't have to spoon-feed you information."

Picard studied the screen. "This 'Selan' who acquired him seems to have been highly placed."

"Yeah. A highly placed sadist," said Crusher grimly. "He was free to indulge himself in his sick experiments, in the name of science. This guy was born in the wrong place and century. He would have been at home in Nazi Germany."

"If you believe in reincarnation, perhaps he was," said Picard, still skimming the computer readout. "Now, if you want to discuss luck, here's the place to do this. Apparently a Klingon raiding party rescued Riker, and they didn't even know he was there."

"They knew that Rombus Three was a Romulan outpost. Really, that was all they needed to know. The Klingons have been pretty systematic over the last year or so. There's this new young turk who's making his influence felt, name of Worf."

"Wharf? Like where ships go?" asked Picard.

Crusher shrugged. "I suppose. Actually, it's appropriate, because when he showed up, that's when Riker's ship came in . . . so to speak. This Worf has been something of a firebrand. Getting the Klingon Council stirred up, trying to convince them to strike at the Romulans preemptively, wherever and whenever they can. And Worf's got a crew of Klingons who agree with him. They've got their own little strike force going. Now, officially the council is disapproving of their actions."

"Officially," echoed Picard. "Unofficially, though . . ."

"Unofficially, my guess is they're ecstatic. I mean, these are Klingons, Jean-Luc. If they didn't secretly approve of what one of their own was doing, I doubt this Worf fellow would still be drawing air."

"Agreed," said Picard. "So Rombus Three was simply the next stop on Wharf's agenda, and Riker was the beneficiary."

"Riker and a handful of other guests, in various states of disrepair, who are being returned to their respective governments. Riker is Starfleet. Terminus is the closest convenient point for us to pick him up. The Klingons said he was in pretty bad shape, though. It'll be walking on eggshells with him for a while."

Picard nodded, scanning Riker's personal history. "He has a wife and son, I see. Have they been notified?"

"Word's been sent, yes. In fact, I was thinking . . ."

His next words were drowned out by the blare of the red-alert siren. Crusher was across the room in a heartbeat, Picard right after him. They emerged onto the bridge.

From tactical, Lieutenant Tasha Yar said briskly, without waiting for Crusher's inquiry, "Shields came up automatically, sir."

At conn, Lieutenant Commander Data was studying his readings. "We are getting readings of a major source of unidentified energy bearing 223 mark 7. All readings are off the scale."

"Is it a ship?" demanded Crusher, settling into his command chair. "A natural phenomenon?"

"I do not think it is natural," said Data after a moment. "Whatever it is, it is most definitely sentient, since it appears to be heading directly for us."

"On screen, full magnification," said Crusher.

A moment later it was there, moving toward them at incredible speed.

Then it stopped.

It came to such a complete and utter halt that it almost defied believability.

"All stop," said Crusher quietly after a moment.

The starship glided to a halt and hung there in space, facing the glowing entity.

Its size varied from moment to moment, fluxing in no discernible pattern. Sometimes it was round, and then it seemed to square off, then it was back to round, followed by oblong.

"Mr. Data," Crusher said in that mild way he had when he was becoming impatient. "Now would be a superb time to give me a clue as to what it is we're looking at."

"I cannot say for certain, sir."

"Take a wild guess, then."

Data turned, his soft blue eyes looking puzzled in his tanned face. "Guess, sir?"

"That's right, Mr. Data. Best guess."

"I guess," said Data cautiously, "that it is waiting to see what we will do."

"It is not answering any hails, sir," said Tasha Yar. After a moment, she added, "I have a phaser lock, sir . . . just in case."

"Let us hope that doesn't become necessary," said Captain Crusher. "Mr. Data . . . ahead on impulse. Take us just to the right of the object, but don't get within five thousand kilometers of it. Let's see what happens if we try to go past."

Slowly the *Enterprise* glided forward. Sublight drive felt like an achingly long crawl compared to warp, but Crusher wanted to make no sudden moves.

Moments later, the choice was taken out of his hands, for the gleaming object suddenly started to expand, to split and reassemble itself into . . .

"A barrier, sir!" said Yar.

She was correct. Whereas before their path had been unobstructed, now a great, glittering barricade blocked their way. It was shimmering and interlocking, like a massive chain-link fence, and it dwarfed the great starship.

"The readings match those of the previous obstruction," said Data.

"Meaning we still don't know what the hell we're looking at."

"That is correct."

"Hmm." Crusher pondered the problem a moment. "We could try going above it or below it. This is space, after all. I seem to recall something about it being infinite in all directions."

Picard shook his head. "If something wants to stop us from going on, we can presume it will move with us."

"Very likely," agreed Crusher. He rubbed his forehead. "Tasha, please shut off the red alert. It's giving me a headache."

Picard breathed a silent thanks. He didn't understand how anyone could think with that hellacious noise going on, but it wasn't his place to complain about it.

And suddenly, the barrier disappeared. It still existed and impeded the *Enterprise*'s path . . . but it was no longer visible. The front viewscreen had suddenly blinked out, to be replaced by a field of solid white.

"Viewer malfunction?" demanded Crusher, not ecstatic about some sort of glitch in the system turning up at such an inappropriate time.

Ensign Chafin at Ops frowned. "No, sir. All systems read normal."

"Look!" said Picard.

Words were starting to appear on the screen, one after the other, each about a second apart. A flabbergasted Picard spoke the words out loud as they showed up.

Three words.

"'Simon . . . didn't . . . say,'" Picard read.

Crusher stared at him in confusion, and then back at the words. There they were, in an ornate black lettering that had a gothic look to it. "Simon didn't say?" he repeated, perplexed. "Who the hell is Simon?"

"It is quite likely a reference to the children's game Simon Says," Data surmised. "A group of two or more participants imitates the actions of a leader. Each action must be preceded by the words 'Simon says.' Without that two-word cue, anyone performing the action is disqualified from proceeding further."

"Thank you, Mr. Data," said Crusher. "Far more than I needed to know." He glanced at Picard. "Now what?"

Picard rubbed his chin and said simply, "We wait until Simon says."

The words vanished, to be replaced, one by one, with a new comment. Picard read it out loud: "'You're in for a long wait.'"

It took a moment for the full impact of that to register. "Whatever is out there heard what you said, Number One," said Crusher. Then he turned to face the screen and said, "If you could hear him, then you can hear me. This is Captain Jack Crusher of the *U.S.S. Enterprise.* Please identify yourself and give the reason for your impeding our progress."

"What would you like to know?"

The voice had come from behind them.

Standing up by the turbolift was a singularly bizarre being.

He was dressed entirely in black, except for a white formal shirt with elaborate ruffles on the breast, and more ruffles dangling from the cuffs. An ascot tie was knotted with a gleaming diamond stickpin. He sported a black cutaway morning coat, with tails that hung to just behind the knee. A cream-colored waistcoat was buttoned across his flat stomach. His black trousers were immaculately pressed, and his black shoes gleamed.

His face was triangular, and he had a shock of curly black hair. Over his right shoulder was a casually held walking stick. On his face was an expression of amusement, and clearly it was the *Enterprise* crew that was the source of his smug delight.

He looks like a magician, thought Picard, *or like something that fell off the top of a wedding cake.*

They stared at him a moment, and the odd figure repeated, "What would you like to know?" His voice was low and silky and mocking, almost foppish. To emphasize the question, he swung the walking stick off his shoulder and pointed it at Crusher.

Tasha Yar's reaction was immediate. The moment she saw something being pointed at the ship's captain, she launched herself at the possible threat. It was not for her to make any value judgments as to the likelihood of attack, or even the wisdom of her engaging in an assault upon a being who had penetrated the starship's defenses so effortlessly. She had one imperative: Protect the captain.

What did not matter, unfortunately, were her attempts to intercede.

The strange being snapped his fingers. That was all that was required, and Tasha Yar froze in place.

"Let her go," Crusher commanded.

The intruder did not acknowledge that Crusher had spoken. Instead he walked casually around Tasha, studying her from every angle as if examining a specimen. "A fascinating portrait of hostility, don't you think?" he inquired.

"I said let her go."

The intruder's face darkened. "You, sir, are hardly in a position to give orders."

"This is my ship," shot back Crusher. "It is my job to extend courtesies normally given to guests, whether they are invited or not. It is also my job to give orders. I will not engage in one aspect while ignoring the other, and you *will* release her."

"My my my," said the intruder, with the tone of a parent having caught a child raiding a cookie jar. "A pity that you consider such belligerence to be necessary. It is certainly not necessary. Nor," and he lowered his voice dangerously, "is it wise." He allowed that to sink in a moment, and then shrugged expansively. "However . . . just so you do not get the wrong impression of me . . ."

With an elaborate flourish, he waved in Tasha's direction. Yar unfroze, unaware of the passage of time. All she knew was that her target was no longer in front of her, and she paused momentarily. The intruder, who was behind her now, swung his cane and rapped her smartly once on the buttocks. Tasha spun to face him, her eyes narrowing and her gaze as hard as diamond and about as cold.

"Stay where you are, Lieutenant," said Crusher firmly.

"Yes, do, Lieutenant," the intruder advised. "Your captain has your best interests at heart, I can assure you. You have been warned, you see. I don't dispense warnings lightly. Nor do I dispense them twice."

Picard took a step forward, subtly but deliberately placing himself between the intruder and Crusher. "Who are you?" he demanded.

The intruder turned and looked at him as if seeing him for the first time. "Ah. Jean-Luc Picard," he said.

"How do you know me?"

"Who doesn't?" asked the intruder nonchalantly. "The man with the most promising career in Starfleet . . . until he was court-martialed and found negligent in the *Stargazer* incident. Busted in rank, as I recall. That must have hurt, didn't it."

Picard felt all eyes upon him, but he gave not the slightest indication of what was going through his mind. Instead he said, "I'm still waiting to learn your name."

"Names are *so* important, are they not? Tools of remarkable power if wielded properly." The intruder, his cane back across one shoulder, walked slowly around the bridge. He dragged his finger along one railing, checking for dust and nodding approvingly when none was found. "My name, dear chaps . . . is Trelane. I am part of the Q Continuum."

"The what?" Crusher now said.

"The Q Continuum," continued Trelane. "A collective of beings similar to myself."

"All insufferable, you mean?" muttered Tasha.

Trelane laughed loudly at that. It was the laugh of someone pretending that he had appreciated a joke, when what he really enjoyed was the prospect of making one squirm for having dared utter it. "I mean, my dear lieutenant . . . and you, Commander, and Captain, and all of you . . . that we are all-powerful. We are incredibly advanced, and concerned about all life-forms throughout the cosmos. We do not take our advanced status lightly, I assure you. We are omnipotent in the most positive sense of the word."

"There is no 'positive sense' to that word," replied Picard.

"Spoken like someone who has never been omnipotent. I can tell you from firsthand experience that it is, in fact, absolutely splendid. Now . . . to the business at hand."

He had circled around the bridge and stopped several feet away from Crusher. Picard was still subtly but definitely placing himself in the path of any possible attack on Crusher . . . not that he truly anticipated having any better luck against forestalling such an eventuality than Tasha had had.

"The *Enterprise,* Captain, is a ship of destiny. It always has been. It always will be. You can comprehend that, can't you?" He smiled broadly. "And other ships in the Fleet will take their cues from you. Since you are the first one to make these journeys, the first one to chart the farthest points . . . why, it's important, don't you see?"

"What is important?"

"Why . . ." And he showed his teeth. "That you suffer, of course."

Crusher stared at him.

Picard felt a fury rising in him that he could barely contain. He took a step forward and said angrily, "You just want to make us suffer? What's the point?!"

Trelane's head snapped back and he laughed merrily.

"My *dear* Picard," he chortled, *"that* is *the point!"*

And he vanished.

TRACK **A**

4.

Dr. Beverly Howard shut off the computer screen and looked up at Picard. "So that's what I missed, eh?"

Picard nodded, but found that he was having difficulty looking straight at Howard. *God, she hasn't aged a day,* he thought. That sweet face, the red hair in its tight curls.

And the way she was looking at him. Studying him, assessing him, comparing him to the man he once was. To the people they both were.

He felt skin brushing his hand, and looked down. She had rested her hand next to his, the edges rubbing against each other. A casual, meaningless gesture, and yet it was enough to send what amounted to a seismic jolt through the ship's first officer.

Was he reading too much into it? Or was he not reading enough?

Picard stood, straightening the lines of his uniform, and focused his attention on the sickbay, which was bustling with activity. Howard's head nurse was busy overseeing the administrative duties, and making sure that all the medical equipment was correctly calibrated. The fact was that all of that had been attended to before the *Enterprise* was launched, but it was standard operating procedure for any new CMO to make certain, personally, that everything was up to snuff.

"It was a rather impressive display," Picard concurred.

Beverly steepled her fingers and said, "Do we have any idea what this Trelane wanted?"

"None at all," Picard said grimly. "He issued no ultimatums, offered no conditions. He simply showed up, effortlessly penetrating our defenses; spouted some sadistic threats; and vanished . . . along with the barrier that was blocking our way. It was almost as if . . ." He frowned, trying to figure the best way to put it. "It was as if, once he had us, he didn't know what to do with us. Like he hadn't fully thought things out."

He looked to Howard for her reaction, but her expression had changed subtly. She was no longer looking at Picard, but instead over his shoulder at something else. He turned to follow her gaze and saw Captain Crusher standing in the doorway to Beverly's office. His hands were draped behind his back, as if he had no clear idea of where to put them. He rocked on his heels slightly, giving the appearance of standing on the deck of an ocean vessel.

There was an uncomfortable silence for a moment, and then Crusher cleared his throat and said, "Getting settled in, Doctor?"

"Yes. Yes, Captain, quite well."

"I hope it wasn't too much difficulty, asking you to take a shuttle from Farpoint Station and meeting us en route to Terminus."

"Difficulty? Not for you." She smiled without letting it affect any other part of her face. "It was grotesquely inconvenient for me, of course. Stripped-down, high-speed

shuttles are not my idea of the most pleasant way to travel.
I wasn't ecstatic about it, nor was my support team."

Crusher shifted uncomfortably. "Starfleet rerouted us to
Terminus. I didn't have all that much choice, Doctor."

She opened her mouth and it was clear that she was
about to press the matter. Point out that Jack could have
argued with Starfleet on it. Requested that another ship be
routed to Terminus, or at least asked that the *Enterprise* be
given a more reasonable ETA. Something, anything, along
those lines.

But then she glanced at Jean-Luc, and the message in his
eyes was clear: *Let it go.* She considered the silent advice
with equal quiet, and then allowed her face to soften into
the far more pleasant lines she bore when she wasn't feeling
the blade of anger knifing through her, as seemed to
happen so easily these days.

"Whatever you felt was best, Jack," she said quietly.
Then, as an afterthought, she added, "You might want
to check out Farpoint Station in the near future, though.
There's something . . . odd going on there."

"Odd?"

She shrugged. "I can't really say more than that. It's
nothing I can put my finger on. It's just . . . it's worth
checking."

"If you say so," said Crusher, "then it will be done."

"Thank you." She smiled. "It's good to see you, Jack.
I . . . have to admit, when I got off the shuttle and it was
Jean-Luc waiting to formally greet me instead of you, I was
wondering if I'd see you at all during my tenure here."

"Things have been hectic. Jean-Luc brought you up to
speed?"

She nodded at the computer screen. "Definitely. I've
never heard of this 'Q Continuum.' Have you?"

"No," said Crusher, "but Data's done some research and tracked down an earlier reference to a Trelane."

"Excellent," Picard said, leaning against Beverly's desk. "What has he got?"

"You're gonna love this," said Crusher, pacing the room in his customary manner. "Nearly a century ago, the *Enterprise* 1701, under the command of James Kirk, encountered a being calling himself Trelane on stardate 2124.5. Trelane, alternately referring to himself as the 'Squire of Gothos' . . ."

"Gothos?" said Picard.

"The world that Trelane inhabited," explained Crusher. "According to Captain Kirk's log, Trelane had extensive dealings with the *Enterprise* crew before others interceded, permitting the *Enterprise* to continue on her way."

"What others?"

"Trelane's parents, apparently."

"Parents? Are you sure?"

"Ohhh yes. That fact is supported by the log of Science Officer Spock, in which Trelane is classified as . . . so help me . . . a small, naughty boy."

Picard shook his head. "That's one of the truly amazing things about Kirk's *Enterprise*. They seemed incapable of having a normal day."

"For them, the abnormal was normal." Crusher slapped his hands together and rubbed them briskly, as if he were cold. "Well . . . I'll be on my way, then. Number One . . . I'll expect to see you on the bridge when you can tear yourself away. Doctor, a pleasure as always."

"Yes, of course. Jack . . ." She hesitated. "We can make this work. I know we can because, deep down . . . it's good to see you again."

He smiled in spite of himself. "Same here."

Picard looked from one to the other, suddenly feeling that perhaps he should be in another room . . . or perhaps on another starship. He cleared his throat, about to suggest that maybe he should leave so that the captain and chief medical officer could become reacquainted.

At that moment Howard's chief nurse stuck his head in. "We'll be ready for you in about five minutes, Doctor."

"Oh . . . Geordi, this is Captain Jack Crusher. Captain, this is my head nurse, Geordi La Forge."

"An honor, sir," said Geordi, shaking Crusher's outstretched hand.

"Geordi's been with me for several years now," said Beverly. "I'd be lost without him. Best nurse in the field."

Crusher was immediately struck by how engaging a young man La Forge was. His face was pleasant and open, his brown eyes gentle. Clearly La Forge was topflight nurse material: he had a way about him that immediately put one at ease. If he looked down at you as you lay flat on your back, and told you that everything was going to be just fine, you'd very likely believe it.

"Thank you, Geordi," she said.

That was when there was a scream in the sickbay.

Howard was on her feet so quickly that she banged her knee on the underside of her desk. She grimaced in pain but staggered forward, following the others out.

The scream had issued from the throat of one of the medical technicians, and the reason for it was that one of the bulkheads was melting.

There was no hint of a red alert or any sort of alarm klaxon, which meant only one thing: Whatever was causing this insanity was somehow originating from within the ship. Crusher hit his signal comm and shouted, "Security alert! Security teams A and B to sickbay, immediately!"

He started forward but suddenly Picard was blocking his way. He had once again placed himself in between his captain and a danger that was presenting itself.

And the danger was very evident. The bulkhead wall was indeed melting away. . . .

No. Not melting . . . at least, not in the sense of being subjected to intense heat. Picard could see now that it was distorting and stretching, as if it had been transformed into putty and was now being subjected to stress from the other side. It was bulging, elongating. . . .

"There's someone in there!" said Picard.

Clearly he was right. The shape of a human head was starting to push through the puttylike wall. They could see the indentations of the eyes, a mouth that was open wide in a silent scream. Lower down were hands, pushing against the straining wall, and now there was the hint of a shoulder. . . .

The security team charged in, Tasha Yar at the forefront. Crusher was amazed at the woman's speed; if there were any shortcuts anywhere in the *Enterprise,* Yar knew precisely where they were and how to use them. She and the team had their phasers out, but Crusher put up a hand. "No one move," he snapped. "Let's see what—"

Then the wall tore.

There was a sound that was like a thunderclap, combined with a massive tearing and, insanely, a distant sound of shattering like a thousand heads smashing through a thousand windows.

A body thudded to the floor.

The others gaped at it, for it was clothed in a Starfleet uniform. There were a few small stylistic differences, but otherwise it was clearly Starfleet.

It was a man. As the others looked on, he managed to

pull himself to all fours. He was breathing heavily, his chest rasping, as if he'd just run a great distance. He was slender, his black wavy hair tinged with gray. His face was narrow, and his dark eyes burned with a furious intensity. It was that gaze that he now turned on the *Enterprise* crewmen.

He moaned softly. He repeated a word over and over again, and it sounded somewhat like, "Where?"

Crusher took a step forward around Picard, seizing command of the situation. "I am Captain Jack Crusher. You're on board the *U.S.S. Enterprise.* Please explain how you—"

He stared up at them. "Captain . . . who?" Then his scrutiny fixed on Picard. "Picard . . . ?"

Picard blinked in surprise. He looked to Crusher for guidance, and Crusher simply shrugged. "This is your day for being recognized."

"Yes, I am Commander Jean-Luc Picard." Feeling something more should be added, he said, "And this is Dr. Beverly Howard . . . and Head Nurse Geordi La Forge."

"Now, who the blazes are you?" demanded Crusher. "Are you associated with Trelane? Why are you wearing a Starfleet uniform?"

With what seemed to be incredible effort, the newcomer managed to get out, "I . . . am Q . . . and you have absolutely *no* idea . . . how screwed up this is."

And then, having used the last of his strength, Q slumped forward and hit the ground, unconscious.

TRACK CHANGE

TRACK **B**

1.

Hikaru Sulu lunged forward, his sword just grazing the chest of his opponent.

The opponent, clad in fencing white, backed up slowly across the rocky, uneven terrain. The trees rustled overhead, and far, far below, waves could be heard crashing against the shore. On the plateau where the battle was raging, Sulu was advancing, the point of his sword flicking from side to side.

His opponent continued to retreat, did so until he could go no farther. Sulu came in quickly, his sword little more than a silvery flash of metal.

The man in white parried, spun out of the way, and—remarkably—thrust back and under his arm. It was a novel and daring move.

Sulu blocked it easily, and with a quick angling of his wrist, sent his opponent's sword clattering to the ground. The man in white made a grab for it, but Sulu's blade was between him and his own weapon, and there would be no reaching it this day.

Sulu touched his sword to the collarbone of his opponent and said quietly, "You're dead."

"It would appear so," replied his opponent. He stood and removed his headgear, to reveal a balding head with closely cropped white hair on either side. "The match is yours."

"As it should be," replied Sulu. "After all, you must have respect for your elders, Picard."

Picard nodded, and then smiled wanly. "I appreciate the advice."

Sulu regarded him thoughtfully for a moment. "Something is bothering you, isn't it, Captain."

"Very perceptive, Commodore," replied Picard. "Something is indeed bothering me, and damned if I know what it is."

"If it's your fencing, there I can help you," Sulu told him, unable to resist adding, "Believe me, if I were you, I'd be concerned. Your technique is incredibly rusty."

"I've been rather busy," Picard said dryly.

"Excuses ill become you, Picard."

"I'll work on it."

"That's better."

Slowly Picard walked around to the edge of the cliff and watched the waves far below crashing against the breakers "My father claimed that he could tell when there was going to be a severe weather change just by the way his knees or elbows might ache at any given time."

"That's a simple physiological reaction to a weather condition," said Sulu. He was busy running through a series of practice thrusts and parries. "That has nothing to do with premonitions and such."

"Perhaps premonitions," said Picard, "come from the ability to look at a hundred small things at once, and notice that one of them is out of kilter. But because there are so many things, it is difficult to ascertain just precisely which thing it is."

"Until the problem becomes fully blown, at which point," Sulu lunged forward, stabbing at air, "you say to yourself . . ."

"'How could I not have seen it coming.'" Picard nodded. "Absolutely right." He turned away from the cliffside and faced Sulu. "My apologies. I don't normally blather on in this fashion."

"Don't worry about it," said Sulu. "I'm always here, whenever you need a sympathetic shoulder. We're a fraternity, we starship commanders. No one else carries our responsibilities. No one else deals with the sort of burdens we have to face. And it seems as if, with each passing decade, they make it harder for us. Your crew complement is, what? A thousand? With a maximum of seven thousand? Including children and entire families?" Sulu shook his head. "I wouldn't want to have to deal with your problems."

Now Picard whipped his sword through the air, enjoying the sharp hissing sound it made. "What about you? With the older, slower warp configurations. The dilithium crystals that constantly had to be replaced because they couldn't be reenergized. No holodecks to provide you with an alternative to daily starship life. No families to give you a sense of grounding; after all, in space . . . where there is neither up nor down . . . we have artificial gravity to anchor us physically, but family gives us our emotional grounding."

"You're absolutely right, Picard." Sulu smiled lopsidedly. "So, after seven years aboard this ship, how many of your command crew is married, again?"

Picard winced. "Touché."

"Isn't it interesting," said Sulu, "that even given the opportunity to have families aboard ship, your senior officers—you not excluded—still make the choice of avoiding entanglements."

"It isn't simply a matter of choice. Even with all the amenities, starship life isn't the easiest, or even the safest. Facing the hazards of space . . . it's not like living on a planet, where you can . . ."

"Be destroyed by a space probe. Be conquered by the Borg." Sulu started ticking off examples on his fingers. "Be raided by Romulans. Be subjected to natural disasters like earthquakes, or have your sun go nova, or—"

"All right, all right!" Picard laughed, putting up his hands in defeat. "Touché again. Point taken and made. There is no safe haven."

"No," said Sulu gravely. "There's not."

Picard sighed. "I admit, there were roads not taken. Options not explored. Don't think that I haven't dwelt on those from time to time. Still . . . I had a firsthand exploration of what happens when one second-guesses one's actions."

Sulu cocked his head and regarded him curiously. "What sort of firsthand exploration?"

"A near-death experience. I don't really wish to discuss it. Let's just say that it cured me of my regrets. Thinking endlessly about all sorts of ways things might have gone . . . it seems rather a waste of time, don't you think?"

"Ah, but Captain . . . all of mankind's greatest achievements started with two simple words: 'What if?' Don't be too quick to dismiss their usefulness."

"I'll try to take your advice," said Picard. He straightened his back, unconsciously adopting the stance he always struck when he was in his Starfleet uniform. It was as if he was physically preparing to reassume his responsibilities. "End program," he said.

The rocks, the brush, the distant crashing ocean . . . and Commodore Hikaru Sulu . . . all vanished. The only thing remaining was the small holodeck room itself, its gleaming yellow lines crisscrossing around the wall, floor, and ceilings.

Picard headed out the door, and hadn't managed to get two feet when Crusher's voice called his name. He stopped and turned, smiling pleasantly. "Yes?"

"I've got Professor Martinez settled in," said Crusher. "And she asked me to pass on her appreciation. She's quite pleased with the guest quarters."

"Not a problem," said Picard.

"She was most complimentary, Captain," said Beverly Crusher. She smiled in that impish way she sometimes had. "And to be perfectly honest, Jean-Luc," she said in a lowered voice, "I think she finds you rather attractive."

Captain Picard raised an amused eyebrow. "Really," he said neutrally. "Thank you for the tip, Doctor. Your concern is, as always, noted."

"Just watching out for you, Captain," she said. "I knew you'd be interested." She took a step closer and dropped her voice to an even more confidential level. "It would not surprise me if she gratefully accepted any invitations to dinner you might choose to extend."

Picard regarded her curiously. "Beverly, why this sudden morbid interest in my social life?"

Crusher put a hand to her chest in mock astonishment. "Jean-Luc, I'm shocked . . . *shocked* . . . that you would insinuate such a thing."

"Oh, are you?"

"Yes, absolutely. There's nothing 'sudden' about it. I've *always* taken a morbid interest in your social life." And with that, she smiled and headed on her way down the corridor.

Picard shook his head. It might or might not have been his imagination, but he couldn't help but feel as if, ever since that time when they'd been able to read each other's minds, Beverly Crusher was acting like a woman who was insufferably pleased with herself. . . .

TRACK **B**

2.

Professor Andrea Martinez sat at the bridge science station, Commander Riker directly behind her. "As you see from ship's logs," he said, "the *Enterprise* has had more than her share of encounters with temporal anomalies."

"True," she said. Martinez had a round, thoughtful face, and deep-set gray eyes. Her hair, blond with gray streaks, hung in a sprightly way around her shoulders. She stroked her chin thoughtfully. "But there's only one that has an actual explanation behind it . . . this one, on Sarona Seven, that Paul created."

"Paul? You mean Dr. Manheim? You knew him?"

Martinez nodded. "I was his research assistant fifteen years ago. A brilliant man. He was the one who shifted my field of interest from black-hole event horizons to temporal phenomena. A shame things didn't work out for him." She frowned. "There are all these others, though, and frankly, Commander, that's why I . . ." She paused and turned, looking at him with amusement in her eyes. "I'm sorry, would you mind? You're breathing down my neck. . . ."

"Sorry." Riker took a step back, and then "felt" some-one's gaze on him. He turned and saw Deanna Troi, look-ing quickly away but with an unmistakable smirk on her face.

Picard walked onto the bridge and said briskly, "Mr. Data, estimated time of arrival at the Ompet Sector?"

"Twenty-two hours, eleven minutes," Data said, with no need to glance at his instruments.

Picard nodded approvingly and strolled over toward the science station. "Professor, how is your research coming?" he asked.

Martinez looked up, and Riker saw an immediate shift in the woman's no-nonsense expression. Her face softened ever so slightly, and the edges of her eyes crinkled up. Amused, Riker thought, *The old dog has still got that way with women.*

Picard, for his part, didn't even seem to acknowledge the clear difference in the way Martinez regarded him. Per-haps it was that apparent indifference that women found alluring.

"Interestingly, as I was telling Commander Riker here." She turned and said, "Is there a place where we can chat more comfortably?"

"Of course," he said graciously.

Moments later Picard, Riker, Troi, Data, Worf, and Martinez had retired to the conference lounge.

"I have a confession to make," began Martinez. "I asked specifically for the *Enterprise* to be the ship that trans-ported me out to the Ompet Oddity. I even called in favors from Starfleet."

"That would explain our being ordered out of our way to get you," said Picard, making no attempt to hide his curiosity. "Why us, Professor?"

"Because this ship has been practically a magnet for

temporal curiosities," said Martinez. "The average starship might encounter, at most, one such circumstance
during a tour. More often, none. But you people make
unexplained time twists seem as common as a head cold."

"I'm sure you're exaggerating."

"I'm sure I'm not." She pulled out a computer notepadd
and skimmed it. "On stardate 42679.2, you encountered a
time loop en route to Endicor. On stardate 43625.2, you
encountered another temporal anomaly . . . possibly a
Kerr loop of superstring material, but it was never determined for sure. Then we come to stardate 45020.4 . . ."

"There was no encounter with an anomaly on that date,"
Data said.

"True. But you did meet a Romulan named Sela . . ."

"That nonsense," Picard said briskly. "Granted, I cannot deny her remarkable resemblance to the late Tasha Yar.
But her claim that she was Tasha's daughter . . . that Tasha
was somehow tossed back two dozen years in time, when
we saw her die . . ."

"Can you say for certain that one of your encounters
with a temporal anomaly might *not* have resulted in such a
paradox occurring?" asked Martinez.

"You're asking about 'might-have-beens,' Professor, in a
galaxy of infinite possibilities," Riker spoke up. "For all we
know we 'might have been' all killed in our sleep and been
replaced by exact duplicates with all our memories intact.
But what's the *likelihood* of such a thing?"

"All I'm saying is that, considering your ship's history, I
would not rule it out," said Martinez. "Like this instance:
On 45652.1, you literally blinked out of existence for 17.4
days while you were trapped in a recursive causality loop.
Captain," and she stared at him blankly, "what in *hell* is a
recursive causality loop?"

"A temporal phenomenon that caused us to repeat a series of events," said Picard.

"I know. I know because this," and she tapped the notepadd, "explained as much. You're encountering things so bizarre, you have to coin phrases in order to explain them. Not to mention that I have absolutely no clue as to how an explosion of *any* kind . . . such as the collision with the *Bozeman* that you say created this 'loop' . . . could conceivably cause such a phenomenon." She looked from one officer to the other with a raised eyebrow. "Thoughts?"

"It was an extraordinary circumstance," offered Data.

Her mouth twitched. "I daresay. For what it's worth, you folks are carrying on a grand tradition. The original *Enterprise* NCC-1701 did its share of time traveling, being the first to develop the slingshot effect. In that ship's history there are at least two instances of time travel." She glanced down again. "The first was on stardate 3113.2, when the ship was tossed back in time to the nineteen-sixties, allegedly after a near-collision with a black hole." She looked up. "Subsequent attempts to duplicate such an occurrence, under controlled scientific conditions, did not succeed. Temporal distortions in the vicinity of black holes? That's a given. But being thrown centuries backward in time? There's no grounds for that."

"Infinite possibilities, Professor," said Picard. "As you yourself observed, how are we to say anything is not possible?"

"Indeed, Captain. There was one other incident, on stardate 3823.7, in which an ion storm, combined with a transporter malfunction, exchanged several *Enterprise* crewmen with counterparts in a parallel universe."

"But that didn't involve time travel. How is that an 'unexplained temporal phenomenon'?" asked Troi.

Martinez leaned back in her chair. "First, because although it was vaguely possible that an ion storm could conceivably, remotely, cause such an exchange . . . it's not bloody likely. As unlikely, if not more so, as an explosion causing a recursive causality loop, if you catch my drift. Second, the current scientific theory is that parallel universes are, in fact, alternate time tracks. Separated from our own by dint of the various decisions that sent history in different directions. But that separation is not always one hundred percent, as Captain Kirk could attest, were he here. Or Sela might point out, if you actually believed her. You cannot, however, ignore the records of one of your own officers, and I'm quite certain that Lieutenant Worf could attest to his own experiences."

Worf shifted uncomfortably. He had been silent up until then, but now he was forced to nod in agreement. "I can easily see where parallel universes could be viewed as alternate time tracks," he said. "You have all read my full reports on my . . . difficulties . . . upon returning from the Klingon competition. I would be inclined to say that 'alternate timelines' is certainly accurate enough. Each variant universe in which I found myself seemed different from our own due to specific moments in its history that deviated from ours. Even the most drastic . . ."

"Which one was that?" asked Riker.

Worf looked at the first officer. Oddly, in his report on the affair, he had found himself unable to mention the brief, viewscreen encounter with the *Enterprise* that was a refugee from a Borg-infested universe. There had been Riker, beard and hair unkempt, terror gushing from him like a fountain, begging, pleading, refusing to return to his own, nightmarish cosmos. Worf was very aware that, during the first major Borg incursion, it had been a margin of bare seconds that allowed the *Enterprise* to turn the Borg's destructive incursion against the Borg themselves.

Two, three seconds the other way, and their own universe might just as easily have been the one in which the Borg were "everywhere."

It was an awareness that had cost Worf a few nights of sleep . . . particularly when he would look over to his sleeping son and imagine the child existing in that sort of universe. Worf had seen little need to inflict that knowledge upon anyone else.

"The one in which I was married to Counselor Troi," said Worf without hesitation.

Deanna had to smile at that. "How horrible it must have been for you," she said in dry sympathy.

"And Mr. Worf's troubles were also set off by a not-quite-explained anomaly. All right, Professor, you've made your point," said Picard. "But let us say for the moment that you are correct: that the *Enterprise* is, for some reason, a sort of magnet for temporal oddities. Why would you say that is?"

She spread her hands and shrugged. "I haven't a clue," she said. "The point is, though, that if something *is* going to happen upon visiting the Ompet Oddity, this would be the ship to which it would happen."

"Now there's a cheerful thought," said Deanna.

Picard turned to Data. "Mr. Data, do we have any further research available on the Oddity that we can make available to Professor Martinez?"

"No, sir," said Data. "It is, in fact, the professor who has written the first major extrapolations about it."

" 'Major'? You do me honor, sir," said Martinez, sounding amused. "Without firsthand observation, it's been guesswork up until now. Conclusions drawn from long-range scans and probes after the initial mathematical findings that revealed its existence. I'm just damned lucky that the science council felt I was the best person for the job of inspecting the Oddity up close . . . and that I, then, had the luxury of waiting for your availability, as I said."

"You were fortunate that the Oddity has continued to remain in existence for so long a time," said Data. "It has been our experience that such anomalies tend to be short-lived."

"What can I say?" She smiled. "Some things are just destined to be."

As the others left the conference room, Martinez lingered by Picard a moment and said, "Captain . . . I was wondering if, by chance, you are free for dinner tonight."

"I'm afraid not, Professor," said Picard. "I am otherwise engaged for this evening."

She sighed, making no effort to hide her disappointment. "A previous date?"

"Actually, my dining companion is unaware."

"A surprise. How marvelous. I love surprises."

"I used to love surprises," said Picard ruefully, "until the unpleasant surprises started to outnumber the pleasant ones."

"Jean-Luc! This is a pleasant surprise."

Picard stood outside Crusher's quarters, a bottle of wine in one hand, two glasses in the other. "May I come in?" he asked.

She stepped aside and gestured for him to enter, and he did so. "To what do I owe the honor of this evening?" she asked.

He turned to face her and said, with a touch of sadness, "Beverly, we both know to what this 'honor' is owed."

"Yes." Her face darkened, and her normally cheerful nature . . . which had been exaggerated, even artificially exuberant in recent days . . . evaporated. Her hands wandered as if she were unsure what purpose they served at the ends of her wrists. "I . . . spoke to Wes earlier. He has a great deal on his mind these days."

"Don't tell me he forgot."

"No." She shook her head. "No, he remembered. And thank *you* for remembering, Jean-Luc."

"As if I could ever forget."

He poured the wine in silence, filled the glasses halfway for himself and Beverly. They raised the glasses, but then paused a moment, the space between their glasses filled with far more than just emptiness.

"To Jack Crusher," said Picard. "Husband, father, friend . . . and missed by all. In commemorating the one day of his death, let it always remind us to celebrate all the days of his life."

Beverly nodded, and clinked glasses. But she found that—as she did so—she lowered her eyes, unable to meet Picard's gaze.

Although they spent the rest of the evening together and made small talk, there was more silence in their words than either would admit.

TRACK **B**

3.

In the silence of space, it roared at them.

The *Enterprise* hovered a safe distance from the Ompet Oddity, a shimmering array of blue and red hanging in space. From deep within . . . if such a thing could be considered to have depth . . . there seemed to be some sort of source of light, flickering and tantalizing.

Martinez watched from the science station, and she slowly became aware that she couldn't remember the last time she had taken a breath. She forced air into her lungs to play it safe; certainly passing out on the bridge wouldn't do much for her image.

"Reading a high degree of accelerated graviton activity," Data said, "as well as a high neutron flow. In many ways, the readings are similar to several other temporal disruptions we have encountered."

"And the cause of the Oddity?"

"Unknown, sir."

Picard dwelt for a moment on the curious nature of the universe. For some reason, it made him think of a time, in

61

his youth, when he had been at Starfleet Academy in San Francisco. He had not been there for three days when there was an earthquake. It was not unexpected, of course: instrumentation detected it many hours before it arrived, and everyone had had more than enough time to get to shelters. Nevertheless, there was still the distant sensation of the ground shifting beneath them. And Picard remembered thinking, *If you can't even count on the ground beneath your feet to remain stable, what in the world* does *remain stable?*

If he'd only known then what he knew now. Namely, that there seemed times when the entire fabric of the universe was being held together with spit and baling wire.

"Is the probe prepared?" asked Picard.

"Yes, sir." Data ran a quick triple check. "All telemetry readings are on-line."

"Launch probe."

The probe hurtled out of the *Enterprise,* leaving a shimmering stream behind it as it sped, straight and true, toward the heart of the Ompet Oddity.

In a low voice, Riker said to Picard, "What do you think the probe will reveal, Captain?"

"If I knew that, Number One, we wouldn't have to launch a probe," Picard said reasonably.

Riker smiled at Picard's deadpan response, but then his expression turned serious. "Suggest we go to yellow alert, Captain." When Picard turned and looked at him questioningly, Riker continued, "If there's one thing I've noticed about these anomalies, it's that they seem to respond rather poorly to being annoyed. They suck us in, they blow up, they spit out alternate versions of us . . . *some*thing."

"And your concern is that a probe might constitute an annoyance."

"It has occurred to me, yes."

Picard was forced to agree. "Yellow alert, then."

As the *Enterprise* quietly braced herself for a possible emergency, Data calmly counted down the time until the probe made contact with the Oddity. "Ten . . . nine . . . eight . . . seven . . ."

In the Ten-Forward lounge, Guinan was calmly serving out a drink . . . and suddenly her hands trembled with such fierceness that the glass tumbled right out of her hand. Mr. Barclay was the unfortunate recipient of the cascading liquid as it hit his uniform front and dribbled down him.

But his sudden condition of wetness was of secondary concern. What was first and foremost in his mind was the fact that the normally sure-handed, unflappable Guinan had suddenly lost all her dexterity.

"Are you all right?" he asked urgently, worried she was having some sort of a fit.

Guinan was staring at her hands, as if they had suddenly taken on a life of their own. And then they had assumed a defensive posture, blocking her head as if warding off something.

Then her conscious mind caught up with her subconscious.

"Oh no," she said, "not again," and for the first time she was feeling genuine dread. For not only was she getting a sense of *him* again . . . but there was something else as well. Something beyond even her ken, and her ken was considerable.

"Three . . . two . . ."

Data stopped counting.

Picard frowned upon the abrupt cessation. "Mr. Data, what's wrong?"

"We have lost contact with the probe, sir," said Data.

Picard rose from his seat. It was a silly move, of course. It wasn't as if, once he was standing, he had a better shot at seeing the probe. Nevertheless, he was on his feet as if it made a difference, and he said crisply, "Did it enter the Oddity?"

"No, sir," said Data. "It vanished a moment before entering it."

"Are you sure?" Professor Martinez now asked.

Data looked at her with the closest to surprise that his normally expressionless face could come. "Of course," he said.

"A malfunction?"

"I do not believe that it . . ." Then Data stopped, looking at his instruments. Had he been human, he would have been utterly perplexed. "Captain . . . I am reading the probe again. Its position has shifted. It is now at 218 mark 4. It is relatively stationary."

"Relatively?" Riker now said, sounded confused. "Relative to what?"

"Minute changes in its trajectory. It appears to be moving almost rhythmically approximately two meters, back and forth."

"Give us a view of it."

The viewscreen shifted, the Ompet Oddity momentarily vanishing to be replaced by the new location of the probe.

They saw what appeared to be a meteoroid hanging in space. The upper portion was a mile wide, and flat, with the underside tapering downward.

And there seemed to be something moving on it.

"Full magnification," said Picard.

The closer image now occupied the screen.

Martinez's jaw fell to somewhere around her ankles. "What the hell—?" she managed to stammer out.

On the viewscreen, she was seeing something that made

a temporal anomaly such as the Ompet Oddity look positively routine.

There was a man on the surface of the asteroid. He looked utterly normal and human, and did not seem the least bit deterred that there was no atmosphere, no gravity, no nothing. He sported black trousers, thigh-high buccaneer-style boots, and a white shirt with flared sleeves.

There was a small barrier consisting of a net made, apparently, from standard string or rope.

The probe was there as well. Gleaming and round, it was being batted back and forth over the net. The man was appearing on one side and then the other and back again, exuberantly striking the probe on either side before it could land.

"What the hell is going *on?!*" demanded Martinez.

"I believe," Data said slowly, "that it is a volleyball game. The object is to—"

"I think she knows what a volleyball game is, Mr. Data," said Picard. "Readings?"

"None, sir," said Worf.

"Instrument failure?"

"I can confirm what Lieutenant Worf said," Martinez told him. "I'm not getting any reading at all! As near as the instruments can tell, there's no one there."

"An illusion?" suggested Picard.

And the strange being turned as if, in airless space, Picard's worries had carried to him.

A split instant later, he was standing on the bridge.

"Do I *seem* like an illusion to you?" he announced.

Before Picard could speak, however, Guinan's voice came over his comm unit. "Guinan to Picard," she said quickly and without preamble. "Is *he* up there?"

From the tone of her voice Picard knew precisely which "he" she meant. Q, however, was nowhere to be seen.

Merely this . . . person. "Not at the moment," he said, "but stay alert, please."

Slowly he rose to his feet. "I am Captain Jean-Luc Picard," he said carefully. "Identify yourself, please."

The other bowed slightly. "General Trelane . . . retired. Once the humble Squire of Gothos. Greetings and felicitations to all of you."

Slowly Trelane circled the bridge, nodding approvingly. When he spoke, his voice echoed and soared, as if he were addressing the upper mezzanine at a theater. "Well, I must say . . . this is something of an improvement. Everything has a very calming look about it. Muted colors rather than those stark primaries. Very impressive. Very relaxed." He spun on his heel and loudly proclaimed, "Yes, an excellent job! You will not find a word of protest from me. Indeed, you will not."

He stopped and stared openly at Worf.

Worf scowled back.

"Oh dear," said Trelane. "Not quite human, are you. A bizarre form of Nubian, perhaps?" he asked.

Worf started to bristle, and then immediately realized he wasn't sure why he was doing so. The question had no meaning to him. He was reacting more to the tone than the words.

Trelane waved dismissively. "No matter," he said. "Captain, I congratulate you! A fine vessel, with an . . . interesting . . . crew."

"I'm pleased you approve," Picard said neutrally. "Now if you would be so kind as to—"

"What can she do?" Trelane demanded.

Picard frowned. "Pardon?"

"The old one moved like molasses," sniffed Trelane. "Is this one terribly faster than the first?"

"If you mean the first starship named *Enterprise,* yes. Do

you mean to tell me you are familiar with the original *Enterprise?"* Despite Trelane's bizarre manner and uncomfortable resemblance, in attitude, to Q . . . despite the fact that he was a trespasser and intruder . . . nevertheless the historian in Picard found that nugget of information a fascinating one.

"Oh yes, quite," said Trelane. Suddenly he yanked his sword from his scabbard and swept it through the air with such panache that Riker ducked, lest he be decapitated. Worf prepared to lunge, but Picard gestured for him to remain where he was since Trelane was not attacking. Instead he was gesturing with it. "It was a grand and glorious battle royale!" he declaimed. "A daring tale of resourcefulness and treachery . . . the former mine, the latter theirs, of course . . . which I might share with you valiant chaps on some future stormy night. For now—" He extended his sword straight forward, as if pointing the way. "—let's see what this mighty vessel can do."

Abruptly the *Enterprise* hurtled forward, as if propelled from a slingshot.

In Ten-Forward, everyone was hurled out of their seats like so many poker chips. Guinan lunged and grabbed the edge of the bar and watched helplessly as her bottles cascaded off the shelves.

In engineering, Geordi La Forge watched in helpless horror as all velocity meters went right off the scale. The warp engines, however, pulsed normally as if nothing were unusual.

Not since the *Enterprise* was hurled into Borg space had Picard felt so completely powerless on the bridge of his own ship.

The captain was slammed back against his chair, as were

his other officers. Worf lost his grip on the railing and crashed back against a bulkhead.

Picard didn't know how much of the pressure upon him was some sort of genuine unexplained g-forces at work, and how much was being provided courtesy of Trelane himself. Ultimately it didn't matter, since the result was the same either way.

Trelane, for his part, seemed utterly unaffected. His sword still outstretched, his dynamic posture undisturbed, he was crowing, *"Tally-ho!!"*

Stars streaked by, a dazzling blur, spiraling around them as if they were plunging headlong into a galactic whirlpool. Picard was certain that he heard the very hull of the ship screaming in protest, and any moment the entire vessel was going to fly apart.

"Stop!" he shouted.

"Make me!" Trelane challenged.

And then Picard's eyes widened as he saw a huge ball of light heading straight toward them, straight on a collision course. There was no opportunity for evasive maneuvers, because at the speed they were traveling, to see such an obstruction was to be practically on top of it.

Even Trelane seemed startled. He drew back his sword and just barely had time to shout, *"Have at you!,"* stabbing forward toward the star on the screen, and the next thing they knew, they were enveloped in it.

There was a soundless explosion from all around them.

And when the lights, and their vision, cleared up, all was as it had been. The *Enterprise* was back at its previous position, and everything was exactly the way it was before Trelane had, on a whim, sent the *Enterprise* careering at impossible speeds across the galaxy.

Actually, not *exactly* the way it was before.

Q was standing directly in front of Trelane, holding Trelane's sword by the blade. He was shaking his head and sighing heavily.

"Showing off again?" he asked.

Trelane shrugged. "As you say." He didn't seem particularly upset that Q had interceded. Without a word he took the sword by the hilt and replaced it in his scabbard.

Professor Martinez gaped at the new arrival. He was slim, black-haired, and sporting a Starfleet uniform.

The bridge crew was pulling itself to its collective feet. Worf was up first, and he was unable to contain an audible growl when he saw who had newly arrived. Trelane seemed rather taken aback by the ferocity of Worf's reaction, but Q was not the least bit perturbed.

"Don't worry about him, my lad," he said to Trelane, indicating Worf. "He's almost as amazing an anomaly as that out there." He gestured expansively. "Do you like it, Picard? It's my protégé's latest work."

"We should have known!" Riker said fiercely. "Your 'protégé' could have gotten us killed!"

"Oh, nonsense. He was in perfect control. I was monitoring from a distance, and if there'd been any real danger, I would have stepped in sooner."

"Your assurances," Picard informed him angrily, "are less than assuring."

Martinez felt very much as if she had walked into the middle of a mystery. "Is he like you?" she asked Trelane of Q. "Are you like . . ." She turned helplessly to Picard, her face a question mark.

Picard, feeling decidedly sour, said, "Q, Professor, is a powerful being . . ."

Q held up a scolding finger. "Ah-ah, Jean-Luc. 'All-powerful.'"

"Being," continued Picard as if Q had not spoken. "A member of the Q Continuum, who seems to feel that it's his purpose in life to annoy us."

"Not my *sole* purpose," Q demurred. "I like to spread myself around."

Worf rumbled, "What he excels at spreading is—"

"Not now, Lieutenant," Picard said quickly, having no desire to escalate the war of words that always seemed to break out between Worf and Q whenever the latter showed up. Picard's major interest at that point was getting back to something that Q had just said. "Are you telling us, Q, that *he* . . . made that?"

"It's something of a hobby of mine," said Trelane. He was continuing his tour of the bridge, his hands draped behind his back. "I make them all the time."

Then he turned to face Picard squarely, and for a moment . . . just a moment . . . there seemed the slightest disruption of his veneer of politeness. "It's perfectly clear to me that you must absolutely adore them," he said. His voice was low and silky and not particularly inviting.

Now Riker stepped forward, so that he and Picard were on either side of Trelane. "Why is that clear?" asked Riker.

"You keep becoming involved with them," said Trelane matter-of-factly. "I make one here, and there you are. I make another over there, and there you are again. I whip up my little temporal enigmas, and there you come, again and again. It's getting so that I almost expect you to show up." He sighed, sounding like a bored fop, and waved a handkerchief in his face as if he had a case of the vapors. "It's a massive sort of kismet, I suppose."

"Yes, Jean-Luc is nothing if not predictable," sighed Q. "For example, now he'll say—"

"Q, I want to talk to you alone," Picard told him

brusquely . . . and then he was rather annoyed to see that a couple of the bridge crew actually looked like they were trying not to smile. He turned and immediately saw why. Floating behind his head were a set of silver balloons, which bore the words: Q I WANT TO TALK TO YOU ALONE. Judging from the reaction of his people, they had doubtlessly snapped into existence a second before Picard had actually uttered the words.

The crewmen very quickly—since they knew what was good for them—composed themselves. Q gestured grandly in the direction of the captain's ready room, and Picard strode briskly through the door. Q was right behind him, and the door hissed shut.

Picard turned to face him . . . and Q was right there, practically on top of him. He was grabbing Picard by the uniform front and for a split instant the bewildered starship captain thought that the omnipotent being was physically attacking him.

But that impression quickly evaporated when he saw Q's expression. It was one of barely contained desperation. Clearly he was trying to maintain his usual facade of smug distance, but in this instance he was not succeeding particularly well.

"Picard," he said, low and intense. "You've got to help me."

"What?" was all Picard could get out.

"He's driving me *insane,*" Q informed him. "I can't *take* it anymore."

And Picard did something then that he had never done before. He laughed in Q's face.

Q sighed heavily and released Picard, making no pretense at his disgust over the captain's reaction. "I should have known you would think this was an amusing situation." He sauntered across the room, regaining a measure of his usual swagger, and flopped down onto the couch. He adopted a pose in which he was rubbing his temple, giving great physical testimony that he was clearly feeling beleaguered from all sides. "A race as minimally developed as yours *would* find this funny. Back during the times when your people were crouched around fires while animals peered from the forest, the concept of high humor involved the tribal leader openly scratching his nether regions. A pity you haven't substantially evolved beyond that."

"You have to admit to a certain irony in this instance, Q."

"I don't have to admit to anything, Picard, but you do."

Picard raised an eyebrow. "Oh, do I?"

"Yes. You have to admit that you owe me."

"I owe you?" said Picard, bemused. "How the devil did you come to that conclusion?"

"Easily, Picard." Q put one hand over his heart and flapped his fingers several times as he said, "Thump . . . thump . . . thump."

And Picard knew instantly what Q was referring to. Picard blanched slightly, and braced himself against a wall. For Picard, it was the equivalent of being in a situation that was most certainly a dream, and then discovering that he was, in fact, wide awake.

"That . . . happened?" he whispered.

"What 'that' are you referring to?" asked Q.

In an uncharacteristic display of open anger, Picard slammed an open palm onto his desk. The materials atop it shuddered under the impact. "No games!" he snapped. "Not about that! Not ever!"

Q's expression softened just a bit. "All right, Picard. Two opponents, two"—he made a few jabs with his fists—

72

"sparring partners, coming clean with each other. You are, of course, referring to the incident when your mechanical heart failed you."

Picard nodded, waiting for Q to continue.

"And in your coma, you suddenly discovered yourself in an area of white haze. And then you heard," and he smiled slightly in a manner that would give any rational person chills, "that hated voice, telling you that you were dead, that you were in heaven . . ."

"And that you were God," Picard finished. "I didn't believe it, of course."

"I'm not surprised. The thought of you going to heaven . . ." Q shuddered slightly. "Well . . . it's clear they'll let just about anyone in."

Picard's eyes narrowed. "For someone who was imploring me for help just moments ago, you're getting pretty damned cocky."

"What can I say, Jean-Luc? You're such an easy target." Then Q grew serious again in that mercurial way he had. "And I led you through an incident in your life that you regretted, and you had the opportunity to do things differently. And you discovered that you wound up with even *more* regrets. So you put things back the way they were before. Huzzah, huzzah, and all was right with the world once more. And you want to know if it *really* happened. You won't like the answer."

"I'll risk it," said Picard.

"The answer is: Yes and no."

"That's no answer."

Q shrugged. "It may not seem like much of one to you, but it's the best I can provide you. You won't understand any answer beyond that."

"More of your condescens—"

Speaking so sharply that Picard could practically feel the voice bisecting him, Q said, "Picard, despite humanity's overall inflated opinion of itself, you are going to have to face up to the reality that there are concepts of time and space that are, and will likely remain, beyond your comprehension." He shook his head in disgust. "And you accuse *me* of arrogance? Picard, I could blast this ship out of existence if I felt like it. I could grow hair on your head. Turn your crew into embryos, force Worf to recite doggerel. I could turn your ship inside out, your reality outside in. I am not being condescending, Picard . . . not that I'm incapable of it, you understand, but this simply isn't one of the times. Now, what I most definitely *am,* Picard, is arrogant. Why? Because I have *reason* to be. I have a *right* to be. So . . . *mortal* . . . what's *your* excuse?"

There was a long silence, and Picard stood there with his arms folded. "Are you through?" he said finally.

Q rolled his eyes. "I *knew* I could count on you for a dazzling riposte."

"I simply wanted to say that you've made your point. Whether time changed or not, whether *I* changed or not . . . it would appear that you did me a tremendous service by laying to rest one of the more . . ." Picard sighed heavily. ". . . the more nagging aspects of my life. So I suppose that, in a sense, I do 'owe' you."

"Good." Q slapped his knees and rose. "I'm glad we're agreed on that, then."

"But frankly, Q, I'm not exactly certain of what you're expecting here." Picard now uncrossed his arms and draped them behind his back. "Debt or not, I'm not about to order my crew to make themselves available for this . . . this person's amusement." He frowned, still clearly befuddled over the situation. "Would you mind telling me how in the world you became involved in this . . . enforced association?"

Q sighed heavily. "I would mind, yes. Unfortunately, it's a fair question. The problem is that to explain would take lengthy descriptions of all manner of Q Continuum affairs. Not to sound *condescending"*—he rolled the word around in his mouth—"but I don't see where it would benefit either of us to give you all the . . . what's the expression? . . . the gory details."

"In terms I can understand, then," Picard said dryly.

"Very well. Trelane is a child. He encountered the *Enterprise* some years ago, back under the command of Kirk. You can read all about it, I'm sure, so I won't waste your time with it here. That was a mere century ago, and although he has matured slightly since then, he still has quite a ways to go. . . ."

"You mean until he becomes a paragon of proper behavior such as yourself."

"Exactly," said Q, choosing to ignore the sarcasm in Picard's voice. "Now I am . . . to use a term to which you can relate . . . Trelane's godfather. All members of the Q, at some point or another in their existence, must take a fledgling Q under their wing and guide them toward the glorious and enviable fate that awaits them. I have a long association with Trelane's parents, and it was I who was chosen for this . . ." He tried to keep the groan out of his voice and did not entirely succeed. ". . . honor of shepherding Trelane."

"For how long?" asked Picard.

"As long as it takes. In human terms, it's a span of time that's staggering to contemplate."

"Did you go through such a process yourself in your developmental years?"

"Well, of course," said Q. His attention appeared to wander a moment. "I haven't thought of good old Q in quite some time. After shepherding me, he left the Continuum for a while. In fact," and he frowned, "I don't think he's come back yet. Something about a vacation."

"Now there's a surprise," said Picard. "What I would suggest, Q, is that you handle Trelane in whatever manner your mentor handled you." He couldn't resist adding, "Only try to do a better job."

"Ha. Ha. Ha." Q rose and crossed to face Picard. "Look, Jean-Luc. I could have just popped in on you unannounced. I know how much you simply *adore* when I do that. You immediately get all defensive, because you don't want your precious crew to think that you're losing control of the situation. So instead I kept him occupied for a time, and endeavored to skew matters so that we would run into each other by 'happenstance.' All this just to try and catch you in a good mood . . . presuming you ever have one."

Picard tilted his head slightly, regarding Q with sudden suspicion. "Are you saying that you somehow *forced* Professor Martinez to request the *Enterprise* for this mission?"

"Picard, you of all people should know: When I want to force something, it's obvious. You wouldn't have to ask the question; you'd *know.* Let us simply say that I put certain matters into motion with a confident idea of how they would turn out. If you want more of an answer than that, Picard, you're not going to get it."

"All right, all right," said Picard. "Enough shadow dancing, then. What are you saying? That you want Trelane and yourself to stay here for a time, to observe us?"

"To interact with you. To talk with you. To understand

76

you. Trelane made something of a muddle of it last time. He fancied that he was studying humanity, but it was rather like a child pulling the wings off flies and then claiming he's an entomologist."

"Yes, I understand." Picard stabbed a finger at him. "But you'll have to be with him every moment. I don't need him going off on his own and harassing my crew."

Q tossed off a salute. "Understood, *mon capitaine.*"

"I want you to understand, Q . . . I'm doing this against my better judgment."

Looking surprised, Q said, "What a startling coincidence. That's precisely what God muttered to me when he created humanity."

Picard simply stared at Q with a dour expression. "Ha. Ha. Ha."

"I'm not joking, Picard," said Q, deadpan.

"So you're no longer claiming to be God, but simply saying that you knew him."

"He's a tough fellow to *know,* in the strictest sense," said Q, keeping such a perfectly straight face that Picard started to get chills. "Doesn't say much. Prefers to let His actions speak for Him. Ohhh, I advised Him against it, of course." He closed his eyes and shook his head wearily. "I said to Him, G— . . . He has this thing about not wanting His name spoken in direct address. Eccentric. G—, I said, you'll regret it. Humanity, I mean. They'll give you nothing but headaches, I warned Him. Stick with the animals. They don't talk back, they won't start wars, and they won't think that the simple trick of mastering upright locomotion or producing the occasional memorable musical comedy gives them license to run an entire planet into the ground. Well, He saw fit to do otherwise . . . although

I did pitch in here and there in putting together life on Earth."

"Oh really," said Picard, not buying it for a second. "And just where, in all aspects of creation, can your hand be seen?"

Q smiled toothily. "Why, Picard . . . who do you think came up with the duck-billed platypus?"

TRACK B

4.

Trelane's first hours aboard the *Enterprise* had been relatively peaceful. Indeed, even promising. Picard found himself having to admit that Trelane's presence might be one of the most phenomenal scientific finds in quite some time.

Professor Martinez and Commander Data spent a lengthy period of time discussing matters of temporal anomalies with Trelane. It turned out that the erstwhile "Squire of Gothos" had developed something of a fascination with matters of relative time flow.

"It stems from his first encounter with the original *Enterprise*," Data had explained to Picard in the captain's ready room, as Riker stood near at Picard's request. "He had been observing Earth rather closely, or so he thought. It turned out that he was watching events of several centuries past. He had forgotten to allow for the amount of time required for light to travel. That realization led to a strengthened fascination with the relative passage of time."

"That fascination led, in turn, to his creating a variety of temporal anomalies," said Martinez. She seemed awe-struck even to be putting forward the explanation, as if she could scarcely believe it. "To a being like Trelane, the entire universe is his petri dish."

"And *we* kept running into these anomalies he created?" Picard said incredulously, appearing far less enthused about the wondrousness of the situation than did Martinez. "What are the odds on something like that? Don't answer that," he amended quickly, upon noticing the slight disfocus in Data's eyes that always seemed to precede some lengthy and unwanted explanation. "It was rhetorical."

Data nodded, unperturbed.

"Trelane claims that it's coincidence," said Martinez. "Q backs him up on it."

"Perfect," said Riker, unimpressed. "A being of incredible power and questionable behavior swears to something, and a similar individual vouches for him. That's like Kodos claiming he didn't perform any executions, and his alibi is that he was making the rounds of British pubs with Adolf Hitler."

"You don't have to sound quite so sarcastic, Commander," observed Martinez.

"There is always the possibility," said Data, "that the *Enterprise* continues to remain a source of fascination for Trelane. Although there is no way to prove it . . . particularly if he himself does not admit to it . . . it is possible that Trelane finds himself repeatedly drawn back to the *Enterprise.*"

"Much like a child picking at a scab," said Riker.

Picard glanced at Riker, and a small smile actually played across his lips. "I can't say I exactly appreciate the analogy, Number One," he said drolly, "but it may indeed be valid. I am pleased that matters seem to be proceeding smoothly, particularly since I had great trepidation about permitting Q and Trelane to remain here."

"I would have liked to see you try to force them to leave," said Martinez.

Picard let the remark pass. "Let's keep a close eye on matters, though, shall we? If problems occur, we should deal with them before they become unmanageable."

Meantime, down in Ten-Forward, Geordi was seated at a table with Beverly Crusher, chatting over drinks. He noticed that she seemed just a shade out of sorts, and asked about it.

She smiled wryly. "For someone who's allegedly blind, you see a great deal of subtlety."

"I'm a subtle guy, Doctor," he said.

"Nothing's wrong," she lied, feeling Jack's long-dead gaze drilling into the back of her neck. "Just having an off day."

Geordi was about to press the matter when he saw Crusher's surprised look at something over his shoulder. He turned around to see what she was staring at.

Trelane had sauntered into Ten-Forward. It was hard not to notice him, because a fanfare of music that seemed to come from everywhere sounded throughout the lounge.

All over the place, heads were turning.

He stood there for a moment, his hands on his hips, looking for all the world like a pirate standing confidently on the deck of his galleon.

"Well!" he said. "This *is* impressive."

Guinan was standing behind the bar, her eyes narrowed to slits. Beverly Crusher saw in Guinan something that she was not accustomed to: uncertainty. The fact that Trelane was associated with Q was certainly enough to put Guinan on guard. And indeed, Trelane seemed to ooze arrogance with even greater facility than did Q.

He turned and looked at Guinan. Immediately his face fell in disapproval.

"You're her, aren't you," he said with a notable lack of enthusiasm.

Guinan nodded.

He studied her, giving her such intense scrutiny that it was as if he were mentally disassembling her molecule by molecule. "Q told me to be wary of you," he said finally. "But to be perfectly blunt, I'm not sure why."

Guinan put on a wide smile that belied the caution she felt. "You wouldn't want to know," she said.

Trelane laughed. It was not a pleasant sound.

"Guinan," he said, "I am making every effort to be on . . . how did Q put it? . . . my best behavior. But that does not mean that I must tolerate rudeness. I despise rudeness." He leaned forward slightly, his face darkening. "I think that you may have been displaying a rude tone."

"No," she said. "If I'd been rude, you wouldn't be thinking I might have been. You'd *know*."

"Ah, but I believe you have been rude. And I believe that you owe me an apology."

"Really," said Guinan. "Do you also believe in the Easter Bunny?"

"Uhm, listen," La Forge now said, stepping in quickly. "Perhaps it would be better if . . ."

Trelane did not even afford him a glance. "Do not interfere. This is none of your concern."

"Look, Trelane," Geordi said firmly, "I'm making it my concern."

Guinan felt a tingle of alarm. Verbal sparring was one thing, but Trelane was proving unconscionably thin-skinned. That could be dangerous. "Geordi, don't—" started Guinan.

Now Trelane did look at him, and he was scowling fiercely. "Go away," he said, and waved dismissively.

Geordi vanished.

Beverly let out a squawk of alarm. Instinctively she hit her comm badge and called, "Crusher to La Forge." She wasn't at all sure she would get any sort of response, because for all she knew Trelane had just tossed Geordi into the heart of a sun somewhere.

What she heard was unexpected. The high-pitched scream of a woman came over her comm badge. After that, nothing.

Then Guinan did something extraordinary. She actually vaulted over the bar, her long red robe swirling around her. She did it effortlessly, as if gravity had little or no interest in her. She stood toe-to-toe with Trelane, and Beverly started to take a step forward. Without looking at her, Guinan put out a commanding hand, and Beverly stopped dead in her tracks. In some distant part of her mind, she wasn't sure if she didn't want to move or that she couldn't move.

"Bring him back," Guinan said firmly.

"And if I don't want to?" replied Trelane challengingly.

"Now!" said Guinan.

Trelane regarded her with a raised eyebrow for a moment, and then said with an air of boredom, "Oh, very well." He made a flippant gesture of his laced wrist, and Geordi La Forge reappeared in a flash of light.

He was sopping wet. His hair was glistening with water droplets, and his drenched uniform was clinging to his body. Curiously, he had a somewhat bemused expression on his face.

"Geordi!" exclaimed Crusher. "What happened?! I heard a scream, and—"

"It's . . . it's okay, Doctor," said Geordi, slightly bewildered.

"Where did he *send* you?"

"Uh . . ." He coughed slightly. "Counselor Troi's shower."

Beverly felt her cheeks burning. "Oh" was all she could think of to say.

"Don't worry." He tapped his VISOR. "I didn't see anything."

And Trelane, switching moods, laughed loudly as if they were all the best of friends. He clapped Geordi on the back and proclaimed, "Here is a man with a sense of humor! You could all take lessons from him! Guinan! Drinks for everyone here, on me!"

Guinan looked at the dripping Geordi, who was valiantly trying to maintain his good humor. But she could tell how mortified he was. Likewise she was chagrined on behalf of Troi. Yet there was Trelane, smug, self-satisfied, the personification of mean-spiritedness.

And on top of all that, he'd just given her the perfect setup line.

In the spirit of striking back on behalf of her friends, Guinan took a pitcher of water . . . and her life . . . in her hands.

"Whatever you say," Guinan proclaimed. "Drinks on you," and she upended the pitcher over Trelane's head.

Beverly and Geordi jumped back so as not to get caught in the cascading liquid, although in Geordi's case it was really somewhat moot. Guinan, Beverly would later realize upon recollection, did not get a drop on her. But the doused Trelane was a soaking, drenched mess. His hair was now matted, the fluff was gone from his ruffles.

And there was roiling fury in his eyes.

"You . . . !" he growled, and started toward Guinan. Guinan struck a defensive pose, her arms snaked in front of her as if warding off a serpent.

Which was the precise moment that Q showed up.

He entered in typical fashion, in a burst of light. Everyone froze, and Geordi felt a sense of dread.

Q looked from Guinan to Trelane and from Trelane to Geordi . . . both of whom had puddled considerably on the floor by that point.

He clapped his hands and rubbed them briskly.

"So!" he said. "Everyone getting along?"

Trelane, so furious that his hand was trembling, pointed at Guinan and said, "Look what she did to me!"

Guinan did not lessen her defensive pose. If she was at all intimidated by the collective power facing her, she did not show it.

"Guinan did this to you?" asked Q, stressing Guinan's name with some incredulity.

"Yes!"

"Well . . ." And Q shrugged. "You probably had it coming, then."

Geordi tried to fight down an explosion of laughter. He was only partly successful and it came out as sort of an aborted hiccup.

"Q!" said Trelane, stricken. "How can you side with her against—"

"I'm not siding with anyone," replied Q. "I'm simply stating fact. Oh, now, don't blubber." He snapped his fingers and instantly Trelane and Geordi were dry, along with the floor under them. "We need to talk," he said, and with another small gesture they had both disappeared.

Which was excellent timing, because a second later

Deanna Troi stormed into Ten-Forward. Her hair was wet, and her uniform sported large damp areas.

Her fists were clenched, her expression one of more fury than anyone had ever seen from the normally unflappable counselor.

"All right! Where is the little weasel?"

"Which one?" asked Crusher.

"Either!!!"

On the top of the saucer section, Trelane sat with his arms resolutely folded, his face set.

Q was talking to him. Actually, not "to" so much as "at." Trelane was listening with half an ear and nodding every time he heard Q pause, on the assumption that it was at these moments that he was expected to agree.

There was a long pause. Trelane looked up, and for a moment . . . just a moment . . . he felt genuine fear. For Q was scowling darkly, and he looked angrier than at any time Trelane could recall.

"You weren't listening to anything I said," Q accused him.

"That's not true," Trelane said quickly.

"It *is* true! I just said you had a leg growing out of your stomach, and you nodded!"

"I thought it was metaphorical," Trelane told him, not sounding particularly convincing.

Q strode toward him. "Get up," he said.

Trelane drew his arms tighter across his chest. "I don't want to," he said, rallying his rebellion.

"I said *get up!*" Q grabbed Trelane by his lapels and hauled him to his feet, and never had Trelane so genuinely feared for his continued existence as at that moment. "Treat them in a high-handed manner, and that does not bother me. Heaven knows they bring it upon themselves

86

with their pomposity. But you are never . . . *never* . . . to treat me as anything less than your superior! I have been assigned as your mentor! It is a sacred responsibility, and one that I take extremely seriously, and I will not be challenged or ignored! Is that clear?"

Trelane tried to pull away from him.

Q shook him.

There are few things as disconcerting to any creature as being rapidly shaken back and forth. Trelane was no exception to that rule. His feet skidded out from under him, and he was entirely in Q's power.

"Is that clear?!" Q demanded again.

Trelane nodded wordlessly, and Q released him. Trelane thudded to the ground.

There was nothing said for a long moment. And then Trelane looked up at him, and there was a world of hurt in his expression. His voice was barely above a whisper as he said, "I thought . . . I thought you *wanted* to be with me."

Q sighed deeply. "Of course I want to. It's just . . ." Then his voice trailed off. "We'll discuss it later. All right?"

Trelane nodded wordlessly, not trusting himself to speak. He did not want to let his voice break in front of Q. Never in front of Q.

Then Q vanished, and the only sound . . . which, of course, could not be heard in the vacuum of space . . . was a choked sob.

All things considered, it took Deanna a remarkably short time to calm down.

She had returned to her quarters, gotten her hair properly coiffed, her uniform dried out. She was about to head up to the bridge when she jumped back slightly in surprise. Q was standing between her and the door.

His manner, however, was decidedly unthreatening.

"Counselor Troi," he addressed her rather formally. "I know that believing me is not something with which you would have tremendous experience. Nevertheless, believe me when I say you have my most heartfelt apologies."

She could sense nothing from him, of course. But he *seemed* sincere, and she decided to allow for the surface possibility. She nodded. "All right," she said. "Accepted." She watched as Q seemed to shift his weight from one foot to the other, as if uncertain as to what to say or do next. "Would you like to sit down and talk?" she asked.

"No. No, not at all." He sat down.

She waited.

"I lost my temper with him," said Q, "and I don't know why. I don't like not knowing why I did something. It ill behooves one who is omniscient to have that sort of gap in knowledge."

"Similar personalities tend to conflict," said Troi. "You get impatient and angry because, unconsciously, you see your own shortcomings mirrored in the other individual."

"Hmm." He considered that, stroking his chin. "A pity that does not apply in this case."

"Why not?"

"Because I have no shortcomings."

She let it pass. Instead she steepled her fingers and said thoughtfully, "Trelane is trying to get reactions. He's trying to test authority. He wanted to see what Guinan—whom you respect—"

"Far too strong a word," Q said immediately.

Deanna ignored him. "He wanted to see what Guinan would do. What I would do, and Geordi, and so on. He's inquisitive and probing and—"

"An irritating youth."

"A youth." She considered that a moment. "With the

life span of your kind, 'youth' is extremely relative. Let me guess, though. Trelane is standing on the cusp of what would be, for him, adolescence."

Q sat up a little straighter, and looked marginally impressed. "Excellent deduction, Counselor. That is quite right."

"Adolescence, Q . . . that's a frightening concept, even to an immortal. And it is not unusual for human near-adolescents to have moments of regression. Intimidated by the thought of growing up and the inherent responsibility, there are lapses. Displays of behavior that are age-inappropriate."

"Meaning that the closer Trelane gets to adulthood, the more he may cling to the ways of childhood."

She nodded.

Seemingly genuinely interested, Q said, "And how would you recommend dealing with such a situation?"

"There's several ways," she said. "And one way in particular might be the best."

"Out of the question," said Picard.

Q had made himself nauseatingly comfortable on Picard's sofa. He was fully reclined, his legs draped over an armrest. Deanna was seated nearby, and Picard was pacing.

"Frankly," continued Picard, "my first inclination is to simply ban him from the ship. Thus far his only saving grace is Professor Martinez, and her claims that her discussions with Trelane about temporal physics are bringing her own research quantum leaps forward. But what you're proposing now, Counselor . . ."

"Trelane is in a situation where he is looked upon as a child . . . even by beings who are centuries younger than he," Troi pointed out. "What he needs is people who will look up to him. Who could potentially look up to him, even treat him as an authority figure."

"Yes, but . . . introduce him to the children of the *Enterprise?*" Picard shook his head. "It's too dangerous."

"I'll be with him the entire time, Jean-Luc," Q said confidently. "I can control him."

"I'm not entirely certain of that," Picard said ruefully.

"Picard," Q informed him, "if I were not capable of keeping Trelane in check, then there is a very great likelihood that your beloved Guinan might be scattered all over the sector by this point. He was absolutely furious at the way she treated him. And I can tell you that I myself found it somewhat galling taking Guinan's side, but the fact is that the little creep did indeed have it coming to him. And if Guinan was the one who gave it, then so be it. Not only is it my power that's keeping Trelane under wraps in the somewhat pathetic quarters you generously assigned, but it was I who held him in check after Guinan decided to give him an early bath time. That's another you owe me, Picard."

"Nonsense. The situation wouldn't have arisen if you hadn't brought him onto the ship."

Q shrugged. "Pishtosh. I won't be dragged into arguing niggling details."

"Captain, if he's carefully monitored and controlled," said Deanna, "it might very well do him a world of good. Ultimately, Trelane wants to be in control, and feels threatened every time he realizes that he, in fact, is not in control."

"I thought you couldn't read him," said Picard.

"Captain," she said, sounding slightly wounded, "I do have a few degrees that don't require empathic ability, you know. I'm giving you my professional assessment of

Trelane, based on my personal observations of him now, and some reading I did on his case from the original *Enterprise* logs. In my opinion, Trelane would benefit tremendously from the opportunity to interact with less-than-omnipotent beings whom he does not find particularly threatening. Children fill that need. For that matter, Captain, it would be a tremendous occasion for the children as well."

"She's right, you know," said Q. "After all, how often do mortal children get to rub elbows with omniscience?"

Picard frowned, drumming his fingers on his thigh. "I'm still not sure I like it."

"You don't have to *like* it, Picard," Q said. "You simply have to allow it. I swear to you on the honor of the Q Continuum that I'll be there every step of the way to make certain that none of your precious human tykes are hurt." He smiled ingratiatingly. "Trust me, Picard. When have I ever steered you wrong?"

It began innocuously enough.

The teacher whom the students addressed as Mrs. Claire was on duty when Q and Trelane arrived. They did not come alone. At Picard's insistence, a security team was along for the ride. In point of fact, Picard knew that if Trelane went berserk, there would be nothing that the security team could seriously do to rein him in. That would be Q's job. The guards were there primarily to send a message to Trelane, namely: *We're watching you. We're taking this seriously. So don't try anything.*

Mrs. Claire had been apprised ahead of time of what was happening, and just what the creatures facing her were capable of. She had tried to act blasé about the matter, blowing it off with a calm "One more child, more or less, won't be a problem." Inwardly, though, she was quaking.

She had thought that her past experience dealing with children in their so-called terrible twos was difficult. That was nothing, though, compared to a child who was capable of putting an end to everyone on the ship, purely at a whim. She had been assured that Q was going to be making sure Trelane didn't try anything quite so drastic, but nevertheless she felt a great deal of pressure.

The children had giggled when Trelane first entered. He was dressed even more formally than before, wearing a large red velvet greatcoat and a black sash over it. A large ceremonial sword hung from it in a scabbard. He scowled at their initial reaction, and something inside Mrs. Claire recoiled in fear.

But then a five-year-old girl had fingered the material in Trelane's coat. When he had looked down at her, she said simply, "That's soooo beautiful." And she spoke with such sincerity and genuine admiration that something in Trelane immediately—to his astonishment—started to melt.

One of the boys ran a hand along the sword and whistled in admiration. "Where did you *get* this?" he said enviously.

"I made it," said Trelane, not without a touch of pride.

"Wow!" said another one of the boys.

Then they began to cluster around him, asking him questions about where he had come from, and how he had made the sword, and that gorgeous coat, and those great boots, and why did he have those ruffles on his sleeves, and what's a squire, and could they get to be squires, and where was Gothos, and could they go to visit it, and was it a wonderful place with trees and skies and lakes and animals, and he had *made the planet?!* Upon learning that, their level of being impressed shot somewhere into deep

92

space. They had never met anyone who could just whip up an entire planet before.

"You are the greatest guy in the whole universe!" said one particularly enthusiastic boy.

"Maybe if you're good, you can all go visit Gothos someday," said Trelane. "Would you like that?"

Naturally this resulted in a chorus of enthusiastic "Yes!" from all and sundry. One lad even went so far as to say, "I wish my father was fun, like you," and this comment elicited a delighted snort from Q, because the boy was Worf's son, Alexander. Q relished the notion of Alexander repeating his desire to his scowling, beetle-browed progenitor. "Father, why can't you be more like Trelane?" he would ask. The boy would be damned lucky if Worf didn't put him through a bulkhead for inquiring.

The first encounter was a smashing success. The children had spoken eagerly about Trelane to their parents. Trelane, for his part, talked in nothing but glowing terms about his day's activities. "What fascinating creatures those little ones are!" he said. "And what a true tragedy that they develop into dour, humorless beings called adult humans."

"A tragedy, yes," commiserated Q.

Trelane appeared to give the matter some thought. "Do you think," he asked gravely, "if I cause them to remain just as they are, forever . . ."

"I don't think that would be wise," Q said quickly. "In fact, I know it would not be wise."

"Oh," said Trelane, clearly disappointed.

Geordi, meantime, was in the turbolift on the way down to engineering, when the lift stopped to pick up a passenger. To La Forge's dismay, the passenger was Deanna Troi.

"Uh . . . hi, Counselor," he said.

She nodded and smiled as the turbolift continued to its destination. "Hello, Geordi," she said. She looked at him curiously. "Is something wrong?"

"No. No, not at all." Then he paused, reached over, and hit the manual override, bringing the turbolift to a stop. "Uhm . . . look," he said uncomfortably. "I . . . uh, I just wanted to let you know how sorry I was about before . . ."

"Oh, that." She laughed. "Geordi, it wasn't your fault. You didn't expect to show up in my shower. It was Trelane's rather childish idea of a joke, that's all. You just had the poor fortune to be caught in the middle."

"I just wanted you to understand that I was . . . well, disoriented," he said. "That jump screwed up my VISOR for a moment, and with that and the water suddenly all over me . . . and then I slipped, and . . . "

"And naturally you grabbed on to the nearest thing for support, which happened to be my . . . "

"It all happened so fast," he told her.

She sighed. "Geordi," she said. "When I screamed, it was purely because I was startled, which I think is somewhat understandable. As for the rest of it . . . well, we Betazoids are not overly burdened with modesty when it comes to our bodies. I'm very comfortable with my physicality, and with my sexuality. What you saw and what you . . . grabbed . . . doesn't matter to me. I know it wasn't done from prurient interest, or out of an attempt to hurt me or cause me distress. What matters is that *you* not be so upset about the incident that you feel uneasy around me, or cause yourself undue anguish because of perceived transgressions against me. All right?"

He smiled. "All right, Counselor."

He reached over, activated the turbolift again. It glided to Deanna's deck and she stepped off. Just as she did so, Geordi said, "Oh . . . Counselor?"

She turned. "Yes, Geordi?"

What are you doing Friday night? went through his mind. But very quickly he said, "Nothing. Uh . . . nothing."

She regarded him oddly for a moment, and then she smiled, stepped back, and allowed the doors to hiss shut.

The next day's interaction between Trelane and the children started as promisingly as the previous day's had. The security crew was still present, and was alert as ever. There was a certain degree of relief, though, over the fact that no intervention had been required that first, crucial day.

Mrs. Claire was reading to the children about Winnie-the-Pooh that day. Trelane was listening with rapt interest as well. Q, nearby, felt something that—in a mere human —would have been termed "nausea." A. A. Milne was not exactly to Q's taste.

"Excuse me," he said, desperately needing a break from what he felt to be the oh-so-cute cloyingness of the prose. "I'll be right back." And he vanished in a burst of light.

The security guards stiffened in alarm. It was the first time that Q had been out of Trelane's presence since the detail had been assigned, and they were braced for trouble. Trelane, however, did not seem particularly inclined to provide any. He continued to listen to the story, although his expression wasn't exactly of the same caliber of rapt attention as the children possessed.

And then he said abruptly, "We should go on our own expotition."

Mrs. Claire looked up at the interruption. She didn't bother to correct Trelane on the correct pronunciation of the word "expedition," for all Trelane was doing was repeating the Milne term. Instead she decided to play along. "Well, Trelane, that's not a bad idea. If you could organize an expotition, where would you go?"

"Anywhere I felt like," said Trelane. He rose briskly and announced in that booming, slightly irritating manner he had, "In fact, I think that's where we'll all go now! Anywhere I wish."

"I don't think we can," Mrs. Claire said evenly.

The children, however, were not keyed in to her concerns. "Can Pooh and the others come along?" one child asked.

"Absolutely!" crowed Trelane.

"Now, wait a minute, Trelane," said Mrs. Claire.

"Wait a minute?" He laughed derisively. "Not a minute will I wait, woman. I shall do as I choose, when I choose. I find these charming small individuals to be extremely pleasant company. And if I, in my humble manner," and he bowed deeply, "can provide entertainment for them, then I shall do so."

He gestured. That was all it took. Just a single gesture . . . and probably not even that. Considering Trelane's overdeveloped sense of the dramatic, he might have been doing that just for show.

A small yellow bear appeared. He simply popped into existence with the oddest of sounds. He looked around, scratched his head, and said, "Oh, bother."

There were more popping noises in rapid succession. Within seconds, the schoolroom was packed with small, animate stuffed animals.

The lead security guard immediately hit his comm badge. Trelane, however, saw the movement. "I did *not* give you permission to do that!" he snapped.

A kangaroo leaped through the air, her large feet slamming into the head of the security guard.

The other guards immediately went for their phasers. Mrs. Claire let out a yelp. The children surged forward and mixed in with their beloved friends from the beloved storybooks.

The guards froze, uncertain what to do, unwilling to open fire with the children in the way.

"Your behavior has been abominable and bellicose!" Trelane archly informed the guards. "Proper manners simply must be taught." He snapped his fingers.

The animals charged.

Worf looked up from his station and said, "Captain . . . security reports that they are under assault by . . ." He paused in confusion. ". . . a plush yellow bear."

Picard moaned softly and headed for the turbolift door.

"And associates," Worf added.

Deanna Troi tried not to laugh.

Riker, endeavoring to keep to the gravity of the situation, was on his feet immediately. "Mr. Worf, with me," he said briskly. One step behind his captain, he headed for the turbolift, the confused Klingon right behind him saying in bewilderment, "A plush yellow bear?"

"Something we should be able to handle, Worf," said Riker. The turbolift slid shut behind them.

"I suspect he has a very little brain."

Q arrived at about the same moment that Worf and Riker did. To their astonishment, a small stuffed tiger was ricocheting from one guard to the other, making loud "grrrrr" noises. An owl was flapping about getting in all of their faces, and a rabbit was bouncing squarely on the head of one of the security guards. The bear, for no discernible reason, was performing mild calisthenics and muttering to himself.

Before anyone could say anything, the creatures had vanished. This prompted a collective moan of disappointment from the children. Trelane, angered, turned and saw Q. "I should have known."

"No, *I* should have known!" Q said angrily. "What did you think you were doing? For crying out loud, Trelane, when are you going to exercise some self-control! Some discipline! When are you going to learn to think before you do something—and don't say a word, Picard," he continued quickly. "I know exactly what's going through your mind. So save the smart retorts and cleverly ironic observations, because I'm not interested in them right now."

"Then maybe you'll be interested in this," said Picard. "I have had enough, and more than enough. I want him off my ship. I want you off my ship. You've abused the courtesies extended you, and stretched tolerance beyond reasonable limits." Picard was well aware that he was standing in a schoolroom in the middle of the *Enterprise,* engaging in a conversation that would be better served in privacy. For some reason, it didn't matter. His anger was so towering, so consuming, that he didn't mind if everyone in the ship was a witness to it. "It is no longer of relevance to me if Trelane is cooperating with Professor Martinez. I don't care if he's telling her the secrets of the universe. This ship and its personnel are not here for your amusement, your edification, or your whim. I want him gone. I want you gone. Now." His voice lowered, a sure sign of his anger, for Picard did not get enraged in loud and demonstrative fashion. Instead he got quieter, more intense. "I said *now.*"

Trelane took a step forward, and he glared at Picard with unconcealed contempt. "Q, we do *not* have to tolerate such treatment."

"No," said Q very softly, very dangerously. "We do

not." There was an uncomfortable moment of silence, and then Q sighed loudly. "However . . ."

Trelane looked at him, astounded. "However? *What* however?"

"Trelane," said Q quietly. "There is a basic truth that you still have not quite grasped. If you simply destroy everything that irritates you, fairly soon there will be nothing left. You must learn restraint. Tolerance. I freely admit it is," and he glanced at Picard, "an ongoing learning process. That's all that life ever is. You've led a fairly insulated existence. Your parents, I think, overreacted, after some of your earlier unfortunate escapades. Kept you sheltered, kept you away from other, lesser races. Consequently, you have continued to nurse all of the inappropriate behavior that you would have been well advised to dispense with. So I would have to say that the occasional dressing-down by those who are your inferiors is a needed dash of humility. And I must also say that, throughout all my experiences in this wide space-time continuum, I do not know of an inferior being more capable of meting out a solid tongue-lashing than Jean-Luc Picard. I salute you, *mon capitaine.*"

Trelane looked at Q with such a mortified expression—with such a sense of betrayal—that it was almost palpable. "You . . . you like him better than you like me," he said, stricken and vulnerable.

He spun toward Picard, furious. Before Picard could make a move, Trelane swung a vicious backhand toward Picard.

Reflexively, Picard brought his forearm up and blocked the blow. It glanced off his arm, and Picard shoved Trelane back. He stumbled and fell against Q, who was not in the least bit discomforted by the sudden impact.

"How *dare* you!"

"Get him out of here, Q," said Picard. And in a remarkable display of contempt, he actually turned his back on him. "Enough of our time has been wasted."

"Captain . . ."

Trelane had spoken, but his voice was bereft of the arrogance that had permeated it mere seconds ago. Picard turned back, and saw that Trelane was wringing his hands slightly, looking distraught, confused, even bewildered. He licked his lips, looked as if he was about to say something, then had changed his mind. Clearly he was weighing his next words carefully. Finally he spread his hands as if openly admitting that he was at a loss as to what to do.

"I'm . . . really not so bad," he said. "Once you get to know me, that is. Please . . . you are a truly intriguing species and . . . I really would like to have the opportunity to know you better."

Picard considered the matter for a long moment. He was very aware of every eye upon him.

"I'm sorry, but no," he said finally.

Trelane's reaction was instantaneous. *"Fine! Then be damned with you!"*

His disappearance was violent, an explosion of light and sound that was blinding and deafening . . . and yet, paradoxically, had no heat and made no noise.

Half a ship's length away, Geordi La Forge and the engineering crew staggered in reaction to the seismic shock of it.

In the Ten-Forward room, Guinan clapped her hands to her ears, a move that surprised and confused a number of customers who did not have the capability of detecting what it was that Guinan was reacting to.

All Picard knew was that one moment he was looking at Trelane, and the next he was flat on his back. The world was so disoriented to him that for an instant he thought that perhaps the vessel had lost its artificial gravity.

Long seconds later, his vision cleared and he was chagrined to see Q standing over him, looking entertained. "I'll say this for you, Picard: You haven't lost your knack for handling delicate situations."

"What happened?"

"He had a snit and took off. Unfortunate, really. I had hoped for better." He extended a hand for Picard to help himself up.

"Oh really." In response Picard waved off Q's aid, and instead braced himself against the wall, using that to pull himself up. His vision now fully returning, he saw the rest of his people pulling themselves together. A couple of the children were crying and demanding to know where Trelane was. The toys had likewise vanished. "You know what I think, Q?"

"Of course I do, Jean-Luc," Q cut him off. "After all, that's what 'omniscient' *means,* isn't it?"

"I think—"

Q rolled his eyes. "He's going to tell me anyway."

"—that you simply wanted to cause trouble. No more, and no less, than that. You delight in difficulty, and revel in reactions."

"And you adore alliteration *ad nauseam,"* replied Q. "I've learned to tolerate your little deficiencies. Sooner or later, you are going to have to learn to tolerate mine."

And with that, he vanished.

"Good riddance," Worf rumbled.

"Indeed," agreed Picard.

Trelane was back in the quarters that he had been assigned—the quarters he'd been ordered to vacate—

pacing quickly, his hands tracing vague patterns in the air.

He could not determine at whom he should be the most angry. Q, for not supporting him . . . ?

Picard, for daring to treat him in such an insolent manner?

Or perhaps . . .

Himself.

He looked downcast, not wanting to admit to any potential culpability. But somewhere deep within him . . . he knew. He knew.

In frustration, he thudded his hand against the side of his head. "What is it with me?" he demanded of the empty chamber. "Why is this happening? Why do I *do* this to myself? I . . . I don't *mean* to make problems. I don't *mean* to cause difficulties. I start out wanting to do something, and it seems like *such* a good idea at the time." He started to rub his temples, feeling a distant throbbing. He had begun to pace, and now he stopped in front of a full-length mirror. Trelane stared at it forlornly and continued, "And I want things to go just so. I can see it, right here in my head, how things should be. How I *want* them to be. But nobody else ever sees it that way! So I find myself trying to convince them, and I get more and more frustrated because they just don't get it. They just don't understand. And the next thing I know, I'm starting to lose my temper, or shout, or do whatever it takes to *make* them understand. But no one does. No one *ever does!*"

And then there came a soft voice that startled Trelane mightily. He blinked and looked in confusion at the mirror.

He saw himself looking back, but there was a difference. For one thing, he was dressed completely differently. He was sporting a black suit, and on his face was an expression of haughtiness that surpassed anything Trelane would have thought himself capable of. Instinctively he felt himself recoiling, even as that soft voice said, with utter confidence, "You're wrong. I understand."

Despite his apprehension, Trelane nevertheless felt himself uncontrollably staring at the duplicate in the mirror. "What is this . . . ?" he demanded, endeavoring to disguise his bewilderment with bluster.

"Why, my dear fellow," purred the reflection. "Haven't you figured that out?"

"No," said Trelane. "No, I haven't."

"Well, then . . . I'll explain it to you."

The next thing Trelane knew, two shimmering hands had reached out of the mirror and grabbed him by the front of his ruffled shirt. Trelane let out a yelp of alarm as he felt himself being pulled implacably toward the mirror.

"Stop it!" he shrieked. "Let go! *Let go!*"

The reflective duplicate was smiling, his eyes blazing with a fearsome intensity.

Trelane braced himself against the sides of the mirror, trying to stop his forward path. Then his hands started to slip. *"Q!"* he howled, and then, with no sound at all, Trelane was hauled into the mirror. The reflecting surface rippled slightly, in a manner reminiscent of a lake surface that just had a rock skipped across its top. Then it stopped and smoothed out.

The door to the quarters slid open and Worf stuck his head in. He looked around, scowling. He was certain that he had heard something: the sounds of a scuffle, or perhaps a brief cry. But a quick inspection of the room yielded nothing. There was no indication that anything peculiar was going on. Having satisfied himself that all was well, Worf shrugged and went back out into the corridor.

If he had thought to put his ear against the mirror, and had strained mightily, he might just barely have heard a very distant, and somewhat pitiful, shriek for help. But it never occurred to him to do so. Why should it have? It would have been a very silly notion.

And if there was one thing that Mr. Worf most definitely was not, it was silly.

It was only later, in the privacy of his quarters, that Captain Picard allowed himself the luxury of regrets.

Dammit, he was supposed to be dealing with new life-forms. Why was it that one of the most intriguing and formidable life-forms around had to be so utterly irritating at the same time? If only he had handled it better.

He had spent so much time dealing with Q that one would have thought he'd have developed a thicker skin by this point. Yet not only had Trelane managed to get under that "thicker" skin, but he had done so faster and more efficiently than Q ever had.

How had he managed it?

Picard had the funny feeling that it was Trelane's relative youth. Despite his outwardly adult appearance, Picard had known that they were in fact dealing with a being possessing all the capriciousness of a child. If there was one thing that always set Picard's teeth on edge, it was children.

Which meant that, perhaps, Picard should have been making even *more* effort to be patient with Trelane, rather than letting his temper get the best of him.

It was typical of Picard to be so demanding on himself that no matter how he handled any given situation, he always subsequently examined it from a variety of angles to try and figure out how he might have responded in a way that would have been preferable. It was his fate, it seemed, to go through life constantly second-guessing himself. Always in the privacy of his quarters, though, and always after the crisis was long past. Then the second-guessing could commence. But it was done with a sense of trying to determine how he would handle a similar situation in the future, rather than beating himself up over how he had dealt with whatever was in the past.

The past, after all, was the past. It was set and done. Wasn't it?

TRACK CHANGE

"I . . . am Q . . . and you have absolutely no *idea . . . how screwed up this is . . . "*

TRACK A

5.

Tommy Riker knew he was in trouble even before he walked into the house. He possessed no Betazoid powers of empathy, despite his mother. But it did not take any burst of genius, or a telepath, or even a mild psychic, to know that something was up.

For one thing, his grandmother was standing there, her arms folded, her scowl severe. She was not ten paces away from the front door, and Tommy wondered if she had been standing there, riveted to the spot, waiting for him.

"I sensed you were coming," replied Lwaxana Troi in response to his unspoken thought. "I thought I would brace you, because your mother is definitely not happy."

This, to Tommy, did not seem a particularly useful endeavor on Lwaxana's part. Having Lwaxana Troi prepare him for his mother's ire was somewhat like making ready for a summer squall by first endeavoring to survive a tactical nuclear strike.

Tommy scowled, and it was at moments like that that he

most reminded Lwaxana of his long-gone father. The boy was not even eight years old, and yet his parentage was unmistakable. He looked absolutely nothing like his mother. Oh, every so often there was a slight hint of her around the eyes when Tommy was lost in thought. The rest of the time, though, he was William Riker in miniature. He had straight brown hair, a hank of which seemed to have a life of its own and was perpetually being brushed out of his face. His eyes were dark and filled with a strange intensity that seemed to blaze most brightly when he was confronted with a particularly difficult situation. His jaw was rounded but had strong character to it, and his upper-body strength was particularly impressive. He had the most well developed musculature for a child that Lwaxana had ever seen.

When he spoke, his voice was always of a firm and even timbre. There seemed almost no childlike aspect to it at all, and every so often Lwaxana would wonder whether the child's parentage—the intensely serious and aggressive father, partnered with the studious, thoughtful, and perpetually in mourning mother—had conspired to rob the boy of any true sense of childhood.

"Why isn't Mother happy?" he asked. He pulled off his light jacket (it was fairly balmy outside) and thoughtlessly tossed it toward a chair. Seemingly out of nowhere appeared the towering Mr. Homn, looking gaunt as always. He caught the jacket before it hit the chair, and walked away with it.

"I think you know why, young man." She scowled. "We heard from your teachers today. They are not particularly pleased with your classroom performance."

"They should be."

"They *should* be?" Lwaxana stared at him as if he'd sprouted a second head. "Why in the world should they be pleased that you got into a fight?"

"Because I ended it fast." With a lopsided grin, he swung a brisk right cross through the air. "You should've seen it, Lwaxana. He went right down, boom."

"Of *course* he went right down!" Lwaxana told him in exasperation. "Betazoid males are taught to emphasize contemplative congress! To think with their heads, not with their fists!"

"He was digging around in my brain," Tommy said with undisguised irritation.

"He's Betazoid. Betazoids always read minds."

"Then he should have read that I was going to hit him and gotten out of the way. I can't help it if he just stood there and stopped it with his chin." Tommy blew air between his teeth. "He was making fun of my thoughts. He said they weren't deep or profund—"

"Profound," corrected Lwaxana. "He was probably right, because lord knows your father wasn't especially profound either—"

The moment the words were out of her mouth, Lwaxana would have given her right arm to be able to call them back. For they had been like cold slaps to the boy, who idolized his father's memory. And for all her irritation with the boy, truthfully Lwaxana loved and cherished Tommy Riker, son of William and Deanna Riker, with a ferocity that occasionally frightened even her. How could it be that a woman who was so formidable with her power of thought could say something so thoughtlessly?

Before she could even frame the words *I'm sorry,* Tommy's face had twisted into a ferocious snarl, and he spat out, "Don't you say anything bad about him! Don't you *ever!*" And he ran off past her, thudding into her right leg as he went. It was just enough of a thump to leave no impression that he had done it any other way than deliberately.

She sighed. "How can he be that devoted to a father he never even knew?" Even as she asked, though, she already knew the answer. Deanna's love for William T. Riker was as fierce and unrelenting and unyielding as it had ever been. Clearly, that raw emotion from Lwaxana's daughter had, in turn, been transferred to Lwaxana's grandson.

The thought actually brought a small smile to her lips. Perhaps the boy did have some rudimentary psychic ability after all. No test had been able to measure it, unfortunately, but who knew? Maybe the tests just needed updating.

"I'll see to it immediately," she said firmly to no one, and headed off for her study.

Tommy stuck his head into his mother's room. She was writing something, and seemed rather engrossed in it. His mother was practically the only person he knew who still wrote on paper. In fact, paper was so seldom used that he wondered where in the world she got it from. Paper was part of the old way, though, the traditional way, and Lwaxana was very big on anything having to do with tradition and musty old rituals. It was a love for the old and out-of-date that she had passed on to her daughter, his mother.

He decided that now was not the time to disturb her, but she looked up at him as he made the motion to leave. She was fairly thin, Deanna Riker was. Her eyes were large and luminous, but seemed to stand out against the starkness of her face. She wore no makeup, and her hair was cropped short and graying at the temples.

Their gazes locked for a moment, and then Deanna pointed first to him, and then to the seat next to her desk. Without a word—but accompanied by a rather loud, protesting sigh—Tommy trudged across the room and plopped down nearby her. He sat there, fingers interlaced, waiting for her to finish whatever it was she was doing.

It took her a few long minutes that seemed to crawl by. While Tommy was waiting, he stared around the room. This was her place, his mother's study. It was sacrosanct and untouchable. His grandmother seemed to take extraordinary joy in rearranging everything else in the house incessantly. It seemed to Tommy that never a month went by when there wasn't some new stick of furniture or bizarre decoration turning up in the home of Lwaxana Troi . . . and that, in turn, might likewise vanish months down the line. His grandmother was unquestionably a woman of mercurial tastes.

Deanna, by contrast, was slow, thoughtful, and methodical. Some years back, when he was little (and not the mature kid he had grown into), she had read him a story written by someone on his father's home planet. It was about two creatures that didn't exist on Betazed, called a grasshopper and an ant. The grasshopper loved to dance and sing, and was rather frivolous. The ant, by contrast, was hardworking and serious and, frankly, rather humorless. When he had pointed out the resemblances between the bugs and his grandmother and mother, Deanna had told him that she didn't think he was exactly right about that. But he could tell, though (from long years of practice), that she was actually thinking that maybe, just maybe, he had a point.

Finally Deanna pushed aside her writing and turned to face her son.

She pointed at him. "So what's this?"

Figuring that he had nothing to lose by going for a laugh, he said hopefully, "A finger?"

It was worth a try. Didn't work, though. The edges of her mouth did not so much as twitch.

"You had trouble in school," she said accusingly.

"No, I didn't."

"You beat up Reg Lartin."

"Yes, but it was no trouble. He went down pretty quick."

She moaned softly, shaking her head. "What am I going to do with you?"

"Beat me?"

"No, of course not."

"Not let me go to school." He nodded. "That seems right. I think that's what you should do."

"You hate school," she pointed out. "You'd be thrilled to stay home."

"That's not true," he said with absolutely no conviction. "I love school." It was a fairly worthless tack for him to take, because not only was his mother an empath, but his own skills at dissembling were fairly pathetic. Tommy Riker might have been many things, but a liar—or an effective liar, at least—was not one of them.

"Why did you get into a fight with him?" asked Deanna.

"I already told Lwaxana . . ."

Deanna sighed. "I wish you'd call her 'Grandmother.'"

"She told me not to. She said it makes her feel old."

"Do you always do what she tells you?"

"When I want to."

Realizing that pushing this particular point was going to do little good, Deanna said, "What did you tell her?"

"That Reg was making fun of my thoughts. He said I didn't have depth."

"Do you know what he meant by that?"

"I knew I didn't like the sound of it. And I knew he was making a face while he said it. A big, stupid, dumb face. So that's where I hit him."

She took him gently by the shoulders. "Betazoids," she said, "have minds that work on different levels. So do most

114

life-forms, really, but we Betazoids are more attuned to the inner workings than other species. He was simply commenting that you didn't seem to be as aware of what was going on," and she tapped the side of his skull, "inside here."

"Yeah, well," Tommy said, and clenched a fist, displaying it proudly. Deanna could see the skinned knuckles where the fist had impacted with the other boy's face. "I made him aware of what was going on inside his nose . . . especially when it started bleeding all over the bottom of his face."

"Tommy, this is inappropriate behavior," Deanna said firmly. "Not only are you clearly unapologetic about what you did, but you seem to be reveling in it."

He frowned. *"What*ting in it?"

"Reveling. Being proud of it."

"Oh. Okay."

"Do you disagree with that?"

"No, but at least I understand it." He paused. "Lwaxana said something mean about Dad."

Deanna's face darkened. "What do you mean, 'mean.' What did she say?"

"That he wasn't profound."

She blinked, not exactly sure what to make of that. And then she actually smiled slightly. "Well . . . she's right, I suppose. Your father was many things, but profound wasn't one of them. But you see, Tommy . . . when you love someone, as I did your father, you learn to love them *because* of those things that others would consider faults."

He was looking at her strangely now, with his head slightly askew. "Don't talk about him like that."

"Like what?" She was confused. "What do you mean, honey?"

"You said things like 'was.' You never talked about him

115

that way before. Like he's not here anymore. Like he's dead or something."

Involuntarily, Deanna felt her eyes starting to sting. With the force of her considerable determination, she managed to push the tears back. In a way, she found it incredible that, after all these years, the tears could still come so quickly.

"I'm sorry, honey," she said. She tried to pull him close to her, but he pulled back. He stood there, feet planted, eyes narrow and suspicious. "I am sorry. It won't happen ag—"

"You think he's dead, don't you."

"No," she said.

"Then why did you say 'was'?"

"I wasn't thinking, Tommy. I have a lot on my mind. . . ."

Now Tommy's face went the color of umber, and she knew what he was going to say before he said it. "It's Wyatt. He's still sniffing around, isn't he."

Despite the difficulty of the situation, Deanna found herself trying not to laugh. " 'Sniffing around'? Where did you hear *that?*"

"Lwaxana."

"Hunh." That should not have surprised her. "All right, yes, Wyatt has been calling a great deal. He would like to spend some time socially with me. Tommy, the fact is that Wyatt has been a good friend, even since before you were born. Even before your father and I married. By Betazed contract law, Wyatt could have forbidden the marriage. He was betrothed to me when I was your age. But because he cared more about my happiness than his, he released me from my obligation to him. He did not have to do that. In a way, you owe your life to him," she told her scowling son, "so I would be a bit more polite in regards to Wyatt Miller, if I were you. It's . . ." She tried to find the words. "It's been a long, long time since your father . . ."

"He's *not dead*," said Tommy firmly. There was such conviction in his voice that Deanna found herself actually startled by it. "He's not," he repeated.

"Tommy." She squeezed his hands. "I want to believe he's alive as much as you do. Trust me, I do."

"He's coming back to us. I just got this really strong feeling, that's all."

"When did you get this feeling, honey?"

"I did, that's all. I wanna understand it, but I can't. I can't pretend it makes any sense. I can't pretend *anything* makes any sense. I just . . . I just woke up one night, and I felt like I could see him."

"You woke up." She smiled sadly. "It sounds to me as if it might have been a dream, Tommy."

"No," he said firmly, stomping his foot for emphasis. "No dream. I knew that's what you would say, and what you would think, and that's why I didn't tell you."

"Tommy . . ."

Then Deanna looked up, sensing her mother's impending presence before Lwaxana got to the door. Even if Deanna had not been empathic, she would have had no trouble detecting Lwaxana's arrival. For Lwaxana was running down the hallway, the sounds of her footsteps so rapid that it was clear she was sprinting. What in the world could have happened to be of such import that it would send Lwaxana Troi, daughter of the Fifth House, charging down a corridor like a juggernaut?

Deanna heard something crash, and immediately realized from the placement of the sound that it was the second-century Bel-t'zor vase. It was irreplaceable, price-

117

less. She heard her mother mutter a curse, but Lwaxana didn't even slow down upon having knocked the vase off its pedestal. What in hell was going on?

Lwaxana was moving so quickly that she almost overshot Deanna's study. She skidded past and snagged the doorframe with her carefully manicured fingers. "Deanna," she gasped, trying to catch her breath. Then, so as not to have to wait for her lung capacity to catch up, she thought at her daughter, *Come quickly.*

Quickly where? Deanna replied.

Downstairs. A call for you. You . . . you won't believe it. I don't believe it.

Believe what, Mother? Already Deanna had a feeling what her mother was trying to tell her, but somehow she couldn't bring herself to dare to hope.

There's a Klingon on—

"Stop it!" said Tommy in exasperation. "You're thinking at each other again! I hate it when you do that!"

"There's a Klingon on my call screen," Lwaxana said, managing to have caught her breath sufficiently to speak. "He's got news."

Deanna gripped her desk, her knuckles turning white. "Is he . . . is he . . ." And she could barely whisper the word. ". . . alive?"

Lwaxana looked at Deanna oddly. "Well, of course he is."

Deanna's mouth moved, but no sound came out.

But her mother continued, "I mean, we wouldn't be getting a call from a dead Klingon, would we? That doesn't make any sense. Are you sure you're feeling all r—"

"Not the *Klingon,* Mother!" Deanna shouted in exasperation. "I know the Klingon's alive! Is he calling about Will? Is *Will* alive?"

"I don't know," said Lwaxana. "He wouldn't tell me! He

wouldn't tell me anything about why he was calling! To be perfectly honest, he was extremely rude. His name was Woof, I think."

Deanna was on her feet and out the door, her mother and son following. As they headed down the hallway, Deanna looked forlornly at the shattered vase, which Mr. Homn was already in the process of sweeping up. "Mother, why didn't you just call me telepathically? Why did you run all this way?"

"Oh, that nasty Klingon got me all distracted," she said, her hands fluttering. "He just snapped at me! Barked orders! 'Go get her,' he told me. *Me,* holder of the sacred chalice of Rixx!"

Deanna wasn't listening by that point. Instead she was running, her arms pumping, her legs churning up the distance. She hit the stairs and took them two at a time, so quickly that by the bottom she almost fell and only a quick grab of the banister prevented it. Then she was across the foyer, into the west wing, and to her mother's study where the call screen was.

Sure enough, the scowling face of a Klingon was on the screen. The moment she came into view, he said brusquely, "Are you Deanna Troi Riker?"

"Yes, I am."

He seemed to be regarding her up and down for a moment. For some reason, Deanna put an arm across her breast in what could only be termed a bit of unconscious modesty. What was it about this Klingon's penetrating gaze that was so disconcerting?

"I am Worf," he said finally. "We wish to clarify a situation that has come to our attention. Please speak to this individual."

He stepped aside and Deanna stared at the empty screen for what seemed an eternity.

Then another man appeared on the screen. His hair was long and somewhat disheveled, although clearly endeavors had been made to make him somewhat presentable. He was wearing Klingon clothing, although there were no badges or markings of rank on it. And his eyes . . .

His eyes were those that had once gazed lovingly into her face. That had hungrily scrutinized her naked body on many occasions, and seemed to have the ability to look right into her soul.

"Oh . . . my God," she whispered. She felt her knees going weak, and she braced herself against a chair, lowering herself into it. "Imzadi . . ."

He was staring at her, and he mouthed the word in response. For a brief moment that was, simultaneously, an eternity of love, she thought that he was whispering it in reply, so moved and heartfelt that he was unable to say it.

But in the next instant, she realized with an utterly crushing conviction the truth of it. Because he now said "Imzadi" out loud, and it was clear that he wasn't speaking the word to her as a reply. He was uttering it in the tentative way that someone does when confronted with an unfamiliar term.

"Im . . . zaa . . . dee?" he said again in such a lurching tone that the word almost seemed an obscenity.

She felt the tears welling up, and this time she did nothing to stop them. She heard the sounds of Lwaxana and Tommy arriving behind her, and the gasp from Lwaxana as she saw the image on the screen. The tears burned hot on Deanna's face, and she brought her interlaced fingers up to her mouth and clamped down on them with her teeth, doing so with such force that she drew blood.

"Oh my God . . . Will . . . what have they done to you?" she gasped.

Worf now stepped into the picture once more. "He was a captive of the Romulans. He was tortured."

Behind her, Lwaxana made a low, choking sound. Then, in a voice brimming with fury, she said, "The . . . *animals* who did this . . . they . . ."

"They are dead," said Worf matter-of-factly. "I killed his tormentor myself."

"Good," said Lwaxana with such viciousness that it would have stunned Deanna, had she been listening.

But she was not. Instead she was staring at the screen, at the battered and haunted image of the man she had married. The man she loved. The man that she was finally, finally giving up for lost . . . and now he was back. He was alive. Whatever they had done to his mind could be repaired. However they had managed to twist and torment his soul . . . whatever abyss they had tossed it into . . . Deanna was suddenly filled with the utter conviction that she could make it right. She could nurse the shards of her husband's spirit back to health. The one thing that she could not have done was bring him back from the dead. Whatever gods there were, though, had decided that she would not have to. Her beloved husband, the father of her son, had been returned to her, and no matter what he had suffered, they would deal with it. They would overcome it.

If they were together, that was all that counted.

"Is that . . . Dad?" whispered Tommy.

All Deanna could do was nod. Trying to control the trembling in her voice, Deanna said, "Will . . . Will, it's me. It's Deanna. Will . . . we can get through this. You and I, and our son." She brought Tommy around so that he was clearly visible to the screen. "This is Tommy. You were . . . you were gone before he was born. I've told him all about you. He's very anxious to meet you."

"The *Enterprise* is en route to Terminus, where we will

transfer him over to Starfleet hands," Worf informed her. "I have consulted shipping schedules, and there is a Klingon freighter in proximity to Betazed that could be diverted to pick you up and rendezvous with the *Enterprise.* You would have to be prepared to leave immediately . . ."

"Yes. Yes, of course. In an hour. I can be ready in an hour," said Deanna. "Will . . . oh God, Imzadi, I—"

"Very well," said Worf briskly. "Make your preparations for departure." And the screen blinked out.

"What did I tell you?" proclaimed Lwaxana. "That Woof fellow. Just plain rude." She turned to Deanna. "Darling, I would come with you . . . but I have responsibilities here that I can't . . ."

"No, Mother, it's all right," said Deanna. "I . . ." Her voice choked. "My God, I want to say and do half a dozen things all at once in all different directions. I . . ."

Lwaxana reached out and folded her into her arms. Deanna clutched her and started to sob openly, making no effort to stem the floodgates that had opened in her eyes. She reached out to her son and pulled him in alongside. Tommy, however, remained dry-eyed, and when he spoke his voice was muffled and unintelligible. Regaining momentary control of herself, Deanna said, "What, honey?"

"I'm coming with you," said Tommy.

"Oh, honey . . . no, no, I don't think that you . . ."

"I *said* I'm coming with you," Tommy said firmly.

"Young man," said Lwaxana firmly, "this is your mother's journey. She's in enough emotional turmoil already, and she certainly doesn't need you along as additional distraction. You are staying here with me, and that is absolutely, positively, final."

Tommy's jaw set into a determined expression.

* * *

The Klingon freighter departed from its detour to Betazed promptly one hour and ten minutes later. Along for the ride was a new passenger, a Betazoid female named Deanna Troi Riker . . .

. . . and her son, Tommy.

TRACK A

6.

Q opened his eyes slowly and suspiciously, taking in his surroundings and not saying a word.

Dr. Beverly Howard noticed that he was awake, and immediately summoned Crusher and Picard. Geordi La Forge stood by her side as she waited for them to arrive. Slowly they approached the being who had identified himself as "Q" and Beverly said, "Can you hear me?"

Q regarded her with curiosity. "If I couldn't hear you, then how could I reply? Woman, what *have* you done to your hair?"

"I . . . what?" She touched the orange curls . . . and then gasped to find that her hair had suddenly snapped into a straight, shoulder-length 'do.

"Much better," Q said with no patience. He started to rise from the bed and noticed for the first time that he had restraining straps on his arms. He looked up at her with a contemptuous stare and said, "You *can't* be serious." With that, he sat up fully, the straps simply having blinked into nonexistence.

At that moment, Crusher and Picard entered. Captain Crusher stepped forward, arms folded, face set. "All right," he said, "what's this all about?"

Q didn't answer at first. Instead he stared in quiet bemusement at the scene before him. "So let's see if I understand this," he said, as if Crusher hadn't even spoken. "You're the captain of the *Enterprise* . . . and you, Picard, are the first officer . . ." He looked at Beverly. "And you are still ship's doctor?"

"That's right."

"Dr. Beverly Cru . . . no." He snapped his fingers to remind himself. "Dr. Beverly Howard. Yes, of course." He glanced at Howard's head nurse. "And Geordi La Forge and his big brown eyes instead of that noxious piece of metal. Too bad; the metal was an improvement." Before La Forge could ask what Q was talking about, Q had already made it clear that he had lost interest in conversing with the head nurse. Q's face dimmed, as if eclipsed. "All right, then. We haven't time to lose."

"Would you mind telling me what's going on, first?" demanded Captain Crusher.

"Truthfully, I don't think you'd really want to know. You've encountered Trelane?"

"Yes," said Crusher ruefully.

"All right, then. Listen to me carefully. I will fill you in, although to be perfectly blunt, it probably won't do you a damned bit of good. But if your entire existence is going to be collapsing, I suppose you're entitled to know precisely why that is."

"Collapsing?" Crusher was incredulous. "Just from Trelane? He's merely one being. How can you possibly—"

"No," said Q, easing himself off the medical bed. He found to his distress that he was limping slightly. "No, he's not *merely* anything."

"I don't know what you're—"

"No, *Captain,*" Q said with undisguised contempt, "you don't know, and since you don't know, we would all be better off if you kept your mouth shut and listened for a brief time."

"How dare you—"

"Don't waste your posturing on me, it's of no relevance," Q said brusquely. "Now, listen to me carefully. Are you familiar with the concept of parallel time tracks?"

"There's been some bits and pieces of theory bruited about," said Picard. "Nothing major, though."

"Hunh," grunted Q. "Well, let me tell you right now that you are up to your backsides in something major at the moment. Now: Trelane . . . you met him. You spoke with him. Just as I'm speaking with you now." He started to pace. "You refer to the universe. That's not quite right. It's a multiverse, filled with beings similar to yourselves. Many things are different, however."

"And which of these multiverses is the real one?" asked La Forge.

Q stopped pacing and stared at him. "Then again, many things remain the same . . . such as your race's unsurpassed ability to ask stupid questions." Before Geordi could think of a response, Q had already moved away from him. "Events vary, the flow of time varies. Indeed, the major consistency is the inconsistency. There are, however, several major constants cutting throughout the multiverse."

He stopped then and said to them casually, "I just want you to realize that I'm revealing the secrets of the universe to you. Don't file this away in the same section of your tiny minds along with trivialities such as recipes for banana walnut bread, or memories of the first time you experienced intercourse. We're talking matters of importance here. Do you understand that? Good. Now . . . one of the true constants is chaos. To you, chaos is a theory. It's a matter of the mind. But when you're dealing with beings from the Q Continuum, the line between theory and fact is the same as the line between the shore and the ocean. No matter how you draw the line, the ocean will lap onto the shore, and the shore will erode into the ocean. Are you still with me?"

Fascinated by the intensity and urgency of what he was saying, the officers simply nodded.

"Chaos is real," Q said. "As real as this ship, and you, if you know where and how to look for it. Chaos is one of the core fabrics of reality. It lurks in that center of real unreality that we of the Q Continuum refer to as the Heart of the Storm. And if you are able to tap that incredible power, then nothing can stop you. The cost, however, is . . . considerable."

"And what is the cost?" asked Crusher.

"Sanity," said Q flatly. "And that's just for starters."

"And you're saying that this Trelane managed to tap into this . . . this chaos . . ."

"It should not have happened," said Q. "You see, Jean-Luc, that's what you never understood about the Q Continuum. . . ."

"What are you talking about? I never . . ."

"Right, right." Q waved him off. "Of course. You never heard of us before. One of the main reasons for the existence of the Q Continuum, Picard, is to guard against just such an eventuality. We have existed since before time out of mind, Picard. All things in this great multiverse exist to serve a purpose. And the reason that the Q Continuum exists is so that all of you may . . ."

His voice trailed off, and suddenly Q looked wary. He moved toward the middle of the sickbay, his gaze darting around. He had tensed, as if expecting to be assaulted from any direction, or perhaps from all directions.

". . . exist," he finally finished. "But now . . . now it may all be coming to an end."

"What do you mean?" asked Crusher.

Q looked at him disdainfully. "You're just chock-full of useless questions today, aren't you. I mean, Jackie, that the Q Continuum is in trouble. Like some lesser being, we have found ourselves under duress. Under assault. Under the gun. We are . . . to use an archaic, but once-popular Earth vernacular . . . screwed. And one of our own has been wielding the screwdriver."

"Trelane," said Picard.

"Trust you, Jean-Luc, to provide finally an anticipatory answer instead of another dunderheaded question. Yes, Trelane. But not the Trelane of your universe . . . or even mine, for that matter. This is a Trelane who has weathered the Heart of the Storm. This is a Trelane who actually managed to cut off, isolate, the Q Continuum from the rest of the multiverse. Interfering in our function for the first time in the collective memory of creation. This is—"

"The end."

Q spun, for Trelane was standing there looking as nonchalant as he ever had. He was dressed differently this time, though. He was all in black, but his clothes now had the severe cut of a military uniform. There were red-trimmed flares along the cuffs, and he wore a blood-red half cape off one shoulder.

"Trelane!" snapped Picard. He was about to summon security when Trelane made a casual tossing gesture of his hand, and in the next instant they were all frozen. Only Q and Trelane were left free to move.

"What did you hope to gain by telling them all this?" asked Trelane.

Cautiously, Q backed up, his hands in a defensive mode before him. "I wished to give them knowledge," said Q, "for knowledge is power."

"Oh, I don't know about that," said Trelane. He seemed more amused than anything else by Q's caution. "I would have to say that power is power. You can know if a bullet is heading for your brain. You can know when it has struck you and penetrated. All the knowledge in the cosmos won't stop the power of that bullet."

"And nothing can stop you, is that what you're saying?" demanded Q.

"Well, I didn't say that, now, did I?" Trelane smiled. "But then again . . . far be it from me to disagree with my esteemed mentor."

"Don't discount knowledge," said Q. "Because if you had any genuine understanding of what you were doing . . . then you wouldn't do it."

"Twaddle!" exclaimed Trelane. "Stuff and nonsense! I understand precisely what I'm doing."

"Oh yes?"

"Yes." He raised his hands. "I'm killing you."

And with that, he lashed out at Q, beams of power dancing from his hands.

Q twisted sideways, tearing open the fabric of reality and stepping through. The beams collided around him but didn't quite get him.

"Ha!" shouted Trelane, delighted. "Superb! Not realizing the hopelessness of your position, you *are* going to make a challenge of it after all! How splendid!"

And with that squeal of joy, Trelane matched Q's feat and followed him.

In the depths of space, thousands of kilometers away from the *Enterprise,* Q had gathered some motes of cosmic dust beneath his feet in order to give himself some traction. His mind was racing with possibilities.

It was not racing fast enough, though, for Trelane appeared in the void with him, facing him. His laugh was quick and high-pitched and not especially rational.

"Did you really think you could escape that easily?" demanded Trelane. "Did you truly think that jumping the dimensional barriers could hide you from me?"

"I wasn't looking to hide from you, Trelane," retorted Q. "I was taking my time to determine how I could stop you without utterly destroying you. I owe that much to your parents, who have always been quite decent to me. I wish that some of their fundamental decency had managed to transfer itself to you. They deserved better."

"They deserved what they got," shot back Trelane. "You all deserve what you got! It's your own fault, Q. If you had had the brains to be with the rest of the Continuum when I locked it off, you wouldn't be here, facing me. But no. You had to be gallivanting about."

"I was gallivanting about taking care of you!" Q told him. "Or have you forgotten that?"

Indeed, it appeared for a moment that Trelane had. A brief expression of confusion crossed his face. Then he shrugged. "Ah well. The humans have an expression that relates to that: No good deed goes unpunished. And your punishment, Q, will be very . . . *very* . . . severe."

With that he gestured and the world around Q seemed to explode.

Captain Crusher and Commander Picard were not sure what had just happened. One moment Q and Trelane had been there, the next minute . . . gone. After confirming that everyone in sickbay was none the worse for the bizarre experience, they had been en route to the bridge. Halfway there, however, they had gotten an alarmed call from security head Tasha Yar, urging them to return to the bridge. Under ordinary circumstances, this might have been viewed as a bit of serendipity. But they were to learn rather quickly that these were far from ordinary circumstances.

They arrived just in time to see what it was that had caused consternation for the head of security. Data, who had taken the command seat in the absence of the captain and first officer, now rose and headed for his own station. He spoke while in motion, still the picture of calm. "When the anomaly began to form," he said, "I had the *Enterprise* moved to what I felt to be a safe distance."

"Good work, Mr. Data," said Crusher, assuming the command chair. He glanced at Picard, but Picard too was staring at the monitor screen with rapt attention.

It had literally sprung from nowhere, as if someone had taken a surgical instrument and sliced right through the fabric of reality. And what they were seeing now was the heart of the universe, cut open and pulsing, raw and open and on view for lesser creatures to observe.

"Detecting massive quantum distortions, Captain," reported Data. "Quantum barriers are in flux all around us. Sensor readings are off the scale."

"Pull us back further," ordered Crusher.

"Unable to comply," replied Data. "Helm is not responding. Captain . . . we are not able to hold our position."

"We're being drawn in," said Picard with a deathly chill to his voice.

Q writhed, screaming under the assault. Somewhere in the distance he could hear Trelane laughing.

He couldn't begin to grasp the nature of the attack.

Before, it had been simply vicious, power against power. But this . . . this was something else. This was something insane. This was puissance beyond anything that Q had ever experienced, and it was just his luck that he was on the receiving end of it.

It assaulted his body, his mind. He tried to twist and tear himself away from it, but he couldn't. Before, he had held his own, albeit briefly, against Trelane. Not this time, though. This time, for the first time, there was a true sense of hopelessness racing through him. It was all he could do not to surrender totally to despair.

"Do you remember, Q?" Trelane taunted him. "Remember a brief blink of time ago, when I needed instrumentation to help harness my powers? To focus my abilities, much like children on old Earth needed training wheels for their bicycles? Weren't those fun times, when I was helpless and capable of being humiliated, and an object of contempt? Remember when I was General Trelane, retired? Well, good news, Q old boy!" Space screamed around him. "The general has come out of retirement!"

Then Q rallied. *"No!"* he shouted. "I will not be treated in this manner! I won't permit it!"

"What a shame," replied Trelane. "I wasn't asking for your permission."

Q tried to block, to counter . . . to strike deep into the core of Trelane, find a weak point and exploit it. Trelane could be hurt, he could be stopped. This Q knew. What he did not know was how to go about it.

"Full reverse!" shouted Crusher.

No good. The mighty engines of the *Enterprise* howled, but had no other effect.

Space had fully opened in front of them now, and the massive time vortex seemed to be summoning them.

Within seconds the entirety of the viewscreen was consumed by the swirling mass of temporal energy. They had no more hope of breaking away than an insect did in a hurricane.

This can't be happening! Q thought desperately. He had lost fights before. He had been humiliated before. But even then, even at those times when he was at his lowest ebb, he was always able to think, *Somehow, somehow, I will even the score.* He had always moved beyond imminent defeat to the inevitable, desirable reckoning that would come once he had had the opportunity to regroup and plan anew.

Not this time, though.

Trelane battered him with power that was drawn from beyond the realm of reality, beyond the realm of coherence. He was literally being torn apart by incoherence.

It took but the slightest nudge, and suddenly Q was utterly consumed by the fury of the temporal anomaly that Trelane had effortlessly snapped into existence. He desperately tried to hang on to his consciousness, clutching at it as a sinking man might grasp at the last rays of sunlight before the inky depths of the ocean enfolded him for all eternity.

A voice was coming from all around him, from inside him and outside him, through every molecule of his being. That being, of course, was far greater than he ever permitted the mere mortals of the *Enterprise* to see. The form he wore was as much a matter of convenience as anything else, having the same relation to the reality of him as the tip of an iceberg did to the mass of ice that hovered below the surface.

"It's something of a pity, Q," said the voice, Trelane's confident, sneering voice. "You know . . . in another reality, we might have been friends, you and I. You've been around for as long as I can remember. You were always there, my parents' closest friend. A pity that you have to be dispensed with if my hold on power is to be finalized. But that, my dear Q, is one of the unpleasant truths of the cosmos. For we've come down to it then, haven't we. We have to decide who is to be better served here: you or me. All things considered, Q, I'm afraid I'll have to vote for me. And since this is not a democracy, but an execution, I fear that my vote is the only one that counts.

"Farewell, Q. Farewell, for now and always."

Q had time to scream once and only once, and then he felt the time vortex pulling him apart. He lost his coherence, in every sense of the word, as he spiraled backward, backward . . .

And he could hear Trelane's taunting voice bidding him good-bye. "Farewell, last free member of the Continuum. Farewell, final defender of order, which was ironic considering how you reveled in chaos. Perhaps that was, ultimately, your weakness and the reason for your downfall. You fancied yourself a rebel, a troublemaker. One would have thought you would embrace the purity of chaos, but that you could not bring yourself to do. That is where your undoing had its roots, perhaps. You were afraid to fully commit yourself to your cause. I, on the other hand, had no trepidation whatsoever. Always remember, Q, in whatever fragment of consciousness you might retain throughout the time stream . . . if given the opportunity to fully apply yourself to the ideal of destruction, I suggest you avail yourself of it. For if you don't, the consequences can . . . and will . . . be fatal."

And then Q did not hear—could not hear—any more.

Space folded itself around the *Enterprise* as the vessel disappeared into the temporal rift. And then a moment later, the rift collapsed in on itself, taking with it the frightening roar that could be heard even in the vacuum of space.

The only thing that could be heard after that was the low, disdainful, and triumphant laugh of General Trelane, the erstwhile Squire of Gothos.

TRACK **A**

7.

"**O**h . . . Geordi, this is Captain Jack Crusher. Captain, this is my head nurse, Geordi La Forge."

"An honor, sir," said Geordi, shaking Crusher's outstretched hand.

"Geordi's been with me for several years now," said Beverly. "I'd be lost without him. Best nurse in the field."

Crusher was immediately struck by how engaging a young man La Forge was. His face was pleasant and open, his brown eyes gentle. Clearly La Forge was topflight nurse material; he had a way about him that immediately put one at ease. If he looked down at you as you lay flat on your back, and told you that everything was going to be just fine, you'd very likely believe it.

"It's a pleasure to have you aboard, La Forge," said Crusher. "In a way, I envy you."

"Me, sir?" Geordi said in polite confusion.

"Yes." He looked at Beverly with undisguised sadness for just the briefest of moments. "Dr. Howard is a remarkable woman. She has many, many superb qualities, and any man who gets to spend extensive time with her can count himself fortunate."

For the first time since she'd arrived on the *Enterprise,* Beverly Howard smiled at her former husband with unfeigned warmth. "Thank you, Captain. That's very sweet. Are you this charming with all your chief medical officers?"

"Yes, I am," he said rather gravely. "As a matter of fact, a couple of the men have complained . . . although one or two were genuinely flattered by the attention."

There was some mild laughter from the others, which was all the comment warranted since it really was a rather mild joke. "Well," said Crusher briskly, rubbing his hands together as if trying to warm them. "I'm sure we all have work to do, and it would probably be best if we all got to it."

They headed for the door, and then Crusher stopped and said, "Oh, by the way, Doctor . . ."

"Yes, Commander?"

"It may not be the most relevant observation I've made today, but . . . I'm glad you're back to wearing your hair that way."

"Thank you, Captain," said Howard, reaching up and running her hands along the long, wavy locks that cascaded almost down to her shoulders. The captain nodded once more in approval, and then he and Picard exited into the corridor.

Beverly frowned then, feeling the hairstyle. "Geordi," she said. "Uhm . . . how long have I had my hair this way?"

Geordi looked at her in some confusion. "I . . . I don't know, Doctor." He laughed lightly. "A while, I think. I didn't know there was going to be a quiz, or I would have paid closer attention. Oh," he said, catching a gesture from one of the medical technicians. "They're ready for you."

She shrugged. Damnedest thing, but just for a moment, she had a mental picture of herself with shorter, curlier hair.

"Must be getting old," she muttered.

On the outermost fringes of the galaxy, there was Q.

He was no longer in human form, or any form that would be remotely recognizable to the crew of the Enterprise.

For that matter, he would not have been recognizable to anyone from the Q Continuum, for he was nothing more than an insensate haze of free-floating energy with no discernible pattern.

He did not know when he was, or where he was.

He did not know what he was, or why he was.

He had no genuine sense of himself.

He had only the dimmest, faintest sense (if only he could discern things) that he (if he could remember what he was) had lost (if only he could remember what it was to have so that he could understand loss) something that was very important (if only he could weigh the relative importance of things).

None of this was within his capacity, however.

So all he could do was float and wait until he was capable of understanding . . . whenever, or if ever, that might be.

TRACK A

8.

Picard found Captain Crusher in Ten-Forward that evening. This was something of a surprise, for Jack was not one for hanging around Ten-Forward. Crusher was a good man, a solid leader, one in whom his crew was able to take confidence. But socializing, partying, chitchat . . . these things were not his forte.

Yet there he was.

Picard stopped at the bar. Yeoman Johnson was working the bar that night. "The usual, Commander?" she asked.

"Yes, Caryn, thank you," said Picard. Moments later he was heading toward Jack, who was seated alone by the observation window. "Mind if I join you?" he asked.

Jack shrugged, not even looking up.

Picard sat opposite him, nursing his synthehol and making no particular endeavor to down it. "What's on your mind, Jack?" he asked.

Crusher looked up at him, seeming a bit bleary-eyed. "You really, really have to ask?"

Not really, no. "Her?"

"This is going to be a hell of a lot tougher than I thought, Jean-Luc," he said. "Seeing her . . . it brought up all the old memories in a way that I thought wasn't possible. I mean, you think you've got the wounds healed, you know? You think that the ache is dull and meaningless. That's until you're confronted with the source again, and then bam. It all falls apart on you."

Picard sighed. "I'm sorry, Jack."

Crusher leaned forward and dropped his voice even lower, so much so that Picard had to strain to hear it. "You know what I think? I think she still blames me for Wesley's death."

"Oh, Jack, I don't think that—"

"She does," Crusher said more forcefully. "She does, and you know that she does. And she's right to do so."

"Jack! It was an accident, that fall of his. She—"

"But it wasn't just any fall, was it."

Picard looked at him askance. "What do you mean?"

Crusher stared down into his drink as if waiting for it to talk back to him. "He was only four, Jean-Luc."

"There's no good age for a child to die, Jack. . . ."

"Only four," said Crusher, as if Picard had not spoken. "But he climbed that tree behind the house like he was born to do it. Climbed and climbed, to the highest branches. To the branches that couldn't hold his weight . . ."

"Jack, don't do this to yourself."

"He didn't cry, you know. Not on the fall . . . you think he'd have done something. Some high-pitched shriek or something, but there was nothing. Beverly was in the house, and she didn't hear a scream at all. All she heard was a thud. What in God's name must that have sounded like, Jean-Luc? That little boy's body hitting the ground."

Picard put down his drink and rose, taking Jack firmly by

the arm. "Let's go, Captain. I think it would be better if . . ."

Crusher didn't budge. This presented Picard with something of a problem. On the one hand it wasn't going to do much for the crew to watch the captain come completely unglued in the Ten-Forward lounge. News of that sort tended to spread rather quickly. On the other hand, Picard couldn't exactly grab Crusher by the scruff of his neck and drag him out, kicking and screaming, against his will. Hoping to effect something remotely approaching damage control, Picard slowly sat down again. "Captain," he whispered in the hope that, at the very least, Crusher would automatically drop his own voice to a similar level. "We can discuss this elsewhere."

To his relief, Crusher did indeed lower his tone to a whisper. But the effect sent chills down Picard's spine, because it sounded as if Crusher were speaking from beyond the grave. "I wonder which is worse, Jean-Luc," said Crusher. "The sound that Beverly heard when he hit the ground . . . or the sound that I conjure up in my all-too-vivid imagination."

Picard had no answer.

"He lived long enough to tell her why, you know." Crusher smiled lopsidedly. "He looked up at her from that broken little body, and he said . . ." Crusher's voice caught, and his jaw was twitching.

"Jack, please . . ."

"He said, 'Wanted to climb high enough . . . to see Daddy.'"

Other crewmen were now glancing in Crusher's direction, able to tell from wherever they were sitting that their captain was in some sort of distress. At that point, though, Picard was beyond being concerned about how this was going to look to the crew. His primary worry was trying to pull his friend back together again.

"It wasn't your fault. . . ."

"I should have been there."

"You couldn't know. . . ."

Crusher looked up at him levelly, the inebriating sensations of the synthehol falling away from him. "If I had been there," he said flatly, "it would not have happened."

"Jack, for God's sake, you can't second-guess every moment of your life. You can't look at one path and say, 'I should have followed it because look how much better things would have turned out.' Look at us! A perfect example. If you had stayed on Earth, not pursued your career, then what the hell would have happened when the *Stargazer* was ambushed at Maxia Zeta, eh? Bad enough that the ship was lost. But if you hadn't been quick enough of mind to develop the Crusher maneuver, all hands would have gone with her."

"If I hadn't been there, you would have come up with something."

"Rubbish," replied Picard. "The court-martial board certainly didn't agree with you." Even though it was a painful topic for him, he pushed forward. "You came through for me then, too. You were the hero who, to be blunt, saved his captain's ass. I could have gotten a lot worse than reduced in rank, I assure you. For that matter, I owe my continued career to you. Who do you think would have been remotely interested in having me aboard their ship as Number One, eh? The taint of a court-martial decision against me. The stench of defeat clinging to me."

"You were railroaded, Jean-Luc," said Crusher firmly. "It's politics. All politics. There were still people in Starfleet who felt you were rushed along. Grumbling I still hear about how you should never have gotten a captaincy at twenty-eight. It's rubbish.''

"Yes, well, 'rubbish' is the right word," said Picard ruefully. "If I ever had managed to get another assignment, it would probably have been commanding a garbage scow or freighter somewhere. You saved me from that, Jack. And when you eventually took command of the Fleet's flagship vessel, you asked for me as your Number One.''

"It was no big deal.''

"It *was* a big deal, Jack," said Picard firmly. "Don't think I'm unaware of it. I know about your telling Starfleet Command that if you didn't have the power to choose whomever you desired as your command crew, then you were not interested in helming this vessel. My God, Jack . . . that was a hell of a thing to do. A hell of a thing. Not one man in a thousand would have that sort of loyalty to a friend.''

"What else was I supposed to do?" Crusher replied. "You can talk about Maxia Zeta and the Crusher maneuver . . . lord, I hate that name . . . all you want. But we both know that you saved my life the year before, on that away mission. If not for you, then my butt would be planted six feet under instead of in the command chair of the *Enterprise*. Not that there would have been anyone at home to care when my body came back, of course.''

"Oh, Jack." Picard sighed. He had thought that he had finally managed to get Crusher away from the self-destructive moroseness that seemed to have an intractable grip on him. "Now, come on. You and Beverly didn't divorce until several *years* after Wesley's death.''

"Yes, but that was the turning point. That's where it all changed. You know what I think? I think that every time she looked at me from that moment on, she couldn't do it without affixing blame to me. And why shouldn't she? She couldn't possibly have blamed me any more than I did. In a way, I envy you tremendously. After the court-martial when you were planetside, you had a chance to spend more time with her than I ever did." He leaned forward, curious. "Did she tell you then she was planning to leave me?"

"Jack, why do this to yourself?"

"Did she tell you?" His tone was growing more insistent, and a bit louder. Picard needed to do something to quiet him.

"No, she didn't," said Picard. "Jack, we didn't really spend all that much time together, Beverly and I. Not really. And most of the time I was there, I was just . . . an occasional shoulder for her to cry on."

"Which is more than I was," said Crusher. "Jean-Luc, if I had any part of my life I could do over again, it would be that. What was I thinking, going back out into space so quickly? She needed me. She acted as if she were dealing with it, as if she had her emotions under control. She managed to convince herself so thoroughly that she convinced me, too. What a selfish bastard I was. No, not selfish . . . gutless. Because I couldn't stand the way she'd look at me. . . ."

"Enough, Jack." And this time when Picard said it, it was with sufficient conviction that it managed to penetrate through Crusher's despair. "It's enough."

Jack Crusher nodded. "Yeah," he said, staring at his reflection in the viewing window. "Yeah, I guess it is enough, isn't it." He rose. "I think I'm going to turn in, Jean-Luc."

"That would probably be wise."

He smiled lopsidedly. "You know . . . you do make a fairly good shoulder to cry on. Beverly was damned lucky to have you."

"We were all fortunate to have what we did have, Jack.

The things that we didn't have . . . those are lamentable, of course. But we can either dwell on them, regret them pointlessly . . . or learn from them and move on."

"And I think moving on is exactly what I'll be doing," said Crusher. He patted Jean-Luc on the shoulder and walked out of Ten-Forward. The eyes of the crew were upon him as he went, but he seemed to walk with a measure of confidence that was reassuring to those watching.

The only one not watching him at that point was Jean-Luc Picard. Picard had downed his drink in one shot, and now he sat staring at the empty glass and wondering where he was going to go next, given the situation.

Except that he really wasn't wondering at all.

He knew.

Beverly Howard was up late reading in her quarters when the door chime sounded. Her first instinct was that there was some sort of medical emergency to which she was being summoned, but she quickly realized that was not the case. Otherwise they would simply have called her on her comm unit.

She knew who it was.

She wasn't exactly sure how she knew or, for that matter, what her feelings on the subject were. All that she knew was that her heart was suddenly speeding up. Reflexively she took her own pulse. She stood up because she wanted to be eye to eye with him when he entered. Then she decided that that was going to look too formal, too stiff. So she sat. But it was a nonchalance that felt forced and awkward. So she crouched, half-propped up on one knee. That, of course, didn't help, because it was the worst of all. She'd gone from looking stiff, and then awkward, to flat-out stupid.

In the meantime, the door chimed again.

She stood again and took position behind her chair, leaning on it. She was well aware that she was sending a subliminal message, hiding as she was behind the furniture. But if she delayed much longer, then it was going to seem damned weird when she finally let him in, because the obvious question was going to be "What kept you?" She could pretend she was in the shower. Great idea. All she had to do was pull off her uniform, jump in the shower, get wet, jump out, toss on a robe, and answer the door . . . by which point the man on the other side would very likely be back in his quarters, in bed and sound asleep.

The hell with it.

"Come," she said.

The door slid open and, sure enough, Commander Jean-Luc Picard was on the other side. He was half-turned away, and it was clear that he had been about to leave. "Oh," he said. "Hello. I . . . thought perhaps you were asleep."

"I was," she lied with brisk efficiency. "I fell asleep reading. Come in, please, by all means."

Picard nodded and entered, the door sliding shut behind him. His hands were draped behind his back as he glanced around. "Settled in, are you?"

"Yes."

"Well, that's . . ." He cleared his throat. "That's good. That's very, very good."

"I'm glad you approve." She gathered her emotional strength and, looking as casual as she could manage, strolled from behind the chair. "I mean, I could have simply lived out of suitcases for the next few years, but that wouldn't have seemed much like a show of faith."

"No. No, I daresay not."

They stood there, facing each other uncomfortably for a moment.

"So," he said finally.

"So," she echoed.

He paused another moment and then said, "Beverly," and she could tell from the change of his tone that he was about to get down to business. She had a fairly clear sense of what that business was, but she said nothing to deter him. Indeed, what was there to say?

He licked his lips, which had suddenly gone dry, and said again, "Beverly . . ."

"Yes, Jean-Luc?"

"I don't know . . . if it was particularly wise for you to take this assignment."

"Really," she said, in that way she had that was her way of saying, *This is going to be good.*

The subtext was not lost on Picard, but he chose to press ahead. "I don't think you realize quite how difficult all of this is going to be on Jack. He did nothing to stand in your way for this position, even though he could have. That's not the sort of man that Jack Crusher is."

"Is it the sort of man you are, Jean-Luc?"

"What do you mean?"

"You know what I mean," she said. He seemed slightly . . . just slightly . . . disconcerted by the question, and his reaction gave her a certain feeling of empowerment. She came out from behind her desk and said, "If you were in charge, and I wanted the assignment . . . would you try to block me, taking our history into account?"

He considered the question for slightly longer than either of them felt comfortable. "No," he said. "I'd like to think not. Still . . . you know how Jack feels about you."

"It's over between us, Jean-Luc. It has been for some time."

"I know you believe that, and I know he wants to believe that. But Beverly, the man I saw tonight . . . he still loves you. Deep down . . . hell, not even all that deep down. Fairly close to the surface, actually. I could see it easily. In fact, anyone who was looking could see it."

She stepped in close to face him, and he could smell the scent of her, that perfume she wore. Her eyes glistened in that way that he remembered so clearly he could still call it to mind late at night in the darkness of his quarters. He was amazed to see how accurate his recollection was. The lips, full and firm, and the sweet taste of them, and that first shock of recognition when his mouth had covered hers all those years ago. The recognition that something was happening between them that neither of them had anticipated. Indeed, that neither of them wanted, because it was another difficulty in lives already way overcomplicated.

But it was also something neither of them could stop.

It had started so unexpectedly. They had run into each other again at some deathly dull Starfleet gathering. He was unsure how to approach her, for she still wore the grief of her son's passing like a shroud, and furthermore Picard was all too well aware of the deteriorating state of her marriage to Jack. Beverly, for her part, had been unsure of what to say to Picard, for the *Stargazer* trial had been well publicized and Beverly had felt tremendously embarrassed on Picard's behalf.

At the gathering, they had trod carefully in their conversations, each desperately trying not to say the wrong thing. Eventually the party had broken up, and Picard had offered to walk her home, for neither of them had brought a date with them. It was a lovely night, the air brisk and unseasonably cool.

They made the walk in silence, and in silence he brought her to her door. "Well," he had said, feeling as awkward as a teenager on a first date and not comprehending why he felt that way. "This was . . . very nice."

"Yes, it was."

They stood there a moment more, and then, impulsively, he had leaned forward and kissed to the right of her mouth, just on the underside of her jaw. It was an odd place to kiss her, and he was wondering why he had done so when he abruptly realized that he had not pulled back after the simple, friendly social kiss. His lips were right where he had placed them, and he was *nuzzling* her, for God's sake, she was Jack's wife, was he out of his mind . . . ?

She gasped slightly, and he waited for her to pull back, waited for her to protest, to hit him, to do *something* other than what she was, in fact, doing, which was nuzzling him back.

Then they pulled apart only for as long as it took them to bring their mouths together. His chest was pressed against hers, and he wasn't sure if the heart he felt pounding was his or hers against him. It didn't seem to matter too much, though. Not half as much as the sudden, mutual realization that the reason they'd had such difficulty talking to each other was because talking was not what they were interested in doing. Their bodies were quantum leaps ahead of their minds.

Things had moved rather quickly after that.

They had managed to be discreet, at least. Picard thanked God for that. Even though the marriage was already deteriorating . . .

Even though Jack had as good as abandoned any hope of saving the relationship, instead burying himself deep into a career newly revitalized by his actions on the *Stargazer* . . .

Even though, even though . . .

None of it mattered, because the simple fact was that Jean-Luc Picard, once the best and brightest that the Academy had to offer, had gotten wildly sidetracked from his chosen career. He had seemed a man of destiny, but it now appeared that the destiny was to have a torrid affair with the soon-to-be-ex-wife of his very likely soon-to-be-former-friend.

It was at that point in his life that Picard, in fact, had it in his power to be happy. The feelings between himself and Beverly Crusher, shortly to be Howard once again, had grown. Had become deeper and fuller and richer. He could have chosen to leave Starfleet, found something to do on Earth. Despite Beverly's training in the Starfleet medical corps, she seemed rather content to seek out assignments on Earth, or perhaps on nearby colony worlds. Picard could join her. They could be together.

There was something fairly significant preventing it, however.

The guilt.

Picard was filled with happiness that he felt he did not deserve. Consumed by guilt over whatever part he might have played, real or imagined, in the breakup of his friend's marriage.

Finally, Picard couldn't take it anymore. He had gone to Starfleet Command and, tossing aside whatever shreds of dignity or self-esteem he might have had left, practically begged for an assignment off Earth. On the next available vessel that would have him. Even at his reduced rank he was still a commander, but he was willing to take a position usually designated for a lower rank, if only it would get him the hell off-planet, and quickly.

He called superiors, he called in favors, he even called in the one man whom damn near everyone who was anyone in Starfleet respected: Boothby, the Academy grounds-keeper. It was Boothby, naturally, who got the job done, and within twenty-four hours of making the decision to leave, Picard was gone.

His departure from Beverly was a hurried affair, and also

a complete fabrication. He'd told her he had no choice, that Starfleet was shipping him out. Beverly nodded, understanding and conciliatory, and he had always wondered if she knew. But he'd never had the nerve, or the rebuilt self-esteem, to ask her.

Not until now.

"Did you know?" he asked.

Dr. Beverly Howard looked at him with curiosity. "Know what? That you ran out? That you sought out the assignment from Starfleet? Oh, Jean-Luc, of course I knew."

"But you said nothing."

She shrugged. "What was there to say?"

"You let me go."

"I couldn't stop you even if I wanted to."

"And did you want to?"

She paused. "You helped me, actually."

"I did?"

"Yes. Because I'd been hiding since Wesley's death. Hiding from the galaxy. I felt . . . You're going to laugh."

"Never."

"I felt like . . . if I left Earth . . . I'd be abandoning Wesley. Abandoning my baby. Leaving him to just . . . just be dead without me to be with him." She felt the sting in her eyes and refused to acknowledge it, choking it back. "Isn't that the most stupid thing you ever heard?"

He saw the tears beginning to swell, and he reached up with a tenderness that he would have thought he could no longer summon. Gently he wiped the tears away. "No. No, not at all."

"Ohhh," she moaned softly. "You bastard, I swore I wouldn't let you see me cry. And I won't."

"You won't cry?"

"No, I won't let you see me. Computer, lights out."

The lights in her quarters went out. "Beverly," said Picard with a touch of reproval. "I can't see to leave."

Then he felt her hands at his chest, and from the darkness, she said in a voice low and hoarse, "I don't want you to."

There were a hundred good reasons for him to get out of Beverly's quarters as quickly as his legs would carry him. And there was only one reason . . . a fairly lousy one, in fact . . . for him to stay.

Unfortunately, that was the one that won out.

TRACK A

9.

When Jack Crusher returned to his quarters, he slowed before the door opened. He heard something . . . something odd. Something light and airy.

He heard music.

He glanced around to see if others passing by heard it as well, but there didn't seem to be any reaction from them. He didn't want to start sandbagging his own people and saying, "Do you hear that? Do you hear the music?" He would have sounded as if he were losing his mind.

He entered his quarters, ready for anything.

Trelane was seated in a corner. He was strumming on a large, ornate harp.

Crusher's first impulse was to order the bizarre being to get out of his quarters, to get off his ship. But something halted him. It was the music itself. The music that floated through the air was angelic. Trelane's fingers caressed the strings, and it almost seemed to Crusher as if the notes were tangible. That they were wrapping themselves around him, soothing him and easing the turmoil in his soul.

"You may find this difficult to believe, Captain," Trelane informed him airily, "but you and I are going to be the most excellent of friends."

"You're right about that, Trelane," Crusher said warily. "I find that very difficult to believe."

"Ah, but it's true." Trelane stopped talking for a moment, closing his eyes and seeming to drink in the loveliness of the music that rolled from his fingertips. "I am the first to admit, Captain, that I do not excel at first impressions."

"Excel?" Crusher was astounded. "You brought my ship to a halt, you threatened us, you—"

"I know very well what I did, Captain, so your litany of charges is unnecessary." His hands never stopped gliding across the strings. "Let us just say that I was upset. Upset about matters beyond your ken. Can we start over, Captain?" he asked with a heavy layering of melodrama. "Would that be possible?"

"I don't know," said Crusher carefully.

"You allow for doubt!" Trelane exclaimed joyously. "How absolutely smashing! Tell me, Captain . . . what do you think of my musicianship, eh?"

"You play very well," Crusher was forced to admit.

"I come by it naturally. Never had a lesson. Hard to believe, isn't it." He looked up at Crusher. "Would you like to play?"

"I can't."

"Oh, but I insist."

Crusher wasn't particularly sure how it happened, but the next thing he knew, he was seated where Trelane had been. The large instrument was tucked serenely between his legs. "This is crazy," said Crusher.

"It's a crazy universe, Captain!" Trelane said stridently. "And we have two choices in dealing with it. Either we can submit ourselves to the insanity of creation, and let it take us wherever it may so desire. Or else we can try to beat it at its own game. As for my humble self, I prefer the latter. Play us something, Captain. Play what's in your heart."

With a shrug, Crusher lifted his hands to the harp strings. He had absolutely no idea what he was supposed to do. As a result, he was that much more astonished when his hands seemed to start operating on their own. He didn't have to give it any thought. It was all completely instinctive. His hands floated across the strings. Each touch was sure and steady, and he seemed to know automatically where all the right notes were.

He played no particular tune, no song with which he was already familiar. It was an aimless, wandering melody, and yet somehow it seemed to have meaning to him. It evoked images for him, sensations that seemed strange and yet, somehow, in some odd way, were familiar to him.

Trelane sat across from him, and his eyes were misting up. He removed a handkerchief with a flourish from his breast pocket and dabbed at his eyes. "Play on," he encouraged, and Crusher did so with growing confidence. He lost track of the time, nor would he have ever been able to accurately reproduce the song that he played. He wouldn't even have been able to say for certain how he knew that he was finished. He only knew that he was, and when he lowered his hands from the harp, Trelane burst into enthusiastic applause.

"What did you make me play?" demanded Crusher.

"Make you?" Trelane seemed appalled, even offended, by the very suggestion. "My dear captain, I made you play nothing. Nothing, on my word of honor. I gave you the facility, yes. The dexterity, the knowledge. All of those, my gift to you to try and atone for my boorish behavior earlier. But the music that you produced . . . that, Captain, came

from within you. Tell me: Did it sound at all familiar to you?"

"A little, yes," admitted Crusher. "Damned if I could tell you where from . . ."

"I'll tell you where it's from. The music, Captain Crusher, was an expression of your soul. It seemed familiar to you because, in a very real sense, it *was* you. The you that you try not to let out."

Crusher was still seated behind the harp. Trelane drew a chair over and sat a couple of feet away from Crusher, studying him intently. "What a lonely soul you are," he said sadly. "You have the heart of a warrior . . . something that I can respect. If you had been born at the right time, you would be capable of leading armies across vast plains. Of striking deep into the heart of your enemy, unslowed by their lamentations and cries for mercy. What a great human tragedy it is, Jack Crusher . . . that you missed your opportunity."

Crusher turned his gaze to him and shook his head slowly. "You are something else, Trelane. With your posturing and overwrought declarations. Is this part of the pain you said you wanted to cause?"

Trelane leaned closer. "And would you like to know what the greatest tragedy of all is, Jack?"

"Not especially, no."

"The greatest tragedy is that you indeed are a very lonely soul . . . and you don't know why."

"And you do."

"Of course," said Trelane.

"So are you going to share this great knowledge with me?"

Thoughtfully, Trelane shook his head. "No. No, I don't think I shall. Not yet. It's knowledge that I don't think you're quite ready for. But take heart, Captain. I will tell you, in time. Although I must warn you: You may not like what you hear."

With that comment hanging in the air, Trelane vanished.

He reappeared standing on the edge of the *Enterprise* saucer section, and he smiled broadly.

"Ah, Q," he said. "You would have been so proud of me. I've learned your lessons extremely well. For that, Q, I thank you. Rest in peace, knowing that you have done well. Or, better yet. Rest in . . . pieces."

He laughed loudly at his own joke, and even in the airlessness of space, his chortled glee carried.

TRACK A

10.

Picard slowly opened his eyes with that sense of disorientation one always has when one awakens someplace new. But then he heard the soft snoring near the crook of his elbow, and it came rushing back to him in a gentle, glowing haze.

"Ohhh . . . dear," he said softly.

He flexed his fingers and came to the slow realization that he had lost circulation in his right hand. Gently, gingerly, he pulled the arm out from under Beverly's head. She twitched briefly in her sleep as he accidentally tugged at a hank of her hair, and then his arm was free of her head. She settled back down onto the pillow, her eyes still closed, as Picard raised his arm straight up and shook the hand out briskly. He felt a quick tingling and tried making a fist.

"Want me to kiss it and make it better?" came the tender voice from next to him.

He looked over at her, and her eyes were still closed. There was, however, the trace of a smile on her lips.

159

"Go back to sleep," said Picard.

"Like hell. I go on duty in fifteen minutes."

He frowned and checked the chronometer in the darkened room. She was right.

"I have an internal clock that's as punctual as anything on this ship," she said with a touch of pride. "I set it, I wake up to it, I go to sleep by it."

"Do you make love by it?" he asked.

Now she did open her eyes, twinkling merrily in the darkness as if they generated their own light. "In a sense. It was high time, after all, and it's been a long drought."

"You mean you haven't since . . ."

She shook her head. "No, Jean-Luc. Not since you."

"Hmmph." And then the slow realization began to dawn on him. He sat up, propping himself up on one elbow. "Beverly . . . did you want to come to the *Enterprise* because—"

"Of you?" she completed the question for him. "Now, that's a massively egotistical thing to wonder."

"You didn't answer the question," he couldn't help but observe.

"Truth?"

"That's always preferable."

"The *Enterprise* was a terrific opportunity. My career had been comatose long enough. I will always mourn the loss of my baby, but it was crippling me. So when I decided to apply myself, I threw myself into it completely. God, I haven't put in hours like that since my residency. 'Sleep' was this thing that I used to do, but gave up for the good of my career. Then when the *Enterprise* assignment came up, I gave it . . . what's the expression Jack used to use?" She frowned, and then her face cleared. "The full-court press. Got my name and résumé submitted as a long shot. My work was impeccable and my record spotless. No one doubted I could do the job, but I wasn't sure I had the length of service chops. And then there was Jack to consider."

"So tell me . . . did you think that having him making the decision would work *for* you, or *against* you?"

"I had it pinned down to one of those two," she said dryly. When Picard made it clear with his expression that he expected more of an answer than that, she said, "Let's just say that I was hoping to catch a break."

"So my being on this ship had nothing to do with your wanting the position."

"My, Jean-Luc, your ego knows no bounds, does it." She sighed sadly as if greatly disturbed to discover this weakness in her old lover.

"Once again you don't answer the question."

"If the answer were no, you'd be disappointed, and if the answer were yes, you'd be even more insufferably egotistical than you already are."

"You are masterful at sidestepping things, aren't you."

"All right, all right." She sighed heavily. "If I tell you that finding out you were the second-in-command was a very strong additional incentive, will that satisfy you?"

He gave it a moment's thought. "I suppose it will have to." Then, with a heavy sigh, he said, "You know . . . this cannot become a regular thing."

"Whatever do you mean?"

"Don't act coy, Doctor. It does not suit you. I'm referring to this. Us." He pointed to the both of them. "How in God's name would Jack feel if he knew?"

"I don't know."

"Yes, you do."

"Yes, I do," admitted Beverly with a sigh. "But am I supposed to totally sublimate how I feel . . . how we feel . . . because it's going to upset my ex-husband?"

"That's not the way to think of it," Picard told her. "Think of it as exacerbating an already potentially incendiary situation between yourself and the captain of this vessel."

She lay flat on her back and stared up at the ceiling. "When you put it that way, the choice is pretty clear, isn't it."

"Unfortunately, yes."

"Well . . . that settles that, then." She turned to look at him. "I'm glad we had this talk, Jean-Luc. I mean, I'm glad about everything we had. But I think it was important that we hash this out and get things straight between us. If we're going to be serving together on the *Enterprise,* it's important to know where we stand in terms of whatever we do . . . or don't do . . . in this relationship." She took a deep breath as if a weight had been lifted from her. "Okay, so . . . would you like to shower?"

"You can go first."

She smiled. "Who said anything about going one at a time?"

As Geordi La Forge was walking past Dr. Howard's quarters, he noticed the door sliding open. This was the perfect opportunity to discuss some administrative matters with her, before the usual hustle and bustle of sickbay life arose to distract her. He turned quickly and headed toward her quarters, saying, "Doctor!"

To his surprise, he bumped squarely into Commander Picard, who was clearly just leaving. To his even greater surprise, Dr. Howard was still inside and clearly just finishing adjusting her uniform top.

It took him somewhere around two seconds to work it out.

"Oh," he said.

Picard shot him a look that seemed to say, *I knew it.* But

Beverly, sounding not the least put out, said, "Come in, Geordi. What can I do for you?"

Taking his cue from Howard, Geordi stepped in as Picard walked out. The door slid shut behind Geordi, and then he just stood and stared at Howard.

She looked up at him with a bland expression. "What can I do for you, Geordi?"

"Um . . . I forget," he said, which was true enough.

She sighed. "Okay, look . . . Commander Picard and I are old friends."

"Look, Doctor," he said, shifting in place uncomfortably, "it's none of my business."

"No, it *wasn't,* but I suppose it is now."

"But I don't want to come across as judgmental. I mean, who am I to render those kinds of verdicts?"

"For one thing, you're my friend," she said reasonably, "and what you think matters to me. So I didn't want you to think that I had just met Commander Picard and the next thing you know . . ."

"I didn't think that. And even if I did, well, hey . . . you're both adults."

"We are." Crusher smiled. "The other thing, of course, is that some people might perceive it as having some sort of impropriety. This may seem like a huge ship, Geordi, but in terms of a community, a thousand people is pretty small. We don't need a lot of gossip and misinterpretation going on, particularly this early in the game."

"Which is a roundabout way of saying that you'd rather no one heard it from me."

She nodded. "That's right."

Geordi winked at her. "Don't worry, Doc. As far as you need be concerned, I didn't see a damned thing."

"Thanks, Geordi. By the way, seriously, what did you want to discuss before?"

"Just some minor stuff, really. Nothing that can't wait."

"Good. In that case, I'll be down in a few minutes. Oh, by the way . . . the engineering chief, Argyle, is due for a physical. She keeps 'forgetting.' I'd like you to go down and remind her personally. Use that famous La Forge charm."

"You got it, Doctor."

He left her quarters, and only then did Beverly let out a long "Whhhewwwww . . ."

"Do you have any idea how busy I am here?" demanded Chief Argyle. "Excuse me, please." She stepped around Geordi to get to her workstation.

Geordi La Forge kept right behind her. "Yes, Chief, I'm very aware of it. Everyone on the ship is aware of it."

"Hah, that's a laugh," she said, her thick Scots brogue making every word sound as if she were singing it.

"It's true," he said. "I haven't been here all that long, but whenever I ask anyone about anything when it comes to how this ship runs, they all say the same thing: Gotta go to Argyle. Check with Chief Argyle. Argyle's your woman."

She looked away from her work as if seeing him for the first time. "Go on with you," she said skeptically.

"Do I look like I'm lying?"

She studied his eyes carefully, looking for some hint of dissembling. "Either you're remarkably sincere or remarkably smooth, I'll give you that."

"A lot of people count on you. Is that so difficult to believe?"

"Well," and she straightened her uniform, "engineers don't always get much recognition. Not that I do this job for the recognition. You understand that, don't you."

"Of course, Chief."

"I do it because I love it. That's the important thing. I

love it and it needs to be done. You were right about that. Even people who never heard of me count on me."

"That's right. That's why it's such a shame, that's all."

She looked at him askance. "Why what's a shame?"

"What?" He seemed surprised, as if it were so obvious that her asking about it was nothing short of astounding. "Why, that you're not taking care of yourself. You work so hard down here that you could work yourself sick, and then where's everyone going to be?"

Her lips thinned and her eyes narrowed. "Now, what a tragedy that would be."

"I think so, at any rate. Of course, if you feel different, well, that's your prerogative. I won't take any more of your busy time."

He turned to leave, and Argyle said, "Nurse La Forge."

Geordi turned. "Yes, Chief?"

"You are *definitely* a smooth one. Please let our esteemed chief medical officer know that I'll be up within the hour, provided," she held up a warning finger, "that it doesn't take up too much time."

"I'll tell her," said Geordi, and he gave his most ingratiating, woman-killing smile. Argyle was not immune to it, for she actually flushed slightly at his open appreciation of her.

As Geordi headed out of engineering, he noticed the odd-looking officer who was going toward the door at the same time. Geordi stopped and stepped aside, gesturing for the officer to precede him.

"Thank you, Mr. La Forge," said the officer.

Geordi followed him out. "You know my name?" he said.

"Of course. I am aware of all new arrivals to the *Enterprise* crew."

"You have a good memory."

"I have a positronic brain."

Then Geordi snapped his fingers, remembering. "Of course! I read about you in medical journals! You're Lieutenant Data!"

"Lieutenant Commander," Data corrected him. "Although you may feel free to call me Data. I find I prefer it, since it implies a familiarity that I consider rather appealing."

"Oh. Okay then." Geordi whistled appreciatively. "Lieutenant Commander Data, the first and only human-oid. A positronic brain in a human body. Incredible."

"Many have said so," Data said. "However, I must admit that, although I understand the excitement intellectually, I have difficulty sharing in it. Since I have been what I am for as long as I can recall, to me there is nothing extraordinary about me."

"I guess there wouldn't be, to you. But to the rest of the medical community, it's nothing short of astounding. Dr. Soong working with the Daystrom Institute and creating you . . . well, it's . . . incredible."

"You already said that," Data pointed out.

"Sorry."

"Apologies are not necessary. I cannot take offense." Data began to walk, and then slowed down his pace so Geordi could match it. Data frequently had to remind himself not to walk so briskly that he left others striving to keep up. "I can, however, make observations about the vagaries of human existence. For example, the fact that science progresses with remarkable speed. What would have seemed mere fiction yesterday is fact today."

"Hey, I'm living proof of that."

"Are you?" Data asked him curiously.

"Absolutely. You see, for most of my life, I was blind."

"Indeed." He looked at Geordi's eyes. "Your vision does not appear to be impaired now."

"That's because it's not. For a while I was outfitted with all sorts of prosthetics. A sensor web for a time; and then there was a VISOR, a piece of metal they strapped across my face. But it gave me headaches you wouldn't believe."

"Why would I not believe you?"

"They were really bad headaches," Geordi said simply. "I stopped using it, and for a while I just lived in darkness. You wouldn't have recognized me, because I was so bitter during that period of my life. But then they developed this cloning technique that actually enabled them to grow eyes for me. Real eyes that they then implanted. You couldn't tell, could you."

"Not at all," said Data readily.

"Anyway, I wound up spending so much of my life around the medical profession, I just got interested in it. I encountered so many doctors and nurses, and I finally decided that caregiving was the direction I wanted to take my life. And one thing led to another, and here I am."

"This must be an exciting time for you."

"Oh, believe me, sir, it is. Believe me," he said to Data as they headed off down the corridor, "I can't think of any place I'd rather be, or anything I'd rather be doing, than where I am and what I'm doing right now."

How much time?

How much time had passed?

Centuries? Millennia? Eons?

O floated, the first, faint glimmerings of self-awareness starting to stretch to him, like an embryonic child first becoming aware of his mother's voice.

There was . . . a very distant shouting.

He didn't know what it was, but he could sense that somehow it had meaning to him. However, for him to realize that it had meaning to him, it was also required that he had a sense of himself for it to have meaning to. . . .

It was all rather confusing, really.

What he did not know, or understand, or have any real hope of understanding, was that the dim, faraway noise he detected was the beginning of humanity. It was difficult to say what precisely it was that had caught his disconnected attention.

Perhaps it was a human life-form being ripped apart by a great clawed beast.

Perhaps it was the howling of a newborn child.

Perhaps it was the first woman being raped, or the first man being murdered.

Impossible to say, really. But it caught his attention, it most definitely did.

For about a millisecond.

Then he drifted off again.

TRACK CHANGE

TRACK **B**

5.

Chafin snickered as Lieutenant Commander Geordi La Forge tried to concentrate on the readings from the engineering station. "So you just, like, popped in on Troi? Out of nowhere? And she was—?"

"Tom, I'd *really* rather not discuss it, okay?" said Geordi. "It's not one of the greatest moments of my life, and it certainly wasn't one of hers."

"Yeah, well, it would have been one of mine."

Geordi turned and looked at Chafin, gazing at him through his VISOR. "Tell me something, Tom. How long has it been since you had a date?"

"A date?" Chafin frowned. "That's where you spend time with a woman, right? In a romantic situation?"

"Too long," Geordi confirmed. "Way too long."

"You had no business doing it."

Martinez was regarding Captain Picard with a look of pure, flashing anger. Across the table from her in the

173

conference lounge, Picard's fingers were interlaced and resting in front of him. Riker, the only other occupant of the room, was seated nearby. He was not especially pleased at Martinez's accusatory tone, and this was reflected in his face. Picard, for his part, seemed much calmer, but no less firm.

"What I did, Professor, I did for the good of this crew and this vessel," he said firmly. "That is of paramount concern to me. The risk to permitting, and even condoning, Trelane's actions was unacceptable to me."

"Oh yes," said Martinez with barely contained sarcasm. "That's right in the ship's mandate, as I recall. 'To seek out new life, as long as we're not at risk.'"

"Your tone is not appreciated, Professor," Riker now spoke up. "The captain did what was necessary for everyone's sake, including yours. I'll gladly acknowledge your superiority in all matters theoretical, but when it comes to dealing with beings like Trelane on a practical basis, then likewise you should be willing to allow for the notion that we just *might* know what we're doing."

Martinez frowned. "Look, I'm not trying to undercut anyone here. Hell, if I were trying to do that, I'd be loudly complaining about this on the bridge or in Ten-Forward, instead of requesting a private meeting. I just wish there had been some better way to handle it, that's all."

"I agree, Professor," said Picard evenly. "Unfortunately, there was not."

Martinez sighed loudly. "All right. Fine. I've vented my spleen, and you replied. Believe it or not, I appreciate it. Some civilian scientist comes along and starts complaining about how you're doing things . . . hell, some captains would have just blown me out a photon-torpedo tube and be done with me."

"The day's young," Picard said.

The deadpan comment actually drew a smile from Martinez.

"As long as we've got you here, Professor," continued Picard, "I would ask how much longer we're looking at observing the Ompet Oddity. We're trying to be flexible, of course, but I hadn't intended on making this my life's work."

"Barring unforeseen complications, another eight to ten hours, I should think. That will enable me to fully chart the gravitational fluxes." She shook her head. "Not to sound like I'm harping on it, but that was the sort of information I was trying to get out of Trelane. After all, he claimed that he was responsible for many, if not all, of the odd temporal anomalies you people keep smacking into. That would have made him quite knowledgeable about them. But he would only tell me things in dribs and drabs. Frankly, it was impossible to tell whether he was simply being coy, or whether he wasn't really sure *how* he was doing the things he did, but didn't want to admit it."

"Given a choice, I'd guess the latter," said Picard. "One thing that was painfully evident about Trelane is that he was, and is, a very unrefined talent."

"That's certainly backed up by log entries from the original *Enterprise*'s meeting with him," confirmed Riker. "For instance, he was perfectly capable of creating food, but it had no taste."

"If that's part of the criteria," Martinez said in amusement, "then my mother qualifies as an omnipotent being."

"Don't all mothers?" remarked Picard.

This drew a laugh from Martinez, and Picard couldn't help but observe that she really was a rather striking and pleasant woman. If only this Trelane and Q business had not arisen to bring Picard and Martinez to loggerheads. Who knows how things might have gone? That was certainly Q's way, to show up at the worst possible times. Then again, what time was ever a *good* time for Q to put in an appearance?

Riker was smiling as well. But then he put in on a more serious note, "He also generated fire that produced no heat, in a fireplace."

"So he understood enough of the surface mechanics to produce an effect, but none of the underlying dynamics." Martinez nodded thoughtfully. "Which would certainly support the theory that he *didn't* necessarily know what he was doing."

"He just did it." Picard nodded. "It would also support the reasons for Trelane having a 'mentor' in Q. The notion of any entity possessing that sort of power without a clear idea of how to use it . . ."

"It's rather frightening," said Riker.

"I never thought I would say this, but there are times when I certainly don't envy Q his lot in life. Well"—he looked from Riker to Martinez—"I presume we are done here."

There were nods from the two of them. Riker rose and headed out of the conference lounge, followed by Martinez.

"Mr. Worf," said Riker briskly, upon walking onto the bridge.

"Yes, sir."

"Kindly inform Starfleet that Professor Martinez feels she will be finished with her observations and research of the Ompet Oddity within . . . ten hours." He glanced at her for confirmation. She nodded. "Presuming there are no further startling developments with it, our orders are to proceed to the planet Terminus, there to drop off the professor, where she will be meeting with several of her colleagues to give her full report."

"Aye, sir."

"Thank you, Commander, for all your help," said Martinez.

"My pleasure."

As Martinez headed for the turbolift, Riker noticed that Picard had not emerged from the conference lounge. He headed back for the conference lounge, and the doors slid shut behind him so that he was unaware of what happened when Andrea Martinez stepped into the turbolift.

Her shriek was brief and cut off by the closing doors. It was enough, though, to alert the rest of the bridge crew. The crew had about two seconds to react before the bridge disappeared.

"Captain—?"

Picard's gaze, which had been directed inward, flipped toward Riker. "Yes, Number One?"

"Are you all right, sir?"

Picard considered the question a moment, and then he sighed. "She was right, you know."

"Right about—?"

"I should have handled the business with Trelane better."

"I don't see how."

"Nor do I, and that's the most frustrating aspect. Here we were faced with two beings of inordinate power and ability . . . and I end up ordering them off the ship because I wasn't able to ride herd on their disruptive tendencies. How much of it was genuine concern for the ship's safety, and how much of it was my ego bristling over my rules of discipline being trampled?"

"You had no choice, Captain," Riker said firmly. "If Trelane was flouting rules of conduct and authority right at the outset . . . there's absolutely no telling where matters might have gone from there. I seriously doubt they would have improved. In fact, I can guarantee they only would have deteriorated."

Picard nodded. "I am aware of that. I do not, however, have to like it. Nor is it possible for me not to feel regret. 'Of all sad words of tongue or pen, the saddest are these . . .'"

"'It might have been,'" completed Riker. "Shakespeare said it all, didn't he."

"Almost all," Picard said. "That was John Greenleaf Whittier."

Riker didn't even hesitate. "I knew that," he said with a straight face. "I just wanted to see if you did."

"Indeed," Picard replied with mock indignation.

And that was when an all-too-familiar flash of light flared into existence, immediately capturing their attention.

Q was standing there, and he looked genuinely perturbed.

"Have you seen him?" he demanded.

Picard did not even bother to point out that Q was ignoring the captain's orders to keep the hell off his ship. Such matters were usually of little-to-no consequence when it came to Q, but in this instance his concern seemed so genuine, so overwhelming, that it fully seized Picard's attention. He didn't have to ask who the "him" was that Q was inquiring after. "Not since earlier, no."

"Hmm." Q began to pace. "We have a problem."

In unison, Picard and Riker chorused, *"We?"*

"Yes, 'we,' Jean-Luc. After your little hissy fit, Trelane disappeared."

"I didn't see you objecting to my 'hissy fit' at the time."

"That may very well have been my oversight," admitted Q. "If I had responded in an appropriate manner, such as turning you into a dachshund or a bidet or a nice gazebo or

178

something equally useful, this might not have cropped up. But since I simply stood by . . ."

"*Stood by?* You *agreed* with me!"

"How many of these endless digressions are you going to toss into my face, Jean-Luc? For someone who possesses a mortal life span, you do seem to adore wasting time."

"Fine, what*ever,*" said Picard in exasperation, which was how he seemed to say most things whenever Q was in the vicinity. "So Trelane vanished and now you can't find him."

"That's correct, and unfortunately, that could be extremely dangerous. A being with power such as his, left to his own devices, hurt and bewildered and angry . . . the consequences could be catastrophic."

"What do you suggest?" said Picard, slightly impatient. "We can't search the galaxy for him."

"I'll have to attend to it, then. Don't you go worrying yourself about it, Jean-Luc. As always, I'll clean up after the mess you've made."

Picard's mouth fell open, and he was about to issue a sharp retort when he thought better of it. *What's the point?* was all he could think.

Instead he turned on his heel and stepped out onto the bridge, Riker directly behind him . . .

And when Riker slammed into Picard from behind, he almost knocked Picard flat. For the briefest of moments, Riker was befuddled as to why Picard had come to a halt.

Then he understood.

The bridge was gone.

Not gone, actually, but transformed. It now bore the look of a medieval torture chamber. There were brick walls instead of bulkheads, and the floor was dirt. An unpleasant stench hung in the air, and the only illumination was provided by flickering torches on either side of the room.

The entire bridge crew was chained to the wall, and gagged for good measure. Worf was struggling the most aggressively, yanking at his chains and making inarticulate grunting noises. Data was meticulously testing the strength of the chains, link by link, but having no more success.

They looked up at Picard, their desperate eyes peering over the gags that muted them.

"You know," said Q after a moment, standing behind Picard, "call me crazy, but I don't think we're going to have to look too far to find Trelane after all."

TRACK **B**

6.

Professor Martinez was not paying any attention as she stepped through the doors of the turbolift, and as a result was caught completely off guard upon discovering that the lift was not, in fact, there.

By the time she did realize this, it was too late. Gravity —even the artificial gravity of the *Enterprise*—had already taken hold, and Martinez plummeted down the shaft. She screamed as she plunged, clawing at thin air as if she could dig her fingers into it. At one point she felt her frantic hands brush against the shaft wall, but it was hideously smooth and there was absolutely nothing for her to get a grip on.

It seemed to her that she fell and screamed forever, but it was, in fact, only a few seconds.

Then she stopped.

The panic in her mind was so overwhelming that it took her a few seconds to notice that she was not, in fact, still falling. She was floating, hovering in the air, and it was only then that she came to the realization that she was no longer plummeting.

Her first thought was that she was dead and, rather fancifully, in the process of floating to heaven.

Her second thought was somewhat more practical, although no more correct: namely, that the *Enterprise* life-support system had some sort of fail-safe to negate gravity upon detecting a falling body. The ship did not, in fact, have that fail-safe, although it would not have been a bad idea.

Her third thought was bang on target.

"Trelane," she whispered.

"At your service," came the suave voice.

Light flared up next to her. Trelane was standing there, unperturbed by the lack of physical support. He seemed quite at ease in the weightlessness. Far more so than Martinez, who had to fight the urge to grab at him for bracing. The light was being provided by an elaborate candelabrum that Trelane held in his right hand.

She tried to make her voice sound calm and even. She was only marginally successful. "What . . . what are you doing?"

"Doing?" He acted as if the question made no sense to him. "Whatever do you mean?"

"Why did you make the turbolift disappear? Why am I just . . . just floating here?"

He took a "step" toward her, the candlelight causing shadows to dance across his face that gave him an almost satanic visage. "Are you afraid?"

"Well . . . yes."

"Oh, good!" he said joyously. Sounding almost conversational, he said, "The range of human emotions is such a fascinating one. I want to sample all of them. I myself have never known fear, of course. Triumph, anger, frustration, yes. Of these have I sipped deeply from a most bitter chalice," he told her with an air of tragedy, thudding his fist against his chest. Then he shifted mood again, speaking with an almost distant, morbid curiosity. "But fear. Fear is truly impressive. So what happens? Does your heart race? Your breath shorten, your body become covered in perspiration? All these?"

She nodded, trying to push away the terror, trying to convince herself that all she had to do was remain calm and she would not wind up splattered all over the bottom of the turbolift shaft. Unfortunately she was not at all successful in convincing herself of that.

"Do you know what's fascinating?" he asked.

She'd thought it was a rhetorical question, until the annoyed expression on his face tipped her that he was anticipating an answer. "Wh . . . what's fascinating, Trelane?"

"Well, from my understanding of human emotions, these exact same symptoms are also present when it comes to displays of passion. Tell me . . . why do you think that is?"

"It's . . ." She licked her lips, which had become extremely dry. She felt her throat closing up. "It's . . . it's part of human physiology. It just . . . it just happens that way, that's all."

"Oh, not good enough, Professor!" Trelane said in obvious disappointment.

Martinez fell.

She shrieked as she went, but it was barely out of her throat before she had stopped. Trelane had allowed her to drop all of a yard before halting her descent. Then he floated her back up to eye level with him, and she saw in his gaze something that truly terrified her.

His eyes were almost dead. The only hint of life behind

them was a cold, flickering, and distant sense of amusement.

"Do better than that, Professor. You'll have to do much better."

And her nerves snapped.

"I don't know *what you want me to say!!*" she screamed. "Tell me what to say! I'm not a mind reader! I'm not a psychologist!"

It was as if a light had snapped on over his head.

"You know . . . you're right! You're such a fascinating, good-natured woman . . . but you're not a psychologist *or* a mind reader."

He snapped his fingers.

In her quarters, Deanna Troi leaned forward, taking Ensign Cavalieri by the hand. "Now why don't you tell me what's really troubling you, Joseph," she said.

He looked at her thoughtfully and said, "You already know, don't you."

"I have a strong feeling," she said, which was something of an understatement. "But why don't you tell me. I think it would be better if you said it."

"Well," he sighed, "I guess the reason I have problems with long-term relationships is that I just have this constant fear of abandonment. That no matter how much a woman says she likes me, she might just up and leave me at any moment."

Deanna Troi vanished.

Cavalieri sat there, staring at the empty air. Then he flexed his hands to verify for himself that she hadn't simply turned invisible but was, in fact, gone completely. Then he said tentatively to the empty cabin, "Is this . . . uhm . . . is this, like, some sort of demonstration . . . ?"

* * *

Deanne rematerialized in the turbolift, a couple of feet away from Andrea Martinez. It took a moment for her mind to fully grasp what had happened. As soon as she did, there was one brief, searing moment of blind panic as she tried to find purchase where there was none.

"Oh, *do* stop thrashing about," said Trelane with mild annoyance.

"Help me," Martinez was whispering, *"madre de Dios,* Counselor, help me. . . ."

"This isn't about helping you," Trelane informed her. "This is about helping me. Helping me to understand, to grasp, to grow, to fully comprehend the dazzling variety of emotions and passions that form the human soul. I was seeking the good professor's help, my lovely Deanna, but I regret that she was, in fact, of little-to-no use. Oh, she was a charming enough conversationalist when she felt I could be of use to her. Asking question after dreary question about all manner of things. But when I wanted her to be of use to me, then she began to whine and blubber." He lowered his voice to a confidential level. "It was, quite frankly, rather embarrassing. You were lucky to have been spared it. In fact . . . there's no guarantee you'll be spared it in the future. Don't worry, my dear Counselor Troi. I'll protect you from further such disgraceful displays."

He made a casual gesture in Martinez's direction.

She fell.

The shriek followed her down, down the shaft, the screeching mingling with Deanna's own. The cessation of Martinez's howl was accompanied by the sickening thud of a body hitting the bottom.

"Deanna," Trelane said severely, "I suggest you keep control of yourself, or I'll be forced to seek out someone else familiar with the workings of the human mind. You, in turn, will keep Professor Martinez company. I doubt you'd want that."

With an effort that cost her much, Deanna calmed herself and faced Trelane.

"Much better," said Trelane. "Once you've fully composed yourself, we can continue." He approached her, regarding her with rapt attention, and ran a finger down the line of her throat. "I'm sure it will be quite educational for both of us."

TRACK B

7.

Picard looked in horror at the nightmarish image into which his bridge had been transformed. The bridge: his nerve center, the place that was the essence of the *Enterprise* herself, changed into some sort of hideous, nightmarish travesty of itself. In an insane way, Picard felt violated.

He was surprised at the hoarseness of his own voice as he spun to face Q and said, "Change it back!"

But there was a look of surprise on Q's face. "I'm trying," he said. "I'm trying, but I don't seem to—"

"Do it, Q! *Now!*"

"Shut up, Picard!" Q shouted with a ferocity that he had never before displayed.

That was when Picard realized that there was something akin to genuine fear in Q's eyes. *This is beyond anything he's experienced,* Picard realized, and that thought in turn was followed by the horrified speculation, *What could possibly be beyond what* he *has experienced?*

Q immediately composed himself. He closed his eyes and seemed to be drawing into himself, finding some calm center to tap, some inner resource upon which to draw. His breathing (if a creature such as Q could actually be said to be breathing, as opposed to putting on some sort of illusion of same) slowed; his eyelids fluttered.

When he opened his eyes again, the bridge was back to normal.

The crew members were still in their positions of imprisonment, but their bonds were gone. Worf's hands were over his head as if they were still cuffed to the wall, and he had been pulling on them up until the second that Q made them vanish. As a result he stumbled forward, although he managed to right himself quickly.

Immediately Worf turned to face Q, and he took an angry step toward the powerful being. For one of the few times in his life, Q looked extremely vulnerable. The transformation of the bridge had clearly taken a good deal out of him.

"Stay back, Mr. Worf!" Picard said sharply.

His sense of duty and fealty to his captain served to nail Worf's feet figuratively to the floor.

But he was still clearly seething. "Captain, what did he do?"

"Nothing, you throwback," Q snapped, leaning against the railing. "Nothing except get you out of chains . . . where I would be more than happy to return you to, if you so desire."

Worf growled in response.

"Mr. Data, report," Riker said briskly.

"The alteration came with no warning, sir," Data told him. "No change in energy readings, no triggering of any automatic alarms. One moment everything was normal and the next, we were as you saw us."

"Trelane," said Q. "It had to be."

"Or Trelane with someone aiding him," Worf commented darkly, and the direction of his glance made it painfully clear just precisely who he thought had been of assistance.

"Oh, puh-leeease," retorted Q. "I am no one's helper."

"Now there's an understatement," muttered Riker.

Q turned to him. "Look, Riker, I don't like this any more than you do! But you can't go blaming me for this!"

"You're the one who brought him here!" Riker pointed out.

"If you're going to carp . . ."

"Q!" said Picard fiercely. "Where *is he?*"

"I don't know!" shot back Q. "Do you have any clue how difficult it is for me to say those three words in sequence, Picard? I . . . don't . . . know."

"You would be amazed, Q, how little your feelings of difficulty mean to us," Worf told him.

"Red alert," said Picard, realizing that they were getting nowhere fast. "Security teams, all decks. Find Trelane. That's all I want done, Mr. Worf. Don't attack him. Don't challenge him. Just find him. Furthermore, I want all hands reporting in. Every man, woman, and child accounted for. I want to hear from everyone."

"Troi to bridge!" Deanna said.

There was no response.

"You see?" said Trelane, regarding her calmly in the turbolift shaft. "I could tell that you were trying to decide whether to call for help. So don't you feel better now? I invited you to try and summon a cavalry, and you did so. They're not coming, of course. Blocking transmissions . . . my dear woman, I thoroughly mastered that trick a century ago. Certainly you don't think I'm going to have difficulty with it now, do you? So there it is, my dear. I have been nothing but candid with you. I presume that I can anticipate an extension of similar courtesy from you."

Deanna composed herself. When she gazed at him fully once more, it was with as calm an air as if they were relaxing in her quarters.

"Of course," she said, her voice sounding as if it were coming from a great distance. "I will be more than happy to extend whatever courtesies I can."

"Superb! Now . . . I was discussing with the late, unlamented Professor Martinez the curious link between extreme desire and extreme fear. I was wondering why that was. She gave me some nonsensical, utterly boring tripe about human physiology. I don't care about the human body. It's a rather wretched, flimsy, vulnerable thing. It is the *mind,* my cherished Deanna, that is my passion. My obsession. The mind from which all the most fascinating aspects of humanity stem. So . . . tell me . . . what link is there between fear and desire? And have a care, for . . ." He made a significant downward gesture.

Deanna Troi was unafraid. If she had possessed any apprehension, she had tucked it away where it would do her no harm. The major problem was trying not to think about the broken body of the woman lying at the bottom of the turbolift.

"It's an intriguing question," she said. "It would not be surprising to me that fear and desire have much in common. One carries a healthy portion of the other."

Her matter-of-fact tone intrigued him. He stroked his chin thoughtfully. "Continue, pray."

"Well . . . when it comes to romantic relationships, there is a great degree of personal risk."

"As there is in a duel to the death!" proclaimed Trelane.

"No, not precisely. In that instance, you're simply dealing with the survival instinct. All the attention is being focused on one imperative: Don't die."

"Much as you're doing now."

"In a way," she readily allowed. "But an amorous relationship between two . . . or more . . . people is infinitely more complicated. There are many more shades of meaning. Also, there's the exposure."

Trelane's eyes glistened darkly, like stone striking flint. "You refer to nudity. Sex."

"Not exactly, no, although that's part of it. I meant the emotional exposure. Leaving yourself open to rejection. That's a very vulnerable state in which to be. Plus, yes, sex is an element to be considered as well. There's no other time when, as a species, we leave ourselves more open to hurt than when we're making love. A single look, a gesture, can take on a world of meaning. When it comes to the sex act, believe me: One poorly timed yawn can ruin an evening. An uncontrolled giggling fit can destroy a relationship. I've seen it happen."

"So because of all these elements," Trelane said, "there is fear that mistakes will be made. Gaffes committed. Feelings bruised."

"Exactly."

"It sounds terrifying!"

"In a way, it is. It is also rewarding. There is nothing in this universe worth gaining that does not require some risk to obtain it, up to and including love and happiness."

"This is immensely interesting, dulcet Deanna. You understand so much. And you have made me understand as well! Fairest one," he said breathlessly, "I shall make a gift to you, for you have given me some measure of insight into humanity. Just for that, I shall give you some feeling for what it is to be like unto a god."

"Oh, that's . . . that's quite all right," said Deanna, trying not to slip into nervousness. "Commander Riker was in a similar situation, and it didn't work out very well. So if you're offering me powers or something like that . . ."

"Oh, no! No, certainly not. I wouldn't want to burden you with something as overwhelming, and potentially disastrous, as that."

"If you want to do something for me, then I would certainly not mind being returned to my quarters."

"Oh, in time. In time." As if he were an eminently pleased child, he grinned and said, "Here's what I have planned for you, sweet Deanna. You are going to . . . are you ready?" he asked, interrupting himself.

"I suppose I am."

"Good! Because, Deanna, here's what's going to happen. I know you'll find it terribly stimulating."

He drifted over toward her and brought her face slowly forward. *Remember the center of calm!* her mind screamed at her. Even so, it was all she could do not to tremble in fear as the omnipotent creature brought his lips to just under her ear. He chewed gently on her lobe, and then whispered very softly.

Deanna Troi had had men whisper in her ear any number of times in the past. But she couldn't recall any man who had failed to produce any breath from his mouth. She heard the voice, but there was no feeling of warm breath against her head.

This absence of minutiae was quickly forgotten, however, as she heard Trelane tell her the offer he was making her.

"You," he disclosed to her delightedly, "are going to decide who lives and who dies."

* * *

On the bridge, they were a quarter of the way through hearing from all crew members when Data turned in the Ops chair and said, "Captain . . . I think you'd best hear this."

Picard sat forward. "Go ahead."

"Uh, Captain? This is Ensign Cavalieri. This just happened, and, well, at first I thought maybe she was just trying to make a point. I mean, I don't know what she's capable of, and maybe—"

"Ensign, report," Picard said firmly.

"Counselor Troi vanished, sir."

It was rather annoying that Q was standing next to Picard, looking for all the world as if he belonged on the bridge. Yet Picard felt the briefest measure of relief that Q was, in fact, there.

"Vanished?" he said.

"Yes, sir. Into thin air."

"Excellent. Thank you for reporting in, Ensign. Bridge to Counselor Troi," he said without even pausing for breath.

Silence. But only for a moment, because Picard had half-expected that he would get no response. "Computer, locate Counselor Troi."

"Counselor Troi is in turbolift shaft A," replied the computer.

In all the years that Picard had captained the *Enterprise,* he'd never gotten a response quite like this one. For a moment he thought that perhaps Trelane's screwing around with reality had muddled the computer. "She's in a turbolift?" asked Picard.

"Negative," the computer informed him primly. "She is positioned in the shaft, between decks fifteen and sixteen."

"Oh my God," whispered Riker.

Immediately they moved to the turbolift shaft. The doors did not open. "Manual override!" ordered Picard.

Riker flipped open the manual override panel and triggered the safety switch. Still nothing happened.

"Would you like me to do it?" offered Q.

But now Worf was at the door. He jammed his fingers in between, gritted his teeth, and grunted. The doors hissed open under the Klingon's strength.

Worf staggered forward slightly, and came within a hairsbreadth of toppling into the shaft. For that was all that was there before him . . . the darkened shaft. There was no turbolift in sight.

But before Worf could be in serious danger, Riker and Picard already had grabbed him by the arm and uniform back, and pulled him to safety. Q, standing nearby, murmured, "You needn't have worried. He would probably have just landed on his head and been spared serious injury."

Riker leaned forward, bracing his hands on either side of the shaft. For the briefest of moments he felt as Orpheus must have, shouting into the black hole that led down into Hades, howling the name of his beloved as she was sent hurtling back to her doom.

"Deanna!" he shouted.

Far below, Deanna looked up as Riker's voice echoed and reechoed in the shaft. She wanted to shout back to him, to cry out, to thank God that they'd realized where she was.

But nothing happened. Deanna suddenly found herself paralyzed, unable to move or speak or respond in any way.

Trelane still hovered there, except now he looked fairly cross. "They are becoming rather tiresome," he said, making no effort to disguise his annoyance. "Come, my dear. We shall retire to some place where we can relax and explore your newfound dominion over life and death."

They vanished.

A half second before they arrived, Guinan knew.

She'd been whip-sharp tense all morning, certain that there was major trouble in the offing. And for the past few minutes, her senses had been running riot. It was as if she wasn't sure where to "look" first. Loungers in Ten-Forward were regarding her with curiosity and concern, for Guinan was clearly not in her best frame of mind that day.

But as soon as her little bailiwick was about to be invaded, the imminence and proximity of the threat focused Guinan completely. She had barely enough time to shout, *"Everyone out!,"* and then there was no time anymore. Trelane blinked into existence, Deanna Troi at his side.

Deanna unfroze, discovering that her faculties for speech had been returned to her.

"Guinan to bridge!" Guinan called. "Trelane is down here!" As she spoke she came from around the bar, heading toward Trelane. "Now, you just stay right there and don't cause any trouble."

"I might say the same for you," replied Trelane, and he snapped his fingers.

Guinan came to a halt, not budging. Stock-still. On her face was an expression of sincere surprise.

"Let her go, Trelane!" said Deanna.

"Why should I?" asked Trelane, looking genuinely befuddled. "I don't like her. Since I don't like her, and she doesn't like me, then what is the point? We'll both be aggravated. And certainly if one of us is going to suffer inconvenience, I would much rather that it be her. Unless . . ." And his expression became crafty, his voice almost snickering. "Unless *she* is going to be the one whom you choose to die. I can arrange it for you, if you wish."

And with a wave of his hand, Guinan found herself outside the bay window of Ten-Forward, looking in.

He had released her from her paralysis and deposited her in the cold, unforgiving vacuum of space.

TRACK **B**

8.

There were shrieks and shouts of astonishment from the crew members in Ten-Forward as Guinan, wide-eyed, pressed against the glass, frantically banging on it even though, of course, she had no hope of getting through. Indeed, the sounds of her thumping fists weren't even audible because the glass was so thick.

"Troi to transporter!" shouted Deanna.

"Oh, puh-leease," Trelane said in that high-handed manner he had. "Have you forgotten? No one chats when I don't want them to. Guinan's little call for help didn't reach anyone either. This is my game, Counselor . . . and my rules. Now . . . someone here is going to die. It will be your choice, so that you can have a feeling for what it's like to be godly. If you wish it to be Guinan, then so be it. We leave her out there another, oh, twenty seconds or so, and that will be—as they say—that. If you desire it to be another, though, then choose. But choose quickly. My patience is wearing a bit thin, and I

197

am simply *swamped* with other engagements to attend to."

Guinan clawed at the window.

Staring down into the depths of the shaft, Riker said, "I thought I saw something. Some sort of flash. Similar to when Q appears and vanishes. Trelane must be with her."

"Of *course* he's with her, Riker," Q said with disdain. "Unless your precious counselor is in the habit of hovering in turbolift shafts of her own volition."

"Computer, locate Counselor Troi," Picard said, deciding that double-checking would probably be the smart thing to do. If Trelane was accompanying her, as he doubtlessly was, then her location was extremely subject to change.

"Counselor Troi is in the Ten-Forward lounge."

"I'll meet you there," said Q, and he vanished in a burst, as Picard and the others headed for the emergency exit.

"You're trying my patience, Counselor," said Trelane.

"Bring her back in here! *Now!*"

His eyes hardened. "You know . . . I'm beginning not to like your attitude."

At that moment, Guinan suddenly reappeared in the middle of the Ten-Forward lounge. She was on the floor on her hands and knees, and then she rolled over onto her back, gasping. She was trembling uncontrollably from the cold that had invaded every pore of her body. But none of that stopped her eyes from blazing with fury when she looked upon Trelane, even though her teeth were chattering too hard for her to voice the curse she would have loved to hurl at him.

Deanna started to move toward her, but Trelane angrily snapped, "Stay where you are!" It was then that she saw the somewhat surprised look on Trelane's face, as if he were startled by Guinan's abrupt return rather than being the cause of it.

"All right, Trelane. You have a lot of explaining to do."

Trelane turned to face Q, who had abruptly popped into existence in Ten-Forward.

Q had been displaying his customary smug expression of superiority, but when he looked at Trelane closely, there was just the slightest hint of a crack in his facade.

No less startled was Trelane. "What are *you* doing here?" he demanded. "I already disposed of you."

"What are you talking about?" said Q. "And . . . what's happened to you? You're different. You . . ."

Trelane clapped his hands in realization. "Oh, of *course!* That's it! How fallible of me! With all this temporal jumping about, I'm getting somewhat muddled! I haven't disposed of you *yet*. It's going to happen and, at the same time, it's already happened. This is all terribly new for me, you see. Keeping all of this business straight. It's remarkably strenuous."

"Answer my question, Trelane," ordered Q. "What have you done to yourself? What's changed you?"

"Would you really like to know?" asked Trelane eagerly. "It's incredible news, really. Tell me . . . are you familiar with the Heart of the Storm?"

Q took a step back, making no attempt to disguise the horror he felt. His voice barely above a whisper, he said, "You . . . you didn't."

"But I did."

"You *didn't*. You . . ."

And then Q understood. Then it all made sense.

"You're not Trelane," he said. "Not my Trelane."

"A grotesque oversimplification of a remarkably complicated situation," said Trelane tragically. "I am, in fact, *my* Trelane. My own being, with my own priorities. My own values." And then his voice lowered and, with unconcealed, naked fury, he said, "And my own need for vengeance. Against you. Against the *Enterprise.* Against anyone and anything that treated me with loathing or contempt during that time when I was less than what I am now."

At that moment, Picard, Riker, Worf, and a half-dozen security guards burst into Ten-Forward. But Q put up a peremptory hand. "No need, Jean-Luc," he said. "I am handling this." He turned back to Trelane and said firmly, "You are coming with me right now. We're going back to the Q Continuum. . . ."

"You posturing buffoon!" shot back Trelane. "Don't you understand anything yet? There *is no Continuum!* There's nothing! I disposed of it! I sealed it off! It's done, finished . . ." And with a thick accent, he added, "Kaput!"

For a second, Q seemed to have forgotten about Trelane. Instead it appeared as if he were reaching out with his mind, as he dispatched a silent summons to his fellow residents of the Q Continuum.

The answer, or lack of such, was immediate. From where Picard was standing, he could see the look of pure horror on Q's face.

"You see?" asked Trelane. "It's just you and me now, Q. But that is going to change very, very quickly."

He stretched out his hands, energy crackling from his fingertips.

It was all Q could do not to scream as he felt himself buffeted by forces that previously had been mere theory to him. Energy that he had heard of, even observed from a safe distance. But he had never been subjected to the sort of unrelenting, unstoppable, utterly terrifying barrage of power that was hitting him now.

Ten-Forward seemed to swirl around him, as he felt his hold on reality slipping. The fabric of the universe was shredding around him.

He heard Picard shout his name as he sought desperately for a way out. He needed time to think, to regroup. To form a plan for dealing with this immense and unstoppable power that Trelane had given himself. The child in the tinderbox had the match, and Q had to figure out a safe way to blow out the flame without sending a spark flying onto the wood and consuming them all.

In his agony, in his confusion, in his desperation, Q took the only option that he could. He prayed that Trelane wouldn't notice as Q "selected sight." He looked beyond where he was to all the fabrics of all the realities that wove together to make it unique. To make it a reality unto itself. It was not something that he did often. It was a highly developed skill, one that only the most advanced and knowledgeable of the Q possessed.

And as he saw the threads of those fabrics, he saw also the infinitesimally small spaces between the threads.

A blast of force knocked Q completely off his feet, momentarily ruining his concentration. He tried to stagger to his feet, and through the fabric of reality strode Trelane.

Suddenly Q came to a startling realization: This might be it. Pathetic enough that he had decided that retreat was the only workable option. But now even that piteous alternative might not be allowed him.

That was when Q got the briefest of reprieves.

"Fire!" shouted Picard, and it was only then that Q realized that Picard had deployed his security forces to ring Trelane. He appreciated Picard's gesture, even though there was every possibility that it might also be Picard's last.

Q realized that he was faced with a choice. He could stay

on the *Enterprise,* slug it out with Trelane without any opportunity to regroup and form a plan. Or he could get the hell out of there, which would have the drawback of leaving Picard and his intrepid band—who were knowingly using the equivalent of a peashooter against a rampaging elephant—to their own devices.

But if the Continuum had really been closed off, then he, Q, might represent the last hope of the galaxy, if not the universe.

"Sorry, Picard," he muttered. And he turned the threads of the fabric of reality.

Trelane, for his part, was barely staggered by the phasers. He was more startled than anything else. Startled by the temerity of the *Enterprise* gnats to attack him. Plus the light of the phasers was somewhat blinding.

But then, through the phaser fire, he spotted Q making his escape. Q appeared to be stepping sideways, his body pivoting on an unseen axis and becoming two-dimensional, and then one-.

With a roar of fury, Trelane unleashed a blast that was, unfortunately for Trelane, not enough to stop Q from leaving. Instead all it did was hasten his departure, as Q was smashed through his escape route at high velocity, vanishing into the ether of alternate realities.

Trelane, utterly furious, turned toward Picard and gestured. The phasers vanished, to be replaced by limp, dangling flowers.

"You," said Trelane dangerously, "are a very annoying little man. Are you aware of just how easily I could destroy you?"

"Yes," said Picard. "But you won't."

This certainty actually seemed to amuse Trelane. "Oh, really. Why won't I?"

"Because you're a sadist," Picard told him. "Because

you enjoy the hurting and the torturing of other beings more than anything else. And if you kill me, then you won't be able to hurt me anymore. Where's the fun in that?"

But now Troi was by his side. "Captain, don't," she said warningly, knowing the barely controlled fury that was raging through Picard. "Trelane is a creature of almost unlimited power."

"'Almost'?" retorted Trelane. "And here I thought you were a bright woman. *'Almost,'* you say? Try 'unlimited,' woman."

Deanna had not intended to pique Trelane's already considerable ire. But now that she inadvertently had, she was starting to see a desperate possibility for something. "Well, you . . . you couldn't bring someone back from the dead, certainly."

"Of course I could," said Trelane defiantly. "I can do anything I want."

Making a silent prayer, Deanna said, "Well . . . what about Professor Martinez? You couldn't bring her back."

Picard was chilled to the bone when he heard Deanna's comment, and looked to Riker, who was as wide-eyed as he himself was. Dead? Martinez? The professor *dead?* Was Trelane that far gone, that out of control, that he would dispose of a helpless life so casually?

Trelane seemed to be considering what Deanna had said.

And then he laughed, very unpleasantly.

"Woman, even for a human, that is a lamentable effort. Reverse psychology on one who is all-knowing? How unoriginal. How utterly pathetic."

Then Deanna did something extremely unusual.

She stepped forward angrily and said, in a very sharp tone, "You lied to me."

"How now?" he said indignantly. "What is that you say?"

"You said I could choose who lives and who dies. Obviously you did not mean that."

"Of course I meant it!"

"All right, then." She came close to him, almost thrusting her face into his, driven by both desperation and a sense of utterly helpless frustration. "Choosing someone to die is easy. That's not proof of godhood. Any idiot with a phaser, halfway decent aim, and an itchy trigger finger can determine that someone will die. But choosing someone to live after they're dead . . . that is something only a god could do. If you've any interest in impressing me with your divinity, then that's what I select for you to do."

He considered her for a long moment, and even Deanna, with all her training, was unable to slow the rapid thumping of her heart. She wasn't even breathing, although she didn't notice.

Then Trelane sighed tiredly.

"How you *do* go on," he said, and waved his hand.

Professor Martinez snapped into existence, suspended in the air by Trelane's power, the toes of her boots brushing against the floor.

Deanna gasped. Reflexively, Picard took a step forward, but Riker held him back.

Martinez looked exactly like what she was . . . the corpse of a woman who had dropped down a turbolift shaft. Her legs and arms were at odd angles, like a marionette with severed strings. Her head lolled lifelessly, blood covering it, her hair thick and matted, her nose smashed, a visible dent in her skull above her left temple.

"You dishonorable bastard," Worf breathed in Klingon.

Trelane understood and smiled. "Glass houses, Mr. Worf. Now." He rubbed his hands together briskly. "Let's see what's required here."

He put his hands on her face, tilted her head back. "Awake, fair sleeping beauty," he said, and kissed her on the mouth.

Professor Martinez opened her eyes. She moaned softly as Trelane took a step back. "Congratulations, my dear. You are newly living proof of the power of persuasion that is manifested by the so-called weaker sex."

Picard tapped his comm unit and snapped, "Dr. Crusher to Ten-Forward. Medical emergency."

Martinez's voice was raspy and confused. "Wh . . . what happened?" she croaked.

"Look down," suggested Trelane.

"Andrea," Deanna said quickly, trying to intercept the attention of the still-confused woman. She was not fast enough however, for Martinez did, in fact, look down, and saw the shattered husk of her body.

She screamed. It was not much of a scream, because her vocal cords were as damaged as the rest of her. But it was enough to convey the terror in her heart.

It was at that point that Trelane released her, and she crumpled to the floor. The combination of the pain and the horror was too much for her, and she passed out.

The door to Ten-Forward slid open, and Dr. Crusher entered with several technicians and an antigrav gurney. Her first impulse when she saw the smashed body of Professor Martinez was the same as Deanna's, namely to gasp, express shock, even turn away. But Crusher did not even come close to engaging in such an unprofessional display. Her mask of detachment was firmly in place.

Trelane said nothing, did nothing. He merely stood with his arms folded, watching with fascination as Crusher and the medtechs got Professor Martinez . . . or what was left of her . . . onto the gurney. Crusher was barking orders for drugs to be administered to stabilize her patient, and yet she still had time to assure the barely conscious Martinez, "You're going to be fine."

She noticed that Guinan looked unsteady on her feet, and her face formed a question. But Guinan, who was leaning against the bar, shook her head and waved her off.

Beverly desperately wanted to know what was happening. What had Trelane done? How did Martinez become so brutally injured? But there was no time for that. Nor did Picard need the doctor standing around asking an array of questions that would serve only her curiosity, but not her patient. It would wait until later . . . although, judging from the quiet deadliness that Trelane was projecting, she wasn't one hundred percent certain that there was going to *be* a later.

The moment that Crusher and the medtechs had departed, Trelane slowly, sarcastically, applauded. "You certainly do have your medical people efficiently organized, Captain," he said. "Look at them! Brisk, capable, confident. In your many wars and great quests, you must have frequent need of them. How thrilling for you! How smashing to be able to depend on them! I tell you, Captain, I am impressed. Most mightily impressed. So what now, Captain? What new scheme is your little brain hatching? What new argument? What novel attack, what crafty stratagem, what sort of bluster or threat or command, is next from the tactical computer that is the brain of Jean-Luc Picard?" He walked in a half circle around Picard, his arms spread as if declaiming to thousands of spectators. "Faced with an overwhelming foe, against insurmountable odds! How will you deal with it? How will Jean-Luc Picard, captain of the *Enterprise,* next rattle his saber? You come from a long line of military strategists and geniuses, Picard! This ship carries with it a proud tradition of combat and conquest! Go on, Picard! Make your next move! I cannot stand the suspense, or wait another instant!"

Picard's face was inscrutable.

Then, slowly, he walked toward Trelane.

Then he walked past him.

Trelane watched him, clearly trying not to let his confusion show.

Picard walked halfway across Ten-Forward to a booth, and then he sat down. "Number One, Mr. Worf . . . Counselor . . . all of you . . . please, join me."

Riker and Worf glanced at each other, and the security guards shifted uncomfortably.

"I'm waiting, people. Guinan . . . synthehol for my people, please. They look parched."

Still uncertain of what was happening, but acting as good officers and obeying orders, Worf, Riker, Troi, and the security guards joined Picard at the table. There wasn't quite room for all of them, so a couple of the guards chose to stand.

Picard offered no conversation, nor did the officers attempt to provide any. The guards, taking their cues from their senior officers, likewise said nothing.

Trelane strode over to them, all swagger and confidence, and said, "So?"

"So what?" asked Picard.

Guinan brought them drinks on a tray. She didn't even glance at Trelane as she served out the glasses.

"What do you think you're doing?" Trelane wanted to know.

"Nothing." Picard looked up at him, his face carefully neutral.

"Nothing?"

"That is correct. You are simply too powerful for us. We cannot stand against you. We cannot defeat you. So, rather than waste time and energy trying to combat you . . . which is plainly hopeless . . . we will simply sit and wait for you to do whatever you wish."

Trelane laughed uncomfortably. "Certainly you're not serious."

"No, I'm quite serious. I give up trying to fight you. You chased away Q. You brought the dead back to life. Clearly we are outmatched. You've done far too thorough a job of proving your superiority. You certainly have no grounds for complaint in that respect. Do with us as you will, Trelane. Toss us around. Humiliate us. Throw us into the depths of space or down turbolift shafts. Torture us, kill us. Whatever you want. We are your toys, to dispose of as you see fit."

"But . . . but this is nonsense!" Trelane told him. "I won't stand for this! It's contrary to everything that makes you what you are! You're wondrously warlike, exquisitely aggressive! You can't just languish in passivity and expect me to stand still for that sort of ennui!"

"We're sorry," said Picard contritely. "I see nothing else to do."

Trelane stomped a foot in irritation. "There has to be something you can attempt! I know! How about . . . how about if I don't try nearly as hard, eh? Give you the illusion of a chance?"

"Pointless." Picard sighed. "I can't muster any sort of interest in such an engagement. You pretending that we have a prayer? How am I supposed to keep up enthusiasm on my end, then? No. No . . ."

"Stop talking that way!" bellowed Trelane. "I want to beat you fairly!"

"Impossible," Picard told him, almost sounding as if he were commiserating. "You've made your power all too evident. I'm not interested in fighting a hopeless battle, nor being condescended to. You want me beaten? You've done it. I'm beaten."

"Then . . ." Trelane's face was almost desperate, as if searching his memory. "Then . . . then I want to defeat you! That's it! That's the victory you're trying to withhold from me. Ohhh, you're clever, Picard. You're a crafty one, you are! You admit you're beaten, but we both know you're not defeated!"

Picard shrugged. "Semantics. 'Beaten,' 'defeated.' It's all the same."

"No it's not! It's two different things!"

"Who told you that?"

"He did! Kirk! He said he was beaten, but not defeated! He said it as if it meant something! And it *must* have meant something!"

He was speaking so fast and furiously and angrily that spittle was flying from his mouth. A few flecks landed on Picard's forehead. Indifferently, Picard brushed the spittle away and shrugged once more. "All right. Whatever you say."

"Stop saying that!! Stop agreeing with me all the time!"

Picard fell silent. His expression was one of bland submission. As contritely as he could, he said, "I'm sorry. I'll try to do better."

Trelane's jaw twitched, but no sound came out. Veins on his forehead started to distend. His entire body began to tremble with rage, as if the top of his skull were going to blow off. He pointed a quivering finger at Picard.

"You," he said as if damning Picard to hell, "are absolutely of no entertainment value whatsoever."

He vanished.

Riker was about to speak, but Picard put up a cautioning finger and looked at Guinan. She looked somewhat ragged, a bit beaten around the edges. But she was still able to shake her head. "He's gone," she said. "I'd know it if he was still around."

Now Picard let out a long sigh. "Thank God." Then he sat forward and said forcefully to Worf, "Mr. Worf . . . alert Starfleet immediately. Circulate full feed of all related log entries on Trelane. I will prepare a complete detail report to be included. I want the entire sector to be alert to Trelane's existence, and to all the particulars, within twenty-four hours." He turned to Troi. "Counselor, are you all right?"

"A bit shaken, Captain, but fine otherwise."

"And you, Guinan?"

"I could use a vacation," admitted Guinan. "Someplace where space is simply a thing way up on the horizon somewhere instead of right outside my window."

"You handled him brilliantly, sir," said Riker.

"I handled him in the only way left to me, Number One, and it was by no means a sure thing. He could just as easily have blown us to atoms out of spite. We're talking about a creature who may have managed to dispose of Q . . . something that I know won't particularly upset you, Mr. Worf, but he could have been a valuable ally if and when Trelane returns."

"So you think this isn't over."

"Number One, I think this is just beginning."

"Why?" asked Troi.

It was Guinan who answered. "Because Trelane *didn't* blow us to atoms out of spite."

"Exactly," said Picard ruefully. "The reason I believe this isn't over is because we're all still alive. Of all the infinite possibilities in an infinite universe, his leaving us alone for the rest of our voyage seems to be the least likely." He frowned. "He handled this round badly. He knows he did. But if he's a youngster, as Q said . . . then need I remind you that youngsters have a disturbing tendency to learn. And learn very, very quickly."

TRACK SERVICE

Colors cascaded around Q as he spun out of control, spiraling through the multiverse after barely escaping Trelane's onslaught in Ten-Forward.

He reached out, snagged at passing threads, trying to get enough of a grip to pull himself out of his plunge (subjectively, of course; it was all subjective).

He heard a voice shouting, and it was his own, except his mouth wasn't open. So he opened it to make the sound, except by that point the voice had stopped and he was howling into emptiness.

Then a thread (subjective)

wrapped itself around him (figuratively)

snagged him, and whipcracked him (in a manner of speaking)

and the next thing he knew he was up against some sort of an obstruction. But it was flat, and hard, and it had substance, and he was pressing against it with all the force he had, clawing his way through, terrified (no, not terrified, never terrified, just . . . extremely concerned to the degree where he was bordering on frantic), and suddenly he needed air in his lungs, which was damned weird because he didn't *have* lungs in the standard sense and he didn't *need air* in any sense, but there it was, this pounding in his chest that only served to exacerbate his not-terror and elevate it to not-complete-and-total-panic . . .

And then he was through. He hit a floor that seemed mysteriously familiar, in a room that seemed mysteriously familiar. On all fours, breathing heavily, he sucked air *(why?!)* into his chest, and then he realized that he was surrounded by mysteriously familiar boots. He moaned softly, unable to believe that he had come so far— wherever he had come to—only to wind up back on some damned starship again. "Where?" he managed to get out in a voice that sounded only slightly like his own.

One of the booted feet took a step forward and said authoritatively, "I am Captain Jack Crusher. You're on board the *U.S.S. Enterprise.* Please explain how you—"

It took a moment for it all to penetrate. *Enterprise,* he had said, but Crusher was the doctor's name . . . the woman doctor, not a man, and . . .

He looked up and said, "Captain . . . who?," staring uncomprehendingly at a square-jawed, rather bland-looking man. But then he spotted a familiar face. "Picard?"

Picard was wearing a uniform style that was consistent with what he'd been sporting when Q first encountered him. Q tried to process the information. A parallel universe . . . moving at a different rate of time flow . . . it was possible. Such things happened. Picard, in the meantime, was listening to his "captain" natter on about something, and then Picard was looking back at Q and saying, "Yes, I am Commander Jean-Luc Picard." After a pause, he added, "And this is Dr. Beverly Howard . . . and Head Nurse Geordi La Forge."

"Now, who the blazes are you?" demanded Crusher. "Are you associated with Trelane? Why are you wearing a Starfleet uniform?"

Q pulled up the last of his strength. "I . . . am Q . . . and you have absolutely *no* idea . . . how screwed up this is."

And then, strained from the fight with Trelane, fried from the parting blast . . . and blissfully unaware that, in a fairly brief time, he would be floating helplessly at the edge of the galaxy, practically since the dawn of time, and this entire exchange would be erased from the memory of all concerned . . . Q slumped forward and hit the ground, unconscious.

TRACK CHANGE

TRACK **A**

11.

Commander Picard and Dr. Beverly Howard had managed to remain discreet in their continued relationship.

Neither of them had intended for it to continue, or at least neither of them was going to *admit* to it. But continue it had.

They had two things going for them.

First was the fact that everyone on the *Enterprise* knew of the rather tortured previous relationship between the captain and the chief medical officer. The widely held assumption was that most of the normal interaction between ship's command and ship's medical was going to be between Picard and Howard. This much was, in fact, accurate. Captain Crusher made no secret of his appreciation for Picard "running interference." (Jack Crusher had a habit of using old, and even arcane, athletic terms.) Picard, of course, was all too happy to oblige. Consequently, any time he spent with Beverly Howard elicited no interest at all from even the most busy of the ship's busybodies. No more so than the time that the captain might spend in conference with engineering chief Argyle (although there *were* a few rumors floating around about Tasha Yar and Lieutenant Commander Data—but those tended to fall into the realm of more fanciful speculation).

The second thing they had going for them was having Geordi La Forge as an ally. Something of a romantic, La Forge did not hesitate to cover for them whenever it seemed necessary. Through the efforts of the three of them, matters were kept on a fairly even keel.

Nevertheless, Picard continued to worry.

Sometimes he felt as if everyone were looking at him. So guilty did he feel about his activity that at times it seemed to him as if he had a large, glowing sign tattooed on his head that read, I'M SLEEPING WITH THE CAPTAIN'S EX. He fancied that the moment he walked past crewmen, they'd quickly put their heads together, trading the latest gossip or word around the ship, all centered around himself and Dr. Howard.

If he continued down that path, he would certainly slide into paranoia and overcaution.

Other times, though, he was confident that no one was at all suspicious. That he and Beverly were completely above—even immune to—suspicion. At times like that he'd nod to passing crewmen while thinking, *If only you knew.*

That path, however, led to certain overconfidence. And if he was overconfident, that would lead to sloppiness. And if they were sloppy, then, sooner or later . . . probably sooner . . . they'd make a mistake. An unguarded look, an overheard comment that could lead them to exposure.

Consequently, Picard trod an uneasy line between

being deliriously happy and being afraid to be deliriously happy.

He was walking down the corridor, his mind (as was not unusual these days) preoccupied with thoughts of Beverly, when a small boy plowed into him. The child had struck him with such force that Picard was actually staggered. He looked down in annoyance at the youngster. "This is a starship," he snapped, "not a playground."

"Damn right," shot back the boy. "If this were a playground, you'd be watching where you were going."

Picard stared at the child, thunderstruck. He had taken great pains to establish a precise sort of relationship with the *Enterprise* children: He had little patience for them, and they were intimidated by him. Everyone was well served by this quid pro quo, and could go on about their business.

So where did this pipsqueak get the nerve to mouth off at him?

"I should watch where *I* was going?" Picard asked in undisguised astonishment.

"Good," said the boy, "I'm glad we're agreed on that."

He tried to move around Picard, but now the starship commander stepped directly into the boy's path, blocking him. The boy sighed in exasperation. "I thought we had this worked out," he said.

"Well, *you're* a precocious little monster," Picard observed. "Who are you?"

"Thomas Ian Riker," he told him. He crossed his arms tightly across his chest. "Okay?"

That immediately struck a chord with Picard. "Riker. Of course. The duty officer mentioned that you and your mother had come aboard."

"I'm thrilled for you."

Picard's eyes narrowed, and he was fighting the impulse to grab the boy by the scruff of the neck when a raven-haired, but slightly graying, woman ran up behind him. Picard noticed that her gaze flashed, ever so quickly, toward the pips on his collar. Yes, this was certainly a woman who had spent many years involved with Starfleet officers.

"Commander," she said apologetically, "I'm so sorry." She took her son by the shoulder and pulled him against her, partly out of a sense of maternal protectiveness, and mostly to keep him from running off again.

"Your son has a good deal to learn about how to conduct himself aboard a ship," Picard said stiffly. But it was a forced stiffness, because somehow he found himself immediately liking this woman. Even trusting her to some degree. That was probably an automatic response whenever one was around Betazoids. It was said that a Betazoid's mere presence was sufficient to put people at ease.

Besides, the woman had had a hard enough life the past few years, what with her husband missing, presumed dead. Picard couldn't bring himself to rebuke her too harshly.

"I'm very sorry, Captain. Tommy can get a little rambunctious at times. Tommy, tell the commander you're sorry."

"Why?" asked Tommy reasonably. "You already did."

"Tommy . . ." warned his mother.

"Okay, okay, I'm sorry, okay?" said Tommy, not sounding remotely apologetic.

Nevertheless, Picard decided not to press the matter. Indeed, he decided that a conciliatory tone was the one to adopt. "I'm Commander Jean-Luc Picard," he said.

"Deanna Riker," she said. She ruffled the boy's hair. "And you've met Tommy already."

"We had a run-in, yes," Picard said sardonically.

"He's just very excited about being aboard a starship finally," Deanna explained. She squeezed him affectionately. "I suppose you can understand the feeling."

"Oh yes. I felt very much the same when I was young."

"I don't believe it," said Tommy skeptically.

Picard looked at him askance. "You don't believe I felt the same way?"

"No," Tommy informed him with that infinite smugness that only a child can muster, "I don't believe you were young."

Picard tried to think of a comeback, but Deanna quickly pulled on Tommy's arm while saying to Picard, "I'm sorry again, Commander. I'll talk to him . . . *firmly.*"

"That's quite all right," said Picard.

"I bet the kids beat you up all the time," Tommy said. "And did you *ever* have hair?"

"*Tommy!*" Deanna practically shrieked, her face coloring. She headed down the corridor, yanking Tommy so hard that his feet left the ground.

Picard stood there until the voices faded away.

Then he laughed. He wasn't certain which was funnier: the boy's utterly irreverent attitude, or the mother's numbing chagrin.

Either way, it had served to distract him from his various concerns, and for that he supposed he should even be grateful to the boy.

But not *too* grateful . . .

"I have never been so embarrassed in my entire life," Deanna informed Tommy once they were back in their quarters.

Tommy looked bored, resting his chin on one hand. "That's what you always say."

"Don't talk back to me, young man. Your treatment of Commander Picard was absolutely abominable. We are guests on this vessel, Tommy. They are giving us free passage to see your father. Perhaps you would have preferred to travel the entire way on the Klingon freighter?"

Tommy thought of the beds with no mattresses, and the inedible food. He made a face.

"Or maybe," continued Deanna unrelentingly, "I should have just left you home, as I wanted to in the first place. But no, you begged, you pleaded. You promised best behavior. *This* is the best behavior you have to offer? Running around a Federation starship like a maniac and being disrespectful to senior officers?"

"Is it okay to be disrespectful to junior officers?" he asked hopefully, looking for a loophole.

"No!"

"Oh."

She sat down across from him, reached for his hand. He pulled it away quickly. "Tommy," she said softly, "what's bothering you? I mean, here you are on board a starship, which is where you've always dreamt of going. Traveling to see your father, whom we've both missed so very much. It . . ."

Then she frowned. "What's wrong? Tommy, I . . . I mentioned your father, and you . . ."

"Can you ever shut off the empathy?" he demanded irritably. "Can I ever have a thought to myself? Huh?"

"You just . . . you went all tense inside. I don't understand. . . ."

"Why should you understand? *I* don't understand." He

brushed a hank of hair out of his eyes, and it stubbornly fell back over them again.

"Something happened. Something has you concerned."

He stared at his shoes.

"Tommy . . ." she prodded him.

"Was that guy on the screen really my father?"

"Of course."

He shook his head. "I don't believe it."

She tilted her head slightly. "Why don't you?"

"He didn't look right. I . . . I've seen my father up here for so long," and he tapped the side of his head, "and then to see that . . . that guy with the Klingon. I don't see it. It doesn't seem right."

She reached for his hands again, and this time he let her hold them. "Honey, it's understandable that you feel that way. It was a shock for you. It was a shock for me, too. I'm afraid that it's . . ." She paused, trying to find the right way to put it. "I'm afraid it's a reminder that there are some people in this galaxy who will not hesitate to injure or destroy other living beings. But what I want you to remember is not just your father's outward appearance. It's the soul and strength of the type of man who was able to survive the . . ." Her voice caught slightly, but she pushed past it. ". . . the awful treatment that the Romulans inflicted on him. He was so determined to come back to us that it was that dedication that pushed him through it all. That's what we should be focusing on. His character. That's what's important."

"I guess so," sighed Tommy.

She waited. "Is there something else?"

"No," he lied.

She folded her arms in that way she had which Tommy

knew all too well. That silent, reproving manner that said, *You're not fooling me.*

"Well . . . you know that feeling I had?" he asked after long moments of hesitation.

"What feeling?"

"Like, right before Dad turned up . . . I had the feeling that he was *going* to turn up?"

"Oh, that." She shook her head and smiled. "Tommy, people have those kinds of intuitions all the time. You get a 'feeling' that this thing is going to happen, or that thing is going to happen. And nine times out of ten . . . it doesn't happen. But no one gives any thought to those times. You just don't pay any attention to them; you've got more important things on your mind. That one time, though, that something does happen . . . why, that's always going to be what you remember. 'That was just on my mind!' you say."

But Tommy was shaking his head emphatically. "No. No, that's not how it happens with me. It . . . it comes to me in kind of a daydream. You know how the teachers complain that sometimes I'm not paying attention in class?"

"Um-hmm." She nodded, her lips pursed.

"Well, that's because those are the times when one of those daydreams comes to me. And I can see stuff happening, big as life. And I had a bunch of them just before Dad was found. You see?"

"Yes, I see. So tell me, Tommy . . . any other daydreams lately?"

He frowned. "You don't believe me."

"Let's just say I'll need some convincing."

"Well . . ." He seemed hesitant. "It didn't make a lot of sense."

"Such things rarely do."

"Okay. It was . . . well, it was real weird. There was this guy . . . Dad . . ."

"Your father again. I'm beginning to sense a pattern."

"No, it wasn't Dad."

"You said it was."

"No, it . . ." Deanna could sense the boy's overwhelming frustration over trying to put across what was going through his mind. He continued gamely, "It was Dad . . . but it wasn't Dad. He looked like him, but he was different. And . . ."

There was a long pause. "And what?" prompted Deanna.

"And that Klingon, Worf, was there." He looked up at Deanna with haunted eyes, and for the first time Deanna felt a chill go down her spine as Tommy said, "And the Klingon was killing him."

TRACK **A**

12.

Slowly . . . excruciatingly slowly . . . the free-floating discorporated energy-being at the edge of the galaxy was becoming aware.

Ironically, it had been as a result of humans that he had
been awakened from his unconscious slumber. Humans,
those curious, bothersome creatures with whom he seemed
to have formed a bizarre sort of bond.

There had been a vessel . . . a vessel transporting a group
of humans. They had underestimated the force of the
galaxy's boundary, for the barrier was a powerful and
fearsome place. Energies the likes of which the humans had
never experienced inhabited the barrier. They could never
have guessed that one of those energies had once been a
sentient being, and had the potential to become so again.

When Q had first sensed the ship entering, he had been
drawn to it in an amorphous, barely comprehending fashion. He did not understand that it might provide succor, or a
way out of his predicament. All he knew was that somehow,
in some distant way, it interested him.

As the ship had been battered helplessly about in the force of the galactic barrier, Q had stretched out the tendrils of his semi-aware mind. He had found a human, one whose mind seemed attuned to him.

In old Earth legends, ghosts would sometimes possess human beings, seeking the warmth of the living to counter the innate coldness of the dead.

So was it with Q.

He plunged his full essence into the human, hovered there, insinuating himself throughout the human's substance.

The human collapsed. That didn't matter. Even though the human was unconscious, Q was exploring, investigating, seeking out every fiber of the human's being, trying to learn as much as he could.

It was an incredible, heady experience. Q lodged himself serenely in the human's cerebral cortex, and began to grow stronger.

It was an exhilarating, and ultimately short-lived, association.

The ship managed to extricate itself from the barrier, but in short order the human's brain overloaded . . . a consequence of the unrestrained, undisciplined, unfettered power of the Q running rampant through his mind. Q lacked the mental tools to rein himself in. Consequently it was too much for the human to handle. He went berserk, the power of the Q eating him from the inside out, until the ship's captain was forced to destroy his vessel with all hands rather than risk the newly godlike crewman gaining access to any inhabited worlds.

The Q essence, without fully understanding everything that happened, suddenly found itself without a home. Frantically, motivated purely by a primal desire to live, Q lunged back toward the only home he had known for eons . . . the galactic barrier.

And there he hid for two hundred years, as humans reckon time.

Two hundred years, pondering what had happened. Two hundred years to consider the mistakes he had made, to realize who he was, what he was. To realize, in short, what had happened to him.

It began to come back to him, ever so slowly. The merest fragments. Snatches of memory, for he had essentially led two lives. One as an omnipotent being of almost infinite power, and the other as a free-floating field of semisentient energy. Consequently there was a great deal for him to sort out.

Two hundred years . . .

And then another vessel came along.

This one was far bigger, far stronger than its predecessor. It, however, had no more luck than the previous hapless ship.

However, Q was ready this time.

He did not yet know who he was.

He did not yet know what he was.

But he knew that he was getting out this time, and getting out to stay. He had come to a realization. The energies of the galactic barrier, which had protected him, had also imprisoned him. He had become overly dependent on them, so much so that when he had briefly tasted freedom, he had come scurrying back. He did not have the power, the strength, to overcome the forces that held him there. Not on his own. He needed help . . . help that only a human vessel might be able to provide.

Deep within him, something recoiled in fear at the notion of departing this womb, this nurturing environment. But he had to do it. He had to take the step forward, or risk being trapped there forevermore.

The ship entered the barrier, and the barrier fought back with greater ferocity than ever, as if somehow aware that Q *would be making an escape attempt. The ship was hurled about, out of control, its shielding buckling, and Q suddenly became aware that the ship might indeed not make it out at all. NOW, screamed his essence, and Q thrust himself into the ship. He spread himself thin, spread himself all through the starship, shoring it up, boosting the engines, providing it protection while, at the same time, seeking out a human host.*

There were several who seemed to have potential. One, however, was so powerful that he feared he would be overwhelmed, even rejected. There were two others who seemed likely, one a female human, the other male. Arbitrarily, he chose the male.

His energized substance rippled out through one of the consoles, and the human pitched backward. Q embraced him joyously, his isolation evaporating, his sense of complete disconnection dissolving in the pure sense of life that the human possessed.

He meant no harm, did Q. He only wanted to submerge himself once more in a human host. To learn, to grow. That, and he wanted to get away from the damned barrier.

He burrowed deep into the human, and hid.

Or tried to hide, at least. But the human host was not destined to be able to hide him for long. . . .

"Gary!" shouted Captain Kirk.

He moved to his fallen bridge officer. For a moment all of the training he'd received in Starfleet, all the mental preparation he'd been given for dealing with the loss of a crew member, deserted him. How it was important to develop a sort of professional detachment, akin to a doctor's. Care about your people, by all means. Don't disconnect, don't isolate yourself. But don't feel each and every injury. Don't take every death to heart, no matter how tempted you might be, because down that path lies madness.

But this was Gary Mitchell, James Kirk's oldest friend from his days at the Academy. The man he had laughed with and gotten drunk with. The man who'd helped Kirk pull off his ingenious fudge on the Kobayashi Maru exam, and the man whom Kirk still suspected of sending a cute blond technician named Carol Marcus Kirk's way . . . a woman Kirk had nearly married.

This was Gary Mitchell, and James R. Kirk felt a brief moment of genuine fear at seeing Mitchell go down. "Gary!" he shouted again.

Gary moaned in a strangled voice. Kirk helped him roll over . . . and froze.

Lieutenant Commander Gary Mitchell's eyes were glowing.

Glowing with the power of the Q.

TRACK A

13.

"Captain Crusher . . . receiving extremely unusual graviton readings." Data paused a moment, and then turned when Crusher did not respond immediately.

Commander Picard, in the seat next to his commanding officer, turned and looked at Jack in puzzlement. Crusher was staring at the planet of Terminus below them, around which they had just fallen into orbit. But he did not seem to be looking at it so much as looking through it.

Very softly, Picard said, "Jack . . ."

Crusher looked up, blinking in momentary confusion. Picard hoped it wouldn't be necessary to repeat to Jack what Data had just said. To Picard's relief, Crusher said, "Graviton readings, Mr. Data?"

"Yes, sir."

"Significance?"

"Too early to be certain, sir. It might signal the formation of some sort of spatial or temporal distortion."

"Does it present a danger to Terminus?"

235

"Not at present."

"Still, they should be alerted to it. Tasha," he said over his shoulder, "get them on screen for me."

"Aye, sir," said Tasha Yar.

Crusher noticed that Picard was still staring at him. "Is something wrong, Number One?" he asked in a low voice.

"I was about to ask you the same question," replied Picard. He frowned. "Still concerned about that Trelane creature? We haven't seen him since that one time, but . . ."

"I'll admit he's in the back of my mind," said Crusher. "But fairly far in the back. I, um . . . I don't think he'll be causing us any trouble."

For some reason, this made Picard feel extremely uneasy. Jack's rather cavalier dismissal of a being such as Trelane was worrisome. After all, this had been an entity capable of stopping the *Enterprise* in its tracks, throwing up a force barrier to immobilize them. He had made threats about pain and such, and then left those threats dangling as he went off to do who-knew-what. And Captain Jack Crusher was of the opinion that Trelane would not be causing them any trouble?

Now was not the time to press Crusher on the matter, however, for at that moment Tasha Yar said, "We have the proconsul of Terminus, sir."

"On screen, Lieutenant."

The proconsul appeared a moment later. His skin was scaled and beet red, giving him a look slightly akin to a cooked lobster. His eyes looked rather world-weary, as if they'd seen many things that they would much rather have forgotten. There was also a general edginess about him, the mark of someone who was just a shade more obsessed with his own self-importance than was probably good for him.

"This is Proconsul Teffla," he informed them. "You took your own sweet time getting here, *Enterprise.*"

"We had a distraction or two on the way," Crusher said. Then, quickly deciding to change the subject, he continued, "We're getting some curious spatial readings in the vicinity of your northern pole."

Teffla's expression immediately fell. Crusher felt a certain degree of smugness watching the proconsul's facade quickly evaporate when he felt threatened. "Should I alert the populace?" he asked. "Should we evacuate . . . ?"

"As of this point, that would be jumping the gun somewhat," Crusher assured him. "We are maintaining a cautious watch, though, and . . . if you wouldn't mind . . . we would like to monitor it for a time to make certain that it's stable, and that it poses no threat to you."

"That is very good to hear," said Teffla, running his hands down the front of his uniform to smooth it. "I remind you, Captain, that Terminus has been extremely cooperative with the Federation. Being on the edge of the frontier as we are, we have offered our services any number of times as a scientific and tactical observation post. It's comforting to think that the Federation feels we are entitled to similar return consideration."

"You needn't concern yourself, Proconsul. We're on top of it. Now . . . to our reason for being here."

"Ah yes." Teffla glanced around, as if unconsciously concerned that someone was watching him. He lowered his voice to confidential tones and said, "Frankly, I'm relieved you're finally here. This 'Riker' of yours has not been any great problem, of course . . . not in his mental condition. But the Klingon with him, Worf . . . frankly, Captain Crusher, it's been almost nightmarish. He's utterly paranoid."

"Paranoid?" Crusher frowned. "In what way?"

"He sees conspiracies everywhere! He insists on double-and triple-checking identities of all manner of key personnel. He's constructed elaborate password systems. He acts as if he expects attack at any moment."

"Really."

"I told him that Terminus was a secure facility, and he snorted at me. Can you imagine such a thing? Me! Proconsul Teffla!"

"A faux pas of galactic proportions, surely," deadpanned Crusher.

The sarcasm went right past Teffla. "I should say so. I will say this for him, though. If I were in trouble and I needed someone guarding my back, I certainly would not mind having him there," he admitted grudgingly. "His paranoia is extremely irritating, but he has been guarding your man, Lieutenant Commander Riker, as if his own life hinged on it. That's good for Riker, I suppose."

"I'm glad to hear it," said Crusher. "We'll arrange for their immediate transport up."

"Excellent," said Teffla in relief. "Because, frankly, Worf keeps looking at me most suspiciously. I think he thinks I'm going to try something . . . and is considering making a preemptive strike, just in case."

Picard was in the transporter room when Dr. Howard showed up. She stepped close to him and said, "Glad I'm not too late."

"He should be coming through just about any time." Picard glanced over at Transporter Chief O'Brien. "Anything yet, Chief?"

"Still waiting the signal from planet surface, sir," said O'Brien.

As O'Brien studied his console, Beverly let her hand drift

ever so lightly toward Picard's. She said nothing, looked straight ahead to the transporter pads as if her mind was solely on her incoming patient . . . which, to a large degree, it was. The instant that Riker appeared on the pad, she would be all business.

Just for a moment, though, she indulged herself. Her right hand brushed against Picard ever so slightly.

Which was when Jack Crusher entered the room.

"Don't want to go!" howled Lieutenant Commander William Riker.

He was clutching a piece of furniture, looking like a trapped animal. His hair was still wild and disheveled. Worf was certainly no barber, and did not have the time, patience, or finesse to do much with Riker's appearance beyond making damned sure that Riker bathed, since his stench was considerable even for a human. Worf stood nearby, his muscled arms folded across his armored chest, barely able to conceal his impatience.

"You must go," he rumbled. "You are a Starfleet officer. A Starfleet vessel has arrived, and you are scheduled to depart with it."

"I don't want to!"

"You must. It is your duty. Furthermore, your wife . . ." He paused, trying to recall her name, and then it came to him. ". . . Deanna . . . and your son, are aboard ship."

That caught Riker's attention. Somehow the mere mention of her name seemed to penetrate the confused and angry haze that hung over him. "Deanna," he whispered.

"Yes, that is correct. Deanna. She is waiting for you. Do you wish to keep her waiting?"

Riker shook his head in a quick, short fashion, as if afraid that too much shaking might cause it to tumble off his shoulders. Then he stared at Worf with a sort of animal cunning that looked so crafty that Worf felt his opinion of Riker going up a few notches. "Are you coming, too?"

"As a matter of fact," said Worf slowly, "I am."

Riker considered that a moment.

"Good," he said at last.

Crusher slowed as he entered, his eyes narrowing. For an instant, he thought he saw . . .

No. No, that was ridiculous. Picard and Howard were simply standing there. Within proximity of each other, certainly, but there was nothing unusual about that. They weren't so near to one another that it should have sparked any sort of reaction from Crusher, or even the slightest hint of impropriety.

Jack rubbed the bridge of his nose. He was just going to have to start dealing with this. Was he *that* hung up on Beverly that seeing her standing nearby his trusted second-in-command was enough to upset him? This was ridiculous. What was going to happen when the time came, as it inevitably would, that Beverly actually did become involved with someone? Was he going to mope around like some lovesick Academy plebe? Dammit, anyway. He had come so far, accomplished so much . . . too much . . . to let himself get sucked into that sort of futile, pointless mind-set.

Besides . . . Beverly and Jean-Luc? What *was* Crusher thinking? Just how far gone was he, anyway? Picard was old enough to be her . . . well, older than she liked, at any rate. And Jean-Luc, for all his dependability and friendship, was something of a stiff. A fairly passionless man, really, although he did pursue some of his hobbies with a laudable intensity. No, not the sort of man that Beverly would be remotely interested in.

Besides, it was a known fact that divorced women always found themselves invariably drawn to men who reminded them of their ex-husbands. It was painfully obvious that no two men could be less alike than Jack Crusher and Jean-Luc Picard. So it was senseless to dwell on it.

Extremely senseless, because if he didn't get control of this intense, irrational feeling of jealousy where Beverly was concerned, then some very serious problems were definitely in the offing.

"What's the delay, Chief?" Crusher asked.

"Getting the signal now, sir," he said.

"Number One," Crusher said, taking a step closer to Picard, "we have an interesting development. Starfleet has just informed me that I am to meet with the Klingon who is escorting our officer. That fellow Worf I told you about."

"Wharf? Like a pier?" asked Beverly.

Picard was about to tell her "Yes," but Crusher said, "Pronounced the same, but I'm told the preferred English spelling is W-O-R-F. And believe me, if a Klingon tells you that something is preferred, then you'd damned well better prefer it that way, too. Particularly when the word is through the grapevine that Worf is on the fast track for the Klingon High Council."

"Indeed," said Picard.

"Politics in the Empire are oftentimes incendiary. The Klingon-Federation alliance has been an exceptionally beneficial one. I think we all want to keep it that way."

The transporter suddenly came to life. "Two to beam up," affirmed O'Brien.

The beams coalesced and re-formed, and within moments two new arrivals were standing on the transporter pads.

Crusher and his officers weren't exactly sure where to

look first: at the Klingon with his wild mane and fiercer mien, or the haunted-looking Starfleet officer, likewise dressed in Klingon clothes, albeit they were far simpler, with less accoutrements and trimmings.

All in all, they were a rather extraordinary-looking pair.

Crusher absorbed all of it, and then stepped forward briskly. "Welcome aboard the *Enterprise,*" he said, thudding his hand against his chest and then outstretching it in a fair approximation of the Klingon salute. "I am Captain Jack Crusher. This is my second-in-command, Jean-Luc Picard, and my chief medical officer, Dr. Beverly Howard."

Worf returned it in perfunctory fashion, and then said, "I am Worf, son of Mogh. This is Lieutenant Commander William T. Riker. I believe he is one of yours."

Riker walked slowly down off the transporter pad, looking around warily. It was clear from his eyes that something he was seeing lit a spark in his mind. Picard noticed that his shoulders were hunched as if he were perpetually bracing himself for some sort of beating. When he walked, he moved on the balls of his feet, which would enable him to move more quickly to one side or the other. The better to dodge.

What had they done to the poor bastard? Picard wondered. No one should have had to suffer what this man clearly had gone through.

"Lieutenant Commander," said Crusher, "welcome back." He extended a hand toward Riker, and Riker automatically flinched. Crusher stood there a moment, his hand in midair, and then he slowly allowed it to drop to his side. Lowering his voice, trying to sound less authoritative . . . and perhaps less threatening . . . he said, "The first thing we're going to do is have Dr. Howard check you over. Make certain your inoculations are in effect, and that no dangerous . . . whatevers . . . have been introduced into your system."

"An excellent idea," rumbled Worf. "The Romulans may have subjected him to any manner of medical experiments."

"This way, Lieutenant Commander," said Beverly. She took him gently by the arm, ran her fingers down his biceps. He found the motion immediately soothing, and although he clearly didn't trust her unreservedly . . . on the other hand, he seemed to regard her with somewhat less suspicion than he did the others.

"His family is aboard?" asked Worf the moment that Riker had departed.

"Yes," said Crusher. "But I thought it might be wiser to get him settled in a little first."

He let the statement hang there for a few moments, and then slowly, Worf nodded. "You are concerned that his family might find his current condition . . . disconcerting."

"Partly," admitted Crusher. "That, and it also might be a bit overwhelming for him. I think it would suit everyone better if he were eased into the situation. A return to normality is important for him, but first he has to adjust to what normal is."

"I do not know if I agree," replied Worf. "When faced with a difficult situation, the preferable course is to confront the problem. Cut through it, quickly and efficiently. Your brand of delicacy merely prolongs the problem."

"That's an interesting point of view, Worf," Picard spoke up, "and appropriate for the powerful Klingon mind-frame. When dealing with humans, however, it is important to make allowances for our relative . . . fragility."

Crusher fired him a look. But Worf merely grunted. "You

are most likely correct. I have not had a great deal of contact with humans. I trust you will be able to thoroughly instruct me on your shortcomings."

"We have so many," Crusher said dryly. "I hope we have time to list them all for you during your relatively brief stay."

Worf, master of subtlety and sarcasm, replied, "I am certain your best efforts will be sufficient."

Riker lay on the med table, staring straight up into space. Picard and Howard were standing a short distance away, studying him silently.

"I've given him vitamin supplements to bring his system back up to speed," said Beverly Howard. She was studying him with a sort of wonderment. "His stamina is incredible. I'm not sure what kept him going all these years."

"The human mind is a formidable weapon."

"True enough," said Beverly. "And I'll grant you that's probably what kept him alive. Unfortunately, that was also one of the main targets of his captors."

"Is there brain damage?"

"Physically, no. His neural systems are intact. No damage to any of the motor functions. That's physically. Emotionally is another story."

"Any feeling for it so far from your examination?"

She turned to him, her face expressionless. "Jean-Luc, I couldn't even begin to assess the damage. Let's face it, he's been through enough to break a dozen men. The fact that he's verbal is nothing short of miraculous."

Picard sighed. "What do we do?"

"First? First, we do what we can to make him feel like a human being. That means some of the amenities. You have a hairstylist on this ship?"

"He's a Bolian named Mr. Mot. I haven't had to make use of him so far . . . no comments, please, Doctor." He intercepted what was going through her mind. "I understand that he's quite skilled. Unfortunately, he also tends to prattle a bit."

"Some nice, pressure-free prattling would probably suit Mr. Riker about now," said Dr. Howard. "And after that, I suggest a long-overdue reunion with his family is in order."

He looked from Beverly over to Riker. "Do you think that will help?"

She sighed. "Frankly, Jean-Luc . . . I doubt it could hurt." She looked sadly at Riker. "Think of it. Beneath that disheveled hair and edgy, paranoid manner is a man who had once been an extremely gifted and promising Starfleet officer. Who knows what he might have been like if this hadn't happened to him?"

"I guess we'll never know," said Picard.

"So, Worf . . . you've made quite a name for yourself."

Worf was seated across from Crusher in his quarters. "I have worked for my cause, and for my Empire. The manner of personal reputation I've garnered is irrelevant."

Jack leaned back in his chair. "All right, then. I'll grant you that. Nevertheless . . ." He paused. "Okay, listen, Worf. Cards on the table."

Worf looked down at the table with slightly furrowed brow.

Crusher missed the momentary confusion, continuing, "The Federation thinks that you're going to be someone to reckon with. Considering the transitory nature of many alliances, and the past incendiary nature of Klingon-Federation relations . . ."

"They wish to make certain that, should I come into

some sort of power, that I will be generously disposed toward the Federation."

Crusher nodded. "That's it exactly."

"Very wise," Worf said after a moment. "Very foresighted. I can respect that. I take it, then, that you can respect my position as well."

"That position being?"

Slowly Worf leaned forward. The crackling of his leather armor seemed to fill the room. "The Klingon Empire will never be secure until its enemies are destroyed."

"Well . . . that's one way of putting it, I suppose."

Worf dropped his voice down. Crusher actually fancied that his desktop was vibrating in accordance with the basso profundo of the Klingon's voice. "My sources inform me," he said, "that the Romulans are planning major incursions over the next several years against the Federation. Furthermore, they are already engaging in a variety of covert activities designed to split apart the Klingon Empire. Virtually anyone, Captain, could be a Romulan agent."

Crusher stared at him. "I beg your pardon?"

"They have perfected an assortment of surgical disguise techniques. Although I have no proof or specifics, I believe that there is already at least one Romulan operative posing as a Vulcan in some position of authority within the Federation. Likewise, various operatives are spreading themselves through our people as well."

"Those are fairly serious charges, Worf."

"It is a serious situation. I have recommended that the Council begin to compile lists of suspected Romulans throughout the Empire. I am also suggesting that you bring the recommendation to your superiors as well."

Crusher found himself speechless for a moment. Then he said, "Worf . . . I agree that security is of prime importance. And I'm not a great fan of the notion of Romulan operatives insinuating themselves into all walks of life. But what you're suggesting sounds perilously close to paranoia."

Worf tilted his head in such a way that his eyes almost seemed to disappear. "Are you implying . . . ?"

Crusher raised his hands, palms up and facing Worf. "I'm not implying anything. All I'm saying is that what you're proposing sounds as if it could send a wave of suspicion throughout both our peoples. Trust would be a thing of the past. We'd be looking everywhere for possible traitors, scrutinizing our neighbors, turning in anyone who seems the least bit suspicious."

Worf seemed puzzled. "Your point being . . . ?"

"My point is that that isn't necessarily a good thing!"

"With all due respect, Captain . . . I believe you will find that, historically, a little suspicion can be very beneficial. Whereas a little laxness," he added grimly, "can be very fatal."

"Now just relax, Lieutenant Commander," said Mr. Mot as he eased Riker into the chair.

As Riker did as he was told, Geordi La Forge stood nearby. He had escorted Riker down from sickbay, and was now making sure that nothing went at all awry. This was, after all, supposed to be simply a routine haircut. But if there was one thing that Geordi had learned, it was that the routine rarely was.

Riker was not having an easy time of loosening up. He was stiff as a board, and Mot almost had to shove Riker's stomach to get him to sit down. Once he had managed that, he fingered Riker's stringy hair, making no effort to hide his distaste. "Good lord," said Mot, "what did you do, cut it yourself? Or did you just rip it out with your bare hands?"

"Sir," said Geordi, not knowing the barber particularly well but wanting to make sure that his charge was not upset. "Lieutenant Commander Riker has been . . . indisposed for quite some time. I think dwelling on that might not be the smartest idea."

Mot afforded him a barely interested glance. "Oh you do, do you."

"Could you just cut his hair, please?"

Mot sighed, the weight of the world on his ample shoulders. He brought out his cutting implements while proclaiming, "Will someone please explain to me why I subject myself to amateur—"

He didn't get to finish his thought, however, because at that moment he brought a sharp-edged blade into the general vicinity of Riker's throat.

Riker saw the brief glint of light against the metal.

And it speared into his memory with the preciseness and power of a phaser blast.

The Romulan's face was leering over him, and he was being probed with a blade. There were little bits of his flesh being scooped out, and blood was trickling from a dozen wounds. . . .

Riker's hand speared out and snagged Mr. Mot around the throat. Mot didn't even have the opportunity to shriek, because Riker's viselike hand clamped off any possible air intake. Mot did not even fully understand what was happening. All he knew was that, suddenly, he couldn't breathe, and his eyes were threatening to burst out of their sockets as Riker grunted inarticulately.

Geordi was frozen for only a moment. Then he grabbed Riker by the arm, not even wasting time trying to pry the cordlike fingers from Mot's throat. Instead he jabbed a spray hypo into Riker's arm.

The effect was instantaneous. Riker's grip on Mot went slack, as Riker sank back into the chair with the powerful tranquilizer coursing through his system. Within seconds he was unconscious.

Mot staggered back against the wall, rubbing his throat and trying to suck air into his lung. "In all my years . . . I have never . . . *never* . . ."

"You're going to be fine, Mr. Mot."

"How can you say that?!"

"Because you're talking."

"No thanks to him. Thankfully, my people are possessed with an extremely strong larynx."

"Good. So . . ." Geordi gestured to the sleeping Riker. "Get to it."

Mot stared at him in astonishment. "You aren't serious. You expect me to attend to his hair needs after he assaulted me in that manner?"

"I don't think he's going to be causing you any trouble in the immediate future."

"No," said Mot firmly, putting down his barber tools. "I refuse. I have been abused by this . . . this ruffian, and I will not give him the honor of having his coiffure sculpted by me. I, the victim, do not feel like attending to my victimizer."

"Is that your final word?"

"I'm afraid it is."

"All right, then," said Geordi. He reached for the barber's utensils.

Mot froze in alarm. "What are you doing?"

"I'm going to trim his beard unevenly and then give him a lousy haircut." He gave Mot a look of iron. "And then

I'm going to tell everyone on the ship that you did it . . . except you were in a drunken stupor at the time."

Mot snatched the cutting tools from Geordi's hands. He looked daggers at the young nurse.

"Blackmail is an ugly practice," he said as he began to cut Riker's hair.

"Practice makes perfect," replied Geordi.

TRACK **A**

14.

Deanna Troi Riker paced her quarters like a caged cat. Tommy, on the other hand, sat as still as a Buddha, watching his mother move back and forth. She would sit for a brief time, read, lose interest, start to pace around some more, lean against the wall, drum on it, then sit . . . and start the cycle all over again.

"What's keeping him?" she said finally in exasperation.

"Ma, this isn't doing any good, you know," Tommy informed her.

She sighed and sat down again. "I know," she said. "But he's been aboard ship for a while now. Why haven't they let us see him?"

"I'm sure they have their reasons," said Tommy.

"I would certainly like to know what they are."

"They're Starfleet, Ma. They know what they're doing."

She regarded him with an amused smile. "Your confidence in Starfleet is so absolute," she said with a touch of wonderment.

He shrugged. "I guess so."

"Because you idolize your father, of course. And since he is in Starfleet, then naturally Starfleet holds your allegiance."

"Don't you trust Starfleet?" There was genuine surprise in his voice.

With a sigh, Deanna said, "Your father loved the life, as my own father did. I know that. I also know that my father died unconscionably young, and I've spent nearly seven years wondering if your father was alive or dead. A part of me would like nothing better than if no member of my family was ever again associated with Starfleet."

Tommy was silent for a moment, and then he said, "I'm going to join Starfleet."

She smiled slightly. "Well . . . we have plenty of time to make that decision."

"It's not our decision," he replied. "It's my decision."

"All right," she said gamely. "Then you have plenty of time to make that decision. But it's not going to be here and it's not going to be now. Okay, Tommy?"

"But Ma, I think maybe we—"

"Okay, Thomas?"

The stress in his mother's voice was not lost on Tommy, nor was the extremely formal "Thomas" that his mother used only on those occasions when he was in the deepest of trouble. But he hadn't *done* anything. Why was she so mad at him?

At that moment, the door chime rang. The noise so startled Deanna that she leaped to her feet, hand on her chest to steady her heartbeat. "Yes?" she said.

A woman's voice said, "There's a gentleman here who would like to see you."

Deanna froze.

"Uhm . . . hold on a minute," she called.

Tommy was dumbfounded as his mother ran to the

mirror to check her hair. "Hold on a minute?" he said in disbelief. "Ma, for crying out l—"

"Just—" She put out a hand, gesturing for him not to say anything. "Just . . . give me a moment." She paused, endeavoring to compose herself. Then she drew a slow breath and said, "Okay." Loud enough to make herself heard through the door, she repeated, "Okay!"

The door hissed open.

A Starfleet officer, a woman with short blond hair, was standing on the other side. She nodded briefly to Deanna. "Lieutenant Yar, ma'am. Security," she said formally. "I just wanted to warn you that your husband is a bit . . . skittish."

"Skittish?" said Deanna in confusion.

"Jumpy, let's just say. Frankly, if you were someone else, we might consider holding off a little while. But, since you are both an empath and a trained psychologist, well . . ." Tasha shrugged. "We figured you could handle it. Just proceed carefully. I'll be right outside in case you need me."

Deanna didn't understand why she might possibly need the aid of a security officer in dealing with her own husband.

And then he was there.

He was someone more normal-looking than he had been when she saw him briefly on the screen back on Betazed. His hair was neatly styled, his beard trimmed. He was not wearing a Starfleet uniform, but instead simple off-duty fatigues. He was far thinner than she remembered him . . . even, if such a thing was possible, shorter. His shoulders were slightly hunched. He glanced around nervously. This, of course, was perfectly normal for someone who had been through what he had suffered. He was instinctively watching out for an attack to come from any direction. He could not let his guard down for even a split second, in anticipation of having to pay—and pay brutally—for even a moment's laxness.

To Deanna, he looked absolutely wonderful.

"Will?" she said softly.

He didn't appear to hear her at first. Instead he was cautiously staring into the room, as if scoping out every possible angle before daring to set foot inside. She repeated his name and this time he looked at her . . . except he didn't look at her so much as through her. Then, finally, he appeared to focus on her.

She waited for him to say something.

"Deanna?" he whispered.

Her hands flew to her mouth, to stifle the shriek of pure joy that wanted to leap from her. Such a loud noise might startle him, even frighten him. All she could trust herself to do was nod.

And then he spoke two words that caused her world to crack around her.

"Where's Deanna?" he said.

TRACK A

15.

Gary Mitchell was a dim, distant memory.

Q had not intended for matters to get so utterly out of control. His ability to manipulate the power of the Q had been tremendously hampered by his vessel's decision to go utterly berserk. Plus, Mitchell had transferred some of the Q power over to a human woman, and that had not worked out particularly well, either. He'd had the devil's own time extricating the power from her lifeless corpse.

What was insane was that, deep down, Mitchell had *liked* wielding his godlike ability. Oh, he had wailed about it. Seemed frightened by it. But deep, deep in his subconscious somewhere, Mitchell had derived a delirious enjoyment from his ability to manipulate power, to manipulate people. To play God. What was odd was that the human he'd taken over from that first, earlier ship had had the same reaction. Q had thought it a fluke, but now he realized it to be a major flaw of the species. Power corrupted, and absolute power corrupted them absolutely.

(But it hadn't with Riker . . .)

The thought fragment had come unbidden to him. The recollection from another part of his existence, jumbled around with the billions of bits of information that the incorporeal life-form called Q was trying to digest.

(Who was Riker?)

(What was Riker?)

(Where was Riker?)

(*Enterprise* . . .)

But that made no sense. The *Enterprise* was the vessel that he had just been on. The vessel that Gary Mitchell had been on. The ship that Kirk commanded . . .

Kirk.

Kirk had killed Mitchell.

He'd not done so on his own, of course. Mitchell was dead because Q had allowed it to happen. Mitchell's power obsession had grown to such gargantuan proportions that he threatened to overwhelm Q entirely. If Q had not gotten out when he did, he might have been trapped inside Mitchell forever, his own consciousness and power totally subservient to the madness that had been unleashed within Mitchell.

So he had used the woman, Elizabeth Dehner. The woman upon whom Mitchell had foolishly bestowed some of his power. Q had managed to use what little influence he had to get Dehner to turn on Mitchell. She had done so, for she had not been fully corrupted yet. Perhaps the female of the species was more resistant to the temptations of ultimate power.

She had sought to stop Mitchell, and she had battled him, matched him blow for blow, power for power. In so doing she had given Q the room he needed, the opportunity he needed. There on the planet Delta Vega, while Gary Mitchell was in mortal combat with James R. Kirk, Q had started to pull away from him. To withdraw his power, to escape his influence and make a bid for his own freedom.

The power had started to fade from Mitchell . . . and then his subconscious began to pull Q back as he found himself beset by Kirk. It had been a fearsome struggle, the mutated mind of Gary Mitchell doing everything that it could to yank the unwilling Q back into himself. Ultimately, it had been Kirk himself who had settled it. Before Mitchell could integrate the Q power back into himself, Kirk had brought an avalanche of rocks tumbling down upon Mitchell. The momentary distraction was enough for Q to rip himself completely clear, and the rocks had crushed the mortal body of Gary Mitchell. Moments later, Q had reabsorbed his missing aspect from Elizabeth Dehner as well.

As James Kirk mourned the loss of his friend on Delta Vega, Q reveled in his freedom. And then, for a moment . . . just for a moment . . . he contemplated taking over Kirk.

But as quickly as the flittering thought passed through his mind, it was rejected. He sensed in Kirk a personality as strong as, if not stronger than, Mitchell's had been. Q had only just been starting to assert his own fragmented personality, and he was not going to take the risk of being subjugated once more.

Besides, he had spent far too much of his existence being dependent on, or involved with, one thing or another.

So he had stayed on Delta Vega for some time, allowing himself to gather his strength and collect himself. An amorphous, undefined energy being, sorting it all out.

Eventually, he had left.

He had explored the galaxy, slowly reassembling the pieces of his life and existence. He darted through nebulas, skirted black holes. He encountered a variety of energy creatures similar to himself in his travels . . . similar, but different. One in particular was especially repugnant, and tried to instill a sense of fear in Q. This did not work out particularly well; Q was more annoyed than anything else.

Since both beings were amorphous, there was not terribly much they could do to each other. The creature went on its way, vowing hostility and revenge.

Still, the encounter jogged something within Q. It took many more years for it to fully come together within his dispersed mind because, since he had very little understanding of his reason for being, he had very little incentive to concentrate on matters of importance. Indeed, he had only the slightest concept of what "important" was.

Slowly, though . . . ever so slowly . . . the pieces were assembling.

And he felt himself being drawn . . . drawn to a point in time and space that he did not yet fully comprehend.

He hoped he would understand once he got there.

JUMPING TRACKS

TRACK C

The *Enterprise* shields shuddered under the pounding of the three Romulan warbirds.

They were bracketed, surrounded on all sides. What had started out as a rescue mission had gone wrong, horribly wrong. The hell of it was that, as the hopelessness of their situation went through the captain's mind, she came to the bleak realization that—given the exact same set of circumstances—she would do precisely the same thing.

"Captain Garrett!" roared Delhaney from its tactical board, shoving the blood-matted brown fur out of its face. "Front deflectors failing! Rear deflectors at fifty percent and falling!"

"Drop rear deflectors!" ordered Garrett. "Reroute all power to front shields!" Her hands gripped the armrests of her command chair. "Continue distress signal! Helm, bring us around! Keep our front facing them!"

"Helm not responding!" shouted Castillo. In frustration, not knowing what else to do, he slammed his fists down on the helm control. Certainly it wasn't much use for anything else other than as a punching object at that moment.

Another volley ripped from the Romulan warbirds, battering the helpless starship at will. Damper circuits went down, and the science station suddenly blew outward, practically shredding Science Officer Berkholt. Berkholt was dead long before he hit the ground.

A small fire started to rage through the bridge. Moving quickly, Delhaney threw itself headlong onto the fire, its massive body snuffing the flame before it really got started.

Knowing beyond question that the ship was dead, but refusing to admit it, Garrett punched the intercom. "Engineering! Any thoughts on the phasers coming back on-line?"

"Phaser battery casings are cracked, Captain!" came back the engineer's voice. It was laced through with static, just barely comprehensible. "We're trying to lock her down before we've got an uncontrolled radiation leak on our hands!"

Garrett fought the insane impulse to laugh. They had maybe another minute or so of life left to them. The last thing any of them should have to worry about was a slow death from radiation poisoning.

"Captain!" called out Delhaney, still brushing soot off its uniform front. "A fourth Romulan warbird has appeared, right behind us!"

Behind them, where they were unshielded.

"Perfect," said Garrett.

And then the call came up from engineering. "Captain! Two photon torpedoes, locked and loaded!"

Immediately Garrett was on her feet. "Delhaney! Target the one behind us and fire! Now!"

Delhaney didn't even tell Garrett that the computer lock was out of commission. Why add to her aggravation?

Delhaney manual-targeted, breathed a quick prayer, and fired.

The warbird that was diving in behind them was struck on either side, just as it fired upon the *Enterprise.* The shots went wide, one of them even striking a glancing blow off another one of the warbirds.

If the starship had had another forty or fifty photon torpedoes at its disposal . . . or perhaps a couple of fully charged phaser banks . . . it might have had a fighting chance. As it was, the warbirds regrouped and descended upon the *Enterprise,* showing no mercy . . . not that they had been especially disposed toward mercy earlier.

Delhaney was about to report to Garrett that all shields were on the verge of total collapse when a substantial array of photon torpedoes, targeting the central part of the saucer section where the bridge was situated, struck home. Delhaney was blown back from its station, smashing into the walk rail with such velocity that its spine was snapped instantly.

Another blast, and another. The ceiling of the bridge started to crumble, debris raining down upon the screaming bridge crew. Garrett had leaped up from her seat, jumping over Delhaney's body and grabbing command of tactical herself. Quickly she scanned the controls.

They had nothing. They'd have as much success if they climbed out onto the saucer and spit at the warbirds.

The ship lurched wildly; Castillo was thrown from his chair. Ironically, it was the only thing that saved him, for rubble cascaded all over the helm, burying the controls and Castillo. If he'd been in his seat, he would have been killed immediately. As it was, he was "merely" entombed.

Garrett surveyed the bridge. Everyone down. Dead, most likely. It had been so unfair. The crew of the *Enterprise* 1701-C had been a damned fine group. No captain could have asked for better, and they deserved better than this. They deserved to go on and do great things, to have legends written about them, songs sung. They hadn't been out in space all that long . . . not nearly long enough.

They . . . deserved . . . better . . .

The Romulans were closing in, licking their collective chops. They knew the ship had nothing more to give. But they weren't offering surrender, no. Instead they stepped up the fury of their attack, photon torpedoes coming from all sides. The viewscreen was one large square of blinding light. Garrett thought back to the stories of how, when one is facing death, one sees a tunnel of light. That had always seemed a nice, consoling story somehow. A promise that there was someone or something waiting for you on the other side. Somehow, though, she never imagined the light consisting of a barrage of Romulan torpedoes.

She staggered, went down, and suddenly there was a lurching feeling as if the entire ship were . . .

. . . were turning inside out.

There was light, searing light everywhere, and Garrett could not believe that even the unremitting barrage of photon torpedoes could produce a display of such intensity.

The ship teetered, and for one moment Garrett felt as if she were on the brink of something. Standing on the edge of a waterfall, perhaps, and looking down into the cascade of falling water.

Then the ship dropped suddenly, like a roller coaster. Garrett skidded forward, maintaining her place at tactical only through the courtesy of her desperate fingers wrapped around the console.

And in addition to the light and the overwhelming incandescence, there was something else, too. In the back of her mind, she thought she heard something. Something that sounded like mocking laughter, before the light completely overwhelmed them.

And then the warbirds were gone.

Just like that.

Garrett couldn't believe it. One moment the *Enterprise* was doomed, the next . . . they were clear. There was nothing on the screen at all except clear space.

For a moment, she felt a small burst of concern. Perhaps the warbirds had cloaked. It didn't make any sense, of course. She knew that even as she ran a check on all instruments to see if there were any energy traces of them. The warbirds had them cold. There was no reason to leap into hiding—particularly since they couldn't fire while cloaked—unless . . .

Unless another ship, or several ships, had come to the *Enterprise*'s rescue.

Garrett started to pull herself to standing . . . and shrieked. She hit the ground, trembling violently as her body was racked with pain.

She looked down at the lower half of her body and understood immediately. When she had fallen, her leg had caught on something—a chair, whatever. Her upper body had hit the ground at a different angle from the rest of her. Something was terribly wrong with her leg . . . broken, fractured . . . something. That was just wonderful. Lack of mobility was definitely something she needed to have added to her already dire straits.

Part of her wanted just to lie down on the floor and die. The part was attached to her hips. However, her brain was, at least for now, still in command, and it was her brain that ordered the rest of her to haul herself back up to tactical. She put all her weight on her good leg. The shift in position was enough to cause her severe distress, but she forced herself to lock off that part of her mind which registered pain. Up, up, and dammit, move, get up *get up,* you lazy bitch, she shouted at herself. And then she was up and at tactical, and she had made the pain fade to a dull ache that she could at least live with.

The theory that other vessels had arrived was quickly put to rest when the screens read all clear. No sign of any ships at all . . . not theirs, not Klingons' . . . no one's.

Then she double-checked her instruments. She felt blood trickling down into her face and she wiped it away impatiently, still unable to believe or understand what the sensors were telling them. As if they might be mistaken, she looked up at the screen for visual confirmation.

It was true. Damn, it was true. The stars were different. The *Enterprise* had completely changed position.

"How the hell?" she whispered, registering dim surprise at the raspiness of her own voice.

But there was no time to speculate as to the hows and wherefores. She punched up the intercom and spoke again, sounding only distantly like herself. "This is the captain . . . all hands . . . report . . ."

Nothing. Nothing except crackling over the ship's intercom. Were they all unconscious? All dead, perhaps? There was a gruesome thought . . . the last living being on the entire ship. God, what if that was the case? What if it was just her, and seven hundred dead people? And . . . here was the most hideous thought . . . what if she didn't die, and what if they were never found? There they would be, floating derelict, helpless.

The ship of corpses.

She'd go out of her mind. She knew that beyond certainty. She'd either have to haul all seven hundred bodies down to the shuttle bay, try to get the doors working, and blow them out into space . . . or else spend the rest of her life stepping between dead bodies wherever she walked.

There was more blood in her eyes, and with an annoyed growl, she wiped it away again. It was ridiculous, her going on in this manner. For one thing, she had no business assuming that everyone was gone. And for another thing . . . life-support systems were failing. She wouldn't survive much beyond her crew.

She laughed.

She had to laugh. Who wouldn't? When the best news of the day was that life-support systems were failing . . .

She laughed for what seemed a very long time. It was, in fact, two seconds. Then she brought herself under control and, trying to ignore the throbbing in her head, she checked to make sure that subspace, at least, was working. Video send wasn't operational, but voice was still on-line.

"This . . . is Captain Garrett . . . of the *Starship Enterprise,* to any Federation ship. We . . . have been attacked by Romulan warships and require . . . immediate assistance. We have lost warp drive . . . life-support is failing . . ."

She talked and continued to do so, the sound of her voice the only thing keeping her company.

TRACKS **B** AND **C**

Captain Picard looked up in surprise to see Guinan emerging from the turbolift. It seemed so rare to see Guinan any place besides the Ten-Forward lounge. And for her to appear now, on the bridge, unannounced and without any sort of summons . . .

It was most peculiar.

Then again, it might have had something to do with Q and Trelane. Perhaps she was here to warn him about their imminent return. Q had been so thoroughly dispatched that Picard could not help but be concerned. How bizarre that was. Once, Picard would have sworn that it would be a cold day in hell before he would care about Q. Now, though, he would actually be relieved to hear one of Q's sardonic comments.

"Guinan?" asked Picard.

Guinan was staring at Worf with such furious intensity that it was almost startling. Worf didn't realize at first, but slowly he became aware of the scrutiny to which he was being subjected. "Is there a problem?" he rumbled.

Guinan frowned, shook her head. Then she turned to Picard. "We need to talk. Now." She lowered her voice and said urgently, "It's all wrong, Captain. This is not the way it's supposed to be."

He looked at her in confusion. "Very well." He gestured toward his ready room, and she preceded him in. She lost no time in apprising him of the situation.

"Everything has shifted," she said.

"Shifted?" He stared at her blankly. This certainly wasn't at all what he had expected to be discussing with her.

"Everything has changed," she said. "This ship . . . you . . ."

"Me?" If it had been anyone else, he would have thought it some sort of elaborate hoax. "In what way?"

"I don't know . . ."

"You must have *some* idea how things have changed."

Guinan sighed in exasperation. "I look at things . . . at people . . . and they don't *feel* right."

"What things? What people?"

Looking around helplessly, Guinan finally fixed her gaze on Picard. "The bridge . . ."

"What's the matter with it?"

She tried to articulate, but nothing would come. *"It's not right"* was her frustrated reply.

Picard knew that Guinan had been through a lot recently. Being punted out into space, bullied by Trelane . . . it was enough to unsettle anyone. "It's the same bridge, Guinan. It hasn't changed," he said patiently, hoping that he didn't sound too condescending.

Guinan, thoroughly disconcerted, ceased her pacing and sat. "I know that. And I also know . . . it's wrong."

It was too nebulous. He needed something that he could

latch on to, some way to try and see through her eyes what it was that was going on. "What else?" he asked.

She felt as if she were looking deep into herself, trying to pull from her deepest recesses the things that were bothering her. Then something clicked. "Families. There should *not* be children here."

Picard tried not to laugh. Over the past years he had developed something of an acceptance, even a grudging enjoyment, of some of the children who populated the *Enterprise.* Seven years ago, though, he would have been one of the first to agree that there should not be children on the ship. To hear that sentiment coming from Guinan, though, was nothing short of bizarre. "Why should there not be children, Guinan?"

"Because this is a ship of war," she told him.

They were chilling words, words that cut deeply into him. "What?" he whispered.

"Our mission, and . . . Worf . . . Worf shouldn't be there . . ."

Now Picard stood, and there was no disguising the tremendous concern in his face.

Guinan looked down, more vulnerable than he had ever seen her. "I wish I could prove it," she said softly. "But I can't."

"Guinan," Picard said slowly. "We've all been under tremendous strain lately. Perhaps it would be best if you went down to sickbay for a time. Have Dr. Crusher check you over."

She rose and sighed. "There's nothing that she can do for me, I'm afraid. Nothing that anyone can do. There's no action to take . . . and that's another thing. There should be something we can do. But there isn't. It's like it's all being taken out of our hands."

"Guinan . . ."

She raised a hand and shook her head. "It's all right. Thanks for listening to me. It was . . . it must sound very strange to you."

"I'm concerned."

"I know. Don't worry. I'll get it worked out."

Guinan walked out of the ready room, and still felt an unconscionable chill as Worf watched her. She entered the turbolift and went down to Ten-Forward.

She stepped through and stopped.

It had changed back.

Whereas before there had been a number of civilian personnel lounging about, looking utterly informal, now Ten-Forward was filled solidly with uniformed crewmen. Not only that, but the uniforms were back to the way that Guinan remembered, with the slightly flared style and the customary sidearm that was required for all Starfleet personnel to wear at all times. The waiters wore sidearms as well. The lighting was back to the dimmer, more stark environment. There was none of that disconcerting sooth-ing environment she had found herself surrounded by. Instead everyone was alert, battle-ready, prepared at any moment for the sound of a red alert that would tell them . . .

Yes. Tell them that the Klingons were attacking.

Already the recollection of her confusion was fading. A Klingon on the bridge . . . God, she had imagined that there was a . . .

It faded completely, and the only thing that filled Guinan now was an overwhelming sense of relief and well-being.

For one, brief moment, she had done a sort of mental double take. Like one of those odd instances where a word that you've never had trouble spelling suddenly looks completely wrong, no matter how you juggle the letters.

She couldn't even recall the reasons for her being concerned. All she knew was that everything was fine, and her momentary discomfiture was completely gone.

"Must be getting old," she murmured.

TRACK C

On the bridge that Guinan had not just left, Captain Picard finished making an entry in his military log.

He did not, of course, enter any of his concerns about how the war with the Klingons was going. The simple fact was that it was not going well. Private communiques from Starfleet indicated that, as soon as six months from now, the Klingon Empire would triumph over the Federation. It was hard to believe that such a thing was possible.

"Captain," said Lieutenant Yar. "Long-range sensors have detected a ship."

"Able to identify?" he asked.

Tasha Yar frowned, double-checked her readings. "Definitely a Federation starship. Accessing registry. It's . . ." She stopped, trying not to let her amazement show in her voice. "It's the *Enterprise* . . . 1701-C."

Picard slowly turned in his command chair.

Data said briskly, "Sensors confirm design and specifications, Captain. Analysis of hull and engine materials

273

conform to engineering patterns and methods of that time period."

From the Damage Control station, Ensign Wesley Crusher observed, "But that cruiser was destroyed with all hands about twenty years ago."

"Presumed destroyed," Data corrected. "The *Enterprise*-C was last seen near the Klingon outpost on Narendra Three exactly twenty-two years, four months, and five days ago."

"And now it's here," said Riker.

"Mr. Data, is it possible," conjectured Picard, "that it has . . . traveled through time?"

"It is a possibility, Captain," said Data. "I am detecting residual radiation on the exterior hull. However, if any sort of temporal rift did provide a bridge through time for the *Enterprise*-C, it is now gone."

"Scanning the interior of the ship, sir," Tasha said, not taking her eyes from the tactical display. "Heavy damage to warp-field nacelles and hull-bearing struts." She looked up with sadness in her eyes. "No life signs, sir," she said softly.

There was a long moment of silence.

"All dead?" Picard finally managed. "Are you sure?"

"Yes, sir. I'm receiving their automated distress signal, but that's all. Sensors indicate total life-support failure."

"Prepare an away team," Picard said. "See if you can bring the engines back on-line. Get her up and running."

"The Fleet could always use another ship," Riker suggested. "Even if it is a little old."

"Agreed. If we can get her up and running within nine hours, we can escort her to Starbase 105. Otherwise we'll destroy the ship and proceed on our previous mission to Terminus."

Riker nodded and rose to assemble the away team. And

Picard could not help but muse, "As I recall . . . the Narendra Three outpost was wiped out."

"That is correct, sir," said Data.

Picard sighed. "It is regrettable they did not succeed. If a Federation starship had rescued a Klingon outpost . . . it might have averted twenty years of war."

The call from the away team was far less than Picard had hoped . . . but, unfortunately, everything that he had feared.

"I'm standing on the bridge, sir," said Riker, his voice sounding filtered through the air mask he wore on his face. "Everyone is dead. Dr. Crusher says that the captain hung on longer than the others on the bridge crew, but that she died twenty-four hours ago."

"Damn." Picard shook his head. "To come two decades through time, and then die because we were one Earth day late." What he did not say out loud was that these were certainly not the best times for the *Enterprise*-C to flee to. No, not the best times at all.

"Geordi says that the deterioration of the warp core has gone too far. He estimates a repair time of twelve hours at least, and even then it's not a sure thing."

Picard shook his head. "No. No, that's far too much time. Especially with Klingon vessels having been spotted in the area. Return here immediately." He sighed. "It's a pity, but we'll do what we have to."

A short time later, the away team had returned to the ship. At Picard's behest, everyone on the bridge was standing, their heads lowered. Tasha Yar had targeted the *Enterprise* 1701-C at several key points, and merely awaited Picard's order.

Picard was silent for a long moment, and then he said—with the regret quite evident in his voice—"Fire."

Tasha activated the phasers. The lethal beams struck at the ship that was out of its time. They penetrated deep into the warp core, rupturing the containment grid that was already barely staying together.

The result did not take very long as the *Enterprise*-C shuddered. The first signs of its destruction appeared in the engineering section as the hull seemed to be eaten away, dissolving into itself. Tasha Yar sent several more phaser bolts toward the saucer section, and that was all the additional impetus that was required. The old ship blew up, a fireball briefly flaming into existence consuming the vessel, driven by the eruption of the warp core. There was no air to feed it in the vacuum of space, but that did not prevent the fireball from ripping through the *Enterprise,* devouring metal and bodies with equal efficiency.

Within seconds . . . far too few seconds . . . the *Enterprise* NCC-1701-C, commanded by Captain Rachel Garrett, reclaimed the status that it had been accorded for twenty-two years: a memory. All that was left were a few unidentifiable twisted pieces of her hull that would float in space, mute testimony to the passing of a ship bearing a proud and distinguished name.

There was a long silence on the bridge, and then Picard looked slowly at Riker. "Set course for Terminus," he said quietly. "You have the conn. I . . . will be in Ten-Forward if you have need of me."

"Aye, sir," said Riker, carefully maintaining the facade of normality. Determinedly working to maintain the illusion that he was unaware, or simply uncaring, of the awful melancholy of the situation.

Riker knew, though, exactly what was going through his commander's mind at that moment, and it had nothing to do with their next destination. No, Picard was dwelling on a very bleak extension of their own difficult situation these days. A situation where any moment could bring an attack from the Klingons; where any summons for help might be an ambush; where a state of battle-readiness had to be maintained at all times; and where the *Enterprise* NCC-1701-D was one of the few last hopes against a completely militaristic existence in the galaxy.

There, but for the grace of God, thought Picard, *go we.*

TRACK **A**

*S*top him
Stop him

The words floated through the semiconscious haze that was the energy being who had once called himself Q.

He did not, could not understand the origin of the entreaties. It was as if they were coming from within him, but far outside him, all at the same time. But they drove him. Drove him with a compulsion that was peculiar to him, but had no less the sense of urgency.

Something was telling him that it was pivotal he be at a particular place at a particular time. The problem was, he didn't know the where or the when.

That did not stop him from going there.

He floated, unable to resist. It took seemingly forever for him to get where he was going, because the galaxy was vast, and he was having trouble concentrating.

Every time his attention seemed to flag, however, that prod would come along that would nudge him on his way.

Stop him

Who was the "him" that he was supposed to stop? How was he supposed to go about it? It made no sense to him.

But he was moving anyway.

And as he did, more memory bits began to float to him. The jigsaw pieces of his life began, with excruciating slowness, finally to interlock. The holes were still gaping, but he was starting to be able to plug them. To find the fragments that fit and piece them together. His existence, which was a chaotic discord of jumbled bits, finally began to coalesce.

It was happening gradually, but the speed of the process began to increase. Q ceased paying heed to where he was going, the inner compulsion so strong that it drove him without his conscious effort. The preponderance of his study was focused on the intriguing enigma of his own origins.

So when he arrived at the single most important moment in the entire history of the cosmos, he was not giving it his one-hundred-percent, undivided attention.

But he was very shortly thereafter.

TRACK B

Captain Picard entered the Ten-Forward lounge and was almost tripped up by several running children.

Immediately aware of their faux pas, the children stopped where they were and mumbled apologies. It was difficult for Picard to be *too* upset. These particular children, he was well aware, had been some of the more enthusiastic participants in the "Captain Picard Day" the students had put together not long ago. In fact, the small girl who had plowed into him the most forcefully just now was also the one who had spent almost two solid weeks (according to her teacher) crafting a Picard doll. It was a rather silly item, as far as Picard was concerned. A doll of him.

Still, the doll had almost been worth it just for Riker's holding the toy in front of his face and solemnly intoning, "Make it so."

"We're sorry, Captain," one of the children was saying again.

Working to maintain a serious demeanor, Picard said gravely, "Ten-Forward is usually for grown-ups, you know. If Guinan was kind enough to let you in, then it behooves you to be on your best behavior rather than running about."

"Yes, sir," one of them muttered.

A smaller girl informed Picard, "Our teacher says that horses have behooves."

Picard was about to correct her, and then quickly realized that it would simply extend the conversation. "That's very nice," he said with a solemn expression.

They walked gingerly around him and out the door. Picard had no illusions, though, that the moment they were out of his sight, they were probably running down the corridor at warp speed.

He saw Guinan engaged in relaxed and pleasant conversation with a couple of lieutenants to whom she had just brought drinks. Then she turned and looked at Picard, as if knowing that she was going to see him even before she spotted him. Which (knowing Guinan) was not that much of a stretch.

She glided over to him in that way she had. "Hello, Captain," she said cheerfully. "Can I get you a table?"

"Actually, Guinan, I came down because of you."

"Everyone comes here because of me," Guinan told him, smiling. "I give wonderful ambience."

"I've been concerned because of our conversation earlier."

She tilted her head slightly. "Conversation?"

"Yes, about . . ." He stopped.

Something was wrong. Very slowly, he continued, "About . . . how things have changed."

Guinan frowned. Now the tone of her voice altered as

she became aware that something was genuinely off. "Maybe you'd better refresh my memory."

"You . . ." Picard glanced around, as if wanting to make damned sure that no one was listening. "You came up to the bridge and told me that things had changed. That the *Enterprise* was different from the way it was supposed to be. That we were at war with the Klingons."

She fixed him with a stare as if trying to determine whether this was some bizarre attempt at humor or not. "At war?"

"Yes. And you said there were no children on the ship."

"And when did I say all this?"

"Just a few minutes ago."

Guinan gave it some thought. "Picard . . . how would you react if I told you that I've been down here the entire time. That at the point where you say I was talking with you, I was, in fact," and she pointed at Lieutenant Barclay and Lieutenant Gomez, who were engaged in a game of 3-D chess, "kibitzing at that game over there."

"An impostor," Picard said slowly.

"Could be, considering some of the visitors we've had lately."

"But it makes no sense," said Picard. "No sense at all. Why would Trelane—or Q, for that matter—engage in such a charade? It seems utterly pointless. For that matter, I don't think it was an impostor. I can't believe that either Trelane or Q would be capable of creating such a flawless fake."

"You're telling me there's something that a member of the Q Continuum is *incapable* of doing?"

It was a reasonable question, of course. And, unfortunately for Picard, the answer was that they had no real idea of just what the beings in question were capable of accomplishing.

"If it was a fake," Picard said, "then it was nothing short of brilliant. But . . . what if it was not a fake?"

"If it wasn't," said Guinan, "then we have some major problems ahead of us."

"That," Picard said, "may turn out to be an understatement."

TRACKS B AND A

The machine was huge.

Trelane was extremely proud of it. It had taken him an unconscionable amount of time to construct. He had meticulously crafted every circuit, thoroughly contemplated each fragment of his instrumentality.

He clapped his hands in glee as he stepped back to look at it. Did he dare to hope? Was it actually (gasp!) finished?

He made a few marginal adjustments, to make sure that everything was on-line. And as he did so, he could not help but reflect on the circumstances that had brought him to this moment.

James Kirk had been a major disappointment to him. Indeed, the entire crew of the *Enterprise* had been. None of them had really understood what he wanted to do. None of them had seen the pure joy, the great adventure upon which he had wanted to embark.

He had not intended to hurt any of them. None of them.

Why was it, though, that they couldn't understand? Was it that they were incapable of doing so, or were they just perversely *refusing* to do so? What was it that was so difficult for them to grasp?

The fact was that, for all the alleged wonderments that the galaxy had to offer, it was, in fact, a colossal *bore.* There was *nothing to do.*

How many times had he complained of that to his parents? How many times had he voiced his frustration? Did they listen to him? Did *they* understand? No. How often did he say to them, "I have nothing to do"? Did they sympathize? Did they agree? No. "Study your predators," they said. "Brush up on your particle physics," they said. "Clean your quadrant," they said. No, no sympathy at all.

"They mean well, I suppose," said Trelane out loud. "But they just don't understand. They just don't get it."

He had tried to take up hobbies. Somehow, though, they always seemed to lead to bigger problems. For example, he'd developed a fascination for human beings. It seemed harmless enough at first. Indeed, when the *Enterprise* had shown up with its load of helpless, hapless humans, Trelane had been nothing short of ecstatic. Finally he would have the opportunity to implement his endless hours of intense study. He would make them feel at home. He would regale them—and they him, in turn—with boisterous stories of mighty military campaigns. They would all be great friends, comrades . . . why, they'd be so thrilled to encounter him, they'd never want to leave. They might even want to worship him once they saw the extent of his knowledge and power.

Well, *that* had not exactly worked out, had it.

No. Instead they had yelled at him, berated him, abused his hospitality at every turn. And what had been the result? He'd gotten in trouble with his parents.

He'd tried to explain to his parents, but, of course, being parents, they had not understood because parents never do. After all, they felt they were so superior all the time.

But why hadn't the humans understood? That was a source of tremendous aggravation. He couldn't comprehend it. They were, after all, the species that he had catered his interests to. It should not have been that much of a stretch for them to grasp the majesty of the world that Trelane, the Squire of Gothos, had created for their entertainment.

Apparently, though, it was, and they didn't.

Furthermore, Trelane had felt completely mortified by the simple mistakes he had made. That he had made food with no taste, well . . . that was forgivable. After all, he'd never actually *been* to the sodding planet, so how was he supposed to know? The answer was that he wasn't supposed to know. No one could hold him responsible for such a minor gaffe.

That the fire in his fireplace was cold *was* a tad embarrassing, he had to reluctantly admit. That was something he should have remembered. It was simple combustion, after all. Something he'd learned about ages before. That was really the only excuse he could come up with: that it was such old news to him, he couldn't be bothered to remember it.

The most annoying mistakes, however, involved his power source and the time gaffe. The time gaffe had been just plain sloppy, and there was simply no excuse for it. How in the *world* could he have forgotten to allow for the amount of time it takes for light to travel? That was just unconscionable. Here he was watching humanity still toddling around in wooden sailing vessels, while they were arriving at his doorstep in starships.

And then Kirk had destroyed his power source. That had *really* hurt. Even though he had managed to fall back on other instrumentality, that did not remove the sting of being made to feel utterly helpless in front of totally inferior beings.

So that was why he . . .

Suddenly he stopped. Something was up. He sensed it. Had his parents found out, despite all his careful preparations?

He looked around, and then he saw it. It was some sort of amorphous energy being, hovering nearby, as if trying to decide whether it should be taking some sort of action (although what sort of action a floating energy creature would be thinking of taking, Trelane couldn't even begin to imagine).

"Hello," Trelane said in a rather chipper tone. "And what are you doing there, may I ask?"

The creature said nothing. It just wavered in the air.

"Well!" said Trelane. "You've certainly arrived at a propitious moment, haven't you. Excellent timing. You're to be commended. I will tell you what, my amorphous friend. You . . . lucky you . . . will be given the first opportunity to witness the high point of my existence."

He circled his machinery proudly, running his hands across its gleaming metal surface. "This device, you see, is the answer to all of my problems. It's going to tap into the theoretical core of the very universe. Isn't that exciting? And would you like for me to tell you what the result of that tap is going to be?"

Still there was no response. That was quite all right. Trelane wasn't really expecting one.

"What's going to happen," said Trelane, "is that I'm going to be infallible. Because at the universal core is all the power, all the knowledge, all the potency that any being could possibly desire. And it will be mine. Mine to tap into. Mine to do with as I wish."

He spread his arms wide, as if encompassing the entirety of the cosmos as he spoke. "No one will be able to second-guess me. No one will be able to tell me what to do. I tell you, it will be nothing short of glorious. A sublime experience. A consummation devoutly to be wished. And you," he pointed, "you, my noncorporeal observer, will be here to be a part of it. Is this not simply too exciting?"

Stop him

Q did not know how. Unable to touch, unable to communicate, unable to fully understand beyond the most instinctive of impulses. He floated there as this odd creature chattered on to him about a variety of things that did not interest Q in the slightest.

He knew he had to be here, to try and stop something. But what? *What?*

"All right," said Trelane, taking a deep breath. For some reason he suddenly felt nervous. But there was nothing to be nervous about. He was in complete control of the situation. He had created the machine from scratch, and he had a full understanding of the forces into which he was about to tap. So there was nothing, absolutely nothing, to be nervous about.

This did not stop him from feeling just a twinge of uncertainty. After all, something could go wrong. He was trying to obtain control over unimaginable power. Certainly there was *some* margin for error. Some vague possibility that there could be a major botch-up. Not that there was going to be, of course, but it remained a vague possibility.

"Not a problem," he said, and activated the machine.

Trelane . . .

The name suddenly fell into Q's mind, the final key that unlatched the tumblers in his memory. Suddenly it all fell into place, one piece after the other. And there was Trelane, and an eternity of loneliness stretching in back of Q, and a cosmos of chaos awaiting him.

He understood, *damn him, he understood.* . . .

He screamed a soundless scream.

Trelane placed himself flat against the machine. There were no crude on/off buttons, no switches to flip, no relays . . . none of the primitive niceties that adorned the mechanical creations of lesser beings. The machine was, in fact, simply a vast block, with a black surface that seemed to absorb all light. Almost like a black hole, but translated into another form.

The device operated through willpower, and Trelane willed it to life now. He felt the black metal throbbing beneath him, and it filled him with a giddy ecstasy. All of the hesitation, all of the second-guessing, fell away as he knew beyond any doubt that he was doing the absolute right thing.

This would get his parents' respect.

This would gain their attention.

This would be his statement, his message to them that he was grown-up. All the times they'd talked with each other in low voices, thinking he couldn't hear, thinking he wasn't around. Making noises about how they were going to deal with him. About what a slow learner and slow developer he was. That he should be much further along in his abilities by now, and perhaps there was something wrong with him in terms of his personality. Those muttered comments about immaturity.

"I'll show you," he said. "I'll show all of you."

He began to melt into the machine.

And then he saw them.

Q saw them.

He knew immediately, in no manner that he could express or even begin to grasp, that they had materialized in response to his summons. Understanding was flooding over him, with greater and greater speed, as all of his existence began to make sense to him.

He saw the father, powerful, calm, but the concern for his son's latest activity clearly evident. He saw the mother . . .

. . . the mother . . .

. . . a glorious creature, was Trelane's mother. Q knew her instantly, saw the beauty that permeated her. There were stars in her eyes and splendor in her soul. He knew her in ways that he could only begin to comprehend as he was deluged with memories.

Memories, he quickly realized, that had to be of strictly secondary importance to the moment that he was witnessing.

He heard the voice of Trelane's mother. It was a voice that was made for speaking words of love, for whispering in the darkness. A voice for teasing and cajoling, a voice for gentle remonstrations. But that was not the way he was hearing it now. No, her voice was filled with concern, with confusion. She did not fully grasp what was occurring. All she knew was that her child was in some sort of danger, and she had to do something.

"Trelane!" she said in alarm, and then her voice was drowned out by the strident authority of Trelane's father's.

"Trelane!" he said forcefully, for his father was a great scientist; a highly respected, awesomely knowledgeable being. He knew instantly what Trelane was about to do, and knew that it had to be stopped. "Get *away* from there! *Now!*"

"No!" shouted Trelane petulantly, half-merged with the vast machine. "It's mine! I made it! I can play with it if I want to! And you can't stop me!"

And with that, he plunged himself into hell.

Reality crumbled around him, and was replaced with Unreality.

It was as if it were a living, breathing thing, the Unreality of it all.

The Unreality saw the intruder, saw the maggot who thought to explore it, to tame it, to understand its mysteries and command its power.

Chaos stretched far and wide, the laws of physics and sanity mere abstract notions that had no place there.

And into the Heart of the Storm plunged Trelane.

He was greeted rudely.

The assault came quickly, brutally, from everywhere and everywhen. Trelane had pushed through barriers that lesser beings would not have been able to attain, and wiser beings would have known to leave well alone.

And then he saw and he understood and the universe . . .
was and was not

and he was and was not and oh look there was a piece of the universe fragmenting off and there was another growing to take its place and it was constantly shifting

and Trelane did not know where to look first so he

looked everywhere first and everywhere last and in between he looked everywhere else and everywhere was looking back and invading him coming in through everywhere through every aspect of his brain and his heart and soul and everything that made him what he was and would ever be and never was and never would be

and he experienced it firsthand as the Heart of the Storm pulled him up deep into its embrace sucking him in sucking him dry and filling him up with itself and saying to him okay look here's the deal

you want to know you want to know it all you want to feel it all and experience it all and understand it all and command it all well fine that's terrific with me that's okay ginger peachy right a rooney and how's the weather out there oh it's storming out there well that's okay because its storming here too

and Trelane arrived and Trelane left and Trelane was trapped in there forever and Trelane was stopped just in time and Trelane never built the machine and Trelane was never born and Trelane was much younger and this would never happen and Trelane was much older looking back on this and pondering what a fool he had been and it was amazing that he had lived that long and he hadn't lived that long

so here's the deal where were we oh yes everywhere we were everywhere

and there was laughter laughter all around and perhaps it was coming from him and perhaps it was coming from elsewhere and the Heart of the Storm raged and it wasn't just the storm it was the universe the pulsing heart of the universe my God (who?) he had entered the heart of the universe the living breathing core of the multiverse that surrounded him that tied all things together and made them what they were and weren't and should be and shouldn't be

292

so here's the deal and it swamped him submerged him and the raging storm pummeled him and ripped him open and gutted him and turned him inside out and outside in and he was giggling and screaming and howling and crying and bleeding and laughing and being conceived and being born and growing up and dying he was dying and being born again

so here's the deal and it's a fluid deal because look around you look at the universe it's a vast weak place that's constantly expanding expanding far beyond anything it was supposed to be because you see it was never meant to be permanent in any shape or form it was never meant to be anything more than a first draft why it's still a work in progress look at it barely stitched together and why it wouldn't take much more than a pull here or a tug there to get the whole thing to unravel and won't that be nice won't that be ever so nice

to pull it all apart and then stitch it back together again with something that holds better a nice cable stitch perhaps or perhaps stronger wire instead of the flimsy thread that's currently holding it together which could be cut so easily so easily and you just pull on this end and watch that other end of it just slither right out and dangle

it's all so weak you see at least someone comes along and damn where have you been until now Trelane because you've been feeling misunderstood haven't you and no one cares about you and you know what you want to do and why won't they let you well guess what that's not going to be a problem anymore no it's not because there's no way in hell they're not going to let you they won't be able to stop you try as they might try as mightily as they wish it's not going to happen

because you're mine and I'm yours and I'm going to give you precisely what you've always wanted and we're going to make a multiverse that will do them proud except the first thing we do is we get rid of this whole multiverse thing pare it down to one because it's confusing don't you think with all these alternate time tracks and parallel universes and who can keep any of it straight except

well here's a thought here's a notion tell me what you think of this Trelane my baby my angel my sweet thing and let me touch you here and stroke you there in ways that your parents never let you know about and this is going to be absolutely exquisite get this listen to me my delectable thing you're so delicious I could just eat you up and here's what you'll do after I'm through with you you'll understand you'll understand everything because everything is anything and anything is everything and up and down are completely relative and come here let me enfold you let me enrapture you let me do you because I've been waiting here for so long at the Heart of the Storm and it's been forever since I had a lover as succulent as you and you could be the best of all the greatest of all the last time there was one like you my God (who?) that was the end of everything and the beginning of everything and he or she or it or whatever was ultimately destroyed and the universe went with it but that's okay because another one started and another and another and it's getting out of control and it's time it's time to bring it under control again, bring it down to a manageable level because I think we all have to agree that this is getting just a little ridiculous the seams are showing don't you see the seams are what it seems like and oh yes touch me there Trelane and see things as they have always never been

Let me cram it
down you
up you and sideways and throughout your entire being it's here and there and I'm everywhere and you see how it all comes together and how it all comes apart

and we'll come together and when we come apart everything else will too
      You've waited

                    You've wanted
  As have I
        War God
                      Little Boy
    not a little boy anymore all grown up all mine come
to me come and thunder in the Heart of the Storm
           and mine
  give it to me

                 yes everything we
are and want and there's so much need
      what's that
         what's that pulling for you trying to pull
you out and they don't know they don't know what they're
doing they don't know you're mine and come here Trelane
let me show you you've seen some now you'll see all come
to me come to me come . . .

Trelane exploded in infinite directions and in that moment he existed throughout time and space and it was all
revealed to him in a second and he tried to understand it
which was a major and fatal mistake, for when he collapsed
back down, his mind didn't quite make the jump. . . .

Around the machine, time bent and warped. The rest of
the galaxy went on about its business unconcerned,
unhampered . . . but in this little piece of it . . .

It's not that time lost all meaning. Rather, it was a case of
the meaning of time becoming redefined.

Trelane's parents, frantic out of their minds, were only
dimly aware that eternity's march had altered its step for

their benefit. Random bits of chaos leaked in all directions from the machine, unleashing temporal energies the likes of which they'd never seen. But they couldn't concern themselves with that. All that mattered was their son.

For them, years of time passed and they didn't even know it.

For Trelane, it all happened in the course of one second, as seconds are reckoned on a cosmic scale.

Trelane was blown out of his machine, into the arms of his parents. He was not moving and not breathing (which was okay since breathing was something of an affectation anyway). He did not hear his parents shouting at him because he was too busy listening to the whole of creation shouting at him, telling him what needed to be done and who he should do it to.

Finally he looked up at his parents.

He was quite mad.

Not "quite mad" as in extremely angry. No, "quite mad" as in . . .

"Quite Mad."

As a hatter. As a loon. As every psychotic killer or irrational creature throughout the entire history of everything, all wrapped up and combined into one package and tied off with a bow.

Well . . . not quite exactly.

Actually, he was Much Madder than that.

He giggled.

It was not a pleasant noise. Very high-strung, but not nervous, because he had nothing, absolutely nothing to be nervous about.

"Let's play a game," he said softly.

His parents looked at each other, not understanding. Floating nearby, the discorporated Q understood only too well.

"It's called 'Pretending everything is normal,' which it's not, but I'm ever so good at pretending. And we're all going to play. Everyone, in all the multiverses. Won't that be fun?"

"Trelane," said his father very slowly but as firmly as he had ever spoken in his entire existences . . . and there had been more than a few . . . "I want you to come with me. We're going to go to the Q Continuum."

"Whatever for?"

"Because you've had an accident, Trelane," his mother told him. "And they're going to try and make it better."

"Oh, I don't think so," said Trelane. "But if you're so interested in going to visit them, why then . . . you go right ahead."

"Now, Trelane . . ."

"I *said* that you should *go right ahead!*"

There was no noise except for a slight sound that was a combination of a quick sucking and popping noise, and then Trelane's parents vanished. Vanished into the Q Continuum, vanished without the slightest chance at preventing it from occurring . . . not that their resistance would have made that much of a difference.

Even though he had accomplished the deed, Trelane felt no small measure of surprise at how quickly and efficiently he had done so. He felt power surging through him, power beyond imagining. He was going to need some time to sort it all out. Yes. Time. That, and exercise. It was as if he had developed a thousand new muscles, and each and every one was going to have to be flexed and challenged before he was fully accustomed to making them operate.

Almost as an afterthought, he decided that the Q Continuum would be sealed off. Thought was as deed, and the Q Continuum—the endless guardians of spatial order since time out of mind—were closed off. Closed down. Trelane snickered as, in his mind, he could hear their collective howling and anger.

It was of little relevance to him beyond the immediate need to keep them out of his way. He shut off their yowling as easily as he had shut them out of interfering with his affairs.

He turned his attentions elsewhere . . . and there were so many elsewheres to attend to.

And, utterly forgotten, Q sobbed in discorporated frustration.

Trelane was one of a kind.

And the first thing he had to do was make damned sure it stayed that way.

His long-range plans were so masterful, so sweeping, that he felt a little intimidated by them. Which was why Trelane decided to start small. Unraveling the fabric of the universe was not as easy as it sounded. One had to know just where to pull, how hard to tug. Otherwise one might wind up with some sort of stubborn knot and have a much harder time of it than was necessary.

So he proceeded to take steps. What he thought of as cleaning up after himself.

He chose the method. He chose the aspects of the multiverse that most appealed to him.

And then . . . he began.

He stared through the mirror at himself.

The image filled Trelane with a certain measure of disgust. How naive he looked. How miserable. What was going on in this particular timeline that was causing him such dismay?

Trelane watched himself walking around in a cabin aboard the *Enterprise,* looking frustrated and chagrined.

What had they said to him, done to him in this timeline, that was causing him such aggravation? How had the crew of the *Enterprise* managed to bring him low again? And so easily? *So damned easily?*

He felt the fury building in him, and knew beyond any doubt, beyond any question, that they would pay. They would all pay.

He had to make his alternate persona understand that, though.

No. The hell with it. Forget about understanding. He didn't have to settle merely for that. Trelane could handle it himself. Better that way. Much better.

Trelane loved mirrors.

Always had, always would. For mirrors were far more than mere reflections of one's own vanity. They were, in fact, gateways to limitless possibilities. When one looked in a mirror, one did not always see oneself as others saw one. There was a reason for that. It was because one was peering into other dimensions where things were better. Different. More desirable.

Mirrors, each and every one of them, were little shards of eternity, revealing an infinity of truths. They were the closest thing to keys to the multiverse that anyone had.

Trelane drifted into the mirror now and heard himself wailing, "And the next thing I know, I'm starting to lose my temper, or shout, or do whatever it takes to *make* them understand. But no one does. No one *ever does!*"

"You're wrong," said Trelane with utter confidence. "You're wrong. I understand."

Through the darkling glass, he watched himself recoil and stammer in confusion. "What is this?"

"Why, my dear fellow," said Trelane. "Haven't you figured that out?"

"No. No, I haven't," naive Trelane said, looking wary.

"Well, then . . . I'll explain it to you."

It was impossible, what he was about to do. But chaos was about infinite impossibilities, and he tapped into that power, that knowledge that was thundering in his head and filling his body. He reached through the mirror, *through it,* grabbing his counterpart by the front of his ruffled shirt. His counterpart thrashed and struggled, but Trelane merely maintained his same, confident smile.

"Stop it!" shrieked his counterpart. "Let go! *Let go!"* He tried to brace himself against the sides of the mirror, and he howled, *"Q!"*

Trelane pulled once more with finality, and his counterpart was ripped through the mirror . . .

. . . and pulled into him.

How odd. He had known what he wanted to do, but up until the moment that he had accomplished it, he hadn't been quite certain that he could do it.

Indeed, though, he had managed.

He heard, deep within him, a distant and terrified cry, and then there was silence.

Dead silence.

TRACKS **B** AND **C**

Guinan looked out the window of Ten-Forward, suddenly feeling tremendous unease.

Something was happening. Something that . . .

"No," she breathed.

DERAILMENT

1.

Commander Picard lay on his back, staring up at the ceiling. Beverly Howard was cuddled next to him, her breathing slow and steady. Nevertheless, Picard had the feeling that she might indeed be awake. "Beverly?" he said softly.

No answer.

"Beverly," he whispered again.

Without opening her eyes, Beverly said, "So are you going to keep doing that until you're sure I'm awake?"

"Whatever is required, Doctor."

"Go back to sleep, Jean-Luc."

"We need to talk."

"No, we need to sleep. I don't know how you do it, a man your age . . ."

He raised an eyebrow. "A man *my* age?"

". . . but we mere mortals don't necessarily have your stamina. So go back to sleep, please. Doctor's orders."

"I want to talk to you. Commander's orders."

Now she opened one eye a slit. "You are aware, are you not, that the chief medical officer can countermand the orders of the captain himself, based on medical need? And you're just a lousy commander."

He said nothing, but simply stared at her. Even in the darkness of the cabin she could see the intensity of his gaze.

"Oh, bloody hell," she muttered. "Okay, Jean-Luc. What's the problem?"

"What if I decided to leave?" he asked.

"It's your quarters. You can leave whenever you want."

"You know what I mean."

Truthfully, she did not at first. Her thinking was still a bit muddled by sleep. But the tone of his voice penetrated the haze. "You mean leave the *Enterprise?*"

"Yes."

"But . . . you just *got* here."

"As did you."

"Where would you go?"

"It's a universe of infinite possibilities, Beverly. Where wouldn't I go?"

"You wouldn't leave," she said firmly. "You're just using me as a sounding board. Saying things to see how they sound out loud. But I can tell from the tone of your voice that you're already dismissing the idea."

"Not completely," he said, but he wasn't particularly convincing.

"Jean-Luc . . . Starfleet is your life. You got off track, is all. It's not fair that it happened. But that doesn't mean that you should consider the notion of going off track again."

"Perhaps," he observed, "because my plans did go awry, and I survived it . . . it made me more aware that there

306

is, in fact, life outside of Starfleet. A concept that I had not really been willing to entertain since I was a very small boy."

"There is life outside of Starfleet," she agreed. "But not for you. This is your place, Jean-Luc. This is what you were meant to do. It's your destiny."

"I don't believe in destiny. Nothing is preordained. We make our own lives. Destiny is a function of twenty-twenty hindsight, and nothing more."

She was silent for a moment.

"Just out of morbid curiosity . . ."

"Yes?"

"In this rather unlikely scenario, if you did leave . . . did you envision that I would be coming along with you?"

"It had crossed my mind."

"Hmm." She appeared to consider it. "You know . . . it could be interesting, I suppose. Perhaps you could become . . . I know." She snapped her fingers. "You could become a trader. You know, in spices and such."

"A trader? In spices?"

"No, not spices," she said more excitedly. "Archaeological artifacts. That would be perfect. That's always been one of your main hobbies anyway. We could travel around from one planet to another, one dig to another. See what we could turn up. We'd be living a fairly meager existence, of course. Subsisting from one find to the next. Still, it could be tremendously exciting. Seek adventures, thrills. Go wherever we want, do whatever we want. Not be tied in to Starfleet decisions and orders. What do you say, Jean-Luc?"

"It sounds . . . intriguing," he allowed.

"Let's do it."

"What? When?"

"Now."

"What do you mean, now?" He laughed. "We can't just up and leave. We're in orbit around Terminus, we're monitoring this developing spatial rift, we . . ."

"The hell with it," she said. "There's always going to be some excuse, Jean-Luc. We're never going to have *nothing* to do. Starfleet life isn't built that way. We'll always be on our way to something or coming back from something or tied up in something. There's never a convenient time to leave, so we might as well just do it. Come on. We'll head over to Jack's quarters right now and resign our commissions. We'll beam down to Terminus, and I'm sure we can find somebody down there willing to part with a Starhopper."

"A Starhopper? Aren't those a tad cramped?"

"Yes, but they're also affordable. It's not like we have a ton of Starfleet back pay to draw on. Maybe we'll have to stay on Terminus a little while and work off the difference, but we can manage it. We can *do* it, Jean-Luc," she said with growing excitement. "You. Me. The galaxy. No starship. No rank. No fleet. No uniform. Just us. What do you say?"

He stared at her for a long moment.

"You know damn well I'm going to say no, don't you," he said finally.

She sighed. "I strongly suspected it."

He flopped back on the pillow, feeling like a sham. "I was really wondering what it would be like to leave Starfleet. Lead the sort of vagabond life that you were so colorfully describing. At least I was until you pointed out that we could really do it at any time."

"So now you're having second thoughts."

"More than second thoughts, I'm afraid," he admitted. He looked at her ruefully. "I suppose I never really had the slightest intention of leaving."

She patted his bare chest. "That's all right, Jean-Luc. I didn't have the slightest intention of going with you."

Picard threw his head back and laughed, until Beverly Howard's passionate kisses quieted him, and instead distracted him toward other, more meaningful and worthwhile pursuits.

Jack Crusher wasn't sleeping particularly well.

Actually, he wasn't sleeping at all.

He sat at his desk, wearing his robe and endeavoring to make an entry in his personal log. For some reason he was having trouble concentrating. Finally in exasperation he shut off the log and pulled out a deck of cards. He proceeded to engage himself in a stimulating game of solitaire.

This went on for a time until a voice said, "Sleepless?" It came so unexpectedly that Crusher jumped up, not only dropping the cards but banging his knee rather severely on the underside of his desk. He turned to see—to his utter lack of surprise—Trelane standing there, looking rather amused.

He was also dressed rather oddly.

He was wearing a long, black flowing robe and a white powdered wig. Crusher didn't know what to make of it at first, and then came to the realization that Trelane was outfitted as an old-style judge on the British bench.

"Oh. You're back."

"Amazing," said Trelane, "how you are able to make such wonderfully staggering observations of the painfully obvious." He took a step forward, his black robe swirling about on the floor. "But tell me, Jack . . . how good are you on observing more subtle matters, eh?"

"It's too late at night for games like this."

"Oh, it's *never* too late," Trelane said reprovingly. "Not ever. I should think you would be aware of that, Jack."

"What I'm aware of is that it's the middle of the night and I don't feel like trading pithy observations with you right now." Crusher bent over and proceeded to pick up the scattered cards. Then he heard a finger snap from behind him, and the cards were neatly piled in a stack on the desk. He turned to face Trelane and said in exasperation, "Why us? Why have you zeroed in on us? Go bother someone else."

"I've zeroed in on you, Jack, because you provide such an intriguing test case. Life is a series of tests, you see. With each one our patience and durability are probed and examined, and our worthiness to go forward is scrutinized. If we live up to this scrutiny, we continue on life's endless journey toward self-realization."

"Are you going somewhere with this?" Crusher said impatiently.

"Actually, Jack," Trelane said, smiling, "I thought you might be interested in going somewhere."

There was something in Trelane's voice that Jack Crusher considered extremely disconcerting. Furthermore, Trelane then raised his hand and snapped his fingers. For the briefest of moments, Crusher was suddenly seized by the fear that Trelane was about to wipe him out of existence. There was no doubt in Crusher's mind that Trelane was capable of such an action. Indeed, the amazing thing was that he hadn't done it already.

Trelane did not do so, however. Indeed, the finger snap seemed to have little impact on Crusher at all. He felt no different, seemed to have suffered no ill effect.

"What was that about?" asked Crusher.

"Come with me and you'll find out," said Trelane. He turned and walked through the wall.

"Was that supposed to impress me?" Crusher said, although Trelane was no longer in the room. He headed for the door. "Because if that little parlor trick was intended to make me say, 'Ooooh, aaaahh,' then I'm afraid you're going to be sorely disappointed."

Crusher was so accustomed to the door sliding open automatically that he was halfway through it before realizing that it had not opened. There he was, standing half into the corridor, melting through the door as if he were a ghost. Trelane was standing on the other side of the hallway, arms crossed and looking rather insufferably smug.

"Impressed yet?" asked Trelane.

Crusher stepped the rest of the way through. "Mildly," he allowed. Experimentally he turned and slid his hand through the wall. It went through, phantomlike, his hand no more substantial than a flashlight beam.

"All right, more than mildly. Why did you do this, though? What's the purpose?"

"In the words of the window washer, all will be made clear," replied Trelane.

Crusher stood there and watched several crewmen walk past without acknowledging his presence. He looked curiously. "What am I? Invisible? Intangible?"

"More like irrelevant," said Trelane. "Come. This way."

"I'm not going anywhere with you until you tell me what this is all about."

Trelane walked back toward him and put his face very close to Crusher's own. He grinned toothily.

"It's a surprise," he said.

It was all Crusher could do not to step back, but he did not want to display even the slightest sign of weakness in the face of Trelane. "I hate surprises."

"I don't blame you," said Trelane. "Come along now."

He headed down the corridor, and at that point Crusher saw few options left to him except to follow Trelane and see just what was up.

He fell into step behind Trelane, and quickly noticed that Trelane didn't walk so much as march. Everything he did was heightened and exaggerated, even when it was something as simple as heading down a hallway and being invisible while he did it.

"Tell me, Jack," said Trelane, "do you find yourself with an incredible sense of melancholy in your soul? Eh? Do you feel as if you are alone in a vast and hostile universe?"

"No, but I feel as if I'm being unfairly harassed by a very obnoxious alien being," Crusher said.

Trelane stopped and tossed him a thin smile. "Quite," he said. "You can make your jokes, my good captain. You can toss off your witticisms, play the clown if you so desire. But both you and I know that, in your heart of hearts, you are a sad and wretched individual."

"Not just enough that I'm sad. I have to be sad *and* wretched."

"Would you like to know why you are?"

"That's a hell of a question," said Crusher. He trailed his intangible hand along the wall, and wondered why, if he was intangible, he didn't sink through the floor. Just one of those conveniences that Trelane had decided to toss in, Crusher presumed. "How do you expect me to answer it? I haven't admitted that I'm sad and wretched, and you're asking me if I'm interested in knowing *why* I am."

312

"Let's say you are, just for the sake of argument."

"It's not an argument I care to pursue."

Again Trelane stopped and looked at him, and the facade of good humor was fading quickly from him. "Let's say that you are," he said, emphasizing every word.

"All right," Crusher sighed. "It's your game. At least you're playing it with me and leaving the rest of my crew alone."

"Oh, don't worry, Captain. I assure you that at least some members of your crew are more than capable of finding their own entertainment."

This sounded like a rather curious statement. "What do you mean by that?" asked Crusher.

"Ah-ah. Why ruin the surprise. Now . . ." He frowned. "Where was I?"

" 'Sad and wretched,' " prompted Crusher.

"Ah yes." Trelane smiled. "Tell me, Captain . . . are you familiar with theories of parallel universes?"

"It's not my field of expertise, but yes, somewhat," said Crusher. "I've never taken much stock in it, frankly."

"Really. And why is that, exactly?"

"Well, as I understand it, the theory is that whatever decision someone makes, somewhere there's another universe where the decision was made in the opposite manner. It seems preposterous to me. When you take into account the number of beings that populate our galaxy alone, the notion that any one of them can be individually responsible for creating an entirely separate universe . . . it's ridiculous. Whether I get up in the morning at 0700 or decide to sleep in for a couple more hours because I have a head cold hardly seems the stuff of which universes are sculpted. I doubt that natural law would permit something that unwieldy."

"Ah, but natural law is a curious thing, Captain.

You would be amazed at what it allows and doesn't allow. What seems feasible and what is considered out of bounds."

"Do you mind telling me where you're going with this line of conversation?"

"All right. Let us say, Captain, that your description of the multiverse is something of an oversimplification. On the other hand, decisions that might *seem* minor at the time have a sort of ripple effect. A trivial action can have less than trivial results. What if your decision to sleep in that morning resulted in the deaths of millions?"

"You've lost me."

"Well," said Trelane, "you could sleep in, and while you're in bed, the ship is suddenly attacked. Your second-in-command is in charge instead of you, and he makes some sort of mistake that you might not have made. The result is that your vessel is lost with all hands. Now, let us further say that, two weeks from now, your vessel was responsible for saving the population of a planet by phaser-beaming a geological adjustment during major quakes. But you're not there to do the job. Another vessel is not able to reach them in time. Millions die in a quake. You see the possibilities."

"Okay, okay, fine. I see the possibilities."

"Then see this, Captain. That there are, in fact, thousands upon thousands of universes, of which this is merely one. Will you accept that?"

"Fine, anything to get this over with and you out of my hair."

"I, however, agree with you."

"You agree that you're in my hair?"

"I agree with you that it seems rather unwieldy. It trivializes everything you say and do, because to some degree it doesn't matter. Somewhere there's an equivalent version of you who is handling things differently, so it eliminates the need for decision making. This multiverse business should be dispensed with. Now . . . here's where we come to the part that relates specifically to why you're so sad and wretched."

"Oh, good," said Jack Crusher. "I was getting bored out of my mind waiting for it."

"You see, Jack . . . the business about alternate choices and such? That does not apply to you."

"You mean all of this has been moot? Oh joy."

Abruptly Trelane turned on him and spoke with startling ferocity. "I think it would behoove you, *Captain,* to stow your smart remarks and insouciant attitude. This carries more weight than you can possibly realize."

"And why is that?"

"Because in all of the multiverses that coexist, one with the other, separated by boundaries thinner than you could possibly conceive, your actions are not mirrored by parallel versions of yourself."

Crusher was intrigued in spite of himself. "And why is that?"

"Because you're alone."

"Pardon?"

As if he relished every syllable, Trelane said, "Because you . . . are . . . alone. There are *no* other Jack Crushers in any of the multiverses. Through what is quite likely one of the most remarkable flukes in the multiverse, there is exactly one Jack Crusher in existence. And you look at him every time you stare in a mirror."

"Is that so." He tried to sound flip as he said it, but for some reason he couldn't quite muster the offhand manner that he wanted.

Trelane sensed it and said, "Yes. That is so. You've never known or understood that, of course. Not consciously.

Deep within you, though, you've known. You've understood. You've sensed that you are alone, utterly alone in the multiverse. It explains your ongoing sense of desolation. Your feeling of . . . how to put it? Unworthiness. That's it. I like the sound of that. Your unworthiness, because the forces of order which shaped this mighty multiverse decided that you, Jack Crusher, were such an insignificant, unnecessary, redundant individual that only one of you was required. Think about it, Jack. Thousands of Picards. Thousands of Beverlys. That pathetic wretch, Riker? Thousands of him. That arrogant snot, Worf? Him too. All of them, multiplied over and over. Some of them are significantly different. Some of them are near unrecognizable. But they're there. And you . . . are not. No spares were required. No additionals essential. You, Jack Crusher, are the galactic nonentity. The cosmic fifth wheel. The multiverse, in all its permutations, has done just fine without you. In your heart of hearts, you know this. In your heart of hearts you feel unworthy, and have always felt that way. And now, at last, thanks to me"—he thumped his chest proudly—"you understand why that is."

Crusher wanted to laugh. He wanted to brush Trelane off. He wanted to slug him, if such were possible. He stopped where he was and wanted to shout at Trelane, "You don't know what you're talking about! You expect me to take your word for anything? I'm supposed to be upset over what might or might not be in some theoretical opposing universes? If this is the best you can do, Trelane, you might as well push off and bother someone else because it's not playing here. Not at all."

He said none of that, however.

"You've got . . . you've got one hell of an imagination," Crusher told him.

"Quite true," said Trelane. "I can imagine things that you couldn't even begin to grasp. This, however, is not one of those fevered imaginings."

"And may I ask just what precisely my status is in those other universes? Was I of such insignificance that I wasn't even born?"

"Oh, not at all," said Trelane. "You were born. And then you died. Killed, while under command of your great friend, Captain Jean-Luc Picard."

Crusher tried not to give any sign that he was disconcerted by the flat statement. "Oh really."

"Yes. Killed while on an away mission. A fairly brutal, painful death actually. It's a shame you missed it."

Jack could not think of anything to say. He desperately wanted to disbelieve Trelane. He wanted to laugh in his face, sniff disdainfully, spit at him, kick him in the shins . . . something, no matter how childish, to indicate his utter contempt for this creature. To show that he did not care what Trelane said, because it was most likely a lie. And even if it wasn't a lie, there was nothing to be learned from it. Nothing to be gained. If he was dead elsewhere, then so what? Hell, if he was dead in every elsewhere throughout infinity, so what? He was still there. He, Jack Crusher, still survived, and the rest of them could go burn.

None of which did anything to warm the chill feeling that passed through him.

And, as if he could sense it, Trelane said, "What's that Earth expression? 'Someone just stepped on my grave.' That's it, isn't it."

"I don't care what you say," Crusher said icily, drawing himself up, reaching into himself for reserves of emotional strength. Dammit, he would not let this sadistic little monster confuse him or disorient him.

He did not . . . could not . . . know of the manipulative abilities at Trelane's disposal. Could not know of the chaotic traits raging through him that were enabling Trelane to manipulate the probabilities of certain events, the likelihood that people would react in particular ways that would benefit him. Could not know that, in addition to trying to overcome his own inner demons, he was also unconsciously battling the paranormal manipulative abilities of Trelane.

Ultimately, he did not have a chance. But he couldn't know that, either.

Trelane took on an air of outrage, as if he himself were mortified on Crusher's behalf over the fate that had overtaken him, again and again, throughout the multiverse. "It was an abominable circumstance, really. Especially when one considers the reason for it."

"Reason?" was all Jack was able to get out.

"Yes, that's right. The reason. What, have you not figured it out?"

"No," Jack said, his voice low and hoarse. "Perhaps you should explain it to me."

"Right through here. You'll be able to explain it to yourself."

Crusher looked in confusion at where Trelane was indicating. "That's Picard's quarters. What in Picard's quarters is going to make this clear to me?"

Trelane merely stood there and pointed, his arm outstretched, one finger waggling slightly. For some reason, Crusher was reminded of *A Christmas Carol,* with Trelane cast as the ominous, frightening Ghost of Christmas Yet-to-Come.

"Why should I invade Jean-Luc's privacy?" demanded Crusher. "What's the point in that?"

"He will never know."

"That doesn't make it all right."

Now Trelane stepped closer to him, and in his eyes was a blazing fury that threatened to consume Crusher's soul. "And what he did to you wasn't 'all right' either. You are an explorer, Jack Crusher. If you would be an explorer . . . if you would be a *man* . . . then learn that which you are afraid to learn. Learn that which terrifies you, which keeps you awake at night, which gnaws at your mind and rots your heart. Learn, if you have the mettle to handle it."

Crusher moved toward Trelane, thrusting his face into that of the omnipotent being. "I can take whatever you can dish out," he told him. Then he turned and entered Picard's quarters.

There he stood in silent witness, watching his best friend in the world in the throes of passionate lovemaking with the woman whom he had never truly been able to excise from his heart.

He felt the world hazing out around him. He wanted to run from the room. He wanted to hurl himself into the cold depths of space. He wanted to be anywhere except right there, right then, and yet he could not look away.

Jack watched as Beverly did the things to Picard that she had once done to him. Whisper those words that had once caressed his ears alone. Those soft sighs, the little gasps . . .

. . . all for Picard. For Picard.

Trelane was next to him now, and whispering softly, "You are familiar with David and Bathsheba, are you not? From your old Earth Bible? The king who coveted another man's wife, and so he made certain that the woman's husband—a soldier—was placed in a position where he would most likely die in battle."

Crusher was shaking his head. Whether it was in disbelief of what Trelane was saying or in denial of what his own eyes were telling him, even he could not have said.

"In every other timeline, they're together," said Trelane, trying to muster as much compassion as he could. "They were meant to be together. You were in the way, Jack. Always in the way. The wheels of Fate are great, unyielding cogs, Jack, and they grind up whatever gets in their way. In this case, that was you. Now somehow . . . in this universe . . . you slipped between the wheels. You didn't even know you did it. You outwitted Fate, Jack. That is a great feat. But the fates will not be denied."

"Shut up," whispered Jack.

"How is this for demanding? In every other universe, not only did you die . . . but your son, Wesley, lived. A fine, strapping lad. But not here. Not here because, since you lived . . . Fate had to find some way to make certain that Jean-Luc and Beverly were together."

"Shut up."

"So here, your son was targeted. Your son was sacrificed on the altar of destiny so that you could live but, once again, Beverly and Jean-Luc could be together . . ."

"Shut up!" Jack shouted in words that did not reach the ears of the two ardent lovers in front of him. He spun and swung his fist and, miracle of miracles, despite their mutual intangibility, he nailed Trelane squarely on the jaw.

Trelane sailed out through the door, landing out in the corridor, and Jack charged through the door after him, grabbing him by the front of his black judicial robe and hauling him to his feet.

"Why are you doing this, *why are you doing this!*"

"Because I like you, Jack!" Trelane shot back. "Damn you, damn me, I find I actually like you! And I thought that you, the only Jack Crusher in the vast endless thing that is creation, deserved better than to live his life in ignorance." He pushed Crusher back and then stood there, arms wide, offering no resistance. "You would pummel me for that? Pummel away then. Those who bring knowledge have always been treated badly, throughout human history. The legends abound. Strapped to rocks to have their entrails plucked out. Excommunicated. Drawn and quartered. Burned at the stake. Crucified. A dazzling variety of means you've developed, in fact and fiction, to dispose of those who tell you that to which you would rather be blind. Wars have been declared, genocide committed, all in the name of ignorance. You fancy yourselves gatherers of knowledge, but as soon as you encounter that which makes you uncomfortable, you'll do whatever you can to dispose of it, won't you. Hit me then, Captain Jack Crusher. Strike me down, if it would please you. I offer no resistance. Why should I? Ultimately you can do nothing to hurt me, and all the violence in the world cannot erase the truth of what I have shown you."

Crusher stood in front of him, fists poised. "You . . . are an evil creature," he said.

"That is subjective," replied Trelane. "But I submit this to you, my dear Captain Crusher . . . I have never lied to you. Can you say the same of your best friend?"

And he vanished in a burst of light.

Crusher stood there in the corridor, leaning against a wall, and found that he was unable to breathe. He had to force his lungs to start drawing air, make the conscious effort. He had to force himself to live.

A couple of crewmen walked toward him and stopped, staring at him. "Captain?" one of them asked.

They were looking at him, addressing him. With

Trelane's disappearance, Crusher's intangibility had gone with him. There went the one shred of hope that he'd been clinging to up until this moment; namely, that it had been a dream.

Furthermore, Crusher was standing there wearing his pajamas. His mind still in turmoil over what he had seen, it was everything he could do to pull himself together enough to say, "Just having a sleepless night."

"Oh," said the crewman.

Crusher made his way back to his quarters and lay down on his bed, praying that somehow, by some miracle, either sleep or death would claim him.

Neither did.

2.

It was not quite morning as Deanna Riker heard movement through the bedroom door. She had slept on the couch that night, for Will had been so tentative around her that she did not want him to feel threatened. Nevertheless, it had been agonizing for her. She had wanted nothing more than to hold him, to tell him that everything was going to be all right, to remind him of the life that they had shared and, hopefully, would share again.

But every time her husband, her beloved Imzadi, had looked at her, it had been with fear and confusion. She understood the fear, of course. Deep within him was the knowledge of everything they had been, and everything they had meant to each other. So overwhelming and powerful were those feelings that they were frightening to him because he no longer had the mental tools to handle them.

She had to use every discipline she had ever learned to deal with her husband's tentative mental state.

The one on whom it had been hardest was Tommy, of

course. He had wanted his father to be everything that he had imagined he would be. Instead he was little more than a confused shell of what he had been. Riker had watched Tommy warily, listened to the boy when he spoke, but seemed unwilling . . . or unable . . . to give anything in return.

At least he was speaking in coherent sentences. That was something. But they were generally only a few words at a time, and each was brimming with uncertainty.

In the other bedroom Tommy was asleep. She could have slept with him, of course, but she preferred to be closer to her husband. So she had opted for the couch.

He sounded awake now, though. In addition to the sound of his movements, she also sensed things from the other room as well. Confusion, uncertainty . . . but it was focused this time, rather than the free-floating anxiety that she had been perceiving up until this point.

She went to the bedroom door and knocked tentatively. "Will?" she called softly. "May I come in?"

There was no response, and she chose to interpret that as an affirmative. She touched the release code and the door slid open.

Riker was sitting on the edge of the bed, naked. He was holding something across his lap and staring at it. Deanna recognized it immediately for what it was.

A Starfleet uniform. His, to be specific, with the appropriate designations of rank in place. She had deliberately left it in the closet in hopes that he would do exactly this: Find it. Study it. Become comfortable with it.

The uniform had been a large part of what made him what he was. Perhaps it now held the key to making him that again.

"It's very nice," said Deanna. She sat near him on the

bed, and fought down the impulse to run her hands over his body. "Do you like it?"

He nodded slowly. He was feeling the fabric, studying it, turning it over and over.

"Would you like to put it on?" she asked.

"Whose is it?" he asked.

"It's yours."

"No."

"All right," she said readily. "It's a present, from me to you."

He looked so forlorn, so lost, that it was all that Deanna could do not to weep. She was a woman of peace, a gentle woman, a scholar and student of the mind. Violence was not her way. Yet she was appalled to realize that, if given the opportunity to meet the monster that had done this to her husband, she would gladly have strangled him. Given a phaser she would have shot him, a knife she would have gutted him. All that was going through her mind at that moment was a dazzling array of violent images, and that was of no use. That would do her husband absolutely no good.

"Will," she said, and reached for him.

He slid back on the bed, his feet shoving the blankets toward her as his back went up against the far wall. He kept the uniform clutched around him, and regarded her with that same frightened, desperate look that she had come to know and dread.

She rose from the bed and said softly, "I'll . . . I'll be outside if you need me."

He never took his eyes off her as she walked back into the next room.

She made certain to keep her sobs muffled.

3.

Captain Jean-Luc Picard had performed his morning ablutions—showered, shaved, dressed—and was ready to face the day.

But instead he sat at the desk in his quarters, his personal log activated, trying to determine exactly what to say in regards to his concerns about Guinan.

First she had come to him complaining that there had been some sort of peculiar change in the environment. That the *Enterprise* was a war vessel, that there were no children. The ordinarily unflappable woman of Picard's long acquaintance had never been that off-kilter before.

Yet when he had gone to her to pursue the matter further, she had disavowed any knowledge of the encounter.

All the possibilities as to how it could have occurred had been examined and explored, and the fact was that there was still no solid explanation. Picard had quietly ordered a shipwide search in the event that there was an impostor lurking about, but nothing out of the ordinary had turned up. Guinan swore that neither Q nor Trelane was in the vicinity.

What the hell was going on?

"Bridge to Captain Picard," came Data's voice.

"Picard here."

"We have established orbit around Terminus, Captain. Dr. Martinez's associates are there, and are most concerned about her condition."

"I don't blame them. Check with Dr. Crusher for an update on her status, Mr. Data. I'll be up shortly."

"Yes, sir."

Picard shut off his personal log, deciding to leave the business of an entry for later. He had not slept particularly well. Odd dreams had invaded him, including a few about—of all people—Beverly Crusher. "Odd" wasn't the word for those dreams. "Intense" was more appropriate, and "erotic" would have been pretty much dead-on accurate. He was grateful that that mind-reading link was long gone or he'd have a *lot* to answer for.

He rose and went to the full-length mirror, to make certain that his uniform was smooth and presentable. He nodded approvingly, ran his hands down the front to straighten his uniform.

In the mirror, he made the same gesture . . .

. . . a split second later.

It was a little thing, a tiny, insignificant thing. But it was enough to catch his attention, and he did a double take even as he was in the process of turning away from the mirror.

He faced the mirror again, his eyes narrowing suspiciously. His reflection did the precise same thing, acted in perfect mirror imitation of him. For one moment Picard thought that perhaps, just perhaps, he was losing his mind.

He smoothed his uniform again. The reflection matched him accurately. Still, to play it absolutely safe—for these were odd times aboard the *Enterprise*—he ran his hands back up his uniform. If anyone had been watching, they would have thought that he was out of his . . .

. . . uniform.

The uniform was different. In the mirror, it was different. Slightly more formfitting, he could see that now. The collar was . . .

. . . the pips.

His mirror image did the same thing as he fingered the pips on his collar.

In the mirror, he was wearing the insignia of a commander. He was of a lower rank.

It was impossible. Completely, utterly impossible.

He closed his eyes, shook his head, and then opened them again.

The reflection of Picard-as-commander was gone.

In its place was Picard-as-captain, which was the first thing that Picard noticed because, naturally, he was looking at the collar where the pips were.

Then his gaze wandered to the rest of his reflection, and again the world seemed to tilt around him.

Again the uniform was different. More flared, almost militaristic . . .

(What had Guinan said? An *Enterprise* with a more military cast to it? Everyone with sidearms . . .)

His eyes flickered to his reflection's waist and yes, damn, there it was, the sidearm, just as Guinan had said.

His reflection was staring back at him, his own shock and amazement mirrored (naturally) in his face.

"What the hell?" he muttered. "What's happening?" His mirror image was mouthing the same words, and Picard fairly shouted, *"What's happening?"*

He placed his hands flat against the mirror, as if thinking that he could shove his way in.

The door chimed behind him. "Captain," came the voice of Worf. "Are you all right?"

His head snapped around and he called, "Mr. Worf! Get in here!"

Worf charged in, coming so quickly that the door didn't open quite fast enough and he shoved it to hasten it. He was tense, ready to launch himself against whatever it might be that was assaulting his captain.

"Look!" said Picard, and he pointed at the mirror.

His own reflection was pointing back at him. Uniform, gesture . . . everything was perfectly matched. There was nothing remotely odd about it.

Worf stared at the mirror. Then he looked at Picard. It was clear that what he very much wanted to do was to ask Picard what in the world was on his mind. But he felt that, as head of security, he should be able to figure it out on his own. He scrutinized the mirror uncomprehendingly for a long moment, and then he went over to it and straightened it slightly.

"Is that better, sir?" he asked.

"The mirror wasn't crooked, Mr. Worf. I saw . . . something in there . . ."

"Other than yourself, sir?"

Picard nodded slowly. "Mr. Worf . . . be on the alert."

"Yes, sir." He paused. "For what?"

Picard gave the only answer he could. "For anything."

Worf nodded. "I always am, sir."

4.

Tasha Yar nodded. "I always am, sir."

Commander Jean-Luc Picard nodded in appreciation. Then he looked back at his mirror suspiciously. What in the world had just happened? One moment he'd been looking in his mirror, and the next . . .

"Commander?" asked Tasha. "Would you like me to escort you to the bridge?"

"In case I'm waylaid by any more hostile or unpredictable mirrors? I am grateful for the sentiment, Lieutenant." Picard forced a smile. "But I'm sure I can handle this. I'll just make certain to keep my vanity in check."

"All right, sir. If you're certain . . ." Then, satisfied that Picard had the immediate situation under control, she exited into the corridor.

Picard hesitated a moment longer, casting one more suspicious glance in the direction of the mirror. Then he headed toward the turbolift.

He stepped into the lift, and from behind him a voice called, "Hold the lift, please!"

It was a familiar voice, of course . . . that of Captain Crusher. He turned and waited for Jack to catch up.

Crusher was just standing there, however, staring at him. Picard looked at him with curiosity. "Captain, is something wrong?" he asked.

Slowly Crusher walked toward him, and for some reason the entire moment reminded Picard of nothing so much as a shoot-out in the Old West. Briefly he thought of the momentary image he'd seen in the mirror where he was packing a phaser at his side. If he'd had it with him now, he would have had an irresistible impulse to have his hand hovering over the grip.

"Jack?" he said.

Crusher smiled what was definitely a forced grin and said, "Good morning, Number One." He stepped onto the turbolift. "Bridge."

The door slid shut and Crusher studied Picard in a manner that made Picard feel incredibly uncomfortable. There was definitely something up.

"Jack, what's wrong?" he asked.

"Wrong?" echoed Crusher. "Why, there's nothing wrong, Jean-Luc. What gave you that impression?"

"What gave me that impression, Captain, is that you're looking at me as if you're wondering who I am."

"I'm feeling philosophical this morning, Jean-Luc," Crusher said with an undeniable edge to his voice. "Can any of us really know who each other is? In a way, we're all really strangers, aren't we. All of us passing through life. Each of us with our own little fantasies and dark secrets."

"Halt lift," Picard abruptly ordered. The lift slid to a halt between floors. He turned and faced his commander squarely. "Jack, what the hell is going on?"

Crusher raised an eyebrow and made a painfully transparent effort to give Picard a bland look. "Going on? Jean-Luc, what makes you think—"

"Stop it!" Picard thudded his fist against the wall. "What's gotten into you? Are you upset with me about something? Have I offended you in some way? I'd think that you owe me the courtesy of—"

"I *owe* you?" Crusher said incredulously. The lift seemed to fill with the intensity of Crusher's anger. "Commander, I believe that you are out of order. No, I take that back. I *know* you're out of order."

"Jack, I—"

"I did *not* give you permission to speak freely. Nor did I give you permission to halt this turbolift. This is *Captain* Crusher, overriding previous order. Continue to bridge."

The turbolift obediently resumed its journey upward.

"If you have a problem with me," Picard said hotly, "then I wish you would tell me what the devil it is and spare us all some grief."

"Oh, is that what you wish? To be spared grief?" His voice rose, and he fairly shouted, *"Is that what you wish?"*

His fist lashed out. Picard snapped his head to one side automatically, and Crusher missed him clean. His fist smashed with full force into the far wall of the turbolift, and there was an audible crack.

Crusher grabbed his fist in pain, his fingers stretching into a clawlike position. Blood was trickling from the third knuckle of his right hand and he cursed.

Picard was appalled. "Jack—"

"Be quiet, Picard. That is a direct goddamn order, and you will obey it or be court-martialed!"

Picard opened his mouth, but then he saw the fury in Crusher's eyes. He closed his mouth again.

A thought, an unavoidable thought, went through his mind.

He knows. He knows about Beverly and me.

But he couldn't be sure. There was no way at all to be certain, and there was certainly no way to ask. It was the only thing that made sense, but he simply could not bring himself to pose the question.

The turbolift door slid open, the bridge in front of them. Picard stepped out and turned to face Crusher.

"I'm going to sickbay," said Crusher, holding up the hand slightly as if it were necessary to remind Picard of the reason for having to go down there. "You have the conn . . . Number One." The door hissed shut again.

Slowly Picard headed toward the command chair, and he sank into it. The planet Terminus turned peacefully below them. Above their pole was the spatial rift.

He had to warn Beverly. There was no way around it. Use the communicator, obviously. But he could not very well stand in the middle of the bridge and converse. Walking into the captain's ready room would be a definite breach of protocol with the captain not around. He could, however, talk in the conference lounge. It might cause a curious glance, heading into the lounge when there was no one else around. Curious glances he could live with.

He started to rise and head for the conference lounge when Data suddenly spoke up.

"Commander," Data said. "I have just detected a shift in the gravimetric field of the temporal rift."

Picard paused in mid-rise. "And?"

Data turned to face him.

"It's getting larger, sir."

In the turbolift, Jack Crusher flexed his injured hand, grunting in pain. The blood was flowing freely, and he hoped to God that he had not broken the knuckle.

But with the pain came clarity of thought, and deter-

333

mination to do what had to be done. He felt the fury boiling within him, an anger stoked by forces he did not even understand.

He was going to go down to sickbay and do more than just get his hand attended to. He was going to have it out with Beverly once and for all.

He was captain of the *Enterprise,* and he had surrounded himself with traitors.

It was a situation that would not, could not, be tolerated.

5.

Dr. Beverly Crusher looked down sympathetically at Professor Martinez. The woman had healed remarkably well, but Beverly was still resistant to the notion of moving her quite so soon. It was technically feasible, certainly, but . . .

Still, it was worth asking.

"Andrea," she said softly to the woman who lay on the medlab bed, the bioregenerative field humming gently. Her alpha-wave readings seemed to indicate that she was awake, but her eyes were still swelled to slits, so it was difficult to tell.

"Yes, Doctor," came the raspy reply.

"I'm told we're in orbit around Terminus. A number of your colleagues are there, and interested in talking to you about your observations of the Ompet Oddity. However . . ."

"However, you wonder if I'm in shape to receive visitors. Or if I'm even interested in leaving the relative security of sickbay."

Beverly smiled. "Can't slip anything past you," she said.

Martinez considered it a moment. "To be honest, I'd like another twenty-four hours just to heal. I don't want to throw the *Enterprise*'s entire schedule out of whack, however."

"Tell you what," said Beverly. "Why don't I check with the captain and see if it would be okay with him."

Martinez would have nodded if she'd had the strength to move her head. "I would appreciate that."

Beverly tapped her comm badge. "Crusher to Captain," she said.

"Picard here. Go ahead."

The doors to sickbay hissed open at that moment, and Beverly paused in her transmission to see who the newcomer was.

Her eyes went wide, and all the blood drained from her face.

He was standing there, big as life, older than when she last saw him . . . except . . .

. . . except she'd last seen him at his funeral.

She felt her brain starting to shut down and she forced it back into operation, her medical training clicking in and making her notice that his right hand was covered with blood.

"Doctor," came Picard's voice over her comm badge, sounding puzzled. "Are you there?"

"So," said Jack Crusher, and the sound of his voice startled her as much as his physical presence, if not more. At least when she was staring at him she could think that she was having some sort of hallucination. But the voice lent it weight, reality.

"Jack . . . ?" she whispered.

He seemed unaware of her total shock. He gestured to

her comm badge. "He trying to warn you I'd be down? Is that it?"

She started to tremble, a scream endeavoring to claw its way up from her diaphragm and reach her mouth.

He approached her, his entire body tense with barely contained fury. "All right then, Beverly. We're having it out, right here, right now. And don't shake your head at me!" he told her, because that was what she was doing. Her eyes were like saucers, her skin the color of curdled milk. If he'd not been so far gone with his own concerns, he would have realized that he was seeing a woman who was far beyond alarm over the prospect of an uncovered affair. Beverly was clearly petrified.

"You . . . you . . ." she hissed.

"Beverly, what's going on down there?" demanded Picard's voice.

"Butt out, Picard!" snapped Jack Crusher. "This is between Beverly and me!" He faced her and grabbed her by the shoulders, and started to say her name when finally, finally, the scream found its way up. It started small, just the slightest rasp from between her constricted vocal cords. Once the first noise was out, though, it was as if a cap had been removed from a volcano. Beverly screamed, and it was full-throated and unrestrained and as terrified a sound as Jack Crusher had ever heard from the throat of the woman he loved.

He shook her then, trying to get control of the situation. "Beverly! Shut up! Listen to me!"

And she shrieked at him, "You're dead! *You're dead, oh my God, oh God, you're DEAD!*"

It took several seconds for her words to penetrate his jealousy-clouded mind, but when they finally managed to get through, he recoiled as if he'd shoved his hands into a nest of ants. He backed up as Beverly continued to scream, and then Trelane's words came back to him, and he understood, he understood it all. . . .

He bolted from the sickbay, dashing into the corridor and not waiting to see that Beverly Crusher had fainted dead away.

6.

In Ten-Forward, Guinan pitched back against the bar, grabbing her head. She emitted a brief shriek of alarm, overwhelmed by the chaos that assaulted her, and fell into the blackness of oblivion.

In Ten-Forward, Guinan pitched back against the bar, grabbing her head. She emitted a brief shriek of alarm, overwhelmed by the chaos that assaulted her, and fell into the blackness of oblivion.

In Ten-Forward, hostess Caryn Johnson poured another drink and smiled at a pair of incoming patrons.

7.

Commander Riker was heading for the bridge when his comm badge signaled him. He tapped it and said, "Riker here."

"Will," came Deanna's voice, "I . . ."

She sounded confused. "Counselor? What's wrong?"

"I'm not sure," she said. "In my mind, I feel like I'm hearing . . . echoes."

"Echoes?" he said skeptically.

"Like voices, calling to me. Could you . . . ?"

It was a measure of the relationship that they had that Deanna, when faced with an uncertain feeling, would call upon Riker first for help. Not Beverly Crusher, and not Guinan, but Riker.

"On my way," said Riker, and he headed for Deanna's quarters.

On the bridge, Picard heard a male voice say, "Butt out, Picard! This is between Beverly and me!" Heads snapped

around from all over the bridge crew, for no one ever . . .
ever . . . addressed the captain with such clear contempt.

That voice . . .

Even as Picard allowed his surprise at the man's insubordinate tone to register, he realized that there was something there vaguely familiar. Something that he couldn't
put his finger on. He'd heard the voice before; it seemed so
familiar. . . .

Picard was on his feet, Worf issuing an immediate
security alert, when suddenly Beverly's screams came over
the comm badge. Now Picard was heading for the turbolift
when he heard the man's voice trying to say something that
he couldn't make out over Beverly's panicked screams, and
then he heard Beverly saying over and over again, *"You're
dead! You're dead!"*

And it clicked.

"Oh my God," he whispered. "Jack."

8.

Deanna and Tommy watched as Will emerged slowly, tentatively from the bedroom, wearing the Starfleet uniform.

It had actually been Tommy who had managed to convince his father to try on the uniform. His entreaties had been so fervent, so cajoling, so encouraging, that finally Will Riker had actually said, "Okay. Okay." And he did it with a sort of paternal sigh that made Deanna's heart sing. It was all she could do not to clap her hands in joy when Will acquiesced.

Now he stood there, his shoulders still slumped, his bearing very uncertain—nothing like the proud, confident young man who had swept Deanna off her feet those many years ago. But it was a start. It was a start.

"You look wonderful, Will," she said.

He held up his hands, looked at the red-clad sleeves. (They had started with the arms first.)

"Will?" said Deanna cautiously. Something was wrong. She sensed it.

(They had started with the arms. He was remembering now. They had tied him with his hands over his head and just left him to hang there for hours, hours turning to days. And they had his head strapped back so that there was nowhere for him to look but up, up at his red-sleeved arms, and there had been pain until the arms went numb, and then the fingers went white. And every so often they would come around and beat him on the arms to register the degree of pain he was still able to feel as the circulation left them.)

Will Riker grunted inarticulately, clawing at the uniform arms.

"Will!" said Deanna in genuine alarm.

"Dad!" shouted Tommy, and he ran toward his father and grabbed him by the arms.

That was an error. Will Riker shoved his son, shoved him so hard that he sent him flying across the room like a poker chip. With an alarmed cry Deanna ran to Tommy, giving Will more than enough time to bolt out the door.

"Are you all right?! Tommy, are you—" She was trying to pull him from the corner where he had landed, endeavoring to check over his body to make certain that he was not injured.

In humiliation and rage, Tommy cried out, "He hates me!"

"He doesn't!" Deanna said, holding him close. "He doesn't, I swear . . ."

"He does! *He hates me!*"

"He doesn't hate you! He doesn't even really know you yet, it's going to take time, I told you . . ."

"You said that, you keep saying that," said Tommy, trying to choke back the tears. "When is it going to happen? When . . ."

The door slid open and Deanna looked up.

Will was standing there.

His demeanor had changed completely. He was standing with his shoulders squared, his manner confident albeit slightly perplexed as he stared at her. "Deanna?" he said.

"Will?" Slowly she got to her feet, Tommy still trembling slightly in the corner. Clearly, though, he was curious about the sudden change that had come over his father. "Will . . . do you know who I am?"

He stared at her in bafflement. "Of course I know who you are. Are you joking? My God," and his eyes went wide as she approached him. "Your hair . . . what happened to your hair?"

She clapped her hands in joy. She couldn't believe it, but the empathic feelings she was receiving from him verified his words. He knew her. He *knew* her. Her mind touched his, and the word soared from her mind to his . . . *Imzadi* . . .

He blinked in surprise, and out of reflex, he felt the word back to her.

She went to him, took his face in her hands and kissed him, the tears rolling down her cheeks, soaking his face as well.

Automatically he started to respond, and then it was as if he were suddenly regaining control of himself. He pulled his head away from her and said, "What's happened to you? What's going on? Who's that?"

But even before he spoke, she had realized that something was wrong. His body was wrong. It was full and muscular. When she had first seen his bare body, she had had to choke back a sob as she saw the crisscrossing of scars all over his once perfect skin. But her hands were on his back now, and it was as smooth and brawny as it had been years ago when he had left her.

His confusion as to the boy's identity, meantime, only

344

confirmed what Tommy was already certain of. "I told you he hates me!" he said. "He hates his own son!"

"My son!" Riker couldn't believe what he was hearing. "Deanna, what the hell is happening around here?! Who is this boy? Why is your hair going gray? What's going on—?"

Only her long practice saved her as once more Deanna sought out the calm center of her spirit. As insane as it seemed, she had a strong feeling she already knew what the man in front of her would say when next she spoke. "I," she said slowly, "am Deanna Troi Riker. Wife of William T. Riker. That is our son . . . Tommy."

Riker blanched. "What . . . ?" he whispered.

Now Tommy was slowly approaching him, his initial ire dissipating as he noticed something. While his mother was caught up in turbulent emotion and conflicting information, Tommy the Starfleet buff was picking up on minutiae. "Ma . . . he's wearing the pips of a full commander. That's not what he had on before. Ma, what's going—?"

And then something turned over in Tommy's mind. Something clicked, and he said, "You were in my dream."

They had stumbled too far over into a realm that Riker was quickly sensing was beyond his understanding. "Listen to me," he said. "Stay here. Don't move. Don't go anywhere. Do you understand what I'm saying?"

"Yes," said Deanna, choosing not to voice the several dozen questions that were all tumbling around in her head at once.

He tapped his comm badge. "Riker to bridge," he said.

"Data here," replied Data.

"Where's the captain?" said Riker, surprised.

"He is attending to an emergency in sickbay. An unidentified person apparently attacked Dr. Crusher."

"That might not be the only unidentified person around

here today," said Riker, not taking his eyes off Deanna and the boy. "I'll meet him there." He pointed at them once more and repeated, "Stay here."

He headed out the door. As it slid shut behind him, Tommy looked up at Deanna and said in confusion, "I thought the doctor's name was Howard and the captain's name was Crusher. I'm confused."

"You're not the only one," said Deanna.

Commander Riker moved down the corridor at a brisk clip, heading in the direction of sickbay. He turned a corner . . .

Worf was coming from the other direction, and Riker gaped at him. He was dressed in full Klingon armor. His hair was longer and unkempt, and there was a wild and desperate look in his eyes.

"Mr. Worf!" said Riker sharply. "Has everyone around here gone insane?"

Worf was crouched, gawking at Riker as if he were a sideshow freak. He seemed to come to a decision in a matter of seconds.

"You're not him," Worf said. "It's a trick!"

Riker didn't like the edge in the Klingon's voice one bit. "Now, listen . . ." He put up his hands.

Worf's hand was at his belt, and a moment later he'd snapped open the side blades of a *d'k'tahg* knife. "Next time you attempt a disguise," he growled, "try to do a better job of it. Your Riker disguise would be perfect . . . had you not tortured him!"

"Tortured—?!"

"As it is, you will pay for your shabby deceit . . . with your life!"

He lunged toward Riker, blade flashing in the light.

346

9.

When Beverly Crusher opened her eyes, Captain Picard was looking down at her in concern. Several security guards, including Worf, were in the doorway.

She grabbed his arm, squeezed it frantically. "Jack . . ." she whispered. "I saw . . . you'll think I'm losing my mind, my God, maybe I am losing my mind . . ."

"You're not. I heard him," said Picard. He turned to his men and said, "Mr. Worf, return to the bridge. I want you on station there, just in case of . . . just in case," he said. "The rest of you are to look for a former Starfleet officer named Jack Crusher." He kept his voice steady, trying to sound as matter-of-fact about the entire thing as possible. "Computer records will list him as deceased, but either they are inaccurate, or else someone is engaging in an ill-advised masquerade. Get his likeness from the computer and circulate it throughout all security teams. If he's spotted, I want him."

"Aye, sir," said Worf, as he gestured for the teams to get

moving. Moments later the sickbay was relatively back to normal, although the other doctors and nurses kept stealing sidelong glances at Beverly.

"I have never," she whispered, "never been so frightened in my entire life. Not ever."

"It's all right."

"I thought I was dead."

"He wouldn't hurt you."

"No, I mean I thought I was dead." She actually managed a nervous laugh that sounded like borderline hysteria. "That's when you see dead people, after all. When you're dead yourself. It made sense. Oh God, Jean-Luc, it was . . ."

He folded her into his arms. "It's all right," he said tenderly. "It's all right. We'll find him. We'll get this entire confusing mess straightened out."

"Please," she whispered. "Please . . . tell me what happened . . . ?"

"I don't know."

Picard

The voice was in his head, and Picard snapped around, looking for its origin. Beverly, who was just beginning to calm down, looked nervous again. "Jean-Luc? What—?"

Picard, the voice repeated with more urgency, and this time, Picard recognized it.

"Q," he said. He didn't know whether to be incredibly furious or unbelievably relieved. "Q! Is this your doing?"

Oh, do be quiet, Jean-Luc, came the voice with a measure of the old insufferable arrogance, a high-handed tone that Picard would never have thought he'd actually be happy to hear. *It's starting.*

"What's starting?" Picard was looking everywhere, but there was absolutely no sign of—

No.

There.

In a corner of the sickbay, there was the faintest haze . . . an outline, as if Q were being photographed through a thick gauze.

"There he is!" shouted Picard, and pointed.

Beverly looked where he was indicating. "I don't see anything," she told him.

"He's right there!"

No I'm not, Picard. I'm not there yet. I'm still out of phase with your universe. It's taking me a while to remember how to get back into phase. It's like your suffering a stroke. You know what it is you want to do, but you have to relearn the motor functions.

"What the hell is happening around here?"

Oh, it's fairly simple, really. Trelane is destroying the entire universe. Severing the barriers that separate dimensions from one another. He wants to introduce everything into one plane, all at the same time, all overlapping, and sending all concerned parties into a chaos-driven, berserk fight for survival that will take all life as we know it and turn it into an endless celebration of warfare. There was a pause. *Other than that, how is your day going?*

"Damn you, Q—!"

I've been damned already once, Picard. It took me ages to get back. So I'm not interested in a repeat performance. Listen to me, Picard. Listen carefully. It's going to be all up to you. You're an Enterprise *captain. You're the only type of person he'll care about. You're everything he'll want to destroy. And he'll do it. He'll do it because he's completely insane. Prepare yourself, Picard. It's not going to be easy. But then, when is it ever, eh?*

349

Then the voice dropped out of his head, and the hazy image in the corner of sickbay vanished as well.

In a low, unsteady tone, Beverly said, "What . . . what was that all about?"

Picard looked at her. "Fate of the universe."

"Again?" said Beverly.

10.

At that moment, Lieutenant Barclay ran into sickbay, cradling Guinan's unmoving body in his arms. "Help her!" he cried out.

At that moment, Lieutenant Barclay ran into sickbay, cradling Guinan's unmoving body in his arms. "Help her!" he cried out.

11.

Captain Jean-Luc Picard had had a rough morning. He went over it in his mind as he rode the turbolift up to the bridge.

First there was that queer business with the mirror. He had seen two other versions of himself . . . one in which he was a commander, and another in which his uniform style was different, and he was not packing a sidearm. As if to reassure himself once more, he patted the phaser at his side, glad for the customary feeling of security it gave him.

He found his thoughts returning inevitably to the *Enterprise* NCC-1701-C that he had been forced to scuttle. The specter of lost opportunities hung over him, like a shroud.

There was, of course, the surface notion of having to dispose of a ship that might have been useful in the war with the Klingons. The harsh truth was that, in all likelihood, one more ship . . . and an old one at that . . . would probably not have done anything to turn the tide.

But there was the other great loss. The notion that, had the *Enterprise*-C succeeded in its last known mission, battling to save a Klingon colony, then the war might have been averted. Or if the ship had been known to be destroyed in the fight, that too would have been something the Klingons might have respected. As it was, the disappearance of the 1701-C had simply been one of space's odder mysteries. A mystery that had now been solved. Not that that was going to make a tremendous lot of difference in the way that things had turned out.

He thought of the uniforms of his other selves that he had seen in the mirror, or at least had thought he had seen since he had chalked it off to stress. In both cases the uniforms looked to be from a more peaceful time. Oh, maybe it was his imagination working overtime. But the lines had been simpler, the cut less militaristic.

He wondered what his life would be like if he lived in such a universe. A universe where the *Enterprise* and her formidable equipment could be put to more benign use than war. Science, exploration . . . those were the sorts of fantasies he entertained in his more private moments.

Fantasies, however, were all they were, and ever would be.

The turbolift door slid open and he started to step out onto the bridge.

The first thing he saw was a Klingon. A Klingon in a Fleet uniform.

Jean-Luc Picard was just about the fastest draw in Starfleet. It was a reputation he was rather proud of. It had been hard earned, and it was accurate.

The Klingon was just turning to face him when Picard had his phaser in his hand. Time seemed to elongate as the Klingon registered surprise in seeing the captain.

Picard fired, phaser set on kill.

The Klingon lunged over the railing, dropping just under the phaser blast. Picard swung his arm, tracking the

Klingon, who then dropped just out of range behind the command chair.

Picard had no time to see anything else. The bridge had been captured, and his only imperative now was to get away. "Deck fourteen!" he shouted, which was where the armory was located.

The turbolift doors slammed shut. It was only after the lift whisked Picard away that his mind started to develop the mental snapshot he'd taken of the bridge. Only then did he realize that something looked different somehow. But no . . . he must have imagined it. Things had happened so quickly, and his attention had been elsewhere.

All he knew for sure was that, as long as he remained free, the *Starship Enterprise* had a fighting chance. And if he could get to the armory, then he would give whatever Klingons were aboard ship a fight they would never forget.

12.

On the planet Terminus below . . . on every planet Terminus below . . . Trelane stood with his arms stretched wide. A master musician standing on his podium, attentive to the completion of his latest, greatest masterpiece.

"Ladies and gentlemen," he called out to the emptiness around him. "I welcome you to Terminus! The world whose name means . . . The End. The end, and the beginning." He turned in place, accepting the accolades from the cheering hordes that only he could hear. "I am the beginning, and the end! The alpha and the omega! It ends with us and begins with us!"

The glory of the Heart of the Storm surged through him, and as it manipulated him, so did he manipulate others. The god of war, the lord of tempests, master of all. Unbeatable. Unstoppable.

The threads dangled before him. He could see them with utter clarity. The threads not just of universes, but those that were attached to individuals. It took absolutely no effort to tweak them, pull them, make those who were bound at the other end dance to the tune that Trelane was strumming.

Yes. Tune. That was it. That was what the moment needed.

He gestured, and his beloved harpsichord appeared. The instrument glittered in the light of the sun of Terminus. Far overhead, the temporal whirlpool swirled. So much more than just a whirlpool, so much more potent than the time-shifting rifts that he had dabbled in before.

This . . . this was a direct pipeline to the Heart of the Storm. The power fed through to him, kept him focused.

He sat at his harpsichord, took the liberty of cracking his knuckles with a sound that was like thunder on the horizon. Then he brought his hands down to the keys and began to play.

Reality danced to his tune.

13.

Commander Riker backed up quickly as Worf came at him. An angry Klingon under the best of circumstances was not something most people would want to face. Considering that Worf had apparently gone berserk, that only made it worse. As he moved, he hit his comm badge and yelled, "Riker to security!"

Harpsichord music came over the badge. It was a rather sprightly tune that Riker might actually have been able to enjoy, if the circumstances at the moment weren't quite so dire.

The knife flashed and Riker tried to spin out of the way. He was only partly successful, and the blade sliced across his triceps, drawing blood. Riker grunted, turned quickly on his heel. Worf, with practiced ease, flipped the knife from one hand to the other and charged again.

Riker blocked the knife thrust, banging Worf's arm to one side, and then driving the heel of his palm into the Klingon's face. He smashed him squarely on the nose, and Worf roared in anger. The Klingon threw himself against

Riker, still clutching the knife, slamming him against the wall. It took all Riker's strength to stop the knife from descending into his heart as the two men struggled, one up against the other, their bodies trembling from the exertion. No words were said, no noise other than the grunts from the strain of the battle.

Riker managed to snare his leg around the back of Worf's. Seizing the momentary leverage, he shoved hard against the Klingon, and Worf stumbled back. He hit the ground, Riker on top of him, and the impact knocked the knife loose, sending it skittering across the floor.

Where the hell is everybody else? flashed across Riker's mind. In a ship of a thousand people, what kind of odds dictated that this sort of battle would take place and get no attention at all? Nor did he have the time to shut off that damned music from his comm badge. It was some obscure waltz that he could have done without.

The combatants rolled across the floor, punching and gouging at each other, and then slammed against a bulkhead, bringing them to a halt. Unfortunately for Riker, Worf was on top.

The Klingon dug his fingers into Riker's throat and began to squeeze, his jaw set, his eyes wild.

"This," he grated, "is what happens to spies and saboteurs!"

Riker tried to pull a breath, tried to plead for sanity. But the Klingon was too strong. Riker brought his hands up swiftly and boxed Worf's ears. It was a formidable blow and caused the Klingon tremendous pain. It also caused him to redouble his efforts, and Riker felt the world fading into a red haze.

And then Worf suddenly roared in agony, his head pitching back, the pressure gone from Riker's throat. Worf was on his feet, grabbing at his back, clutching spasmodically.

Worf was still thrashing around, and now Riker could see what he was grabbing for. His Klingon dagger was buried deep in his side, and the young boy from before . . . the one Deanna had called Tommy . . . was holding on to it, twisting it, trying to cause even more internal damage.

Worf swung a gloved hand and he connected, knocking the boy back. Tommy skidded but rolled and came quickly to his feet. Worf pulled the dagger out of himself, which was a mistake, because at least when it was in him it was plugging the wound. Now blood began to pour out of the hole that Tommy had carved in him.

"Don't you hurt my father!" shouted Tommy.

"He's not your father!" snarled Worf.

Riker couldn't disagree.

Worf seemed oblivious to, or simply was ignoring, his injury. He came at Riker again with the dagger, and this time he was a hair slower but no less deadly. Riker darted around him, grabbed up Tommy, and barreled down the corridor like a football player. Worf came right after him, letting Riker know in no uncertain terms that this was the way in which all Romulan traitors would be dealt with.

And the music played on . . .

14.

Captain Jean-Luc Picard, his mind whirling, stepped onto the bridge, and was immediately tackled by Lieutenant Worf.

Worf slammed him up against a console even as Picard shouted, "Mr. Worf, are you *insane?!*"

"Who are you?" demanded Worf. Data and other members of the bridge crew were standing behind him. "What have you done with the captain? Or have you taken possession of his body, in which case I am warning you . . ."

"Lieutenant, release me or I will see you *in the brig!*"

There was enough of Picard's commanding presence to bring Worf up short. He still had Picard immobilized, but now there was serious doubt in his face.

From behind him, Data said, "Captain . . . I believe it would interest you to know that precisely thirty-seven seconds ago, you emerged from the turbolift, wielded a phaser, and attempted to shoot Mr. Worf."

"I have no doubt," grunted Picard. "I also, as you see,

have no phaser. Now, if soon-to-be-ensign Worf would kindly release me, I will explain what I believe is happening."

Slowly Worf stepped back, looking cautiously at Picard.

"It would be best to inform everyone at once," said Picard, "because this will affect the entire crew. Put me on intraship."

Harpsichord music promptly flooded the bridge. Everyone looked at one another in bewilderment. "What the devil is that?" demanded Picard.

"Tchaikovsky," replied Data immediately. "An inferior rendering, I might add. The tempo is—"

"Not now!" Picard looked around. "Where's Commander Riker?"

As if on cue, the turbolift doors opened and Commander Riker, ready to start his shift, walked in.

He took one look at Worf standing near Picard.

"Captain, *down!*" shouted Riker without hesitation, his sidearm in his hand, and he fired.

Picard threw himself back, slamming into Worf, knocking the security chief out of the way.

Riker's head snapped around in confusion. He looked for Tasha, looked for Wesley, saw neither. Data looked strange, and he didn't recognize anyone else.

He lunged back into the turbolift, desperately trying to make sense out of what had just happened. The turbolift door slammed shut and Riker was gone.

"One would not have expected such a sequence of events to happen twice in one day," observed Data.

15.

The *Enterprise* continued in its solitary orbit around Terminus. With each new pass the starship moved through another bend in the dimensional flux zone that had been created and orchestrated by the being far below. It was not reading on any instruments, because no instrument existed that could detect it.

The harpsichord music floated up from Terminus, and there was the joyous laughter of someone totally in control.

"Now," said the manipulator, "let's up the tempo, shall we?"

16.

Lugging Tommy, Riker charged down the hallway, the heavy footsteps of his pursuer directly behind him. On his own he might have been able to outrun the wounded Klingon. But there was no way he was going to leave the boy behind, particularly after the risks that the boy had taken on his behalf.

Then he spotted a possible out.

He darted through the large double doors, which hissed shut behind him. "We have maybe five seconds to pull this off!" Riker told him.

Worf stalked down the corridor, clutching his wounded side. He ignored the blood, ignored the pain. It was all secondary to his overwhelming drive to find the impostor. It was all just a Romulan trick, just another shabby, pathetic Romulan trick.

He paused, looking right and left. There was no sign of the fake Riker anywhere. Then he saw a large set of double doors and realized that that was where the impostor had to have hidden himself.

His dagger at the ready, Worf decided on a full-blown, direct, frontal attack. With a roar he charged at the doors, which obediently opened for him. He hit the ground, rolled so that any possible phaser blasts would pass over his head (in case the impostor had managed to acquire a weapon), and came up ready for anything.

Anything except what he, in fact, faced.

In front of him stretched a maze. A maze that seemed to stretch into infinity. The walls were high, at least seven feet tall, and far beyond him they angled upward, climbing some sort of mountain that was far in the distance.

He heard a hissing noise behind him and quickly recognized it even as he spun to see that the doors had indeed closed behind him. Not just closed, but disappeared. The maze was in back of him as well.

He looked up and saw a red sky, harsh and crackling above him.

Immediately he realized where he was. He had never seen one before, but it had to be. This was a holodeck, the latest thing to be made part of standard equipment in starships.

"Computer!" he called out uncertainly. "Shut off simulation!"

Nothing. The sky was no less red, the maze no less daunting.

"Computer, end simulation!"

No response. The air was still.

With a furious snarl, he started to move through the maze, vowing greater and greater revenge with every step.

* * *

In the corridor, Riker sagged momentarily against the wall, letting out a sigh of relief. "That should hold him," he said.

"He can tell the computer to end the program," said Tommy.

"He can tell it so, but I locked it in with a command password. It'll stay for as long as I say it stays. Now," he looked at Tommy, "let's get you back to your . . ."

The word he was looking for was "mother," of course. But he had trouble applying it to Deanna.

Tommy took him by the hand. "Look . . . I don't know what's happening . . . I don't understand . . . and I think I know that you're kind of not my father, except you kind of are. While you're bringing me back to Mom, could you just . . . just talk to me about stuff?"

"Not now," said Riker brusquely. "Come—"

"If not now, then *when?*" said Tommy. "I saved your life! Please—!"

"Okay, okay," sighed Riker. He pulled Tommy along so quickly that his feet almost left the ground. "What do you want to know?"

"Tell me about girls," said Tommy.

As the unheard tempo increased, it started to happen all over the ship. Faster, more out of control, more insane. Crewmen started encountering those long dead, those never born. Uncanny feelings of déjà vu swept over everyone, and the entire crew became aware that something was going on. Something unnatural. Something apocalyptic.

Trelane played on.

Jack Crusher staggered into his quarters, nursing his injured fist.

Wesley Crusher was waiting for him.

Wesley's back was to him when he heard him enter. "Captain," he began automatically, "communications are out and you were miss—"

His voice trailed off as he turned to face Jack. He stared in astonishment at the ship's captain.

Jack, for his part, stared at Wesley. The uniform was close, very close to that of Starfleet, but there were subtle differences. And the boy he didn't recognize at all. He would have remembered an ensign that young.

Alternate world.

Had to be.

Jack drew himself up and said, "Who are you? What's your name? Report, Ensign."

Wesley's jaw was somewhere around his stomach.

"Dad . . ." he whispered.

Jack stared at the boy, looked carefully at the face. He couldn't believe what he was seeing. Yes. Yes, it was him. It was *him. It was him.*

He should have felt anger, or fear, or more confusion. Instead all that Jack Crusher could feel was overwhelming joy. The throbbing in his fist was forgotten. The disloyalty of that damned Picard and his equally damned wife was forgotten. All of it was forgotten because Trelane, wonderful Trelane, the magnificent Trelane, had given him his son back.

"Wesley," he said, and walked toward the boy, arms outstretched.

Wesley backpedaled, frightened out of his wits. He had seen enough pictures of his late father that he knew him on sight. And he was here now, alive, and it terrified Wesley beyond rational thought.

He darted around Jack Crusher's outstretched arms as if trying to avoid the touch of a leper.

"Wesley, come back!" shouted Crusher. "You don't understand!"

Wesley darted into the hallway.

Crusher charged after him.

Wesley was gone.

Jack had moved too quickly for Wesley to have made it out of sight down a corridor. No, the boy had simply vanished. Disappeared back into whatever and wherever his reality was. And wherever that reality was, it was someplace that did not include Captain Jack Crusher. Picard, yes; Beverly, yes. But not Jack. Never Jack.

Rage blinded him, clouded his thoughts, clouded his sanity. The final element had been shoved into his face, the last realization of that which he would never have. No matter how hard he worked, no matter what he accomplished, Wesley would always be beyond his reach. Just as peace was also beyond it, and happiness.

He would never, ever be happy.

And it was all Jean-Luc Picard's fault. Yes. Yes, all his fault.

Somewhere far away, beyond Jack Crusher's conscious thoughts, Trelane reached over and hit a discordant note. And like a severed string, the mind of Captain Jack Crusher snapped.

17.

Deanna Troi felt as if her head were going to split.

There were whisperings coming to her from everywhere. Empathically, from every direction. It was like going up and down the tuner on an old-style radio, trying to block out the static. She had no idea how to turn it down.

The doors to her quarters hissed open and she saw Riker standing there. "Deanna," he said briskly.

She rose. "Will, something terrible is happening. Something . . ."

Then a young boy entered. A boy with tousled brown hair who looked up at her in confusion.

"Mom?" he said.

Deanna stared at Riker.

"Mom," Tommy said again with growing fear. "Where's my mom? Where is she? She was right here, and now she's gone, and you look like her but you're not her! *Where is she?!*"

Deanna looked helplessly at Riker.

"This is going to take some explaining, which I don't

have the time for right now," said Riker. "Keep an eye on him. Keep your door sealed. It's pandemonium out there."

"Can I do anything?" said Deanna.

"Yes. If you go out there, you can get yourself killed. So stay here."

He went out again quickly, leaving Deanna staring in confusion at the boy.

"Do you want to talk about it?" she asked.

18.

After his assault on the Klingon invader had gone awry, Captain Picard had managed to make his way straight down to the armory. As he quickly loaded up on everything that he could carry, he jumped as Commander Riker charged in. Riker skidded to a halt as Picard whirled on him, phaser at the ready.

"Captain, Klingons have captured the bridge!" said Riker. "I was just up there, and barely escaped . . ."

"I know, Number One," said Picard. "I had a similar experience. And I'll tell you what else. We cannot rule out the possibility that some of our own people are cooperating."

"Traitors?" Riker couldn't believe it. "Captain, are you sure—?"

Picard spoke quickly, forcefully. It all made so much sense to him. It was perfectly reasonable once you were willing to accept it. "The war is going badly, Number One. There will always be those who are turncoats. Those who are not with us, Number One, are against us." He stretched out a hand to Riker. "It's up to us, Will."

Riker grasped the hand firmly. "It will be a pleasure to fight by your side, Captain."

"And the first thing we do," said Picard hotly, "is get those bastards off the bridge."

In engineering, it was all Geordi La Forge could do not to pass out.

Something, some sort of waves, was passing in front of the magnetic spectrum of his VISOR. He staggered, buffeted by the waves. They were everywhere he looked. They were like nothing he had ever seen, and he didn't have the faintest idea of how to go about identifying them.

DiStefano came up to him and steadied him. "Are you okay, sir?" he asked.

"I'm . . . something's off with my VISOR," Geordi said, as the haze seemed to clear up for a moment. "I'm heading to sickbay. Have Dr. Crusher take a look at it."

"Good idea, sir," said DiStefano.

Wesley Crusher dashed frantically into sickbay. "Mom!" he shouted, gripping her by the arms. "Mom! I saw Dad! I saw Dad!"

Dr. Beverly Howard stared uncomprehendingly at the almost hysterical boy. "What? I'm sorry . . . 'Dad'? Who are you, Ensign? Are you new here?"

Wesley stared at her uncomprehendingly. "Mom?"

She tried to laugh. "I'm not your mother. I think you have me confused with . . ." Then her voice trailed off as she stared into his face.

Wesley felt confused, cast adrift. It was a truly grotesque feeling when your own parent didn't recognize you.

"What's all the commotion here?" asked Nurse La Forge.

Wesley's head snapped around and he gaped as he stared at Geordi. "Geordi! Your eyes—?!"

"What about them?" asked Geordi affably.

At that moment, Engineering Chief Geordi La Forge entered.

He stopped and stared.

As did Geordi.

In the corridors, Commander Riker—having just left his "son" behind with Deanna Troi—almost ran headlong into Lieutenant Commander Riker.

The lieutenant commander recoiled in fear as he gaped at his counterpart. Then he backed up, shaking his head. "Another trick," he murmured, and then shrieked, *"Another trick!"*

"Wait!" shouted Riker, but it was too late. His double was smaller, weaker, but incredibly fast when he put his mind to it. He dashed down the corridor.

He turned a corner and slammed into himself. They went down in a tangle of arms and legs. The duplicate shoved his legs under Riker and pushed, sending Riker staggering back.

"Don't run!" shouted Riker, and then he looked down at his hand in surprise. He was holding a phaser. Without intending to, he had grabbed it off the man he had tackled. Except that the rather pathetic Lieutenant Commander Riker that he had been pursuing was not armed.

And then he realized his error, for this Riker was not the man he'd been chasing. For one thing, his uniform was different.

For another, he was packing more phasers.

And he was backed up by Captain Picard, also armed.

372

Music echoed in Picard's head, and the words "Kill him" came to his lips.

Riker had exactly one second to act, and he did so. To his immediate right was a Jefferies tube, and he leaped for it, firing a phaser blast as he went. It was just enough to send the other Riker and Picard darting back, and their blast went wide. Then Riker was up the Jefferies tube and gone, crawling along the inner connectors of the *Enterprise.*

"You were slow, Number One," scolded the other Picard.

"Sorry, sir," said the other Riker. "I'm . . . not accustomed to trying to shoot myself."

"You'll have to get accustomed to lots of unusual things before this business is done," said Picard flatly.

19.

In a storage area, Jack Crusher ripped a piece of cloth off from a uniform and wrapped it around his bleeding fist. It still didn't feel any less painful. But at least his hand wasn't becoming increasingly slick from the blood.

He went off in search of his second-in-command.

Beverly Howard felt a chill in her spine and backed up. "Wesley—?" she managed to say. She shook her head in denial. "No, it . . . it can't be . . ."

"Get away from her!" ordered Nurse La Forge, interposing himself between Wesley and Dr. Howard. He stared at the other Geordi. "If this is some idea of a joke—"

"Then I'm not laughing," replied Engineer La Forge.

"Who put you up to this?" demanded the nurse. "Who decided that this would be funny? *Who?*" He crossed quickly to Geordi and, before La Forge could make a move, yanked the VISOR off.

"No!" shouted Geordi, grabbing at the VISOR.

Nurse La Forge held the instrument out of his reach as Geordi lunged for it, missed, hit the floor. The blind man staggered to his feet, reaching out, groping desperately . . .

And the nurse saw the blind eyes. Saw the face, no longer hidden behind the VISOR, and it was *his face* . . .

"Give that back!" shouted Wesley, and he drove an elbow into Nurse La Forge's stomach. The nurse gasped, dropping the VISOR into Wesley's outstretched hand. Wesley came up quickly behind the staggering engineer, grabbed him by the arm, and dragged him out of sickbay, his confused and frightened gaze never leaving the doctor and nurse.

The moment they were in the corridor, he helped Geordi get the VISOR back on. Geordi turned and looked at him.

"Wes?" he said in confusion. "What are you doing here?"

"I know, I should be on the bridge, but—"

"No, you should be in school!"

That was when Wesley noticed that La Forge's uniform was different.

They stared at each other. "What the hell—?" they said in unison.

Beverly and La Forge ran out into the hallway. There was no sign of the two who had been in sickbay mere seconds ago.

The doctor and her nurse looked at each other.

"What the hell—?" they said in unison.

That was the moment that the bridge went berserk.

The security systems erupted, completely out of control. Actually, not technically out of control . . . they were in full control of one Captain Jean-Luc Picard and his second-in-command, fighting the good fight against the Klingon incursion.

Electrical charges ripped out from all the instruments. Data was barely fast enough to avoid being shorted out altogether.

Chafin was knocked cold. Worf leaped over the railing and grabbed him, roaring as electrical discharges struck him. The doors to the conference lounge and ready room were sealed. There was no place to hide from the assault.

And then there was a loud *whooosh* as gas began to flood the bridge. The molecules of the gas interacted with the electrical discharges. It was like being trapped inside of a lightning storm.

There was absolutely no choice. The crew cleared the bridge, eschewing the turbolift and instead darting down the emergency exits.

Unmanned, unprotected, the conn erupted in flames. Systems went out all through the bridge.

The navigation systems locked down and slowly, but irrevocably, the *Enterprise* shifted her orbit. The mighty starship angled downward toward the planet, where it would shortly meet a final and fiery death.

20.

"I'm not waiting here with you anymore!" Tommy Riker shouted at Deanna Troi. "I'm going out there to find my mom and dad!"

He headed for the door, repeating the action he'd taken earlier when he'd decided to go after his father. On that occasion the result had been that he'd managed to save William Riker's life . . . some damned William Riker or other, at any rate. So he was relatively flush with success, and the interests of this woman who was, and was not, his mother were strictly secondary to him.

Deanna came up behind him and grabbed his right wrist. "You're not going anywhere," she said firmly.

Tommy did not hesitate. His intense and undying love for Starfleet had included study of all manner of things . . . including self-defense techniques. Before she could react, Tommy stepped across Deanna's body, causing her to lose her balance just slightly. It was enough for him to shove against the weak point in Deanna's grip: her thumb. A quick twist broke her grip on him, and Tommy followed the move with a swift punch to her stomach. Solid move, solidly executed, and the startled Betazoid went down firmly on her buttocks with a startled gasp.

Tommy was out the door before she could stop him.

Deanna was immediately after him.

Commander Jean-Luc Picard arrived in sickbay to find Dr. Beverly Howard trembling, confused, disoriented. He would have thought that it was because of her confrontation with Jack, but she quickly informed him that such had not been the case. Jack had not shown up, had not been down to sickbay at all.

The cause for her fright, though, was not much of an improvement.

"Wesley," she had said hoarsely. "Wesley was here."

Picard stared at her in confusion. "Wesley? Your . . . your son? Your little boy . . . ?"

She shook her head frantically. "Not little. A teenager, a young man he was . . . my God, Jean-Luc, what kind of an asylum have we signed aboard?"

"I'm going to find Jack," said Picard. "Stay here."

"Where would I go?" she asked.

He strode quickly out of sickbay, and Beverly Howard immediately vanished, to be replaced by an equally distraught Beverly Crusher . . . who turned and saw a confused Geordi La Forge with perfectly functioning eyes, and she jumped at least a foot in the air except he wasn't there anymore, at which point Beverly Howard rematerialized as smoothly as if she hadn't left at all, and she looked around and couldn't understand where Geordi had gotten off to. . . .

Meantime, all around Commander Jean-Luc Picard, everything had gone berserk. Throughout the vessel, there was a sense of total, chaotic panic. Years of Starfleet training seemed shattered as crew members were darting this way and that. Everyone was running, it seemed, though whether they were running from one place or toward another, Picard could not have said. He tried to regain control but, driven by inner demons and fears, many of the officers ignored him. A number didn't even seem to recognize him, and a few looked at him very suspiciously before continuing on their way.

"What's happening?!" Picard shouted over the increasing terror and din.

At his harpsichord, Trelane upped the tempo of his music still more. He smiled peacefully and, when he spoke, his voice echoed within the subconscious of all the pathetic little vermin running around in the ship, which in turn was spiraling downward, although no one was aware of it yet.

"You are fighting for your place in the universe," he said, punctuating the seriousness of the sentiment with a rather impressive musical sting. "No quarter may be asked, and none may be given. For this, my fine young things, is the end for you. This is far more than war. Oh yes, far more. This"—another musical sting—"is the battle for total annihilation. Who will stay? Who will go? Maybe you . . . but maybe no. A charming rhyme, don't you think?"

He ran his fingers briskly down the keyboard, and the music swelled within their minds, and they were going from jumping dimensions to jumping dementia.

Faster and faster the boundaries deteriorated. Trelane giggled. If he was having this much fun with three universes . . . just imagine the amusement value from collapsing three hundred. Three thousand!

The experiment was shaping up to be a spectacular success.

* * *

The human-oid called Lieutenant Commander Data moved smoothly through the surging tide of humanity that had once been the efficient, coherent unit called the crew of the *Enterprise*.

He was heading for engineering, to the backup control stations, to see what could be done about the current dire situation in which the ship had found itself.

But as he approached engineering, he saw someone coming from the other direction. His head tilted slightly, as did the other's.

From another direction came a third.

The three Datas—two android, one human—stopped and looked at one another.

"Interesting," said Data.

"Interesting," said Data.

"Interesting," said Data.

Commander Picard, heading in one direction, came across Deanna Troi going in the other.

"Mrs. Riker!" he began.

"Captain!" she began. Then she stopped and frowned. "'Mrs. Riker'?"

"'Captain'?" he said.

Suddenly a phaser blast fired, nailing Picard from behind. He hurtled forward, crashing into Deanna Troi. They both went down.

Picard moaned as Deanna struggled out from under him. She looked up in shock to see Jack Crusher stalking toward them, a phaser in his hand and murder in his eye.

"That was on the lowest setting, Picard!" he shouted. "Murdering bastard! We'll bring you up a notch at a time!"

Picard was clutching his ribs, and Deanna threw herself

protectively in front of him. "Keep away from him!" she said.

"This is between him and me!" growled Crusher. "Don't worry, Mrs. Riker. I'm not going to kill him. I'm just going to . . . to break every bone in his damned body! Think she'll love you when you're just a boneless mass of meat? Huh?"

Picard staggered to his feet. Crusher brought his phaser up, at an increased setting, ready to blast through her to get to him.

And suddenly Crusher was lifted completely off his feet. He struggled in midair, his arms thrashing about helplessly, as Lieutenant Worf pivoted quickly and tossed him down the corridor as if he weighed nothing.

Crusher hit the ground and skidded, coming to a halt in front of a small mass of crewmen.

Worf started to advance on him, saying brusquely, "One side! This is a security procedure!"

"Kill the Klingon!"

Worf looked up when he heard that. He wasn't quite sure which was worse: hearing that sentiment, or hearing the voice that mouthed it.

None of the crewmen were wearing Starfleet uniforms akin to his. They all looked far more militaristic and, furthermore, everyone had a firearm.

And at the forefront was Lieutenant Natasha Yar.

"Tasha!" said Worf.

Being called by her name did not slow Tasha in the least. She brought her phaser up and fired. Worf ducked to the left and felt the bolt sizzle over his head.

Worf fired three quick blasts before they could target him. Then he charged down a side corridor, with the rest of the angry mob right after him.

* * *

Deanna watched them go, then turned back to Picard. He was gone.

Picard watched them go, then turned back to Deanna. She was gone.

Everyone in engineering gaped as three Datas, working in perfect unison, sought to override the damaged navigational controls by rerouting them through the backup astronavigational board.

They worked so smoothly, with so little need for back-and-forth, that they were able to discuss matters of somewhat less consequence as they sought to save the ship.

"Tell me," the android Datas (who had a tendency to speak in unison, much to the annoyance of the engineering crew) said to the human-oid, "what is the greatest advantage to having a human body? We have always been curious."

The human-oid gave it a moment's thought. "Sex," he replied.

"Really," said the Datas.

"Yes. I have had frequent liaisons with Lieutenant Natasha Yar." He paused a moment. "I am not supposed to tell anyone else. But since we are, in essence, aspects of the same being, I feel that this is not betraying a confidence."

"Your secret is safe with us," said the Datas.

"Tommy!" Deanna Riker was calling as she ran down the corridor.

She was nearly frantic with worry. The boy had run from their quarters. She had not been able to locate him, and all around her she was getting a feeling of being totally disconcerted. The crush of human anxiety was so palpable that she was almost overwhelmed by it.

She sagged against a wall, trying to catch her breath, trying to screen out the pounding of emotions all around her. Overwhelmed by it all, bereft of her son and her husband, her mind cried out . . .

You're going to be all right, came a soothing voice in her head.

She looked up and stared into her own eyes. Eyes that did not carry with them a world of pain and years of hurt.

"Wh . . . what's happening?" said Deanna Riker, thinking for a moment that perhaps she had spiraled down into the same pit of madness that seemed to have embraced her husband.

"Nothing we cannot handle," replied Deanna Troi. "In numbers is strength."

"Mom!"

Deanna Riker's head snapped around as Tommy ran to her. He hugged her fiercely, saying, "I never thought I'd see you . . ."

"It's all right," she told him over and over, "it's all right."

Tommy looked from his mother to Deanna Troi and back again, as if he hadn't fully believed the resemblance until he saw them next to each other.

"Are you two, like . . . related?" he asked.

"Back away from them, boy."

The crisp order had come from William T. Riker.

It wasn't Deanna Troi's Riker.

It wasn't Deanna Troi Riker's Riker.

It was a William T. Riker whom neither of them had seen. One who, standing next to a man appearing to be Jean-Luc Picard, had phasers aimed at them.

"Will?" said Deanna.

"Will?" said Deanna a second after her.

"You know these women, Number One?" asked Picard.

"I know who they're supposed to be," said Riker. "But it's obviously a Klingon trick . . . because I haven't seen this woman—either woman—in years."

Lieutenant Worf charged down the hallway, the thundering horde right behind him, spearheaded by Tasha Yar.

As stretched as his credulity was at that moment, it should not have come as any surprise to him when, at the end of the corridor, another Tasha Yar was waiting for him.

She did not have her phaser up and pointed at him. Instead she was staring at him with curiosity and a bit of annoyance. "What the hell are you doing in that uniform?" she demanded.

That one sentence, remarkably, clarified a great deal to Worf.

Obviously they were dealing with multiple universes, something that he, Worf, had sizable experience with. Not only had he once become an inadvertent dimension jumper, but he had witnessed firsthand the spectacle of thousands upon thousands of *Enterprise*s emerging from a rift in space.

Unlike that experience, however, the universes were not simply running into one another. They were overlapping, merging, one being made to exist at the expense of others.

All this went through Worf's mind in one second.

In the next second, he immediately discerned three distinct dimensional tracks: There was himself, of course, and his *Enterprise;* there was an *Enterprise* where the crew was at war with the Klingons; and there was an *Enterprise* where time flowed at a slightly different speed (judging by Tasha's older-style uniform), where Worf happened to be on the ship for some reason—as a visitor, perhaps—but was not a member of Starfleet.

In the third second, he made his decision. He stepped forward, grasped her firmly, and lied.

"Ishara told me to tell you that she regrets all the unhappiness between you."

Tasha's eyes widened. Worf's invoking the name of her estranged sister was absolutely the last thing that she had expected.

"We are about to be attacked," he said. "Are you with me or no?"

And Tasha Yar, head of security of the *Enterprise,* yanked out her phaser. "No one attacks anyone on my ship and gets away with it. We could use some cover to fall back, though. Darkness, perhaps."

"Excellent idea."

He and Tasha fired at the overhead illumination. The lights blew out, plunging the entire corridor into darkness. Down the hallway could be heard the crew screaming for Worf's head, but by the time they got their bearings, Worf and Tasha were long gone.

21.

Trelane's hands thundered down on the keys, driving up the sound level. The harpsichord music deteriorated into an earsplitting cacophony, and the only thing that was louder was the laughter of Trelane.

A pair of eyes watched from hiding as the two Deannas faced the collective judge, jury, and executioner called Jean-Luc Picard and William T. Riker.

"Listen to me," said Deanna Troi slowly. "Both of you. This is not the way."

The music chorused in the heads of Picard and Riker, allowing the words to get through but drowning out the sincerity, the sentiment, the thought and order behind them.

"It's another pathetic Klingon trick, Captain," said Riker with confidence. "They've got operatives disguised as a woman who I knew years ago. Obviously they're doing it so that I'll hesitate when I see them, instead of doing what needs to be done."

"Foolish," said Picard.

"We take them prisoner?"

"No time. No facility." Picard raised his phaser, and Riker matched the action. "And, frankly, no patience."

"Stop it!" shouted Tommy. "Don't hurt them!"

"Tommy, get out of the way!" his mother warned him, pushing him to one side.

"Ready," said Picard. "Make it merciful, Number One. A clean shot."

"It's more than they'd do for us."

"Agreed. Do it anyway."

"Put the phasers down," said Deanna Troi. "You're making a mistake."

"Aim," said Picard.

And suddenly a red and black blur blocked their path.

They weren't sure exactly what it was. It moved faster than either of them had ever seen a person move, and the roar that came from his throat was barely akin to human.

He broadsided Picard, hurling him back into Riker. His voice was filled with fury as he howled, *"Don't you hurt my wife!"*

Picard tried to bring his phaser up, but Lieutenant Commander Riker twisted it away from him. Then Riker brought his foot up into the pit of Picard's stomach, doubling him over. Picard gasped, and then Commander Riker shoved Picard out of the way so that he could get a clear shot.

He was too slow.

Lieutenant Commander Riker, longtime prisoner of the Romulans, husband of Deanna and father of Tommy, fired. He did not display any of the hesitation or trepidation that had haunted him since his rescue. In the firestorm of battle, with the life of the woman he loved at stake, there was absolutely no indecision.

The blast hit Commander Riker squarely in the chest. And Commander William Riker, pride of Starfleet, fighter of Klingons, onetime lover of a Betazoid woman he had not seen for years . . . saw nothing else ever again. His molecules lost cohesion and, within seconds, he was wiped out of existence.

Riker turned toward Picard, but now Deanna Troi grabbed him by the arm and cried out, "No! Don't!" And to Picard she cried, "Run!"

Riker would not be stopped. He continued to fire, but the blasts missed Picard because Deanna was yanking on his arm. It gave Picard enough time to fall back and disappear down the corridor.

He turned to his wife, took her face in his hands. "Are you all right? Did he hurt you?"

"No." She shook her head, her voice barely above a hush.

"I couldn't let him hurt you." The words seemed to surprise him, a self-realization. "I . . . couldn't let him . . ."

She held him close.

Deanna Troi didn't know whether to be happy or jealous. She settled for being cautious. "Let's go," she said. "This is far from over."

Picard, having just seen his second-in-command blown to atoms, ran down a corridor as fast as his legs would carry him. Suddenly he heard voices . . . one of them deep and rough, and he recognized it immediately.

There was a Jefferies tube nearby, and Picard clambered up it quickly. Then he twisted around, staking out a position . . . and waited.

The voices drew closer, closer. There was the Klingon's voice, yes, and a female voice talking with him.

My God . . . it was Tasha. Tasha Yar had betrayed them. All of a sudden it made perfect sense. That was how their security had been breached. That was how all those impostors had been allowed to run rampant throughout the ship.

Natasha Yar, traitor to the Federation, pawn to the Klingon Empire.

He wasn't sure who he was going to enjoy shooting more.

22.

Far away from the Captain Picard who was poised in the Jefferies tube, ready to fire upon lieutenants Worf and Yar, another Captain Picard was dumbfounded when Wesley Crusher, in an ensign's uniform, ran up to him and grabbed him by the arms.

"Captain!" he said, too distraught to notice the minute differences between this Captain Picard and the one under whom he had served. "My . . . my father . . ."

It was a mental effort for Picard to jump past the fact that Wesley Crusher was still at the Academy, repeating his final year. To take in stride that Wesley's father, rather than being more than a decade deceased, was running around the *Enterprise* as if he owned the damned ship. For Picard realized that, if he was going to survive this madness, he was going to have to adapt as quickly as possible to the changes thrust upon him.

"What's happened, Wes? Calm down," said Picard firmly.

"I was in sickbay," said Wesley. "I was . . . I was making sure Mom was all right . . . and then this man who . . . but it can't be my father, my father's dead . . ."

Wesley looked close to cracking, and Picard shook him, trying to snap him back to reality. "Is he down there?" demanded Picard.

Wesley nodded.

Picard turned and ran toward sickbay, Wesley right behind him . . . until he vanished.

Engineering was rather quiet.

The only thing that could be heard was the steady thrumming of the *Enterprise* engines, and the steady efforts of the three Datas to stop the ship from plunging into the planet's atmosphere.

All around them was silence, due mostly to the fact that—as various engineering crew members had cracked either because of the strain, or the seductive unheard call to chaos that worked subliminally—the Datas had, one by one, knocked everyone cold . . . up to and including Geordi La Forge, who had come in shouting about how he should be able to see, and it wasn't fair, and . . .

Well, he hadn't sounded like himself at all. It had upset Data (as upset as Data ever got about such things), silencing his longtime friend and associate. On the other hand, at least Geordi wasn't embarrassing himself further by carrying on so.

The android Datas said, "This sabotage goes beyond simple computer malfunction."

"I agree," said the human-oid. "Clearly there is an outside interference that is causing all of our repair efforts to be stymied."

"What shall we do?" asked the androids.

The human-oid gave the matter a moment's thought.

"I am afraid we shall die," he replied.

Jack Crusher, phaser trembling, eyes crazed, stood over Beverly.

"So how long was it him instead of me?" he hissed. "From the very beginning? Was that it? Was our whole relationship just some sort of cosmic joke?"

Beverly couldn't speak. She shook her head desperately. "No," she whispered, terrified of what might happen next.

The staff was gone. They'd run off, seized by the madness that appeared to have swept the ship. But Beverly's determination to stay with her patients was so overwhelming that she had remained at her post despite the fear, despite the confusion.

She had constantly felt as if there was something just out of the corner of her eye . . . another her, but when she turned to look, it would be gone, vanished like the morning mist.

A poem, a very old poem, leaped to her mind: *I thought I saw upon the stair, a little man who wasn't there. He wasn't there again today. Oh, how I wish he'd go away.*

The doors to sickbay hissed open, and Captain Picard entered slowly. "Jack," he said slowly. "Put the phaser down."

"Well," said Jack Crusher. "Well, well, well. Look who's here. My best friend in the entire universe. How are you, pal?"

"Jack," said Picard carefully. "You don't want to do this."

"Don't worry, Picard," replied Jack Crusher cheerfully. "I'm not going to. And yet . . . I'm going to. Isn't that wonderful? I can do whatever I want. Psychiatrists call it 'Niven syndrome.' It's a total disassociation of action from responsibility, in the belief that nothing matters. And you know what? It doesn't. How's this for a bit of logic: I might be doing myself a favor here. Maybe I'll create my own separate timeline . . . one in which Jack Crusher does blow your brains out . . . and one in which he doesn't. Wouldn't that screw up fate something fierce."

"Please, Jack . . . put it down."

"You said that. It didn't impress me much before, and it sure doesn't now."

Suddenly Beverly lunged toward him. Instinctively, immediately, Jack swung the phaser around toward her.

Picard came at him.

Jack brought the phaser back around at Picard, because he didn't want Beverly out of commission when he took down that murdering slime, Picard. He wanted her conscious and watching. He lashed out with a quick snap kick that caught Beverly in the side and knocked her flat. And then he fired at Picard.

But the kick caused him to be slightly off balance, and it was enough for Picard to dodge the blast. Picard moved quickly and ran full tilt into Jack, hoping to jar the phaser loose. He didn't succeed. Crusher clutched the weapon like a lifeline.

Picard looked deeply into Crusher's eyes, and it was at that moment that he knew that there was no hope, none whatsoever, of talking sense into this man. Whether he be ghost of the past, or a demon spit up from hell . . . whatever he was . . . there was no reaching the good man who had been called Jack Crusher.

They grappled, body against body, angling for leverage. Picard was keeping the phaser up and over Crusher's head, unable to tear it free, but at least keeping it aimed away from himself.

Quick-thinking, Beverly grabbed a spray hypo and adjusted the dial, loading it with enough Somnol to tranquilize an army of berserk Jack Crushers. She approached them carefully, trying to slip in, not wanting to get the wrong man.

Picard managed to get his palm under Crusher's chin. He braced himself and thrust upward, slamming Crusher's head against the wall. Jack barely grunted in acknowledgment. Picard did it again, and a third time, and stars exploded in Jack Crusher's eyes. Suddenly he twisted his head away and Picard's hand slipped off.

Jack Crusher sank his teeth into Picard's forearm.

Picard let out a yell, yanked his arm away, and Jack Crusher slammed his forehead forward. He head-butted Picard squarely on the bridge of his nose, and suddenly everything in Picard's sight was a haze of white pain.

With a triumphant yell, Jack viciously backhanded Picard, knocking him flat. He brought the phaser around, and then Beverly came at him with the hypo.

He caught her wrist just before she was able to jam the hypo into him.

Picard was on the floor, trying to clear his head. He stumbled forward, went to one knee.

Crusher twisted Beverly's arm back and she cried out in pain as she dropped the hypo. It clattered to the floor and Crusher kicked it away. Then he pulled her close and hissed in her ear, "You picked the wrong man."

Then he flung her away.

Pumped up by anger and rage, he threw her as hard as he could against a medlab table. Beverly's legs got tangled up in each other and she tried to stop her fall.

Her head struck the edge of the table with incredible force and there was a sharp *crack* . . .

And Jack Crusher realized he'd just heard *the sound.*

Throughout his life he had wondered about the sound of his son's death. The sound of a skull shattering, a neck breaking. The sound of a body thudding lifelessly to the ground, no longer a living, breathing person but instead a sack of dying or dead cells. He had pondered the question with his good friend Jean-Luc Picard not a very long time ago. Which was worse: to have heard it, or to imagine what it was like?

He didn't have to wonder any longer.

Beverly hit the ground, her eyes still open in shock, as if to say, *That's it? That's how I die? From something as stupid as that? I've taken falls before, and good God, I knew life was fragile, who knows better than a doctor, but that was it? How utterly useless.*

For just a moment, just the briefest of moments, there was a spark in her eyes—eyes, the mirrors of the soul—and she whispered, "I've never stopped loving you . . ."

And then she was gone. The mirrors were still in place, but the soul reflected in them had departed.

"Beverly." Picard could barely get her name out, and it was only at that hideous moment, in this insane shifting of universes, that he realized he had no idea *which Beverly it was. . . .*

Crusher stood there, staring at his hands. Staring at the hands that had taken Beverly's life. Then he aimed the phaser at Picard. Picard, on his back, didn't move.

And when Jack Crusher spoke, he sounded the most lucid, the most calm, that Picard could ever remember.

"You know," he said in slow wonderment, "that thing she just said . . . 'I've never stopped loving you' . . . you heard her say that?"

"Yes, Jack," said Picard, choking back tears.

PETER DAVID

"You know what? I think she was talking about me. I'm sure of it. Yes. She was definitely talking about me."

Picard said nothing.

"I'll be damned," said Jack Crusher. And then, matching action to words, he reversed the phaser and blew his own head off.

396

23.

Worf and Tasha Yar looked up and down the corridor carefully. In the distance they could hear screams, and cries of hysteria, and demented laughter. They were nearby a holodeck, and for a moment he considered taking refuge in it. But hiding would not accomplish a thing.

Tasha wiped sweat away from her brow, and realized that her uniform was starting to get soaked with sweat. "Is it getting hot in here?" she asked.

"Klingons are less sensitive to changes in temperature," he informed her. Nevertheless, he placed his palm flat against the bulkhead. "I believe you may be right. The wall feels warmer than before. I wonder—"

Tasha turned to face him. "We're not going another step until you tell me where you know Ishara from."

"You have to take my word that I do."

"The Klingon masquerading in the Starfleet uniform tells me to take his word for it. That's rich."

Suddenly there was a thud from a Jefferies tube nearby.

Immediately Tasha and Worf were on the alert. Then there was a grunt . . . a couple . . . and the sound of punches being landed.

"Who's in there!" demanded Worf. "Come out!"

There was an abrupt crashing and thumping, and then Captain Picard tumbled out of the Jefferies tube, blood pouring from his nose. A second later, Commander William T. Riker slid out as well and stood over Picard. Picard glared at Riker, and then at Tasha and Worf.

"Commander!" said Worf, and then, more cautiously, he said, "Commander?"

"Yes, Worf, it's me," said Riker. "I know it's a little hard to follow sometimes."

"That," rumbled Worf, "is an understatement."

"I just happened to be crawling past in the Jefferies tubes and noticed a somewhat familiar face about to fire on a very familiar face. So I thought I would intervene."

Tasha Yar was looking from Picard to Worf to Riker and then back to Picard. "I . . . I don't understand . . . sir," she said to Picard. "Are you all right?" And she extended a hand to help him to his feet.

He batted it away angrily. "I'm not interested in help from a traitor." Then his eyes narrowed craftily. "Or are you actually a duplicate as well? Is that what's going on here? Is it? *Is it?"*

"I'd sure like to know," said Tasha.

Riker was staring at Tasha in wonderment. "We . . . seem to be trapped in some sort of . . . bizarre temporal warp . . ."

"No, Commander," said Worf. "I've encountered this type of dislocation before. We are experiencing dimensional jumping. You, Tasha, told me that in your reality Jean-Luc Picard is the first officer, and this man . . . William Riker . . ."

"Was tortured by Romulans for seven years," finished Tasha.

Riker and Worf looked at each other. "Sounds pleasant," said Riker, trying to be nonchalant.

"In our dimension," Worf continued, "Jean-Luc Picard is the captain, and Commander Riker is his first officer."

"And who are you?" asked Tasha.

Worf caught himself before giving the answer. "Assistant security chief," he lied.

She nodded.

"In our dimension . . . as is obvious . . . the Klingons and Federation are allies. But this man . . . and our pursuers . . . are from a dimension where the Klingons and Federation are at war."

"A fine fairy tale," sneered Picard.

"Get up," said Riker, gesturing with his phaser. Picard slowly did as Riker instructed, and then Riker continued, "Okay, Mr. Worf. You seem to have a thorough grasp of this. Any thoughts as to what we do now?"

"Yes," said Worf. He aimed a phaser at Captain Picard. "The first thing we do is use him as hostage."

At that moment, their pursuers appeared at the far end of the corridor.

Tasha Yar gaped as she saw for the first time who was leading the mob that was out to lynch Worf.

"Oh my lord," she murmured to Worf. "It's me . . . but with a really bad haircut. My God, I look like a boy. . . ."

The other Tasha was no less startled, but she rallied herself and shouted, "Surrender!"

Immediately Riker threw his arm across Picard's chest. "All right!" he shouted, putting a phaser to Picard's head while trying to tell himself that this was not Picard, *this was not Picard.* "You're going to be doing the surrendering. Otherwise . . . he dies!"

There was a moment of dead silence.

And then Picard spoke, in a voice that was firm and flat and utterly filled with conviction. A voice of authority.

"Kill them," he said. "That is a direct order. Start with the Klingon, but kill all of them." And then his voice raised to fever pitch. *"All of them!"*

"You heard the captain!" shouted the Tasha Yar with a really bad haircut. "Kill them!"

"Nice plan, Worf," muttered Riker.

Sickbay was an appropriate place for Captain Jean-Luc Picard to be for, at that moment, he felt extremely sick.

He had just seen Jack Crusher die . . . again.

And Beverly . . .

Picard cradled her broken body in his lap. He said her name softly. . . .

Picard . . .

He looked up, and this time Q was more defined. Picard could see him, etched in black and white as if he were a line drawing.

I hate to disturb you during your dramatic time of grief . . .

"Shut up, Q," Picard said tiredly. He felt very, very old.

If you wish me to shut up, then I will, came the petulant response. *If, on the other hand, you have the slightest interest in saving the cosmos, then listen carefully. You may have noticed that everyone on this ship has gone somewhat berserk. But you, and a few others, have been spared this rather hideous fate. That,* mon capitaine, *is because of my kindly influence screening out some of the more mind-bending effects of the pure chaos being unleashed upon you. My control is limited, however. So I suggest you get your ass over to the nearest transporter room.*

"And transport where?"

Terminus. Don't you see, Jean-Luc? There are certain junction points in the universe. Places where reality is already stretched thin, and all the multiverses can come together. Terminus is one of those points. And Trelane is waiting.

"What is he waiting for?"

A challenge, Jean-Luc. A final challenge. And you'll have to give it to him. In a cosmos of infinite choices, Jean-Luc . . . you have no choice. No choice whatsoever.

"Kill the Klingon!" shouted Tasha Yar, and they advanced.

And then Riker did something rather odd. He shouted a word that didn't seem to have anything to do with anything.

"Thelonius!" he bellowed.

The doors to the holodeck slid open in response to the preencoded password that Riker had programmed. Worf only had the briefest glimpse of something that looked like a huge maze. And then Riker shoved as hard as he could, sending Picard hurtling into the midst of the maze. "Riker 1, override, deencode, close!" He spoke so quickly that for a moment he was worried that he might have slurred the words. But no, the computer had understood perfectly. Before Picard could get back out, the doors slid shut again, and the computer wiped out Riker's code word. The doors would then stay closed until such time that Riker, and only Riker, came up with a new code word.

Riker wasn't going to do that, however.

He was going to get the hell out of there, and he did, with Tasha Yar and Worf directly behind him.

Their pursuers skidded to a halt in front of the holodeck.

"You five!" shouted the Tasha with the bad haircut. "Follow them! The rest of you . . . help me get this damned thing open! Gomez, hot-wire the door, now!"

Inside the holodeck, Picard stood in the midst of the maze, looking around. "End simulation," he ordered.

The simulation serenely remained in place.

"This is Captain Jean-Luc Picard!" he called out. "On my authority, end simulation. Override code zed—"

He didn't get further than that, however, for there was a low snarl from nearby. He turned.

A Klingon, in full battle armor, was crouched there.

Picard's lips drew back in a wolflike sneer. "So you're the one behind all this, you Klingon bastard."

"Romulan impostor!" shouted Worf, and charged.

Locked in hatred, they came together for the final battle.

"Number One!"

Riker spun in response to that familiar voice.

Coming down the corridor at a brisk run was Captain Picard. He was carrying a white canvas bag slung over his shoulder.

"Captain?" said Riker cautiously.

Picard nodded. "Mr. Worf," he said to the Klingon, and then he saw Tasha, and hesitated only a moment before he said, "Lieutenant. Come along."

"Where, sir?"

"Transporter room," said Picard. "We're going to end this thing right now . . . by taking it to the source."

24.

It was a vast and barren plain.

Trelane and his harpsichord stood out in stark relief against it. He did not even look up from his music as the sound of the transporter beams whined nearby him.

"You certainly took your time," he called out.

The gravelly terrain crunched beneath Picard's boots. He walked slowly toward Trelane, and stopped several feet away. "You did not make it easy getting here."

"Fie," replied Trelane. "So you experienced a few minor inconveniences aboard your petty starship." His fingers fluttered across the keys. "Then again, there's an old saying: God does not give us more than we can handle."

Picard circled the harpsichord. "You . . . are not God," he said.

Trelane looked up at him and smiled ingratiatingly. "The day is young," he said.

"The day is over," said Picard. "The insanity is over. The destruction is over. The chaos is—"

"Over, yes, I get the idea," said Trelane, starting to look

just the least bit impatient. "My, you are a repetitive fellow, aren't you. So tell me . . . how is dear Jack Crusher?"

"Dead," said Picard tonelessly. He looked up at the red sky. Far, far in the distance, he could see the faint outline of the *Enterprise.*

The ship was falling.

The ship was dying.

Tasha Yar of the famed bad haircut finally managed to get the holodeck doors pried open. She and the crewmen with her entered slowly, cautiously.

Yar had taken ten steps and quickly realized that finding Picard was not going to present a problem. The small river of blood trickling beneath her boots was a sure tip-off.

They followed the stream, and found Picard and Worf. The combat had been brutal. A knife had been involved, possibly two. There had been a great deal of cutting and slashing, and when the two of them were done, there was more of them on the outside of their bodies than on the inside.

The image of the others burned hotly in Tasha's mind.

"Find those bastards and kill them," she grated.

"Dead, you say?" asked Trelane.

He changed tunes, playing a quick funeral dirge with facility. "Alas, poor Jack. I knew him, Horatio. A man of most infinite jest, of most excellent fancy."

Suddenly he switched music again. It jarred with the setting and the instrument. It was considerably up-tempo and lively. "Do you like it?" asked Trelane. "It's called 'Hit the Road, Jack.' I'm trying to update my repertoire."

Picard reached over quickly, grabbed the keyboard cover, and slammed it down so forcefully that Trelane barely avoided having it close on his fingers. "Now *that* was rude," he admonished Picard.

Picard circled him, contempt on his face, in his voice. "You," he told Trelane, "are the single most pathetic . . . contemptible . . ."

"Here now! Have a care!" warned Trelane.

". . . monstrous being I have ever encountered!"

"Really?" The excessive nature of the criticism seemed to appeal to him suddenly. "I must say, I don't care for the 'pathetic and contemptible' bit. But the 'monstrous' part . . . yes. Yes indeed, I like the sound of that."

"I want you to leave. I want you to go away, and never come back."

"Oh? And how do you propose to make me do that?"

"You're going to do it because I am going to defeat you."

"No," said Trelane slowly, shaking his head and smiling. "Not this time, Captain. Neither defeated nor beaten shall I, the humble Squire of Gothos, be."

"You are not humble," Picard said. "And you are not what you pretend to be. You are another version of him. Corrupted, distorted. You are the ultimate, evil end of all his worst characteristics brought to their extreme."

"How you *do* go on."

"Yes, I will go on," said Picard. "And the universe will go on. But you, Trelane . . . you will not go on."

He reached into the white duffel bag he had slung over his shoulder.

He pulled out a saber. It glinted red from the sky.

Trelane's face split in a grin.

"Are you challenging me to a duel?" he asked in utter delight.

The sword whished through the air.

"Yes," said Picard. "If you have the courage."

* * *

In the transporter room of the *Enterprise,* Riker studied the transporter controls intently. "What do we do now?" Tasha Yar asked.

"We wait," said Riker. "If they break in here, they could use the transporter to bring him back up before he's finished. That's what we have to make sure doesn't happen."

"But what's he *doing* down there?"

Riker thought of Picard's expression when he, Riker, had suggested that he beam down with Picard, or even in lieu of him. Riker had also pointed out the extreme hazard of trusting Q under any circumstance, much less in some ethereal state.

"Q is sincere this time, Number One," Picard had told him, preparing transporter coordinates, the validity of which Riker did not know. "This thing is bigger than both of us . . . but it's mine, Number One, and you are not to interfere."

Then Riker was jolted from his thoughts as he heard a thumping on the transporter-room door, which they had locked. And from the other side came Tasha Yar's voice shouting, "Security! Open up!"

"How marvelous!" crowed Trelane.

He shrugged off his elaborate coat and stood there in his black slacks, knee-high boots, and ruffled white shirt. A sword appeared in his hand and he sliced it through the air.

"Excellent, don't you think? Identical to the one that your Alexander the Great used to slice through the Gordian knot."

Slowly Picard approached Trelane, sword at the ready. " 'Alexander fought many battles, and took of the strongholds of all, and slew the kings of the earth. And he went through even to the ends of the earth, and took the spoils of many nations.'"

"Maccabees!" said Trelane immediately. "I told you, I have been taking great pains in my studies." His voice loud and theatrical, he continued, "'And the earth was quiet before him. And he gathered a power, and a very strong army; and his heart was exalted and lifted up. And he subdued countries of nations, and princes; and they became tributary to him. And . . .'"

Trelane stopped momentarily, his face clouded just for a second.

"'And after these things,'" said Picard harshly, "'he fell down upon his bed, and knew that he should die.'"

He lunged. Trelane parried. The swords crashed together and, from overhead, lightning crackled in response.

They stepped back, each taking a measure of the other's strength and speed, circling warily. The first few clashes were brief, swift. A blur of swords and then a disengage. Picard quickly saw that Trelane was fairly undisciplined, but he was strong and he adapted to each of Picard's attacks. He had the natural confidence that comes from holding all the cards.

"How did you know where to find me, eh?" Trelane inquired.

"Our instruments told us," Picard lied. He was circling Trelane but then he stopped, sword held defensively. "What about the people of this world? Are they being subjected to the same sort of distortions as our ship?"

"Oh, Captain!" Trelane said, sounding almost disappointed. "Don't you understand yet? I *created* this world! Manipulated reality so thoroughly that you believed it to have always existed! People? There are no people!" Suddenly Trelane's appearance completely shifted. "Oh, in

some realities you might talk to me and I'm calling myself
Proconsul Teffla. Just to maintain the charade, you under-
stand," he said, pronouncing the word "shu-RAHD."
Then he snapped back to his own form. "No, Captain
Picard . . . it's just you . . . and me . . . and soon, just
me."

Now he came forward quickly, and his sword moved so
fast that Picard barely had time to parry. When the swords
clanged together the sound echoed across the plain like a
gong heralding the arrival of Armageddon.

"I think they're in here," said Tasha Yar to her forces.
"The door is locked."

"A lot of the doors are locked," said Ensign Sanders.

"I know," said Tasha, "but this is the transporter room. I
just have a feeling, that's all."

"I'll blast it," Sanders said readily, raising his phaser.

But Yar said quickly, "No. There's delicate machinery in
there. I don't want blasts flying all over the place." It was
getting so hot that it was difficult to think. "Cut it open."

Sanders nodded and adjusted the phaser to act as a
cutting tool. The rest of them grouped around him and
watched as he began to cut through.

Picard backed up, and Trelane was right after him.

"What do you think you've proven, Trelane?" demanded
Picard. "When all is said and done, what in God's name
are you accomplishing?"

"Whatever I want," replied Trelane.

"But what you want doesn't make any sense."

"It doesn't *have* to!" shot back Trelane. "The fact that I
want it is more than enough!"

A quick flurry of moves, and Picard was trying to keep

track of everything, trying to remember everything that he had ever learned of fencing. Every practice session with holoimages and real opponents. He tried to anticipate everything that Trelane might do, every move that he might make.

Not good enough.

Trelane's sword skidded down the length of Picard's and struck a glancing blow off his forearm. "First blood!" shouted Trelane, and Picard spun back and away, barely blocking the next blow that might very well have cleaved the head from his shoulders.

Trelane attacked again. No art, no fencing techniques. Big, lazy slices that seemed to move slowly, but arrived much faster than Picard would have expected. A rapid volley of them, and the first five were blocked but the sixth got through, and now Picard was bleeding from his other arm.

Trelane lunged and Picard brought his blade around quickly. The hilts locked together, and Trelane and Picard were shoving against each other. Trelane was laughing, while Picard's face was a mask of concentration.

"Your ship, Captain," said Trelane. "Your beloved ship is falling from the sky. Doesn't that bother you just a hair?"

"But what does it matter?" Picard snapped back. "Wasn't that the point of this entire exercise? That nothing matters?"

"Excellent! You did understand it, then!"

And then Trelane's head snapped back as a fierce blow from Picard's fist landed. Trelane staggered, surprised, and Picard hit him again so hard that it knocked him flat.

"Wrong, Trelane!" shouted Picard over the rolling thunder. "We matter! All of us! Every human life, every *Enterprise,* whether there be one or one hundred thousand.

Everything has value! Everything has meaning! The only thing of no value in this universe is that which has disregard for others!"

Trelane was on his feet, shaking his head in disgust. "I hope the others aren't as sanctimonious as you."

"There will be no others."

"Ohh yes," said Trelane. "Yes, there will. An endless array of playgrounds in which to romp. Universe after universe to fall before me and, unlike Alexander, I shall never have to weep that there are no new lands to conquer."

"No, Trelane."

Trelane's face darkened. "No one will ever say that word to me again."

"No?" said Picard, and suddenly a great calm was falling over him.

His blade moved quickly, a high, rolling attack. Trelane reached high to block it and, while his full body was open, Picard slammed a foot out and caught him square in the pit of the stomach. Trelane went down once more.

"How dare you!" shouted Trelane. *"How dare you!"*

"You have no power here," said Picard.

"I *am* power!"

"No." Picard shook his head. "You are a child, just as you always were."

"No," Trelane said, voice dripping with contempt. "No, I'm the adult now. I am mighty enough to do whatever I want!"

"Being an adult isn't about might. It's about responsibility."

"Don't lecture me!" Trelane lunged forward, and this time Picard did not think. The parry was quick, instinctive, requiring no thought except the movement of the blade, and then Trelane was past him and for good measure

Picard kicked him in the backside, knocking him flat on his face.

Immediately Trelane was up again, and the skies above him were the blackest black, and the ground beneath him was trembling in sympathy with his anger. For Trelane was a god and Picard was nothing but an upstart mortal, and how dare he *how dare he?*

"You are a child with a lit match, and the universe is your powder keg," Picard said. "I'm taking that match away from you."

"You don't have the power to do it," Trelane said.

"Maybe not," replied Picard. "But I do have the responsibility. I am the adult, Trelane. You are the child. And it's time to show you who is in charge."

Inside the transporter room, the whine of the phasers from outside was clearly audible.

Riker, Worf, and Tasha took up positions, aiming at the door. "Remember," said Riker, sweat pouring down him as the hull of the *Enterprise* began to superheat. "Last one alive . . . if it comes to that . . . destroys the transporter console. I've cross-linked it to every other transporter on the ship. They'll all go when this one does."

"Commander . . . it has been a privilege working with you," said Worf. He turned and looked at Tasha. "And you," he said.

Tasha nodded grimly. "Don't worry. When this is over and Picard has pulled a miracle out of his ear, we'll toss back a few drinks and laugh about it."

"That," said Worf, "would be very nice." He paused as the sound of the phaser grew louder. "Have you ever tried prune juice?" he asked.

Tasha stared at him.

* * *

"You will not defy me again!" shouted Trelane, and charged.

"I think you're right. Because after today, it won't be necessary," replied Picard, and blocked.

Trelane's attack was blinding, brutal. They moved down the darksome plain, and the sky crackled overhead, and the great rift of chaos, the artery to the Heart of the Storm, swelled. The blades moved so quickly that no mortal eye would have been able to follow, and whether that was because Picard had moved up to Trelane's level or Trelane up to his, no one would have been able to say.

Picard dropped back, back, constantly and steadily retreating, but one would not have known it. He was losing, Trelane knew, Picard *had* to be losing because he kept going back and back and back across the plain. . . .

Except it didn't feel as if Picard were losing. There was nothing in his demeanor, nothing in his attitude that came across as if he were losing. More as if he were . . .

The thought flashed plainly across Trelane's face, and Picard nodded in confirmation to the unspoken thought.

"That's right, Trelane," he said. "I'm playing with you."

Trelane roared, and the sky roared with him, thunder erupting all around them, for Trelane's fury cut across all dimensions, all worlds, and no matter where you were that day, no matter how many parsecs, no matter how many light-years or worlds or universes away, you felt the fury of the child-god called Trelane.

His sword crackled with the force of his wrath, and his terrible swift sword slashed forward.

It slashed across Picard's forehead, ripping it almost to the bone. Blood poured forth, down into Picard's face, seeping into his eyes. He staggered back across the darksome plain. The last thing he saw before becoming completely blinded by his own blood was Trelane's sword coming toward him.

The transporter-room door flew open and the first person in was blasted back by a phaser. It was hard to tell whether it originated from Riker, Worf, or Yar, for they were firing as one, peppering the entranceway with phaser fire.

The attackers dropped back, firing and ducking, trying to find a break in the barrage so they could enter.

Around them the temperature rose, becoming higher, more oppressive. . . .

We're in hell, thought Tasha Yar bleakly from her defensive point in the transporter room . . . and that was the second-to-last thing she thought before a stray phaser bolt nailed her. The last thing she thought was *I can't get* over *what an ugly haircut that was,* and then blackness claimed her.

25.

As the sword flashed toward Picard, he blocked—not where Trelane's sword was, because that would be useless. Instead his blade moved instinctively to where the fighting computer in his mind told him it would be.

Metal clashed on metal and he blocked it. . . .

The sword flew out of Picard's hand.

"Hah!" shouted Trelane.

He thrust home toward his target, except his target wasn't there.

Picard, completely sightless, threw himself toward where his ears told him his sword had clattered to the ground. It was an utterly desperate move, because the crashing thunder overhead partly obscured the sword's sound. Picard hurled his body with no grace, no artistry, no elegance . . . just desperation. A swan dive . . .

No, a swan song, thought Trelane deliriously. He spun and knew that he was not going to do some polite, genteel thing like allow Picard to scramble to his feet, no no, he was going to *cut him into bloody ribbons while he lay there because* **he was Trelane and could do whatever he wanted!**

SO THERE!

Picard hit the ground, his desperate fingers reaching out—and they touched the hilt. He grabbed it, but his blood-slicked hands caused it to roll away. He thrust forward on his belly, grabbed the hilt, and he knew that right then Trelane was behind him and he was right there *right there* and there was no time.

Picard did not even turn around. He grabbed the hilt in reverse. His back open and unprotected, with Trelane looming over him about to run him through, Picard shoved the sword backward, the blade passing under his right arm and thrusting upward at an angle.

Hikaru Sulu, a holodeck creation, had effortlessly blocked the unorthodox move because it was so clumsy and inefficient.

General Trelane (retired), the Squire of Gothos, the omniscient, the omnipotent, the god . . . never saw it coming.

The sword rammed deep into him, penetrating his chest and coming out the other side.

And Picard's sword spoke.

"I'm sorry, son," came the voice of Q. "This is the only way."

Trelane screamed, a high-pitched, alarmed, pathetic thing not at all worthy of a god. The Heart of the Storm thundered in fury, but there was nothing that it could do.

For the sword was not simply the power of Q, the sword *was* Q, fully materialized and shape-shifted, and now he had slipped into Trelane, slipped through his guards and defenses, waited until Trelane was so confident of victory, so filled with his own power and arrogance, that he had dropped his guard ever so slightly. And it had been enough for Q to stab deep into the heart of the Heart of the Storm.

Power and energy crackled from Trelane, out of control, pouring from the gaping wound that Q had carved into him. Picard had released his grip and rolled away, wiping the blood from his eyes and trying desperately to stanch the wound.

Chaos rained.

The portal to the Heart of the Storm roiled, crackled, and blood-red droplets poured from it, spattering the darksome plain. Trelane, trembling, writhing, looked upward in slack-jawed, wide-eyed supplication as the Storm broke, pouring down in torrents. Tears poured from Trelane's eyes, tears that matched the red liquid cascading from far overhead, and he sobbed uncontrollably, and he clutched at the sword that was Q and tried to withdraw, begging, pleading, promising that he would be good and don't do this, please, don't do this . . .

Q did not listen. He didn't ignore him, but neither did he listen.

Trelane's form crackled, uncontrolled power being discharged, his body jumping and twisting about. He fell to the ground, thrashing on his back, and he screamed to Picard, *"Help me! Don't you see? It was all in fun!"*

In an infinity of universes, in an infinity of infinity of choices . . . there was nothing that Picard could do.

The darksome plain was soaked with red, and then Trelane emitted a primal scream that was heard from the beginning of eternity through to its end.

And then he blew apart.

It was an explosion without noise, fire without form. It

had no force, and yet was powerful enough to knock Picard back. He rolled across the ground, burying his head in his arms, almost curling up in a fetal position.

Trelane's hysterical cries combined with the roar of unrestrained Chaos, and there was a massive clamor like a million voices screaming in unison, from every point in the cosmos, *It's not fair we were so close so close* . . .

A door slammed.

It was not remotely a sound that Picard had expected to hear. A door? What was that about? It sounded fairly heavy, metal most likely.

He looked up.

The sky was dusky red, and the darksome plain was likewise. But there was no sign of the portal to the Heart of the Storm.

Or of Trelane.

Only Q.

He sat where Trelane had been, his back to Picard, his shoulders moving slightly in a rhythmic motion. And there was a sound that reached Picard's ears then that he had never thought he would hear.

Q was crying.

Nothing loud or demonstrative. Just very soft, almost to himself. And by the time Picard had staggered over to him, Q's face was completely dry and showed no sign of any emotion. He seemed preoccupied.

"Are you all right?" asked Picard.

"I simply . . . sent a message," Q told him. "To myself, in the past. Telling me where and when to be. I won't understand the source of the message, and I'll comprehend it only on a very basic level. But I'll be there, so that I can learn what I need to learn." He paused. "It's rather circular. I don't expect you to grasp it."

"Good." Picard looked skyward. "Is he . . . dead?" asked Picard.

Very slowly, Q nodded once. "We make a great team, don't we, Picard," he said in a deathly monotone. "Between the two of us, we saved the universe. Make a hell of a log entry, don't you think. Captain's log, stardate yakkity-yak. Got up. Brushed teeth. Charted some stars. Saved the universe. Had dinner. Brushed teeth, went to bed."

"Q . . . ?"

Q sighed. "Yes, Jean-Luc."

"You called him . . . 'son.'"

Slowly Q turned and looked at Picard. In that same carefully neutral voice he said, "Don't be ridiculous. That was . . . simply a term spoken from an elder to a younger."

"Indeed," said Picard. "It's just that, in many ways, he reminded me of you. And when you said 'son' . . ." Picard's voice trailed off.

"I've attended to your ship, by the way," Q told him. "Plus, with Trelane's . . . departure . . . everything has been sorted out. It wasn't your Beverly, by the way. Just thought you'd be interested to know . . . although, somehow, I don't think that's going to make you feel all that much better."

"You're right," said Picard slowly.

And then, as if continuing the thought, Q said, "His mother was . . . is . . . a magnificent creature."

Picard looked at Q. "Oh?" was all he said.

Q nodded. "And his father is a respected, sterling member of the Q Continuum. I mean, Picard, honestly . . . if I were Trelane's father, the implication would be that his mother had an illicit affair with me. Such a thing would be . . . unthinkable. Would it not, Picard?"

"Yes," said Picard. "Unthinkable."

"As you say, *mon capitaine,*" said Q.

And he vanished, leaving Picard alone on the darksome plain.

LAST STOP

1.

Lieutenant Tasha Yar was not exactly sure what happened.

When she regained consciousness, she was in sickbay. Slowly she propped herself up on her elbows, and then felt a flash of pain. Nurse Geordi La Forge then stepped into her range of sight and said gently, "Lie down. You've been hurt."

"No kidding," she murmured, and did as she was told. "What happened?"

Geordi just shook his head. Now there was a trembling in his tone, as if he were fighting back something. "I don't know. I don't want to know. They found you in the transporter room with major phaser burns. They brought you here and . . ." He took a deep breath to steady himself. "I think maybe you should just rest. Okay? I'll be back later. We've . . . we've had a lot of injuries. And . . . we'll talk later, okay?"

"Am I going to be okay? Where's Dr. Howard? I mean,

nothing personal or anything, but I'd like to hear it from her."

Geordi blinked back the tears in his perfect eyes. "That, uh . . . that won't be possible right now."

"Why not?"

"Because," he said with the sigh of one who would never stop feeling the hurt, "Dr. Howard is dead."

Commander Jean-Luc Picard made no acknowledgment when the signal chimed at his door. It chimed again, and then, very softly, he said, "Come."

The door slid open and Lieutenant Commander William T. Riker entered. Despite the bleakness in Picard's heart, he could not help but notice that Riker's condition had clearly improved. He walked with shoulders more squared, and there was some snap to his eyes.

"Yes, Mr. Riker?" said Picard.

Riker sighed deeply. "I . . . felt I should just come by and . . . and extend my sympathies for your loss, sir."

Picard nodded. He tried to think of something to respond with, but there were no words.

No words.

Feeling that something more should be said, Riker continued, "I . . . I want you to know that before my . . . my situation, I was a great follower of your career."

"Indeed."

Riker nodded. "I know you ran into some trouble. There's few people around who can sympathize with that as much as I."

"You seem somewhat improved now." Picard found that he was actually glad to speak to Riker. The emotional pain from Beverly's death, from Jack's suicide . . . the overwhelming feeling that if only he, Picard, had been there, he might have made it turn out differently . . . it threatened to engulf him. The only thing to do was try to cling to some small shred of normality.

"Somewhat," agreed Riker. "Things are a lot more clear now. I think that, in many ways, I'll always be watching my back."

"That's quite understandable, after what you've been through."

"Yes, well . . . fortunately, I have a supportive and wonderful wife . . . and one hell of a son. Have you seen him?"

"Oh yes. We . . . ran into each other."

"They're great, the two of them. God . . ." He shook his head. "I don't know what I'd do without them."

"Let's hope you never have to find out." He paused, and then seemed really to be looking at Riker for the first time. "Have you given thought to your future? Would you like to return directly to Betazed?"

"I've been giving it a good deal of thought, actually. I'm hoping to stay with Starfleet, if they'll have me."

"Oh, I'm sure they will." Picard drummed a finger on the table. "How does your family feel about that?"

"As I said, supportive . . . but conditional. When I put in my request at Starfleet, it'll be for a ship where families can accompany." He laughed softly. "Considering how long I've been out of commission, I don't know if I'm exactly in a position to make demands. But we'll see what comes of it. I meant what I said: I don't know what I'd do without them. And I have no intention of finding out."

Picard nodded. Then he said after a moment, "I could use you."

Riker looked so startled that Picard was immediately

able to dismiss the notion that Riker had been planning the conversation this way from the start. "You, sir?"

"I am acting captain," said Picard. "My understanding through the grapevine is that Starfleet is seriously considering making me her permanent captain. A return to grace, as it were . . . the logic being that such a traumatic loss . . ."

His voice broke. Respectfully, Riker looked down during the time it took Picard to compose himself. Then Riker offered, "It might make it easier on the crew in terms of command continuity?"

"Precisely, yes," said Picard. He cleared his throat, which had started to sound somewhat husky. "Given that possibility, and given that you are the highest-ranking officer aboard aside from myself . . . I thought you might be interested in the temporary position of first officer."

Riker was speechless.

"I'm hardly in a position to promise anything long-term," said Picard, "not for you, and not for myself. Still, if things work out . . . but, first things first. Are you interested?"

"Absolutely," said Riker, finding the words. "But . . . are you *sure* . . . I mean, for one thing, I doubt Mr. Mot will ever want to give me a haircut again. And there was . . ."

"Think of it this way, Mr. Riker. In some sense, we are both of us 'damaged goods.' Perhaps each of us is precisely what the other needs."

Slowly Riker nodded. "I would be proud to serve with you, sir."

"Excellent." He reached over the desk and warmly shook Riker's hand. It was a good, firm grip. "Then I shall officially welcome you aboard, Number One."

"Thank you, sir."

"How about we meet here at 0800 tomorrow and discuss the particulars of the ship and what you should know."

"Aye, sir. I'll be here."

He got up and walked out of the room, leaving Picard alone once more.

In his solitude, in his loneliness, he could see Beverly, feel the warmth of her pressed against him. And Jack . . . his friend, his commander, the man who had believed in him, and then that belief had killed him.

He felt his eyes begin to sting. He jammed the balls of his hands into them and took a deep breath.

The door chimed again. Trying not to sound impatient, Picard nevertheless said, more sharply than he would have liked, "Yes?"

Riker took a few steps into the room.

"Yes, Number One?" And then, for one terrifying moment, he feared that this was going to be another Riker, and the whole thing was going to start all over again.

But he breathed out a sigh of relief when Riker said, "About what we just discussed, sir . . ."

"Yes?"

"Well, with all due respect . . . you said that I was the highest-ranking officer aboard ship, aside from yourself. But . . . what about Lieutenant Commander Data?"

"Ohhh yes." Clearly this was a subject that Picard did not want to address. "About Mr. Data . . ."

"You're not passing over him because he's a human-oid, are you, sir?"

"No, Number One. I'm afraid that it's not quite that simple. You see, we've been over every inch of this ship, and . . ."

"And?" said Riker in confusion.

"Well," sighed Picard, "it would appear that we have misplaced Mr. Data."

2.

Lieutenant Tasha Yar was not exactly sure what happened.

One second, she and her backup forces had been storming the transporter room. The next moment, the transporter room was empty except for themselves. The Klingon, the fake Riker, the fake version of herself had vanished.

Now Tasha sat in the Ten-Forward lounge, staring at an empty glass. Guinan, looking slightly befuddled but otherwise none the worse for wear in terms of her having passed out earlier, was back behind the bar. The bridge systems were being checked over. Oddly, the planet that they had been in orbit around, and which they apparently had been in danger of crashing into, had vanished completely.

And Picard and Riker were dead.

That was the worst of it, of course. Picard having died at the hands of that Klingon. And a crewman had been witness to a grotesque sequence of events where one of the fake Rikers had blown the real one out of existence. . . .

Or maybe the Riker who had been with the others in the

transporter was, in fact, real, and he had been a traitor who had been plucked out of . . .

Tasha shook her head, rubbing her temples. All that mattered now was that Riker and Picard were gone. The ship was trying to pull itself together. They were still at war with the Klingons. Everything looked bleak, hopeless. . . .

How could things possibly get worse?

Suddenly she noticed that there was silence in Ten-Forward. Everyone had stopped talking. She looked up as she became aware that someone was standing next to her.

She gaped.

Two Datas sat down opposite her. One looked normal. The other looked perfectly human.

"Tasha . . . we may have a problem," they began.

3.

The adult sighed.

"Ah well," he murmured. "I tried to get it all straightened out. Just because I'm omnipotent doesn't mean I'm perfect." He considered making some additional adjustments, and then opted to leave matters as they were. Aside from the one small glitch, everything else was pretty much in order.

Then, to his great surprise, something glittered in front of him.

It was small and delicate, a sparkling globe of light that absolutely commanded the adult's attention.

He reached out, took the light in his hand . . . and was astounded.

"You!" he said.

It was indeed the child . . . or what was left of him. The child as he was in the beginning. Not in the beginning of this misadventure, but The Beginning.

"Now this is a surprise," allowed the adult. "What happened? Were you a morsel that Chaos was not able to digest? So you were spit out? Is that it?

431

"I never thought I'd see you again," the adult told him. "I . . . wasn't sure how to feel about that. I guess you've gone and made that moot, though, haven't you."

The globe seemed to recognize him, be excited to see him, although it didn't quite seem to know why.

Tenderly, the adult held the globe to him. "Don't worry," he said softly. "This time we'll do right by you. Not let matters get out of hand. I promise."

After a moment the child—the child who once had straddled three lanes of eternity, and hence would be called "Treylane," or simply "Trelane"—put forward its first thought.

"What are we going to do today?"

"My boy," said the adult, seeing a universe of possibilities, "there is nothing that we are not going to do today. . . ."

4.

Captain Jean-Luc Picard stood over Guinan in sickbay, and squeezed her hand. "You're sure you're going to be all right?" he asked.

"Fine," she said. "Fit as a fiddle. In fact, I think we're all going to be all right."

He nodded approvingly, and turned toward Riker. Beverly Crusher was just finishing her examination of him, and she smiled reassuringly. "He's a bit dehydrated," said Beverly. "Otherwise, he's fine."

"Good." He looked carefully at Riker. "Is something wrong, Number One?"

Riker shook his head. "Just thinking, sir."

"About—?"

"About . . . paths not taken. Opportunities missed. And about what a great name for a son 'Tommy' is."

Picard smiled. "Is it purely coincidence that you happen to share that name, Commander William Thomas Thelonius Riker?"

"Yes sir," said Riker, deadpan. "Purely coincidence."

"I see. Well . . . carry on, then, Number One."

Riker nodded and headed for the bridge, which had been restored to order. Picard hesitated for a moment, watching Beverly go on about her work, attending to other patients. Trying to relegate the unearthly reappearance of her husband to some sort of bizarre hallucination, because it made it that much easier for her to deal with.

That was fine with Picard. Everyone dealt with the unthinkable in their own way.

As for what she had said, with her dying breath . . . to Picard, or to Jack Crusher, he would never be sure . . . well, he would deal with that in his own way.

And as Picard headed for the door, Beverly suddenly said, "Jean-Luc . . . there's something I've been wanting to tell you."

He stood in the doorway, and turned to face her. "Yes?"

It was a moment that hung there. A moment that cut across other moments.

(Jean-Luc, you're the best friend I've ever had.)

(Jean-Luc, I think it's time I moved on.)

(Jean-Luc, it's about Wesley . . .)

(Jean-Luc, I'm dying.)

(Jean-Luc, I want to have sex with you.)

(Jean-Luc, I love you.)

She frowned, and shook her head. "How odd," she said. "I can't remember what it was."

"That's all right," said Picard with his customary reserve. He stepped out. And as Beverly turned away, she heard him say, "I'm sure it will come to you . . . sometime."

She turned back to ask him why he sounded so strange when he said that . . .

. . . but he was already gone.